VIRGINIA WOOLF
To The Lighthouse

Text edited by
STELLA MCNICHOL

With an Introduction and Notes by
HERMIONE LEE

PENGUIN BOOKS

PENGUIN CLASSICS

UK | USA | Canada | Ireland | Australia
India | New Zealand | South Africa

Penguin Books is part of the Penguin Random House group of companies
whose addresses can be found at global.penguinrandomhouse.com.

| Penguin
Random House
UK

First published by The Hogarth Press 1927
This annotated edition published in Penguin Books 1992
Reissued in Penguin Classics 2019
001

Introduction and notes copyright © Hermione Lee, 1992
Other editorial matter copyright © Stella McNichol, 1992

The moral rights of the editors have been asserted

Set in Monophoto Garamond
Typeset by Rowland Phototypesetting Ltd, Bury St Edmunds, Suffolk
Printed and bound in Great Britain by Clays Ltd, Elcograf S.p.A.

A CIP catalogue record for this book is available from the British Library

ISBN: 978-0-241-37195-4

www.greenpenguin.co.uk

CONTENTS

Bibliographical Note   vii

Introduction   ix

Further Reading   xlv

A Note on the Text   xlvii

TO THE LIGHTHOUSE   1

Notes   227

Appendix I   260

Appendix II   263

Bibliographical Note

The following is a list of abbreviated titles used in this edition.

MS: *To the Lighthouse: The Original Holograph Draft*, transcribed and ed. Susan Dick (Toronto Universitv Press, 1982; Hogarth Press, 1983). Square brackets are used to indicate words deleted in original draft.

TL: *To the Lighthouse*, first British edn (Hogarth Press, 5 May 1927).

Moments of Being: *Moments of Being: Unpublished Autobiographical Writings of Virginia Woolf*, ed. Jeanne Schulkind (Chatto & Windus, 1976).

Diary: *The Diary of Virginia Woolf*, 5 vols., ed. Anne Olivier Bell (Hogarth Press, 1977; Penguin Books, 1979).

Letters: *The Letters of Virginia Woolf*, 6 vols., ed. Nigel Nicolson and Joanne Trautmann (Hogarth Press, 1975–80).

Essays: *The Essays of Virginia Woolf*, 3 vols. (to be 6 vols.), ed. Andrew McNeillie (Hogarth Press, 1986).

CE: *Collected Essays*, 4 vols., ed. Leonard Woolf (Chatto & Windus, 1966, 1967).

Mausoleum: *Sir Leslie Stephen's Mausoleum Book* (1895), introduced by Alan Bell (OUP, 1977).

Introduction

To the Lighthouse is the story of a marriage and a childhood.
It is a lamentation of loss and grief for powerful, loved,
dead parents, which Virginia Woolf wanted to call an
'elegy' rather than a novel. It is, less apparently, about the
English class-structure and its radical break with Victorian-
ism after the First World War. It demonstrates the urgent
need for an art form which could, though with great
difficulty, adapt to and register that break. It is all these
things at once.

Since fiction is not music or painting or film[1] or un-
spoken thoughts, it requires formal strategies if it is to try
and be several things at once. These strategies may be as
complicated as a whole section written from the point of
view of the passage of time, or as simple as a pair of
brackets.

Mr Bankes, for instance, has a conversation in brackets
on the telephone. He is talking to Mrs Ramsay about a
train time. Then he looks out of the window 'to see what
progress the workmen were making with an hotel which
they were building at the back of his house'. The 'stir
among the unfinished walls' reminds him of her incongruities. The work outside goes on, inside another pair of
brackets – '(they were carrying bricks up a little plank as
he watched them)' – while he builds up his version of Mrs
Ramsay's idiosyncrasies. More than one thing happens at
once: what he says to Mrs Ramsay on the phone and what
he thinks of saying; what he sees from his window and
what he sees in his mind's eye; and, in his mind's eye, her

beauty and her incongruities. More than one time coexists: the time of Mr Bankes's narrative, which is under pressure to move onwards ('Yes, he would catch the 10.30 at Euston'; 'He must go to his work'); the moments in which she appears to his mind's eye; and, outside Mr Bankes's brackets, the moment in which Mrs Ramsay is knitting her stocking and talking to James.

A great deal goes on in brackets in *To the Lighthouse*: silent gestures – '(she glanced at him musing)'; identifications of a point of view – '(James thought)'; comments and qualifications – '(For she was in love with them all, in love with this world)'; reminders – '(The bill for the greenhouse would be fifty pounds)'; sudden deaths; a world war. The middle section, 'Time Passes', reads like a long parenthesis between the first and last sections. Its square brackets enclose the facts of death, as if they belonged to another kind of language. As 'Time Passes' comes to a close, its last section bulges with bracketed phrases about the return of life to the house, which will open themselves out into the third part of the novel. While she was writing the third part, moving between Lily on the lawn and the Ramsays in the boat, Woolf imagined finishing off Lily and her painting in brackets: 'Could I do it in a parenthesis? so that one had the sense of reading the two things at the same time?'[2]

Brackets are a way of making more than one thing happen at once. But they also create an unsettling ambiguity about the status of events. What is more 'important', the death of Mrs Ramsay, or the fall of a fold of a green shawl in an empty room? If the novel makes us think of more than one thing at once, and exists in more than one time, which takes precedence? Is the life of the Ramsays in the garden and house enclosed by the outside world as if in parenthesis, as the lighthouse is surrounded by the sea? Or is it the Ramsays that are the main text, and everything else is in brackets?

Often, the outside world – the 'ordinary' stuff of early-twentieth-century British life: tube trains, evening papers, tools for the car, platform speakers, railway tickets, those bricks – impinges on the world of the house, the garden and the lighthouse. Partly this works as a historical contrast: the Victorian family scene has vanished and become a dream-world – post-war modern life is continuing. But Mr Bankes's bricks in brackets don't just make a simple contrast with his inner vision of Mrs Ramsay 'running across the lawn in goloshes to snatch a child from mischief'. The bricks and the building of the hotel are *like* her incongruities – beautiful and busy, ethereal and tough – and they are *like* the way he is thinking about her, putting one thing against another, building up a picture. The novel insists that you notice its structuring devices, its brackets and sections and shifts in vantage points.

While Woolf was in the early stages of *To the Lighthouse*, in the autumn of 1925, she was preparing a lecture called 'How Should One Read a Book?' (a fragment of which is written in the manuscript of the novel). In it, she compares the thirty-two chapters of a novel to 'an attempt to make something as formal and controlled as a building: but words are more impalpable than bricks'.[3] Try, she suggests, to write on 'some event that has left a distinct impression on you', when 'a whole vision, an entire conception, seemed contained in that moment'. As soon as you attempt to 'reconstruct' it in words, you will find that it 'breaks into a thousand conflicting impressions'.

This is like a note to herself on the writing of her new

novel. The bricks are being trundled up the little plank, the construction is under way. The building must be 'formal and controlled'. But the entropic pull towards breakage and fragmentation – 'things fall apart' – is immense. And the difficulty is compounded because what she wants is a basis of strength and structure and an appearance of fluidity and translucence. So the novel has to be *like* Mrs Ramsay, its incongruities held in balance.

By means of Lily's painting, Woolf builds into the novel a commentary on her own processes. Lily's images for her art – 'she saw the colour burning on a framework of steel; the light of a butterfly's wing lying upon the arches of a cathedral' – go back to Virginia Stephen's vision of Santa Sophia on her visit to Constantinople, recorded in her diary of 1906: 'thin as glass, blown in plump curves' and 'as substantial as a pyramid'.[4] That dome shape occurs in the novel in the imaginations of Nancy, and of Lily, who thinks of Mrs Ramsay as 'an august shape, the shape of a dome'. The dome shape, which combines the solid and the ethereal, was the essence of her plan for the book.

From the beginning, Woolf's plan was clear to her. She expressed it to herself from the first through lists and inventories of ingredients that – as for the cooking of the Bœuf en Daube – would have to be held in balance and brought satisfactorily to the boil. When the novel was published in the spring of 1927, she looked back on the 'unexpected way in which these things suddenly create themselves – one thing on top of another in about an hour ... so I made up The Lighthouse one afternoon in the square here.'[5]

The shape of the thing may have come to her all at once

('without any premeditation, that I can see', she said in a letter to Vanessa[6]), but the ingredients had been accumulating for years: since childhood; since the 'Reminiscences' she wrote in 1908 about her parents; since the memoir of '22 Hyde Park Gate' written between 1920 and 1921. As early as October 1924, on the day she wrote the last words of *Mrs Dalloway*, she entered a cryptic, even ominous, note in her diary, 'I see already The Old Man',[7] as though the figure of Mr Ramsay was the next thing she would have to deal with. By the time *Mrs Dalloway* was nearing publication, the ingredients for *To the Lighthouse* were becoming distinct. In her notebook ('Notes for Writing') for 6 March 1925, she envisaged a collection of 'the stories of people at Mrs. D's party' and listed one of them as 'The picture – I think of the sea'. On 14 March she was still thinking of a book of stories, and added to her list (square brackets show deletions):

> *The Past* founded on [images?] ancestor worship,
>   what it amounts to, & means.
>   Some middle aged woman
>   of distinguished parents; her
>   feelings for her father & mother –
>   [ancient?]

A list of eight story topics follows, and then:

> It strikes me that it might all end with a picture.
> These stories about people would fill
> half the book; & then the other thing would
> loom up; & we should step into quite a
> different place & people? But what?

On the next page of the notebook, the notes for *To the Lighthouse* begin:

All character – <u>not</u> a view of the world.
Two blocks joined by a corridor

Topics that may come in:
    How her beauty is to be conveyed by the
impression that she makes on all these
people. One after another feeling it without
knowing exactly what she does to them,
to charge her words.
Episode of taking Tansley to call on the poor.
How they see her.
The great cleavages in to which the human
race is split, through the Ramsays not
liking Mr Tansley.
But they liked Mr Carmichael.
Her reverence for learning and painting.
Inhibited, not very personal.
The look of the room – [fiddle?] and sand [shoes?] –
Great photographs covering bare patches.
The beauty is to be revealed the 2nd time
Mr R stops
discourse on sentimentality.
He was quoting The Charge of the Light Brigade
& then impressed upon it was this picture
of mother and child.

How much more important divisions between
people are than between countries.
[Ev] The source of all evil.
She was lapsing into pure sensation –
seeing things in the garden.
The waves breaking. Tapping of cricket balls.
The bark 'How's that?'

They did not speak to each other.
Tansley shed
Tansley the product of universities had to
assert the power of his intellect.
     She feels the glow of sensation – & how they are
made up of all different things – (what
she has just done) & wishes for some bell to
strike & say this is it. It does strike.
She guards her moment.[8]

On 14 May 1925, the day *Mrs Dalloway* was published, Woolf wrote in her diary that she was 'all on the strain with desire to . . . get on to *To the Lighthouse*'. Again, she gives a list of ingredients, not the same as those in the notebook:

> This is going to be fairly short: to have father's character done complete in it; & mothers; & St Ives; & childhood; & all the usual things I try to put in – life, death &c. But the centre is father's character, sitting in a boat, reciting We perished, each alone, while he crushes a dying mackerel . . .[9]

First, though, she felt she must write the stories she had envisaged in March. They were written by 14 June, and in that time she had 'thought out, perhaps too clearly, To the Lighthouse'.[10] (Why too clearly? Because the structure she had given herself presented problems, or because she felt it was 'too clearly' about her parents? This warning note would affect the development of the novel.)

The eight stories which formed the bridge between *Mrs Dalloway* and *To the Lighthouse* are all set at Mrs Dalloway's party, but the tunes of *To the Lighthouse* are beginning to be played in them. Mabel Wearing in her embarrassing new dress thinks with relief of her 'delicious moments' by the sea at Easter, with 'the melody of the waves – "Hush,

hush," they said, & the children's shouts paddling'. A girl who is about to enter the adult world of introductions and conversations feels as if she is going to be 'flung into a whirlpool where either she would perish or be saved'. Mrs Latham, sitting outside the house in the garden, thinks of the people inside as survivors, a 'company of adventurers who, set about with dangers, sail on'. Mr Carslake looks at a comforting picture of a heath and imagines himself on a walk; he is annoyed because walking almost makes him want to say he believes in God. 'It seemed to him as if he had been trapped into the words. "To believe in God".'[11] All these moments, in which an inner voice or feeling takes the character away from the social context, will be used again in *To the Lighthouse*.

Two stories anticipate *To the Lighthouse* more fully. In one, 'The Man Who Loved His Kind',[12] there is a prickly encounter between a middle-aged lawyer who prides himself on liking 'ordinary people', smoking shag tobacco and despising society, and a woman who dislikes his egotism, truculence and laziness. Out of his type, she feels, 'spring revolutions'. It is a blueprint for the political and sexual conflict between Lily and Charles Tansley, which has not yet occurred in the list of ingredients for the novel.

The other story is called 'Ancestors', and comes from the note to herself about 'ancestor worship'. A middle-aged woman at Mrs Dalloway's party, Mrs Vallance, compares it with her lost family-home in Scotland. Tears come into her eyes as she thinks of her parents, her father's old friends, the flowers her mother loved, her father's reverence for women, herself as a child with 'dark wild eyes', picking Sweet Alice and reciting Shelley's 'Ode to the West Wind' to her father. The parents are dead, but if she had stayed with them in the garden (where it now

seems to have been 'always starlit, and always summer'),
she would have always been happy.[13]

'Ancestors' is a self-pitying, tearful story, and seems to
have provided a warning for Woolf as she began, in June and
July, to build ingredients from these stories into her plans
for the novel. She knows, by now, that 'the sea is to be
heard all through it', and that she would like to be able to
call it an 'Elegy' rather than a novel.[14] Listing her ingredients again ('father & mother & child in the garden; the
death; the sail to the lighthouse'), she is anxious that the
theme may be 'sentimental'. How to thicken and enrich it?
Another list ensues, mixing together, as so often, subjects
and processes:

> It might contain all characters boiled down; & childhood; &
> then this impersonal thing, which I'm dared to do by my
> friends, the flight of time, & the consequent break of unity
> in my design.[15]

(These anxieties over sentimentality and the need for 'thick-
ening' the material were never to leave her. As she came to
the end of the first draft, she asked herself if it was 'rather
thin',[16] and observed that she was going in dread of
'sentimentality'.[17] On publication day she was still worrying
that people would call it 'sentimental';[18] and she asks Vita
Sackville-West the question 'Do you think it sentimental?',[19] before any criticism had time to arrive.) Meanwhile,
she is interested by the 'new problem' she is setting herself with the passage in time and the 'break of unity'.
(And, she is reading Proust, the writer who has exactly
the combination of sensibility and tenacity – 'he is as
tough as catgut & as evanescent as a butterfly's bloom' – [20]
that she is seeking for in her novel.) By July, she is
vacillating between 'a single & intense character of father;

& a far wider slower book'.[21] It needs to be 'quiet', but not 'insipid'. She might 'do something' to 'split up emotions more completely'.

These problems of balance and construction will be re-enacted in the novel, as when Mr Ramsay reads and judges Walter Scott ('That's fiddlesticks, that's first-rate, he thought, putting one thing beside another') or when Lily diagnoses the problem of design in her painting, which is also the problem of understanding the relations between the Ramsays:

> For whatever reason she could not achieve that razor edge of balance between two opposite forces; Mr. Ramsay and the picture; which was necessary. There was something perhaps wrong with the design? ... She smiled ironically; for had she not thought, when she began, that she had solved her problem? (p. 209.)

Similarly, Woolf does not solve all her 'problem' of design in advance. Her early lists and plans do not seem to envisage Lily and her painting, or the dinner party. They focus on the character of Mrs Ramsay and the scene of the journey, and on a kind of 'sentence' which will carry the narrative on 'easily'. They say nothing about a lighthouse, apart from the title, which, unusually for her, she decided on straight away.

She began writing the novel on 6 August 1925, at Monk's House, and wrote '22 pages straight off in less than a fortnight'.[22] But all that summer she was ill with fainting and headaches and exhaustion. 'Can't write', she said in a letter to Roger Fry, '(with a whole novel in my head too – it's damnable)'.[23] Instead she wrote an essay 'On Being Ill', comparing the effects of illness to those of love: 'it wreathes the faces of the absent ... with a new significance. . . while the whole landscape of life lies remote and fair, like the shore seen from a ship far out at sea.'[24] Some writing of the novel went on that summer ('I'm for the Isles of Stornaway', she wrote to Vanessa on 29 September[25]), but she felt dejected and uncertain about the 'personal' aspects of the book ('It will be too like father, or mother'[26]), and it was not until January that she was launched again.

When she went back to it, she remarked in her notebook that 'the idea has grown in the interval since I wrote the beginning'. By now she wants 'the presence of the 8 children, undifferentiated', to bring out 'the sense of life in opposition to fate – ie. waves, lighthouse'. She has thought of 'a great dinner scene' and an engagement after it, of Mrs Ramsay with the children choosing her jewelry in the bedroom, of her descending the stairs and of how 'all is to draw in towards the end, & leave the two alone'. She thinks of using 'poetry in quotations to give the character'.[27]

Once begun again, the first draft of the novel was written, at a rate of about two pages a day, with speed and fluency ('Never never have I written so easily, imagined so profusely'[28]) between January and September 1926. In her life outside the writing of the book there were complications, distractions, involvements: moves from London to Rodmell; the developing relationship with Vita Sackville-West; social life (including a memorable visit to see Thomas Hardy); the demands of the Hogarth Press; the General Strike in May (with which Leonard was closely engaged and which affected the mood, she felt, retrospectively, of 'Time Passes'[29]); phases of illness; and, in July, 'a whole nervous breakdown in miniature'.[30]

As she wrote, her feeling that she was striking oil

alternated with phases of anxiety. But she forged ahead – 'close on 40,000 words in 2 months – my record', she wrote to Vita[31] – and felt that she was setting herself new targets. She noted to herself on 9 March that she was writing 'exactly the opposite from my other books: very loosely at first ... & shall have to tighten finally ... Also at perhaps 3 times the speed.'[32] The dinner party would seem to her 'the best thing I ever wrote'.[33] The 'Time Passes' section, which she would describe as having given her 'more trouble than all the rest of the book put together',[34] pleased her for its strategy of 'collecting' all the 'lyric portions' in one place, so that they 'dont interfere with the text so much as usual'.[35] In the last part, particularly towards the end, she wrestled, like Lily, with problems of balance, feeling that the material in the boat was not so rich 'as it is with Lily on the lawn'.[36] As she completed the first draft, in September, she went into a period of intense depression. Out of it, in a curious state of mind, she began to see 'a fin passing far out',[37] and the image of 'a solitary woman musing':[38] possible premonitions of a next book.

Between October and January she revised the novel, working at the typewriter, and still liking it: 'easily the best of my books'.[39] During the period of revision, she and Leonard went for a winter holiday to a house near St Ives, and she wrote ruefully: 'All my facts about Lighthouses are wrong.'[40] On 23 January 1927 Leonard read the novel and called it 'a masterpiece'.[41] Between February and March she revised two sets of proofs for the American and English editions. Even during this drudgery, and anxiety about its reception, she was still pleased with it:

> Dear me, how lovely some parts of The Lighthouse are! Soft & pliable, & I think deep, & never a word wrong for a page at a time.[42]

Retrospectively, she saw it as a successful endeavour to do the two things she makes Lily do in the last part of the book: understand her own feelings, and create a structure that worked – 'I ... got down to my depths & made shapes square up.'[43]

Her preoccupation with making shapes repeatedly enters the action of the novel, from the cutting-out of objects from the Army and Navy Stores' catalogue on the first page, to the final stroke down the middle of Lily's canvas on the last. The metamorphosing forms of the lighthouse, the making of the dinner party and the completion of the picture are the three dominant shapes of the book. But, other shapes, which vary and change depending on perspective ('So much depends, she thought, upon distance'), enter every scene of the book: the purple triangle of Lily's picture; the wedge-shaped core of darkness that Mrs Ramsay sinks down to in solitude; the 'august dome' that represents her; the line of letters Mr Ramsay sees stretching ahead of him into the distance; the knots of rope and shoelace that are tied and untied; the shape of the sonnet; and the island, 'shaped something like a leaf stood on end'.

These shapes tend towards, or hover on the edge of, the symbolic, but are not quite solved by being read as firmly explicable 'symbols'. 'I am making some use of symbolism, I observe', she observes drily, and warily, as she reaches the end of the first draft.[44] But she rapidly backs off from Roger Fry's suggestion that arriving at the lighthouse 'has a symbolic meaning which escapes me':

> I meant *nothing* by The Lighthouse. One has to have a central line down the middle of the book to hold the design together. I saw that all sorts of feelings would accrue to this, but I refused to think them out, and trusted that people

would make it the deposit for their own emotions – which they have done, one thinking it means one thing another another. I can't manage Symbolism except in this vague, generalized way.[45]

This canny prediction of the next seventy years' criticism of *To the Lighthouse* – 'one thinking it means one thing another another' – could be read as a defensive smokescreen. I prefer to treat it as a useful warning. In her autobiographical writings in *Moments of Being*, she describes the process of 'scene making' as her 'natural way of marking the past', 'the origin of my writing impulse'. 'Always a scene has arranged itself: representative, enduring.'[46] It might be her father sitting in a boat, reciting 'we perished, each alone', or her mother sitting by the window knitting while the children played cricket. These scenes are not codes, they do not 'stand' for something else. 'Representative' is not the same as 'symbolic'. More obscurely, they provide the shapes that are the focal points for strong emotions. So the narrative is made up of scenes which are constructed to centre around certain shapes. This is why the novel is so much about ways of looking (even when there are no human beings on the scene, the scene is being looked at, and the narrative is concerned with vantage points and perceptions), as when Lily looks along Mr Bankes's 'beam' and adds to it 'her different ray', or when Mrs Ramsay observes Mr Carmichael looking at the fruit bowl: 'That was his way of looking, different from hers. But looking together united them.' And the need to look *through*, to make the solid transparent, is repeatedly insisted on. Lily turns Charles Tansley into 'an X-ray photograph', or presses up against Mrs Ramsay, trying to get inside her 'secret chambers', or needs a 'secret sense' (like the lighthouse beam) to 'steal through keyholes' with.

*

We can make an X-ray of *To the Lighthouse*, and examine Virginia Woolf's construction of scenes and the 'squaring up' of shapes, by reading the manuscript of the novel. She had many of the scenes in mind from the start, often in the same order as she ended up with, but an enormous amount of shaping took place between the first draft (we have no typescript) and the first editions.[47] Susan Dick, introducing her edition of the manuscript, points out the most notable shifts. As passages are rewritten, particular images – light, waves, the lighthouse – are developed and thickened ('to bring out the sense of life in opposition to fate'). Narrative which begins as authorially omniscient is persistently shifted inside a character's mental language. Some characters are altered a good deal: there is less emphasis, by the end, on Mrs Ramsay's inarticulacy, or Lily's religious beliefs. Lily begins as a minor character, Miss Sophie Briscoe, a 'kindly and well-covered' lady of fifty-five who sketches hedgerows and thatched cottages and has refused all offers of marriage.[48]

Once Sophie has become Lily, she is allowed, in the manuscript, to be more articulate about her political feelings, just as Charles Tansley is allowed to be more brutally antagonistic towards her and towards the Ramsays. In general, the politics of the novel's first draft are more explicit. Lily's feelings of oppression sitting opposite Tansley at the dinner table, take the form of a debate (more extensive than 'women can't paint, women can't write'), which reads like a preliminary version of the argument in *A Room of One's Own*. Why does she mind what he thinks, she asks herself.

> O it's Shakespeare, she corrected herself – as a forgetful person entering [Hyde Park] Regents Park, [might wonder

why] & seeing the Park keeper was coming towards her
menacingly; [they make on dogs must be on a lead]; might
exclaim Oh I remember/ of course dogs must be on a lead!
So Lily Briscoe remembered that [everyon] man has Shakespeare [behind him]; & women have not.[49]

But she doesn't want to express this 'horror & despair;
annihilation; nonentity' that he makes her feel, because she
'could not bear to be called, as she might have been called
had she come out with her views a feminist'. There is a line
scored all through this passage, and the word 'feminist' is
censored from the novel. But the word, and Lily's argument, will surface two years later in A Room of One's Own.
The fiction and the feminist polemic are deeply intercon-
nected.

If Lily's feminism is subdued in To the Lighthouse, so is
Tansley's class feeling about the Ramsays: he despises
'these upper-middle-class women'; he reads in his own
room about the French Revolution; he is enraged that they
don't recognize that 'he was going to leave his mark on the
world'; he makes Mr Bankes think of the dangers when 'a
reformer' arises; and makes Mrs Ramsay think of the poor,
not as individuals, but in 'blocks'. To her it seems that his
'love of mankind' is directly related to 'his hatred of the
arts'. In the manuscript of 'Time Passes', the solitary
watchers who walk the beach are identified as 'preachers
and diviners', driven to despair by 'the prodigious cannonading' of the war (which has a more emphatic presence in
the manuscript). Lily, in the manuscript of 'The Lighthouse' (in the final draft, too) remembers Tansley lecturing
on peace; and James (in the manuscript only) recalls him as
one of the 'detestable' people – 'the atheists, the socialists,
the pacifists' – whom his father attracted. It seems that
Tansley is being identified (but more explicitly in the first

draft) as one of the 'watchers and preachers' – the pacifists and socialists – who have tried, and failed, to become leaders during the war years.[50]

In the manuscript, there is also more emphasis on the endurance of the working classes, like Mrs McNab, in wartime, putting up with what the 'kings and kaisers' have brought about. Lurking at the edges of *To the Lighthouse* are the 'ordinary people' of Britain: the sick and poor that Mrs Ramsay visits in the town, the one-armed billposter, the circus troupe, the handsome unreliable gardener, the Swiss maid, the cook, the charwomen, the fishermen, the lighthouse-keeper and his son with the tuberculous hip. The Ramsays are Victorian philanthropists – they think of the servants or the fishermen as individuals, not as a class, and Mr Ramsay (like Scott) admires and envies their simplicity. But the Ramsays' dinner parties, their family life, their kind of literature, their domestic arrangements (there seem to be no servants in the house in 'The Lighthouse') are blown away in the war years, and the class that survives is that low form of life that brings the house back from the brink of ruin: Mrs McNab and Mrs Bast and her son George.[51] It's unfortunate that Virginia Woolf is so distant from her working class characters that she describes them as half-witted troglodytes, and can't even remember whether she has called her Swiss maid 'Marie' (on p. 33) or 'Marthe' (on p. 109). All the same, Mr Ramsay's anxieties about whether civilization should be judged by 'the lot of the average human being' – the 'slave class' – and whether Shakespeare is less necessary than 'the liftman in the Tube' is Virginia Woolf's own anxiety: is the General Strike more important than the writing of *To the Lighthouse*?

All this is muted in the final version of the novel, but a political dimension is still implicit. Behind the Ramsay family is a history of imperialism. Mrs Ramsay's relatives govern India, and Mr Ramsay, though socially eccentric and not rich, is part of the educational establishment. He has his own empire, too, the little island of the family. Mr Ramsay's metaphorical leadership of men is partly a comic fantasy, but is also meant seriously. He is heroic, but he is also a tyrant. The mixture of courtly veneration and domination with which he treats his wife is a product of the patriarchal system, as well as being characteristic. Napoleon, Carlyle and the French Revolution are mentioned often enough in the men's conversation to make it clear that a male tradition of imperialist despotism (which Tansley, though a pacifist and a socialist, has as his intellectual inheritance) is being resisted. By whom? By Mrs Ramsay with an alternative language of matriarchy; by Lily with her painting; by William Bankes with his scientific objectivity; by (the probably homosexual) Augustus Carmichael with his mystical, impersonal Persian poetry; and by the children. In *Moments of Being*, Virginia Woolf describes the Stephen children as a republic opposing a tyranny. 'Vanessa and I were explorers, revolutionists, reformers', fighting against their father and half-brothers, both 'as individuals' and 'in their public capacity'.[52] Cam and James's conspiracy against tyranny re-enacts that battle: it is a political war, fought in the interests of a freer society (the kind in which Paul and Minta's marriage could be perceived as a success rather than a failure) which the Ramsays cannot envisage – or control. 'Their children would see some strange things', says Mr Ramsay to Macalister.

But, as always, Woolf buried the polemical substance of the book below what interested her more: intense emotions, the creation of character and atmosphere, the rhythms of perception. Again and again, *en route* from the manuscript to the final version, direct references are eliminated or obscured. These elisions are made in the interests of fluidity, and one of the most striking and intensive developments in the narrative from first to final version is in her shaping of roughed-out ideas. Unfinished phrases and loosely written passages are condensed, lyricized and made rhythmical. A letter to Vita comments on the process:

> Style is a very simple matter; it is all rhythm. Once you get that, you can't use the wrong words. But on the other hand here am I sitting after half the morning, crammed with ideas, and visions, and so on, and can't dislodge them, for lack of the right rhythm. Now this is very profound, what rhythm is, and goes far deeper than words. A sight, an emotion, creates this wave in the mind, long before it makes words to fit it; and in writing (such is my present belief) one has to recapture this, and set this working (which has nothing apparently to do with words) and then, as it breaks and tumbles in the mind, it makes words to fit it.[53]

This process of applying words to a wave-like rhythm shows that Woolf's characteristic fictional tone was the product of a highly engineered and contrived operation. The wordless movement of the wave that it recaptures might be natural and instinctive, but the recapturing process is all hard work. In *To the Lighthouse*, the most spontaneous-sounding lyrical passages have all been much laboured over. Take, for instance, Cam's rhapsody over her father. The manuscript version reads:

> For nothing/ no one [could be more] attracted her more than this strange old man. His hands were beautiful; & his [strong], shapely feet. His voice was beautiful, & his words. [He] Above all, his haste & his fervour; his oddity; his ridiculousness; his burning extreme/energy; & his remoteness; [& his] But what remained intolerable, & would

forever indicate as with the suddenly raising, unknown to himself, of an arm, upright, & monitory, & enough to quell the stormiest passions of her heart, [was] his intolerable [arrogance, his irra] demand upon her, upon James, upon the whole world perhaps; Submit to me.[54]

In the final version, the rhythm has been mastered and the words made to 'fit' it, the texture has been thickened and filled in with allusions to what exists outside Cam's mental language – his quotation, his book, the fish – to make the moment 'deeper and richer':

For no one attracted her more; his hands were beautiful to her and his feet, and his voice, and his words, and his haste, and his temper, and his oddity, and his passion, and his saying straight out before everyone, we perish, each alone, and his remoteness. (He had opened his book.) But what remained intolerable, she thought, sitting upright, and watching Macalister's boy tug the hook out of the gills of another fish, was that crass blindness and tyranny of his which had poisoned her childhood and raised bitter storms, so that even now she woke in the night trembling with rage and remembered some command of his; some insolence: 'Do this', 'Do that'; his dominance: his 'Submit to me'. (pp. 184–5.)

Or take the end of 'The Window', which reads so eloquently and calmly, but which gave her a great deal of trouble. Here is the first version:

She never could say things she felt. So, getting up She stood at the window, with the reddish brown stocking still knitting, & watching the light from the lighthouse. [Now it was so dark that the sea, on either side, seemed like black marble.] It came & went; [h] direct & strange, & over the sea, like a
   And she thought felt/knew [perfectly certain that he] was watching her, & she knew that he was/what/thinking of her,

& [The] more beautiful than ever, & she knew that it would [give him [exqu] great pleasure could she turn & say to him you have made me so perfectly happy; you have] was not necessary to say anything; but no: she could not do it [& that it was enough for her to turn round with her knitting,] [*in the margin*: she knew that he wished him to tell him how she loved him], smiling because she had known he & she turned round, with her knitting, & smiled at him, because – oh of course she was perfectly right; [she] he knew what she felt: & she need only say to him 'Yes: its going to be wet to-morrow.'[55]

She is still making last-minute changes to this in the proofs, hovering between 'partly because she did not mind looking now, with him watching, at the Lighthouse' and 'partly because she remembered how beautiful it often is – the sea at night'; between 'And she felt very beautiful' and 'And she felt herself very beautiful'; and between two endings, which place the emphasis, differently, on Mr. and Mrs Ramsay's feelings:

'Yes, you were right. It's going to be wet to-morrow.' She had not said it, but he knew it. And she looked at him smiling. For she had triumphed again.

'Yes, you were right. It's going to be wet to-morrow. You won't be able to go.' And she looked at him smiling. For she had triumphed again. She had not said it; yet he knew.[56]

The shaping of the final version had a great deal to do with distancing the autobiographical material ('. . . it will be too like father, or mother'). So Julia Stephen's French ancestry is made Italian (though this doesn't prevent her from inheriting a French recipe for Bœuf en Daube from her grandmother!) and her passion for Walter Scott, equal to her husband's, is cut out so that Scott can be used to bolster Mr Ramsay's maleness. In general, the businesslike, efficient side of Julia's character (much in evidence in her tips for good nursing, *Notes from Sick Rooms*) is suppressed in favour of her solitary, brooding, mystical side. Mr Ramsay is no longer seen, like Leslie Stephen, lecturing on agnosticism in ugly halls, as he is in the first version, and some of the awful scenes between the Ramsay children and their widowed father – scenes which her memoirs in *Moments of Being* vividly evoke – are censored.

These autobiographical expurgations should make us wary of reading *To the Lighthouse* too simply as a literal transcription of Virginia Stephen's childhood. Certainly the novel bears a relation to some identifiable sources. The autobiographical reminiscences in *Moments of Being* (written both before and after the novel) are often very close.[57] It seems as if she must have reread her father's 1895 confessional document to his children, *The Mausoleum Book*, since several of the details about his feelings for his lost Julia appear in the novel. Though she did not reread her parents' letters in 1925, she had laboriously transcribed them in the autumn of 1904 for F. W. Maitland's biography of her father, published in 1906. And she did go back to her diary for 1905, the year that biography was being written. (She wrote to Vita in January 1926 saying that she had left the diary either at Long Barn or Charleston, so she must have been rereading it.[58]) The diary contained a record of the Stephen children's return to St Ives in the summer of 1905. She was also thinking about her great-aunt, Julia Margaret Cameron, as she was writing an introduction to a book of her photographs, published in 1926. Cameron's portraits of Julia Duckworth had been hung on the walls of Gordon

Square when the Stephen children moved to Bloomsbury. Now those mournful images were in her mind again, invoking a double memory: of her mother as she was in Virginia's childhood, and of the time, ten years after her death, when she and the other Stephen children were making a new life without their parents.

But where 'is' Virginia Woolf in her retrospect? She 'is' the child Rose, choosing her mother's jewelry in the parental bedroom; she 'is' the adolescent Nancy, making an empire out of a rock pool and drawing in her skirts at the sight of adult passion; she 'is' Cam in the nursery being talked asleep by her mother, and Cam in the boat adoring and hating her father; she 'is' also Lily, painting this book.

But, 'the painting bits', which she feared Vanessa would laugh at,[59] are drawn from Vanessa and from conversations with Jacques Raverat and Roger Fry. And Vanessa, with her family of children and her beauty and shabbiness and privacy 'is' also Mrs Ramsay: 'Probably there is a great deal of you in Mrs. Ramsay.'[60] When Virginia goes to a lecture by Tatiana Tolstoi, she 'is' Charles Tansley, hating the upper classes and 'wishing to excuse my life to Tolstoi'.[61] The deaths of Prue and Mrs Ramsay, going across the fields in their white wreaths, are obviously 'about' the deaths of Julia Stephen and Virginia's half-sister, Stella Duckworth, who died so soon after her mother. But in December 1925, she again finds herself thinking about Katherine Mansfield, 'that faint ghost', whose death in 1923 had brought into her mind the image of 'Katherine putting on a white wreath, & leaving us, called away; made dignified, chosen.'[62] Possibly Lily's almost erotic desire for physical closeness to Mrs Ramsay may be connected to Virginia's growing feelings for Vita, whom she imagines, while she is writing the novel, as like 'a lighthouse,

fitful, sudden, remote'.[63] Mrs Ramsay's dark feelings about
solitude and death 'are' also Virginia's, and also derive
from her reading of De Quincey while she was writing the
novel. (De Quincey was her mother's favourite writer, but
Mrs Ramsay's liking for him is cut out of the finished
version.[64]) Of all these obscure and complicated connec-
tions between the life and the fiction, perhaps the most
surprising – and, it may be, the deepest – is between
Virginia Woolf and Mr Ramsay. The comic, tyrannical,
charismatic father is often described as the enemy in the
novel. But Virginia Stephen used to go walking and de-
claiming poetry, like Mr Ramsay. And when he broods on
the relation between Shakespeare and the liftman in the
tube, or is obsessed about his own immortality ('Ah, but
how long do you think it'll last?'), it is not only Leslie
Stephen's anxieties and egotism she is invoking. 'Murry
has arraigned your poor Virginia', she writes to Vita in
February 1926, 'and Virginia's poor Tom Eliot, and all
their works, in the Adelphi, and condemned them to
death.'[65] 'Murry says my works won't be read in 10 years'
time,' she writes in the diary, next to her joyful exclamation
about the progress of *To the Lighthouse*: 'Never never have
I written so easily.'[66] John Middleton Murry's article on
'The Classical Revival', which described *Jacob's Room* and
The Waste Land as failures that nobody would be reading
in ten or fifty years' time, was as much the source for Mr.
Ramsay's wanting to reach 'R' as Leslie Stephen's lamentations in *The Mausoleum Book*.

But the simple reading is *also* right. *To the Lighthouse is*
about her childhood, her relationship with her father as she
grew up, her terrible grief for her mother and her feelings
of edgy solidarity with her siblings. It has that peculiarly
intimate, deep feeling which comes out of fictions where

childhood memory is being uncovered and appeased, like George Eliot's *The Mill on the Floss*, Katherine Mansfield's *Prelude*, Willa Cather's *My Antonia* or James Joyce's *A Portrait of the Artist as a Young Man*. Virginia Woolf's childhood, family and young adulthood were her essential subjects. She repeatedly wrote about her dead parents (in *The Voyage Out*, *Night and Day*, here, and in *The Years*) and her dead brother (in *Jacob's Room* and *The Waves*). She knew very well what she was doing for herself in writing *To the Lighthouse*, and explained it twice, once in the diary for 1928, about a year and a half after finishing the book, and once, many years later, in the autobiographical 'Sketch of the Past' she wrote for her friends. Both explanations refer to the writing of the novel in therapeutic terms, but one is about her father and the other about her mother:

1928

Father's birthday. He would have been $\frac{1832}{96}$ 96, yes, today;

& could have been 96, like other people one has known; but mercifully was not. His life would have entirely ended mine. What would have happened? No writing, no books; – inconceivable. I used to think of him & mother daily; but writing The Lighthouse laid them in my mind. And now he comes back sometimes, but differently. (I believe this to be true – that I was obsessed by them both, unhealthily; & writing of them was a necessary act.)[67]

It is perfectly true that she obsessed me, in spite of the fact that she died when I was thirteen, until I was forty-four. Then one day walking round Tavistock Square I made up, as I sometimes make up my books, *To The Lighthouse*; in a great, apparently involuntary rush ... I wrote the book very quickly; and when it was written, I ceased to be obsessed by my mother. I no longer hear her voice; I do not see her.

I suppose that I did for myself what psychoanalysts do for their patients. I expressed some very long felt and deeply felt emotion. And in expressing it I explained it and then laid it to rest.[68]

'Laid them in my mind', 'laid it to rest', 'Rest, rest, perturbed spirit!'. 'Laying' is what is done to ghosts; they are exorcised so that they will cause no more trouble to others, but also so that they can be 'at rest' themselves. The writing of *To the Lighthouse* was the closest that Virginia Woolf came, she says, to undergoing psychoanalysis; she invented her own therapy – the narrative – and exorcised her obsession with both her parents. But it also seems, from her repeated choice of words when she describes this process, that she felt the writing of the novel to be a way of pacifying their ghosts.

To the Lighthouse is a ghost story. Mrs Ramsay's feast derives its magical quality from its mythical resemblance to the Dionysian feast for the souls of the dead, at which, at the end of the meal, the priest (in this case Mr Carmichael) would address the ghosts of the place placatingly, and bid them depart.[69] The disembodied voices at the start of 'Time Passes' are the prologue to a more extended version of her early sketch, 'A Haunted House'. And Mrs Ramsay reappears as a ghost ('It was part of her perfect goodness to Lily') at the end of the novel. Like other great modernist works of the time, in which ghosts break into the modern world – Leopold Bloom's son Rudi and Stephen Dedalus's mother in Joyce's *Ulysses*, the ghost of Tiresias in *The Waste Land* and the 'familiar compound ghost' at the end of the *Four Quartets* – this fiction is itself a 'haunted house'.

The mother died; and 'the house was left; the house was

deserted'. The house in St Ives where the Stephen children had spent all their summers since they were born, and with which Virginia Woolf identified her earliest memories of 'the purest ecstasy I can conceive',[70] was given up after Julia's death. Woolf spent a great deal of imaginative time trying to return to it, 'to reach a state where I seem to be watching things happen as if I were there'.[71] She sees her childhood as a 'space of time' which ends on the day of her mother's death; immediately after that, 'St Ives vanished for ever'.[72] Ten years later, the Stephen children went back to Cornwall, walked up to Talland House on the evening they arrived at St Ives, and looked at it again: 'It was a ghostly thing to do.'[73]

> There was the house ... there were the stone urns, against the bank of tall flowers; all, so far as we could see was as though we had but left it in the morning. But yet, as we knew well, we could go no further; if we advanced the spell was broken. The lights were not our lights; the voices were the voices of strangers.[74]

These unhoused ghosts returning to the lost home have a strong Victorian feeling to them. The diary entry reminds me of Tennyson's 'Enoch Arden', with its shipwrecked sailor returning years later to his old home, looking in the window to see another man at his hearth with his wife and family, and creeping away 'like a thief'. 'Time Passes' dwells on the deserted house like the verses of 'In Memoriam' which lament the lost rectory at Somersby:

> Unwatched, the garden bough shall sway,
> The tender blossom flutter down,
> Unloved, that beech will gather brown,
> This maple burn itself away ...

Till from the garden and the wild
A fresh association blow,
And year by year the landscape grow
Familiar to the stranger's child.[75]

'The lights were not our lights; the voices were the voices of strangers.' *To the Lighthouse* has the emotions of a Victorian pastoral elegy. There is a Tennysonian mood to it.[76] One of Mr Ramsay's bursts of quotation, in the manuscript, is Matthew Arnold's 'Thyrsis',[77] the elegy for Arthur Clough, lost scholar and poet. In this Greek lament translated to the fields of Oxfordshire, the poet looks back on his Arcadia from 'the great town's harsh, heart-wearying roar', and longs for the language in which the Greek elegiac poets could invoke Proserpine or Orpheus.

The family setting in *To the Lighthouse* is also a lost garden, often remembered (by Lily or Mr Bankes) from the limbo of the 'great town'. It is, of course, full of classical decorations and allusions – Helen, Demeter and Persephone, Bacchus and Neptune, the feast for the dead and the journey to the underworld. Mr Ramsay's 'little book' (there are more clues to this in the manuscript[78]) is probably his Plato, and the 'undifferentiated voices'[79] of the Greek chorus are imitated in the 'stray airs' of 'Time Passes'. But the Greekness of *To the Lighthouse* is filtered through the nineteenth century. Mrs Ramsay and Prue stepping with their wreaths and flowers across the fields are Demeter and Proserpine as imagined by Swinburne or the Pre-Raphaelites or Julia Margaret Cameron. Mr Ramsay 'doing homage to the beauty of the world' in the person of his wife and child sounds like Pater's rhapsody over the *Mona Lisa* (even more so in the manuscript, where she looks like 'the profound spirit brooding over the waters of life'[80]). (*To the Lighthouse* has a Victorian nonsense comedy in it, too, with Augustus Carmichael as the Dormouse at the Mad Hatter's tea party, and Mr Ramsay bursting out of the bushes at Miss Giddings like the White Rabbit or Lear's 'Old Person of Buda, Whose conduct grew ruder and ruder'.[81])

But the time of Victorian, neo-classical pastoral has passed: this is a twentieth-century, 'modern' novel. The savage break of narrative down the middle of the book, like Lily's line down the middle of her painting, is a break with literary tradition as much as with childhood. 'Time Passes' was her most adventurous departure from traditional representation; it alarmed and liberated her:

> I cannot make it out – here is the most difficult abstract piece of writing – I have to give an empty house, no people's characters, the passage of time, all eyeless & featureless with nothing to cling to; well, I rush at it, & at once scatter out two pages. Is it nonsense, is it brilliance? Why am I so flown with words, & apparently free to do exactly what I like?[82]

This drastic break marks an intensified struggle for form in 'Time Passes' and 'The Lighthouse' (notice how much harder it is to remember the order things take in these parts), as a new kind of language and shape for fiction is invented. The novel is explicit about this process of invention: constant comparisons are made between the form this narrative is taking, and the previous, established forms against which it has to measure itself. So Lily is well aware that 'she could have done it differently of course', and has to justify to Mr Bankes the possibility that a purple triangle might represent the Madonna and Child just as well as a painting by Raphael or Titian. Mr Ramsay's enthusiasm for the 'strength and sanity' of Scott, and Mrs Ramsay's for the shape of the Shakespeare sonnet, build in a challenge to this poetic fiction (as Lily is challenged by the 'formidable' space of her untried canvas) to equal its literary predecessors.

The lost safe-house and garden are the traditions of writing from which the new writer has to travel, out into formidable space. But the new writing keeps trying to find its way back into the past, so that there is an odd tension in the book between the experimental and the nostalgic. In the last part of the book, there is a painful desire, felt in different ways by Lily, James and Cam, to rediscover the true language of the garden, which they associate with Mrs Ramsay. On the first page, James has the colours and sounds of that garden as his 'secret language'. In the boat he tries to get back to the sound of the garden, before the wheel went over a foot, crushing it, and his father's world of rain and greyness took over. This is even more explicit in the manuscript, where the world of his mother's language is described as 'that miraculous garden ... before the fall of the world (& he did really divide time into the space before the catastrophe, & the space after)'.[83] In James's Oedipal narrative, Eden, or Arcadia, 'that miraculous garden' which precedes the law of the father, is a place where 'people spoke in an ordinary tone of voice' and where his mother 'alone spoke the truth'. Cam, too, remembers her mother speaking a rhythmical and nonsensical nursery language of mountains and birds and gardens to send her to sleep, a language which has become a foreign tongue in the adult world but which can be recapitulated in dream or solitude.[84] The novel's task is to make its new language re-embody – through rhythm, images and shapes – that first, vanished language.

To the Lighthouse is about something ending, and it contains a number of endings: Mrs Ramsay's story to James ('And that's the end'); the last volume of *Middlemarch* left on the train by Minta Doyle; the end of Scott's story about poor Steenie drowning that Mr Ramsay reads after dinner ('Well, let them improve upon that, he thought as he finished the chapter'); the little book he finishes as his journey to the lighthouse ends ('Mr Ramsay had almost done reading' – and so have we when we read that); and Lily's 'vision'. *To the Lighthouse* has so much to do with endings because its subject is death, not just people dying and being mourned, but the wish for death. 'If she had said half what he said,' Mrs Ramsay thinks of her husband, 'she would have blown her brains out by now'. She goes into action at the dinner party like a sailor who sets off again wearily, but would almost rather have 'found rest on the floor of the sea'. I don't suppose Mrs Ramsay kills herself (though Lily, in the manuscript, 'had never heard how she had died: only "Suddenly"'[85]), but her deep sense of the cruelty and sadness of being alive are at the bottom of the whole novel.

As well as endings, though, there are recurrences. A number of things happen twice. There are two dinner parties, the one Mrs Ramsay has in mind in 'The Window' (from which her sons and daughters disappear 'directly the meal was over') and the one we see in full. There are two journeys to the lighthouse, the promised and the actual. There are two lighthouses, too, as seen by James: 'For nothing was simply one thing'. There are two paintings, the one Lily starts in 'The Window' and the one she starts again in 'The Lighthouse'. The Ramsays' lives, like the novel, give off 'constantly a sense of repetition'. And Mrs Ramsay returns at the end as the model for Lily's painting, in the same position she took up in 'The Window'. The ending of the novel is poised between arriving and returning, getting somewhere ('he must have reached it') and being finished. This dark book of loss and grief begins and ends with sentences starting 'Yes': yes, and a tentative conditional future ('if it's fine to-morrow'); yes, and an immediately vanished past ('I have had my vision'). The 'yes' of narrative – something shaped, but liable always to shapelessness – keeps having to be reaffirmed.

Hermione Lee

NOTES

1. Woolf wrote an essay called 'Cinema' in April 1926, while in the early stages of writing *TL*, in which she imagined a cinema of the future that would use its 'picture making power' to make thoughts visible, like smoke pouring from Vesuvius (*CE*, II, p. 271).
2. *Diary*, III, 5 Sept. 1926, p. 106.
3. *CE*, II, p. 2.
4. Quoted by Lyndall Gordon in *Virginia Woolf: A Writer's Life* (OUP, 1984, p. 112), who makes this connection between the form of *TL* and her vision of Santa Sophia. See 'The Window', Note 67.
5. *Diary*, III, 14 March 1927, pp. 131–2.
6. Letter to Vanessa Bell, 8 May 1927, *Letters*, III, p. 370.
7. *Diary*, II, 17 Oct. 1924, p. 317.
8. *MS*, appendix A, pp. 44–5, 47–50.
9. *Diary*, III, 14 May 1925, pp. 18–19.
10. ibid., 14 June 1925, p. 29.
11. Virginia Woolf, *The Complete Shorter Fiction*, ed. Susan Dick (Hogarth Press, 1985, pp. 169, 179, 203, 197).
12. ibid., pp. 189–94.

13. ibid., pp. 175–7.

14. *Diary*, III, 27 June 1925, p. 34.

15. ibid., 20 July 1925, p. 36.

16. ibid., 5 Sept. 1926, p. 106.

17. ibid., 13 Sept. 1926, p. 110.

18. ibid., 5 May 1927, p. 134.

19. Letter to Vita Sackville-West, 13 May 1927, *Letters*, III, p. 374.

20. *Diary*, III, 8 April 1925, p. 7.

21. ibid., 30 July 1925, p. 37.

22. ibid., 5 Sept. 1925, p. 39.

23. Letter to Roger Fry, 16 Sept. 1925, *Letters*, III, p. 208.

24. *CE*, IV, pp. 194–5.

25. Letter to Vanessa Bell, 29 Sept. 1925, *Letters*, III, p. 217.

26. *Diary*, III, 7 Dec. 1925, p. 49.

27. *MS*, p. 3.

28. *Diary*, III, 8 Feb. 1926, p. 58.

29. Letter to Vita Sackville-West, 13 May 1927, *Letters*, III, p. 374.

30. *Diary*, III, 31 July 1926, p. 103.

31. Letter to Vita Sackville-West, 16 March 1926, *Letters*, III, p. 249.

32. *MS*, p. 3.

33. Letter to Vita Sackville-West, 13 May 1927, *Letters*, III, p. 373.

34. Letter to Ottoline Morrell, 15 May 1927, ibid., p. 378.

35. *Diary*, III, 5 Sept. 1926, p. 107.

36. ibid., 13 Sept. 1926, p. 109.

37. ibid., 30 Sept. 1926, p. 113.

38. ibid., 30 Oct. 1926, p. 114.

39. ibid., 23 Nov. 1926, p. 117.

40. Letter to Angus Davidson, 25 Dec. 1926, *Letters*, III, p. 310.

41. *Diary*, III, 23 Jan. 1927, p. 123.

42. ibid., 21 March 1927, p. 132.

43. ibid., 7 Nov. 1928, p. 203.

44. ibid., 13 Sept. 1926, p. 109.

45. Letter to Roger Fry, 27 May 1927, *Letters*, III, p. 385.

46. *Moments of Being*, p. 122.

47. There were two first editions, American and English, which contain considerable variations. Even at the proof-reading stage she was making changes. See Appendix II for the main differences between the two texts.

48. *MS*, p. 29.

49. *MS*, p. 136.

50. *MS*, pp. 137, 148, 152, 216, 316.

51. As the name Bast suggests, there is a resemblance to *Howards End*, and to Forster's feeling that the middle classes might be redeemed by an injection of life from below. Mrs Ramsay slightly resembles Mrs Wilcox, and the Ramsays' abandoned house, 'Howards End'.

52. *Moments of Being*, pp. 126–7. On p. 105, she describes the Stephen children as a 'republic'.

53. Letter to Vita Sackville-West, 16 March 1926, *Letters*, III, p. 247.

54. *MS*, p. 290.

55. *MS*, p. 197.

56. 'The Window', section 19, *To the Lighthouse*, first American edn (Harcourt, Brace & Co., 5 May 1927).

57. See note references to *Moments of Being*.

58. Letter to Vita Sackville-West, 7 Jan. 1926, *Letters*, III, p. 227.

59. Letter to Vanessa Bell, 8 May 1927, ibid., p. 372.

60. Letter to Vanessa Bell, 25 May 1927, ibid., p. 383.

61. Letter to Vita Sackville-West, 31 Jan. 1926, ibid., p. 236.

62. *Diary*, II, 16 Jan. 1923, p. 226; *Diary*, III, 7 Dec. 1925, p. 50.

63. Letter to Vita Sackville-West, 23 Sept. 1925, *Letters*, III, p. 215.

64. See 'The Window', Note 102.

65. Letter to Vita Sackville-West, 3 Feb. 1926, *Letters*, III, p. 238.

66. *Diary*, III, 8 Feb. 1926, p. 58.

67. ibid., 28 Nov. 1928, p. 208.

68. *Moments of Being*, p. 81.

69. Woolf would have read about this in her friend Jane Harri-

son's *Prolegomena to the Study of Greek Religion* (CUP, 1903, 1908, 1922). See 'The Window', Note 32.

70. *Moments of Being*, p. 65.

71. ibid., p. 67.

72. ibid., p. 117.

73. Letter to Violet Dickinson, Aug. 1905, *Letters*, I, p. 204.

74. *A Passionate Apprentice*, 'Diary 1905', p. 282. Lyndall Gordon notes that Woolf again returned to Talland House in 1936, the summer she was writing *The Waves* and close to a breakdown.

75. *The Poems of Alfred Tennyson*, ed. C. Ricks (Longman, 1969, p. 954).

76. See 'The Window', Note 77; 'The Lighthouse', Note 20.

77. See 'The Window', Note 40.

78. See 'The Lighthouse', Note 12.

79. 'On Not Knowing Greek' (*CE*, I, p. 5).

80. *MS*, p. 69.

81. *The Complete Nonsense of Edward Lear* (Faber, 1947, p. 14).

82. *Diary*, III, 18 April 1926, p. 76.

83. *MS*, p. 309.

84. The replacement of the maternal, rhythmic language with the law of the father, closely resembles Lacan's account of the child's entry into the symbolic order.

85. *MS*, p. 303.

Further Reading

T. J. Rice's *Virginia Woolf: A Guide to Research* (Garland, 1984), lists 107 articles on *TL*, in addition to 90 general critical books and 257 general critical articles, and there has been a great deal more written since then. Out of all this, essential biographical reading is still Quentin Bell's two volume biography *Virginia Woolf* (Hogarth Press, 1972), to which I would add Noel Annan's *Leslie Stephen: The Godless Victorian* (Weidenfeld & Nicolson, 1984), Lyndall Gordon's *Virginia Woolf: A Writer's Life* (OUP, 1984) and Phyllis Rose's *Woman of Letters: A Life of Virginia Woolf* (OUP, 1978). I list my essential primary sources in the Bibliographical Note.

For illuminating discussions of the narrative methods of *TL*, see Erich Auerbach, 'The Brown Stocking' in *Mimesis: The Representation of Reality in Western Literature* (1946) (trans. W. Trask, Princeton University Press, 1953) and chapter fourteen of Allen McClaurin's *Virginia Woolf: The Echoes Enslaved* (CUP, 1973).

For the mythology of the novel, see Joseph Blotner, 'Mythic Patterns in *To the Lighthouse*' (PMLA, No. 71, 1956, pp. 547ff.); Madeline Moore, 'Some Female Versions of Pastoral: *The Voyage Out* and Matriarchal Mythologies' in *New Feminist Essays on Virginia Woolf* (ed. Jane Marcus, Macmillan, 1981, pp. 82–104); and Maria di Battista, *Virginia Woolf's Major Novels: The Fables of Anon* (Yale University Press, 1980). For Walter Scott in *TL*, see S. Cohan, 'Why Mr Ramsay reads *The Antiquary*' in *Women and Literature* (No. 2, vol. 7, spring 1979, pp. 14–24). For the evolution of the text of *TL*, see J. A. Lavin, '*The First editions of Virginia Woolf's To the Lighthouse*' in *Proof* (No. 2, 1972, pp. 185–211) and *To the Lighthouse: The Original Holograph Draft*, transcribed and edited by Susan Dick (Toronto University Press, 1982; Hogarth Press, 1983). For interesting feminist readings of *TL*, see Rachel Bowlby, *Virginia Woolf: Feminist Destinations*, ch. 4, (Blackwell, 1988) and Margaret Homans, 'Mothers and Daughters in Virginia Woolf's Victorian Novel' in *Bearing the Word: Language and Female Experience in Nineteenth-Century Women's Writing* (Chicago University Press, 1986). There is a useful collection of essays in *Virginia Woolf's To the Lighthouse: A Casebook* (ed. Morris Beja, Macmillan, 1970).

A Note on the Text

The text of this edition of *To the Lighthouse* is based on the original British edition published by Leonard and Virginia Woolf at The Hogarth Press on 5 May 1927, of which a second impression appeared in June 1927 and a third impression in May 1928. In 1930 a 'New Edition' was published; it included a few substantive emendations, and also one new substantive error, 'dower' for 'power' on p. 119 (this edition, p.83; the 'd' is in fact an inverted 'p'; evidently the first letter of the line had worked loose and been wrongly replaced), which was perpetuated in subsequent British editions from The Hogarth Press (1932–77), J. M. Dent & Sons (1938) and Granada Publishing (1977).

The first American edition was published by Harcourt, Brace & Company on 5 May 1927. Later impressions of this edition, and the Harcourt Brace Jovanovich Harvest edition, follow it without variation.

The two first editions, British and American, published on the same day, contain a large number of substantive and accidental variant readings; the substantive ones alone total 174; neither the list in the *Concordance to To the Lighthouse* edited by James M. Haule and Philip H. Smith, Jr (Oxford, 1983) nor that in the *Definitive Collected Edition of the Novels of Virginia Woolf* (The Hogarth Press, 1990) includes all of them. A small selection is given in Appendix II. Some of these substantive variants are no doubt the result of printers' errors, and others may have been introduced by an American copy editor, but the majority must be due to the fact that Virginia Woolf, revising her novel while it was in proof, and marking one set of proofs for return to her Edinburgh printers (R. & R. Clark, Limited) and another set for forwarding to her American publishers, did not alter the two sets of proofs consistently. The original holograph draft, which is housed in the New York Public Library (Henry W. and Albert A. Berg Collection) and which has been edited by Susan Dick (Toronto University Press, 1982; The Hogarth Press, 1983), is of some evidential value, though it represents an earlier stage in composition than the typescript and the revised proofs.

What is certain is that Virginia Woolf never emended the British first edition by collating the American one. The half-dozen substantive emendations introduced into the 1930 'New Edition' are independent of the American edition, and the mis-numbering of subsections 2 to 14 of 'The Lighthouse', though corrected in the American edition (undoubtedly by a copy editor), was not corrected in a Hogarth Press edition until 1943, two years after the author's death. (In Dent's 1938 edition it had been guessingly rectified, again by a copy editor, by dividing the first subsection into two.) There is nothing to show that Virginia Woolf so much as saw a copy of the American first edition.

For these reasons the first British edition has been taken as the basis of this Penguin edition. It has, however, been carefully scrutinized, and a number of substantive emendations have been either adopted or conjectured; a list of these is given in Appendix I, with brief textual notes where these are appropriate. When Virginia Woolf's diction is idiosyncratic (for instance, p. 47.17, 'Tears had flown in her presence', where 'flown' is intended to be the past participle of the verb 'flow', not that of the verb 'fly') it has not, of course, been interfered with. Nor, in the main, has her inconsistent and idiosyncratic punctuation, irritating though many readers will find it (particularly her frequently beginning a subordinate clause with a comma and neglecting to end it with one). Such non-substantive emendations as have been made (for instance, p. 25.21, the printing of the first British edition's 'sand hills' as 'sand-hills', the form which it takes on its two closely following occurrences, or, p. 62.25, the insertion of secondary quotation marks when Mrs Ramsay is speaking aloud the dialogue in the story she is reading to James) have not been listed; though they are few in number it would be unprofitable to draw readers' attention to them.

Stella McNichol 1991

TO THE LIGHTHOUSE

VIRGINIA WOOLF

PUBLISHED BY LEONARD & VIRGINIA WOOLF AT THE
HOGARTH PRESS, 52 TAVISTOCK SQUARE, LONDON, W.C.
1927

Contents

I
The Window 5

II
Time Passes 135

III
The Lighthouse 157

I
THE WINDOW[1]

'Yes, of course, if it's fine to-morrow,' said Mrs. Ramsay. 'But you'll have to be up with the lark,' she added.

To her son these words conveyed an extraordinary joy, as if it were settled the expedition[2] were bound to take place, and the wonder to which he had looked forward, for years and years it seemed, was, after a night's darkness and a day's sail, within touch. Since he belonged, even at the age of six, to that great clan which cannot keep this feeling separate from that, but must let future prospects, with their joys and sorrows, cloud what is actually at hand, since to such people even in earliest childhood any turn in the wheel of sensation has the power to crystallise and transfix the moment upon which its gloom or radiance rests, James Ramsay, sitting on the floor cutting out pictures from the illustrated catalogue of the Army and Navy Stores,[3] endowed the picture of a refrigerator as his mother spoke with heavenly bliss. It was fringed with joy. The wheelbarrow, the lawn-mower, the sound of poplar trees, leaves whitening before rain, rooks cawing, brooms knocking, dresses rustling – all these were so coloured and distinguished in his mind that he had already his private code, his secret language, though he appeared the image of stark and uncompromising severity, with his high forehead and his fierce blue eyes, impeccably candid and pure, frowning slightly at the sight of human frailty, so that his mother, watching him guide his scissors neatly round the refrigerator, imagined him all red and ermine on the Bench or directing a stern and momentous enterprise in some crisis of public affairs.

'But,' said his father, stopping in front of the drawing-room window, 'it won't be fine.'

Had there been an axe handy, a poker, or any weapon that would have gashed a hole in his father's breast and killed him, there and then, James would have seized it. Such were the extremes of emotion that Mr. Ramsay excited in his children's breasts by his mere presence; standing, as now, lean as a knife, narrow as the blade of one, grinning sarcastically, not only with the pleasure of disillusioning his son and casting ridicule upon his wife, who was ten thousand times better in every way than he was (James thought), but also with some secret conceit at his own accuracy of judgement. What he said was true. It was always true. He was incapable of untruth; never tampered with a fact; never altered a disagreeable word to suit the pleasure or convenience of any mortal being, least of all of his own children, who, sprung from his loins, should be aware from childhood that life is difficult; facts uncompromising; and the passage to that fabled land where our brightest hopes are extinguished, our frail barks[4] founder in darkness (here Mr. Ramsay would straighten his back and narrow his little blue eyes upon the horizon), one that needs, above all, courage, truth, and the power to endure.

'But it may be fine – I expect it will be fine,' said Mrs. Ramsay, making some little twist of the reddish-brown stocking she was knitting, impatiently. If she finished it to-night, if they did go to the Lighthouse after all, it was to be given to the Lighthouse keeper for his little boy, who was threatened with a tuberculous hip;[5] together with a pile of old magazines, and some tobacco, indeed whatever she could find lying about, not really wanted, but only littering the room, to give those poor fellows who must be bored to death sitting all day with nothing to do but polish

the lamp and trim the wick and rake about on their scrap
of garden, something to amuse them. For how would you
like to be shut up for a whole month at a time, and
possibly more in stormy weather, upon a rock the size of
a tennis lawn? she would ask; and to have no letters or
newspapers, and to see nobody; if you were married, not
to see your wife, not to know how your children were, – if
they were ill, if they had fallen down and broken their legs
or arms; to see the same dreary waves breaking week after
week, and then a dreadful storm coming, and the windows
covered with spray, and birds dashed against the lamp, and
the whole place rocking, and not be able to put your nose
out of doors for fear of being swept into the sea? How
would you like that? she asked, addressing herself particularly to her daughters. So she added, rather differently, one
must take them whatever comforts one can.

'It's due west,' said the atheist Tansley,[6] holding his
bony fingers spread so that the wind blew through them,
for he was sharing Mr. Ramsay's evening walk up and
down, up and down the terrace. That is to say, the wind
blew from the worst possible direction for landing at the
Lighthouse. Yes, he did say disagreeable things, Mrs.
Ramsay admitted; it was odious of him to rub this in, and
make James still more disappointed; but at the same time,
she would not let them laugh at him. 'The atheist', they
called him; 'the little atheist'. Rose mocked him; Prue
mocked him; Andrew, Jasper, Roger mocked him; even
old Badger without a tooth in his head had bit him, for
being (as Nancy put it) the hundred and tenth young man
to chase them all the way up to the Hebrides[7] when it was
ever so much nicer to be alone.

'Nonsense,' said Mrs. Ramsay, with great severity. Apart
from the habit of exaggeration which they had from her,

9

and from the implication (which was true) that she asked too many people to stay, and had to lodge some in the town, she could not bear incivility to her guests, to young men in particular, who were poor as church mice, 'exceptionally able', her husband said, his great admirers, and come there for a holiday. Indeed, she had the whole of the other sex under her protection; for reasons she could not explain, for their chivalry and valour, for the fact that they negotiated treaties, ruled India,[8] controlled finance; finally for an attitude towards herself which no woman could fail to feel or to find agreeable, something trustful, childlike, reverential; which an old woman could take from a young man without loss of dignity, and woe betide the girl – pray Heaven it was none of her daughters! – who did not feel the worth of it, and all that it implied, to the marrow of her bones.

She turned with severity upon Nancy. He had not chased them, she said. He had been asked.

They must find a way out of it all. There might be some simpler way, some less laborious way, she sighed. When she looked in the glass[9] and saw her hair grey, her cheek sunk, at fifty, she thought, possibly she might have managed things better – her husband; money; his books. But for her own part she would never for a single second regret her decision, evade difficulties, or slur over duties. She was now formidable to behold, and it was only in silence, looking up from their plates, after she had spoken so severely about Charles Tansley, that her daughters – Prue, Nancy, Rose – could sport with infidel ideas which they had brewed for themselves of a life different from hers; in Paris, perhaps; a wilder life; not always taking care of some man or other; for there was in all their minds a mute questioning of deference and chivalry, of the Bank of

England and the Indian Empire, of ringed fingers and lace, though to them all there was something in this of the essence of beauty, which called out the manliness in their girlish hearts, and made them, as they sat at table beneath their mother's eyes, honour her strange severity, her extreme courtesy, like a Queen's raising from the mud a beggar's dirty foot and washing it, when she thus admonished them so very severely about that wretched atheist who had chased them to – or, speaking accurately, been invited to stay with them in – the Isle of Skye.

'There'll be no landing at the Lighthouse to-morrow,' said Charles Tansley, clapping his hands together as he stood at the window with her husband. Surely, he had said enough. She wished they would both leave her and James alone and go on talking. She looked at him. He was such a miserable specimen, the children said, all humps and hollows. He couldn't play cricket; he poked; he shuffled. He was a sarcastic brute, Andrew said. They knew what he liked best – to be for ever walking up and down, up and down, with Mr. Ramsay, and saying who had won this, who had won that, who was a 'first-rate man' at Latin verses, who was 'brilliant but I think fundamentally unsound', who was undoubtedly the 'ablest fellow in Balliol', who had buried his light temporarily at Bristol or Bedford, but was bound to be heard of later when his Prolegomena,[10] of which Mr. Tansley had the first pages in proof with him if Mr. Ramsay would like to see them, to some branch of mathematics or philosophy saw the light of day. That was what they talked about.

She could not help laughing herself sometimes. She said, the other day, something about 'waves mountains high'. Yes, said Charles Tansley, it was a little rough. 'Aren't you drenched to the skin?' she had said. 'Damp, not wet through,' said Mr. Tansley, pinching his sleeve, feeling his socks.

But it was not that they minded, the children said. It was not his face; it was not his manners. It was him – his point of view. When they talked about something interesting, people, music, history, anything, even said it was a fine evening so why not sit out of doors, then what they complained of about Charles Tansley was that until he had turned the whole thing round and made it somehow reflect himself and disparage them, put them all on edge somehow with his acid way of peeling the flesh and blood off everything, he was not satisfied. And he would go to picture galleries, they said, and he would ask one, did one like his tie? God knows, said Rose, one did not.

Disappearing as stealthily as stags from the dinner-table directly the meal was over, the eight sons and daughters of Mr. and Mrs. Ramsay sought their bedrooms, their fastnesses in a house where there was no other privacy to debate anything, everything; Tansley's tie; the passing of the Reform Bill;[11] sea-birds and butterflies; people; while the sun poured into those attics, which a plank alone separated from each other so that every footstep could be plainly heard and the Swiss girl sobbing for her father who was dying of cancer in a valley of the Grisons,[12] and lit up bats, flannels, straw hats, ink-pots, paint-pots, beetles, and the skulls of small birds, while it drew from the long frilled strips of seaweed pinned to the wall a smell of salt and weeds, which was in the towels too, gritty with sand from bathing.

Strife, divisions, difference of opinion, prejudices twisted into the very fibre of being, oh that they should begin so early, Mrs. Ramsay deplored. They were so critical, her children. They talked such nonsense. She went from the dining-room, holding James by the hand, since he would

not go with the others. It seemed to her such nonsense —
inventing differences, when people, heaven knows, were
different enough without that. The real differences, she
thought, standing by the drawing-room window, are
enough, quite enough. She had in mind at the moment,
rich and poor, high and low; the great in birth receiving
from her, half grudging, some respect, for had she not in
her veins the blood of that very noble, if slightly mythical,
Italian house,[13] whose daughters, scattered about English
drawing-rooms in the nineteenth century, had lisped so
charmingly, had stormed so wildly, and all her wit and her
bearing and her temper came from them, and not from the
sluggish English, or the cold Scotch; but more profoundly
she ruminated the other problem, of rich and poor, and the
things she saw with her own eyes, weekly, daily, here or in
London, when she visited this widow, or that struggling
wife in person with a bag on her arm, and a note-book and
pencil with which she wrote down in columns carefully
ruled for the purpose wages and spendings, employment
and unemployment, in the hope that thus she would cease
to be a private woman whose charity was half a sop to her
own indignation, half a relief to her own curiosity, and
become, what with her untrained mind she greatly admired,
an investigator, elucidating the social problem.

Insoluble questions they were, it seemed to her, standing
there, holding James by the hand. He had followed her
into the drawing-room, that young man they laughed at;
he was standing by the table, fidgeting with something,
awkwardly, feeling himself out of things, as she knew
without looking round. They had all gone — the children;
Minta Doyle and Paul Rayley; Augustus Carmichael; her
husband — they had all gone. So she turned with a sigh and
said, 'Would it bore you to come with me, Mr. Tansley?'

She had a dull errand in the town; she had a letter or two to write; she would be ten minutes perhaps; she would put on her hat. And, with her basket and her parasol, there she was again, ten minutes later, giving out a sense of being ready, of being equipped for a jaunt, which, however, she must interrupt for a moment, as they passed the tennis lawn, to ask Mr. Carmichael, who was basking with his yellow cat's eyes ajar, so that like a cat's they seemed to reflect the branches moving or the clouds passing, but to give no inkling of any inner thoughts or emotion whatsoever, if he wanted anything.

For they were making the great expedition, she said, laughing. They were going to the town. 'Stamps, writing-paper, tobacco?' she suggested, stopping by his side. But no, he wanted nothing. His hands clasped themselves over his capacious paunch, his eyes blinked, as if he would have liked to reply kindly to these blandishments (she was seductive but a little nervous) but could not, sunk as he was in a grey-green somnolence which embraced them all, without need of words, in a vast and benevolent lethargy of well-wishing; all the house; all the world; all the people in it, for he had slipped into his glass at lunch a few drops of something, which accounted, the children thought, for the vivid streak of canary-yellow in moustache and beard that were otherwise milk-white. He wanted nothing, he murmured.

He should have been a great philosopher, said Mrs. Ramsay, as they went down the road to the fishing village, but he had made an unfortunate marriage. Holding her black parasol very erect, and moving with an indescribable air of expectation, as if she were going to meet someone round the corner, she told the story; an affair at Oxford with some girl; an early marriage; poverty; going to India;

translating a little poetry 'very beautifully, I believe', being willing to teach the boys Persian or Hindustanee,[14] but what really was the use of that? – and then lying, as they saw him, on the lawn.

It flattered him; snubbed as he had been, it soothed him that Mrs. Ramsay should tell him this. Charles Tansley revived. Insinuating, too, as she did the greatness of man's intellect, even in its decay, the subjection of all wives – not that she blamed the girl, and the marriage had been happy enough, she believed – to their husband's labours, she made him feel better pleased with himself than he had done yet, and he would have liked, had they taken a cab, for example, to have paid the fare. As for her little bag, might he not carry that? No, no, she said, she always carried *that* herself. She did too. Yes, he felt that in her. He felt many things, something in particular that excited him and disturbed him for reasons which he could not give. He would like her to see him, gowned and hooded, walking in a procession. A fellowship, a professorship, – he felt capable of anything and saw himself – but what was she looking at? At a man pasting a bill. The vast flapping sheet flattened itself out, and each shove of the brush revealed fresh legs, hoops, horses, glistening reds and blues, beautifully smooth, until half the wall was covered with the advertisement of a circus; a hundred horsemen, twenty performing seals, lions, tigers . . . Craning forwards, for she was short-sighted, she read out how it . . . 'will visit this town.' It was terribly dangerous work for a one-armed man, she exclaimed, to stand on top of a ladder like that – his left arm had been cut off in a reaping machine two years ago.

'Let us all go!' she cried, moving on, as if all those riders and horses had filled her with child-like exultation and made her forget her pity.

'Let's go,' he said, repeating her words, clicking them out, however, with a self-consciousness that made her wince. 'Let us go to the Circus.' No. He could not say it right. He could not feel it right. But why not? she wondered. What was wrong with him then? She liked him warmly, at the moment. Had they not been taken, she asked, to circuses when they were children? Never, he answered, as if she asked the very thing he wanted to reply to; had been longing all these days to say, how they did not go to circuses. It was a large family, nine brothers and sisters, and his father was a working man;[15] 'My father is a chemist, Mrs. Ramsay. He keeps a shop.' He himself had paid his own way since he was thirteen. Often he went without a greatcoat in winter. He could never 'return hospitality' (those were his parched stiff words) at college. He had to make things last twice the time other people did; he smoked the cheapest tobacco; shag; the same the old men smoked on the quays. He worked hard – seven hours a day; his subject was now the influence of something upon somebody – they were walking on and Mrs. Ramsay did not quite catch the meaning, only the words, here and there ... dissertation ... fellowship ... readership ... lectureship. She could not follow the ugly academic jargon, that rattled itself off so glibly, but said to herself that she saw now why going to the circus had knocked him off his perch, poor little man, and why he came out, instantly, with all that about his father and mother and brothers and sisters, and she would see to it that they didn't laugh at him any more; she would tell Prue about it. What he would have liked, she supposed, would have been to say how he had been to Ibsen[16] with the Ramsays. He was an awful prig – oh yes, an insufferable bore. For, though they had reached the town now and were in the main street, with carts grinding past on the cobbles, still he went on talking, about settlements, and teaching, and working men, and helping our own class, and lectures, till she gathered that he had got back entire self-confidence, had recovered from the circus, and was about (and now again she liked him warmly) to tell her – but here, the houses falling away on both sides, they came out on the quay, and the whole bay spread before them and Mrs. Ramsay could not help exclaiming, 'Oh, how beautiful!' For the great plateful of blue water was before her; the hoary[17] Lighthouse, distant, austere, in the midst; and on the right, as far as the eye could see, fading and falling, in soft low pleats, the green sand dunes with the wild flowing grasses on them, which always seemed to be running away into some moon country, uninhabited of men.

That was the view, she said, stopping, growing greyer-eyed, that her husband loved.

She paused a moment. But now, she said, artists had come here. There indeed, only a few paces off, stood one of them, in Panama hat and yellow boots, seriously, softly, absorbedly, for all that he was watched by ten little boys, with an air of profound contentment on his round red face, gazing, and then, when he had gazed, dipping; imbuing the tip of his brush in some soft mound of green or pink. Since Mr. Paunceforte[18] had been there, three years before, all the pictures were like that she said, green and grey, with lemon-coloured sailing-boats, and pink women on the beach.

But her grandmother's friends, she said, glancing discreetly as they passed, took the greatest pains; first they mixed their own colours, and then they ground them, and then they put damp cloths on them to keep them moist.[19]

So Mr. Tansley supposed she meant him to see that that

man's picture was skimpy, was that what one said? The colours weren't solid? Was that what one said? Under the influence of that extraordinary emotion which had been growing all the walk, had begun in the garden when he had wanted to take her bag, had increased in the town when he had wanted to tell her everything about himself, he was coming to see himself and everything he had ever known gone crooked a little. It was awfully strange.

There he stood in the parlour of the poky little house where she had taken him, waiting for her, while she went upstairs a moment to see a woman. He heard her quick step above; heard her voice cheerful, then low; looked at the mats, tea-caddies, glass shades; waited quite impatiently; looked forward eagerly to the walk home, determined to carry her bag; then heard her come out; shut a door; say they must keep the windows open and the doors shut, ask at the house for anything they wanted (she must be talking to a child), when, suddenly, in she came, stood for a moment silent (as if she had been pretending up there, and for a moment let herself be now), stood quite motionless for a moment against a picture of Queen Victoria wearing the blue ribbon of the Garter;[20] and all at once he realised that it was this: it was this: – she was the most beautiful person he had ever seen.

With stars in her eyes and veils in her hair, with cyclamen and wild violets – what nonsense was he thinking? She was fifty at least; she had eight children. Stepping through fields of flowers and taking to her breast buds that had broken and lambs that had fallen; with the stars in her eyes and the wind in her hair – He took her bag.

'Good-bye, Elsie,' she said, and they walked up the street, she holding her parasol erect and walking as if she expected to meet someone round the corner, while for the first time in his life Charles Tansley felt an extraordinary pride; a man digging in a drain stopped digging and looked at her; let his arm fall down and looked at her; Charles Tansley felt an extraordinary pride; felt the wind and the cyclamen and the violets for he was walking with a beautiful woman for the first time in his life. He had hold of her bag.

2

'No going to the Lighthouse, James,' he said, as he stood by the window, speaking awkwardly, but trying in deference to Mrs. Ramsay to soften his voice into some semblance of geniality at least.

Odious little man, thought Mrs. Ramsay, why go on saying that?

3

'Perhaps you will wake up and find the sun shining and the birds singing,' she said compassionately, smoothing the little boy's hair, for her husband, with his caustic saying that it would not be fine, had dashed his spirits she could see. This going to the Lighthouse was a passion of his, she saw, and then, as if her husband had not said enough, with his caustic saying that it would not be fine to-morrow, this odious little man went and rubbed it in all over again.

'Perhaps it will be fine to-morrow,' she said, smoothing his hair.

All she could do now was to admire the refrigerator, and turn the pages of the Stores list in the hope that she might come upon something like a rake, or a mowing-machine, which, with its prongs and its handles, would need the greatest skill and care in cutting out. All these young men parodied her husband, she reflected; he said it would rain; they said it would be a positive tornado.

But here, as she turned the page, suddenly her search for the picture of a rake or a mowing-machine was interrupted. The gruff murmur, irregularly broken by the taking out of pipes and the putting in of pipes which had kept on assuring her, though she could not hear what was said (as she sat in the window), that the men were happily talking; this sound, which had lasted now half an hour and had taken its place soothingly in the scale of sounds pressing on top of her, such as the tap of balls[21] upon bats, the sharp, sudden bark now and then, 'How's that? How's that?' of the children playing cricket, had ceased; so that the monotonous fall of the waves on the beach, which for the most part beat a measured and soothing tattoo to her thoughts and seemed consolingly to repeat over and over again as she sat with the children the words of some old cradle song, murmured by nature, 'I am guarding you – I am your support', but at other times suddenly and unexpectedly, especially when her mind raised itself slightly from the task actually in hand, had no such kindly meaning, but like a ghostly roll of drums remorselessly beat the measure of life, made one think of the destruction of the island and its engulfment in the sea, and warned her whose day had slipped past in one quick doing after another that it was all ephemeral as a rainbow – this sound which had been obscured and concealed under the other sounds suddenly thundered hollow in her ears and made her look up with an impulse of terror.[22]

They had ceased to talk; that was the explanation. Falling in one second from the tension which had gripped her to the other extreme which, as if to recoup her for her unnecessary expense of emotion, was cool, amused, and even faintly malicious, she concluded that poor Charles Tansley had been shed. That was of little account to her. If her husband required sacrifices (and indeed he did) she cheerfully offered up to him Charles Tansley, who had snubbed her little boy.

One moment more, with her head raised, she listened, as if she waited for some habitual sound, some regular mechanical sound; and then, hearing something rhythmical, half said, half chanted, beginning in the garden, as her husband beat up and down the terrace, something between a croak and a song, she was soothed once more, assured again that all was well, and looking down at the book on her knee found the picture of a pocket knife with six blades which could only be cut out if James was very careful.

Suddenly a loud cry, as of a sleep-walker, half roused, something about

Stormed at with shot and shell[23]

sung out with the utmost intensity in her ear, made her turn apprehensively to see if any one heard him. Only Lily Briscoe, she was glad to find; and that did not matter. But the sight of the girl standing on the edge of the lawn painting reminded her; she was supposed to be keeping her head as much in the same position as possible for Lily's picture. Lily's picture! Mrs. Ramsay smiled. With her little Chinese eyes and her puckered-up face she would never marry; one could not take her painting very seriously; but she was an independent little creature, Mrs. Ramsay liked her for it, and so remembering her promise, she bent her head.

4

Indeed, he almost knocked her easel over, coming down upon her with his hands waving, shouting out 'Boldly we rode and well', but, mercifully, he turned sharp, and rode off, to die gloriously she supposed upon the heights of Balaclava. Never was anybody at once so ridiculous and so alarming. But so long as he kept like that, waving, shouting, she was safe; he would not stand still and look at her picture. And that was what Lily Briscoe could not have endured. Even while she looked at the mass, at the line, at the colour, at Mrs. Ramsay sitting in the window with James, she kept a feeler on her surroundings lest someone should creep up, and suddenly she should find her picture looked at. But now, with all her senses quickened as they were, looking, straining, till the colour of the wall and the jacmanna[24] beyond burnt into her eyes, she was aware of someone coming out of the house, coming towards her; but somehow divined, from the footfall, William Bankes, so that though her brush quivered, she did not, as she would have done had it been Mr. Tansley, Paul Rayley, Minta Doyle, or practically anybody else, turn her canvas upon the grass, but let it stand. William Bankes stood beside her.

They had rooms in the village, and so, walking in, walking out, parting late on door-mats, had said little things about the soup, about the children, about one thing and another which made them allies; so that when he stood beside her now in his judicial way (he was old enough to be her father too, a botanist, a widower, smelling of soap, very scrupulous and clean) she just stood there. He just stood there. Her shoes were excellent, he observed. They allowed the toes their natural expansion. Lodging in the same house with her, he had noticed too, how orderly she was, up before breakfast and off to paint, he believed, alone: poor, presumably, and without the complexion or the allurement of Miss Doyle certainly, but with a good sense which made her in his eyes superior to that young lady. Now, for instance, when Ramsay bore down on them, shouting, gesticulating, Miss Briscoe, he felt certain, understood.

Someone had blundered.

Mr. Ramsay glared at them. He glared at them without seeming to see them. That did make them both vaguely uncomfortable. Together they had seen a thing they had not been meant to see. They had encroached upon a privacy. So, Lily thought, it was probably an excuse of his for moving, for getting out of earshot, that made Mr. Bankes almost immediately say something about its being chilly and suggest taking a stroll. She would come, yes. But it was with difficulty that she took her eyes off her picture.

The jacmanna was bright violet; the wall staring white. She would not have considered it honest to tamper with the bright violet and the staring white, since she saw them like that, fashionable though it was, since Mr. Paunceforte's visit, to see everything pale, elegant, semi-transparent. Then beneath the colour there was the shape. She could see it all so clearly, so commandingly, when she looked: it was when she took her brush in hand that the whole thing changed. It was in that moment's flight between the picture and her canvas that the demons set on her who often brought her to the verge of tears and made this passage from conception to work as dreadful as any down a dark passage for a child. Such she often felt herself – struggling against terrific odds to maintain her courage; to say: 'But this is what I see; this is what I see', and so to clasp some miserable remnant of her vision to her breast, which a thousand forces did their best to pluck from her. And it was then too, in that chill and windy way, as she began to paint, that there forced themselves upon her other things, her own inadequacy, her insignificance, keeping house for her father off the Brompton Road, and had much ado to control her impulse to fling herself (thank Heaven she had always resisted so far) at Mrs. Ramsay's knee and say to her – but what could one say to her? 'I'm in love with you?' No, that was not true. 'I'm in love with this all', waving her hand at the hedge, at the house, at the children? It was absurd, it was impossible. One could not say what one meant. So now she laid her brushes neatly in the box, side by side, and said to William Bankes:

'It suddenly gets cold. The sun seems to give less heat,' she said, looking about her, for it was bright enough, the grass still a soft deep green, the house starred in its greenery with purple passion flowers, and rooks dropping cool cries from the high blue. But something moved, flashed, turned a silver wing in the air. It was September after all, the middle of September, and past six in the evening. So off they strolled down the garden in the usual direction, past the tennis lawn, past the pampas grass, to that break in the thick hedge, guarded by red-hot pokers like brasiers of clear burning coal, between which the blue waters of the bay looked bluer than ever.

They came there regularly every evening drawn by some need. It was as if the water floated off and set sailing thoughts which had grown stagnant on dry land, and gave to their bodies even some sort of physical relief. First, the pulse of colour flooded the bay with blue, and the heart expanded with it and the body swam, only the next instant to be checked and chilled by the prickly blackness on the ruffled waves. Then, up behind the great black rock, almost every evening spurted irregularly, so that one had to watch for it and it was a delight when it came, a fountain of white water; and then, while one waited for that, one watched, on the pale semicircular beach, wave after wave shedding again and again smoothly a film of mother-of-pearl.

They both smiled, standing there. They both felt a common hilarity, excited by the moving waves; and then by the swift cutting race of a sailing boat, which, having sliced a curve in the bay, stopped; shivered; let its sail drop down; and then, with a natural instinct to complete the picture, after this swift movement, both of them looked at the dunes far away, and instead of merriment felt come over them some sadness – because the thing was completed partly, and partly because distant views seem to outlast by a million years (Lily thought) the gazer and to be communing already with a sky which beholds an earth entirely at rest.

Looking at the far sandhills, William Bankes thought of Ramsay: thought of a road in Westmorland, thought of Ramsay striding along a road by himself hung round with that solitude which seemed to be his natural air. But this was suddenly interrupted, William Bankes remembered (and this must refer to some actual incident), by a hen, straddling her wings out in protection of a covey of little chicks, upon which Ramsay, stopping, pointed his stick and said 'Pretty – pretty,' an odd illumination into his heart, Bankes had thought it, which showed his simplicity, his sympathy with humble things; but it seemed to him as if their friendship had ceased, there, on that stretch of road. After that, Ramsay had married. After that, what with one thing and another, the pulp had gone out of their friendship. Whose fault it was he could not say, only, after a time, repetition had taken the place of newness. It was to repeat that they met. But in this dumb colloquy with the sand dunes he maintained that his affection for Ramsay had in no way diminished; but there, like the body of a young man laid up in peat for a century, with the red fresh on his lips, was his friendship, in its acuteness and reality laid up across the bay among the sandhills.

He was anxious for the sake of this friendship and perhaps too in order to clear himself in his own mind from the imputation of having dried and shrunk – for Ramsay lived in a welter of children, whereas Bankes was childless and a widower – he was anxious that Lily Briscoe should not disparage Ramsay (a great man in his own way) yet should understand how things stood between them. Begun long years ago, their friendship had petered out on a Westmorland road, where the hen spread her wings before her chicks; after which Ramsay had married, and their paths lying different ways, there had been, certainly for no one's fault, some tendency, when they met, to repeat.

Yes. That was it. He finished. He turned from the view. And, turning to walk back the other way, up the drive, Mr. Bankes was alive to things which would not have struck him had not those sandhills revealed to him the body of his friendship lying with the red on its lips laid up in peat – for instance, Cam, the little girl, Ramsay's youngest daughter. She was picking Sweet Alice on the bank. She was wild and fierce. She would not 'give a flower to the gentleman' as the nursemaid told her. No! no! no! she would not! She clenched her fist. She stamped. And Mr. Bankes felt aged and saddened and somehow put into the wrong by her about his friendship. He must have dried and shrunk.

The Ramsays were not rich, and it was a wonder how they managed to contrive it all. Eight children! To feed eight children on philosophy! Here was another of them, Jasper this time, strolling past, to have a shot at a bird, he said, nonchalantly, swinging Lily's hand like a pump-handle as he passed, which caused Mr. Bankes to say, bitterly, how *she* was a favourite. There was education now to be considered (true, Mrs. Ramsay had something of her own perhaps) let alone the daily wear and tear of shoes and stockings which those 'great fellows', all well grown, angular, ruthless youngsters, must require. As for being sure which was which, or in what order they came, that was beyond him. He called them privately after the Kings and Queens of England; Cam the Wicked, James the Ruthless, Andrew the Just, Prue the Fair – for Prue would have beauty, he thought, how could she help it? – and Andrew brains. While he walked up the drive and Lily Briscoe said yes and no and capped his comments (for she was in love with them all, in love with this world) he weighed Ramsay's case, commiserated him, envied him, as if he had seen him divest himself of all those glories of isolation and austerity which crowned him in youth to cumber himself definitely with fluttering wings and clucking domesticities. They gave him something – William Bankes acknowledged that; it would have been pleasant if Cam had stuck a flower in his coat or clambered over his shoulder, as over her father's, to look at a picture of Vesuvius in eruption; but they had also, his old friends could not but feel, destroyed something. What would a stranger think now? What did this Lily Briscoe think? Could one help noticing that habits grew on him? eccentricities, weaknesses perhaps? It was astonishing that a man of his intellect could stoop so low as he did – but that was too harsh a phrase – could depend so much as he did upon people's praise.

'Oh but,' said Lily, 'think of his work!'

Whenever she 'thought of his work' she always saw clearly before her a large kitchen table. It was Andrew's doing. She asked him what his father's books were about. 'Subject and object and the nature of reality',[25] Andrew had said. And when she said Heavens, she had no notion what that meant, 'Think of a kitchen table then', he told her, 'when you're not there'.

So she always saw, when she thought of Mr. Ramsay's work, a scrubbed kitchen table. It lodged now in the fork of a pear tree, for they had reached the orchard. And with a painful effort of concentration, she focused her mind, not upon the silver-bossed bark of the tree, or upon its fish-shaped leaves, but upon a phantom kitchen table, one of those scrubbed board tables, grained and knotted, whose virtue seems to have been laid bare by years of muscular integrity, which stuck there, its four legs in air. Naturally, if one's days were passed in this seeing of angular essences, this reducing of lovely evenings, with all their flamingo clouds and blue and silver to a white deal four-legged table (and it was a mark of the finest minds so to do), naturally one could not be judged like an ordinary person.

Mr. Bankes liked her for bidding him 'think of his work'. He had thought of it, often and often. Times without number, he had said, 'Ramsay is one of those men who do their best work before they are forty'. He had made a definite contribution to philosophy in one little book when he was only five and twenty; what came after was more or less amplification, repetition. But the number of men who make a definite contribution to anything whatsoever is very small, he said, pausing by the pear tree, well brushed, scrupulously exact, exquisitely judicial. Suddenly, as if the movement of his hand had released it, the load of her accumulated impressions of him tilted up, and down poured in a ponderous avalanche all she felt about him. That was one sensation. Then up rose in a fume the essence of his being. That was another. She felt herself transfixed by the intensity of her perception; it was his severity; his goodness. I respect you (she addressed him silently) in every atom; you are not vain; you are entirely impersonal; you are finer than Mr. Ramsay; you are the finest human being that I know; you have neither wife nor child (without any sexual feeling, she longed to cherish that loneliness), you live for science (involuntarily, sections of potatoes rose before her eyes); praise would be an insult to you; generous, pure-hearted, heroic man! But simultaneously, she remembered how he had brought a valet[26] all the way up here; objected to dogs on chairs; would prose for hours (until Mr. Ramsay slammed out of the room) about salt in vegetables and the iniquity of English cooks.

How then did it work out, all this? How did one judge people, think of them? How did one add up this and that and conclude that it was liking one felt, or disliking? And to those words, what meaning attached, after all? Standing now, apparently transfixed, by the pear tree, impressions poured in upon her of those two men, and to follow her thought was like following a voice which speaks too quickly to be taken down by one's pencil, and the voice was her own voice saying without prompting undeniable, everlasting, contradictory things, so that even the fissures and humps on the bark of the pear tree were irrevocably fixed there for eternity. You have greatness, she continued, but Mr. Ramsay has none of it. He is petty, selfish, vain, egotistical; he is spoilt; he is a tyrant; he wears Mrs. Ramsay to death; but he has what you (she addressed Mr. Bankes) have not; a fiery unworldliness; he knows nothing about trifles; he loves dogs and his children. He has eight. You have none. Did he not come down in two coats the other night and let Mrs. Ramsay trim his hair into a pudding basin? All of this danced up and down, like a company of gnats, each separate, but all marvellously controlled in an invisible elastic net – danced up and down in Lily's mind, in and about the branches of the pear tree, where still hung in effigy the scrubbed kitchen table, symbol of her profound respect for Mr. Ramsay's mind, until her thought which had spun quicker and quicker exploded of its own intensity; she felt released; a shot went off close at hand, and there came, flying from its fragments, frightened, effusive, tumultuous, a flock of starlings.

'Jasper!' said Mr. Bankes. They turned the way the starlings flew, over the terrace. Following the scatter of swift-flying birds in the sky they stepped through the gap in the high hedge straight into Mr. Ramsay, who boomed tragically at them, 'Someone had blundered!'

His eyes, glazed with emotion, defiant with tragic intensity, met theirs for a second, and trembled on the verge of recognition; but then, raising his hand half-way to his face as if to avert, to brush off, in an agony of peevish shame, their normal gaze, as if he begged them to withhold for a moment what he knew to be inevitable, as if he impressed upon them his own child-like resentment of interruption, yet even in the moment of discovery was not to be routed utterly, but was determined to hold fast to something of this delicious emotion, this impure rhapsody of which he was ashamed, but in which he revelled – he turned abruptly, slammed his private door on them; and Lily Briscoe and Mr. Bankes, looking uneasily up into the sky, observed that the flock of starlings which Jasper had routed with his gun had settled on the tops of the elm trees.

'And even if it isn't fine to-morrow,' said Mrs. Ramsay, raising her eyes to glance at William Bankes and Lily Briscoe as they passed, 'it will be another day. And now,' she said, thinking that Lily's charm was her Chinese eyes, aslant in her white, puckered little face, but it would take a clever man to see it, 'and now stand up, and let me measure your leg,' for they might go to the Lighthouse after all, and she must see if the stocking did not need to be an inch or two longer in the leg.

Smiling, for an admirable idea had flashed upon her this very second – William and Lily should marry – she took the heather mixture stocking, with its criss-cross of steel needles at the mouth of it, and measured it against James's leg.

'My dear, stand still,' she said, for in his jealousy, not liking to serve as measuring-block for the Lighthouse keeper's little boy, James fidgeted purposely; and if he did that, how could she see, was it too long, was it too short? she asked.

She looked up – what demon possessed him, her youngest, her cherished? – and saw the room, saw the chairs, thought them fearfully shabby. Their entrails, as Andrew said the other day, were all over the floor; but then what was the point, she asked herself, of buying good chairs to let them spoil up here all through the winter when the house, with only one old woman[27] to see to it, positively dripped with wet? Never mind: the rent was precisely twopence halfpenny; the children loved it; it did her husband good to be three thousand, or if she must be accurate, three hundred miles from his library and his lectures and his disciples; and there was room for visitors. Mats, camp beds, crazy ghosts of chairs and tables whose London life of service was done – they did well enough here; and a photograph or two, and books. Books, she thought, grew of themselves. She never had time to read them. Alas! even the books that had been given her, and inscribed by the hand of the poet himself: 'For her whose wishes must be obeyed' . . . 'The happier Helen[28] of our days' . . . disgraceful to say, she had never read them. And Croom on the Mind and Bates on the Savage Customs of Polynesia[29] ('My dear, stand still,' she said) – neither of those could one send to the Lighthouse. At a certain moment, she supposed, the house would become so shabby that something must be done. If they could be taught to wipe their feet and not bring the beach in with them – that would be something. Crabs, she had to allow, if Andrew really wished to dissect them, or if Jasper believed that one could make soup from seaweed, one could not prevent it; or Rose's objects – shells, reeds, stones; for they were gifted, her children, but all in quite different ways. And the result of it was, she sighed, taking in the whole room from floor to ceiling, as she held the stocking against James's leg, that things got shabbier and got shabbier summer after summer. The mat was fading; the wall-paper was flapping. You couldn't tell any more that those were roses on it. Still, if every door in a house is left perpetually open, and no lockmaker in the whole of Scotland can mend a bolt, things must spoil. What was the use of flinging a green Cashmere shawl over the edge of a picture frame? In two weeks it would be the colour of pea soup. But it was the doors that annoyed her; every door was left open. She listened. The drawing-room door was open; the hall door was open; it sounded as if the bedroom doors were open; and certainly the window on the landing was open, for that she had opened herself.

That windows should be open, and doors shut – simple as it was, could none of them remember it? She would go into the maids' bedrooms at night and find them sealed like ovens, except for Marie's,[30] the Swiss girl, who would rather go without a bath than without fresh air, but then at home, she had said, 'the mountains are so beautiful.' She had said that last night looking out of the window with tears in her eyes. 'The mountains are so beautiful.' Her father was dying there, Mrs. Ramsay knew. He was leaving them fatherless. Scolding and demonstrating (how to make a bed, how to open a window, with hands that shut and spread like a Frenchwoman's) all had folded itself quietly about her, when the girl spoke, as, after a flight through the sunshine the wings of a bird fold themselves quietly and the blue of its plumage changes from bright steel to soft purple. She had stood there silent for there was nothing to be said. He had cancer of the throat. At the recollection – how she had stood there, how the girl had said 'At home the mountains are so beautiful', and there was no hope, no hope whatever, she had a spasm of irritation, and speaking sharply, said to James:

'Stand still. Don't be tiresome,' so that he knew instantly that her severity was real, and straightened his leg and she measured it.

The stocking was too short by half an inch at least, making allowance for the fact that Sorley's little boy would be less well grown than James.

'It's too short,' she said, 'ever so much too short.'

Never did anybody look so sad.[31] Bitter and black, half-way down, in the darkness, in the shaft which ran from the sunlight to the depths, perhaps a tear formed; a tear fell; the waters swayed this way and that, received it, and were at rest. Never did anybody look so sad.

But was it nothing but looks? people said. What was there behind it – her beauty, her splendour? Had he blown his brains out, they asked, had he died the week before they were married – some other, earlier lover, of whom rumours reached one? Or was there nothing? nothing but an incomparable beauty which she lived behind, and could do nothing to disturb? For easily though she might have said at some moment of intimacy when stories of great passion, of love foiled, of ambition thwarted came her way how she too had known or felt or been through it herself, she never spoke. She was silent always. She knew then – she knew without having learnt. Her simplicity fathomed what clever people falsified. Her singleness of mind made her drop plumb like a stone, alight exact as a bird, gave her, naturally, this swoop and fall of the spirit upon truth which delighted, eased, sustained – falsely perhaps.

('Nature has but little clay', said Mr. Bankes once, hearing her voice on the telephone, and much moved by it though she was only telling him a fact about a train, 'like that of which she moulded you.' He saw her at the end of the line, Greek, blue-eyed, straight-nosed. How incongruous it seemed to be telephoning to a woman like that. The Graces assembling seemed to have joined hands in meadows of asphodel[32] to compose that face. Yes, he would catch the 10.30 at Euston.

'But she's no more aware of her beauty than a child,' said Mr. Bankes, replacing the receiver and crossing the room to see what progress the workmen were making with an hotel which they were building at the back of his house. And he thought of Mrs. Ramsay as he looked at that stir among the unfinished walls. For always, he thought, there was something incongruous to be worked into the harmony of her face. She clapped a deer-stalker's hat on her head; she ran across the lawn in goloshes to snatch a child from mischief. So that if it was her beauty merely that one thought of, one must remember the quivering thing, the living thing (they were carrying bricks up a little plank as he watched them), and work it into the picture; or if one thought of her simply as a woman, one must endow her with some freak of idiosyncrasy; or suppose some latent desire to doff her royalty of form as if her beauty bored her and all that men say of beauty, and she wanted only to be like other people, insignificant. He did not know. He did not know. He must go to his work.)

Knitting[33] her reddish-brown hairy stocking, with her head outlined absurdly by the gilt frame, the green shawl which she had tossed over the edge of the frame, and the authenticated masterpiece by Michael Angelo,[34] Mrs. Ramsay smoothed out what had been harsh in her manner a moment before, raised his head, and kissed her little boy on the forehead. 'Let's find another picture to cut out,' she said.

6

But what had happened?

Someone had blundered.

Starting from her musing she gave meaning to words which she had held meaningless in her mind for a long stretch of time. 'Someone had blundered' – Fixing her short-sighted eyes upon her husband, who was now bearing down upon her, she gazed steadily until his closeness revealed to her (the jingle mated itself in her head) that something had happened, someone had blundered. But she could not for the life of her think what.

He shivered; he quivered.[35] All his vanity, all his satisfaction in his own splendour, riding fell as a thunderbolt, fierce as a hawk at the head of his men through the valley of death, had been shattered, destroyed. Stormed at by shot and shell, boldly we rode and well, flashed through the valley of death, volleyed and thundered – straight into Lily Briscoe and William Bankes. He quivered; he shivered.

Not for the world would she have spoken to him, realising, from the familiar signs, his eyes averted, and some curious gathering together of his person, as if he wrapped himself about and needed privacy in which to regain his equilibrium, that he was outraged and anguished. She stroked James's head; she transferred to him what she felt for her husband, and, as she watched him chalk yellow the white dress shirt of a gentleman in the Army and Navy Stores catalogue, thought what a delight it would be to her should he turn out a great artist; and why should he not? He had a splendid forehead. Then, looking up, as her husband passed her once more, she was relieved to find that the ruin was veiled; domesticity triumphed; custom crooned its soothing rhythm, so that when stopping deliberately, as his turn came round again, at the window he bent quizzically and whimsically to tickle James's bare calf with a sprig of something, she twitted him for having dispatched 'that poor young man', Charles Tansley. Tansley had had to go in and write his dissertation, he said.

'James will have to write *his* dissertation one of these days,' he added ironically, flicking his sprig.

Hating his father, James brushed away the tickling spray with which in a manner peculiar to him, compound of severity and humour, he teased his youngest son's bare leg.

She was trying to get these tiresome stockings finished to send to Sorley's little boy to-morrow, said Mrs. Ramsay.

There wasn't the slightest possible chance that they could go to the Lighthouse to-morrow, Mr. Ramsay snapped out irascibly.

How did he know? she asked. The wind often changed.

The extraordinary irrationality of her remark, the folly of women's minds enraged him. He had ridden through the valley of death, been shattered and shivered; and now she flew in the face of facts, made his children hope what was utterly out of the question, in effect, told lies. He stamped his foot on the stone step. 'Damn you,' he said. But what had she said? Simply that it might be fine to-morrow. So it might.

Not with the barometer falling and the wind due west.

To pursue truth with such astonishing lack of consideration for other people's feelings, to rend the thin veils of civilisation so wantonly, so brutally, was to her so horrible an outrage of human decency that, without replying, dazed and blinded, she bent her head as if to let the pelt of jagged hail, the drench of dirty water, bespatter her unrebuked. There was nothing to be said.

He stood by her in silence. Very humbly, at length, he said that he would step over and ask the Coastguards if she liked.

There was nobody whom she reverenced as she reverenced him.

She was quite ready to take his word for it, she said. Only then they need not cut sandwiches — that was all. They came to her, naturally, since she was a woman, all day long with this and that; one wanting this, another that; the children were growing up; she often felt she was nothing but a sponge sopped full of human emotions. Then he said, Damn you. He said, It must rain. He said, It won't rain; and instantly a Heaven of security opened before her. There was nobody she reverenced more. She was not good enough to tie his shoe strings, she felt.

Already ashamed of that petulance, of that gesticulation of the hands when charging at the head of his troops, Mr. Ramsay rather sheepishly prodded his son's bare legs once more, and then, as if he had her leave for it, with a movement which oddly reminded his wife of the great sea-lion at the Zoo tumbling backwards after swallowing his fish and walloping off so that the water in the tank washes from side to side, he dived into the evening air which already thinner was taking the substance from leaves and hedges but, as if in return, restoring to roses and pinks a lustre which they had not had by day.

'Someone had blundered,' he said again, striding off, up and down the terrace.

But how extraordinarily his note had changed! It was like the cuckoo; 'in June he gets out of tune';[36] as if he were trying over, tentatively seeking, some phrase for a new mood, and having only this at hand, used it, cracked though it was. But it sounded ridiculous – 'Someone had blundered' – said like that, almost as a question, without any conviction, melodiously. Mrs. Ramsay could not help smiling, and soon, sure enough, walking up and down, he hummed it, dropped it, fell silent.

He was safe, he was restored to his privacy. He stopped to light his pipe, looked once at his wife and son in the window, and as one raises one's eyes from a page in an express train and sees a farm, a tree, a cluster of cottages as an illustration, a confirmation of something on the printed page to which one returns, fortified, and satisfied, so without his distinguishing either his son or his wife, the sight of them fortified him and satisfied him and con-secrated his effort to arrive at a perfectly clear understanding of the problem which now engaged the energies of his splendid mind.

It was a splendid mind. For if thought is like the keyboard of a piano, divided into so many notes, or like the alphabet is ranged in twenty-six letters all in order, then his splendid mind had no sort of difficulty in running over those letters one by one, firmly and accurately, until it had reached, say, the letter Q. He reached Q. Very few people in the whole of England ever reach Q. Here, stopping for one moment by the stone urn which held the geraniums, he saw, but now far far away, like children picking up shells, divinely innocent and occupied with little trifles at their feet and somehow entirely defenceless against a doom which he perceived, his wife and son, together, in the window. They needed his protection; he gave it them. But after Q? What comes next? After Q there are a number of letters the last of which is scarcely visible to mortal eyes, but glimmers red in the distance. Z is only reached once by one man in a generation. Still, if he could reach R it would be something. Here at least was Q. He dug his heels in at Q. Q he was sure of. Q he could demonstrate. If Q then is Q – R – Here he knocked his pipe out, with two or three resonant taps on the ram's horn which made the handle of the urn, and proceeded. 'Then R . . .' He braced himself. He clenched himself.

Qualities that would have saved a ship's company exposed on a broiling sea with six biscuits and a flask of water – endurance and justice, foresight, devotion, skill, came to his help. R is then – what is R?

A shutter, like the leathern eyelid of a lizard, flickered over the intensity of his gaze and obscured the letter R. In that flash of darkness he heard people saying – he was a failure – that R was beyond him. He would never reach R. On to R, once more. R—

Qualities that in a desolate expedition across the icy solitudes of the Polar region[37] would have made him the leader, the guide, the counsellor, whose temper, neither sanguine nor despondent, surveys with equanimity what is to be and faces it, came to his help again. R—

The lizard's eye flickered once more. The veins on his forehead bulged. The geranium in the urn became startlingly visible and, displayed among its leaves, he could see, without wishing it, that old, that obvious distinction between the two classes of men; on the one hand the steady goers of superhuman strength who, plodding and persevering, repeat the whole alphabet in order, twenty-six letters in all, from start to finish; on the other the gifted, the inspired who, miraculously, lump all the letters together in one flash – the way of genius. He had not genius; he laid no claim to that: but he had, or might have had, the power to repeat every letter of the alphabet from A to Z accurately in order. Meanwhile, he stuck at Q. On, then, on to R.

Feelings that would not have disgraced a leader who, now that the snow has begun to fall and the mountain-top is covered in mist, knows that he must lay himself down and die before morning comes, stole upon him, paling the colour of his eyes, giving him, even in the two minutes of his turn on the terrace, the bleached look of withered old age. Yet he would not die lying down; he would find some crag of rock, and there, his eyes fixed on the storm, trying to the end to pierce the darkness, he would die standing. He would never reach R.

He stood[38] stock still, by the urn, with the geranium flowing over it. How many men in a thousand million, he asked himself, reach Z after all? Surely the leader of a forlorn hope may ask himself that, and answer, without treachery to the expedition behind him, 'One perhaps'.

One in a generation. Is he to be blamed then if he is not
that one? provided he has toiled honestly, given to the best
of his power, till he has no more left to give? And his fame
lasts how long? It is permissible even for a dying hero to
think before he dies how men will speak of him hereafter.
His fame lasts perhaps two thousand years. And what are
two thousand years? (asked Mr. Ramsay ironically, staring
at the hedge). What, indeed, if you look from a mountain-
top down the long wastes of the ages? The very stone one
kicks with one's boot will outlast Shakespeare.[39] His own
little light[40] would shine, not very brightly, for a year or
two, and would then be merged in some bigger light, and
that in a bigger still. (He looked into the darkness, into the
intricacy of the twigs.) Who then could blame the leader of
that forlorn party which after all has climbed high enough
to see the waste of the years and the perishing of stars, if
before death stiffens his limbs beyond the power of movement he does a little consciously raise his numbed fingers
to his brow, and square his shoulders, so that when the
search party comes they will find him dead at his post, the
fine figure of a soldier? Mr. Ramsay squared his shoulders
and stood very upright by the urn.

Who shall blame him, if, so standing for a moment, he
dwells upon fame, upon search parties, upon cairns raised
by grateful followers over his bones? Finally, who shall
blame the leader of the doomed expedition, if, having
adventured to the uttermost, and used his strength wholly
to the last ounce and fallen asleep not much caring if he
wakes or not, he now perceives by some pricking in his
toes that he lives, and does not on the whole object to live,
but requires sympathy, and whisky, and someone to tell the
story of his suffering to at once? Who shall blame him?
Who will not secretly rejoice when the hero puts his

armour off, and halts by the window and gazes at his wife and son,[41] who very distant at first, gradually come closer and closer, till lips and book and head are clearly before him, though still lovely and unfamiliar from the intensity of his isolation and the waste of ages and the perishing of the stars, and finally putting his pipe in his pocket and bending his magnificent head before her – who will blame him if he does homage to the beauty of the world?

7

But his son hated him. He hated him for coming up to them, for stopping and looking down on them; he hated him for interrupting them; he hated him for the exaltation and sublimity of his gestures; for the magnificence of his head; for his exactingness and egotism (for there he stood, commanding them to attend to him); but most of all he hated the twang and twitter of his father's emotion which, vibrating round them, disturbed the perfect simplicity and good sense of his relations with his mother. By looking fixedly at the page, he hoped to make him move on; by pointing his finger at a word, he hoped to recall his mother's attention, which, he knew angrily, wavered instantly his father stopped. But no. Nothing would make Mr. Ramsay move on. There he stood, demanding sympathy.

Mrs. Ramsay, who had been sitting loosely, folding her son in her arm, braced herself, and, half turning, seemed to raise herself with an effort, and at once to pour erect into the air a rain of energy, a column of spray, looking at the same time animated and alive as if all her energies were being fused into force, burning and illuminating (quietly though she sat, taking up her stocking again), and into this

delicious fecundity, this fountain and spray of life, the fatal
sterility of the male plunged itself, like a beak of brass,
barren and bare. He wanted sympathy. He was a failure, he
said. Mrs. Ramsay flashed her needles. Mr. Ramsay
repeated, never taking his eyes from her face, that he was a
failure. She blew the words back at him. 'Charles Tansley
. . .' she said. But he must have more than that. It
was sympathy he wanted, to be assured of his genius,
first of all, and then to be taken within the circle of life,
warmed and soothed, to have his senses restored to him,
his barrenness made fertile, and all the rooms of the house
made full of life – the drawing-room; behind the drawing-
room the kitchen; above the kitchen the bedrooms; and
beyond them the nurseries; they must be furnished, they
must be filled with life.

Charles Tansley thought him the greatest metaphysician
of the time, she said. But he must have more than that. He
must have sympathy. He must be assured that he too lived
in the heart of life; was needed; not here only, but all over
the world. Flashing her needles, confident, upright, she
created drawing-room and kitchen, set them all aglow;
bade him take his ease there, go in and out, enjoy himself.
She laughed, she knitted. Standing between her knees, very
stiff, James felt all her strength flaring up to be drunk and
quenched by the beak of brass, the arid scimitar of the
male, which smote mercilessly, again and again, demanding
sympathy.

He was a failure, he repeated. Well, look then, feel then.
Flashing her needles, glancing round about her, out of the
window, into the room, at James himself, she assured him,
beyond a shadow of a doubt, by her laugh, her poise, her
competence (as a nurse carrying a light across a dark room
assures a fractious child), that it was real; the house was

full; the garden blowing. If he put implicit faith in her, nothing should hurt him; however deep he buried himself or climbed high, not for a second should he find himself without her. So boasting of her capacity to surround and protect, there was scarcely a shell of herself left for her to know herself by; all was so lavished and spent; and James, as he stood stiff between her knees, felt her rise in a rosy-flowered fruit tree laid with leaves and dancing boughs into which the beak of brass, the arid scimitar of his father, the egotistical man, plunged and smote, demanding sympathy.

Filled with her words, like a child who drops off satisfied, he said, at last, looking at her with humble gratitude, restored, renewed, that he would take a turn; he would watch the children playing cricket. He went.

Immediately, Mrs. Ramsay seemed to fold herself together, one petal closed in another, and the whole fabric fell in exhaustion upon itself, so that she had only strength enough to move her finger, in exquisite abandonment to exhaustion, across the page of Grimm's fairy story,[42] while there throbbed through her, like the pulse in a spring which has expanded to its full width and now gently ceases to beat, the rapture of successful creation.

Every throb of this pulse seemed, as he walked away, to enclose her and her husband, and to give to each that solace which two different notes, one high, one low, struck together, seem to give each other as they combine. Yet, as the resonance died, and she turned to the Fairy Tale again, Mrs. Ramsay felt not only exhausted in body (afterwards, not at the time, she always felt this) but also there tinged her physical fatigue some faintly disagreeable sensation with another origin. Not that, as she read aloud the story of the Fisherman's Wife, she knew precisely what it came from; nor did she let herself put into words her dissatisfaction when she realised, at the turn of the page when she stopped and heard dully, ominously, a wave fall, how it came from this: she did not like, even for a second, to feel finer than her husband; and further, could not bear not being entirely sure, when she spoke to him, of the truth of what she said. Universities and people wanting him, lectures and books and their being of the highest importance – all that she did not doubt for a moment; but it was their relation, and his coming to her like that, openly, so that anyone could see, that discomposed her; for then people said he depended on her, when they must know that of the two he was infinitely the more important, and what she gave the world, in comparison with what he gave, negligible. But then again, it was the other thing too – not being able to tell him the truth, being afraid, for instance, about the greenhouse roof and the expense it would be, fifty pounds perhaps, to mend it; and then about his books, to be afraid that he might guess, what she a little suspected, that his last book was not quite his best book (she gathered that from William Bankes); and then to hide small daily things, and the children seeing it, and the burden it laid on them – all this diminished the entire joy, the pure joy, of the two notes sounding together, and let the sound die on her ear now wth a dismal flatness.

A shadow was on the page; she looked up. It was Augustus Carmichael shuffling past, precisely now, at the very moment when it was painful to be reminded of the inadequacy of human relationships, that the most perfect was flawed, and could not bear the examination which, loving her husband, with her instinct for truth, she turned upon it; when it was painful to feel herself convicted of unworthiness, and impeded in her proper function by these lies, these exaggerations, – it was at this moment when she was fretted thus ignobly in the wake of her exaltation, that Mr. Carmichael shuffled past, in his yellow slippers, and some demon in her made it necessary for her to call out, as he passed,

'Going indoors, Mr. Carmichael?'

8

He said nothing. He took opium. The children said he had stained his beard yellow with it. Perhaps. What was obvious to her was that the poor man was unhappy, came to them every year as an escape; and yet every year, she felt the same thing; he did not trust her. She said, 'I am going to the town. Shall I get you stamps, paper, tobacco?' and she felt him wince. He did not trust her. It was his wife's doing. She remembered that iniquity of his wife's towards him, which had made her turn to steel and adamant there, in the horrid little room in St. John's Wood, when with her own eyes she had seen that odious woman turn him out of the house. He was unkempt; he dropped things on his coat; he had the tiresomeness of an old man with nothing in the world to do; and she turned him out of the room. She said, in her odious way, 'Now, Mrs. Ramsay and I want to have a little talk together,' and Mrs. Ramsay could see, as if before her eyes, the innumerable miseries of his life. Had he money enough to buy tobacco? Did he have to ask her for it? half a crown? eighteenpence? Oh, she could not bear to think of the little indignities she made him suffer. And always now (why, she could not guess, except that it came probably from that woman somehow) he shrank from her. He never told her anything. But what more could she have done? There was a sunny room given up to him. The children were good to him. Never did she show a sign of not wanting him. She went out of her way indeed to be friendly. Do you want stamps, do you want tobacco? Here's a book you might like and so on. And after all – after all (here insensibly she drew herself together, physically, the sense of her own beauty becoming, as it did so seldom, present to her) – after all, she had not generally any difficulty in making people like her; for instance, George Manning; Mr. Wallace; famous as they were, they would come to her of an evening, quietly, and talk alone over her fire. She bore about with her, she could not help knowing it, the torch of her beauty; she carried it erect into any room that she entered; and after all, veil it as she might, and shrink from the monotony of bearing that it imposed on her, her beauty was apparent. She had been admired. She had been loved. She had entered rooms where mourners sat. Tears had flown in her presence. Men, and women too, letting go the multiplicity of things, had allowed themselves with her the relief of simplicity. It injured her that he should shrink. It hurt her. And yet not cleanly, not rightly. That was what she minded, coming as it did on top of her discontent with her husband; the sense she had now when Mr. Carmichael shuffled past, just nodding to her question, with a book[43] beneath his arm, in his yellow slippers, that she was suspected; and that all this desire of hers to give, to help, was vanity. For her own self-satisfaction was it that she wished so instinctively to help, to give, that people might say of her, 'O Mrs. Ramsay! dear Mrs. Ramsay ... Mrs. Ramsay, of course!' and need her and send for her and admire her? Was it not secretly this that she wanted, and therefore when Mr. Carmichael shrank away from her, as he did at this moment, making off to some corner where he did acrostics endlessly, she did not feel merely snubbed back in her instinct, but made aware of the pettiness of some part of her, and of human relations, how flawed they are, how despicable, how self-seeking, at their best. Shabby and worn out, and not presumably (her cheeks were hollow, her hair was white) any longer a sight that filled the eyes with joy, she had better devote her mind to the story of the Fisherman and his Wife and so pacify that bundle of sensitiveness (none of her children was as sensitive as he was) her son James.

'The man's heart grew heavy,' she read aloud, 'and he would not go. He said to himself, "It is not right," and yet he went. And when he came to the sea the water was quite purple and dark blue, and grey and thick, and no longer so green and yellow, but it was still quiet. And he stood there and said—'

Mrs. Ramsay could have wished that her husband had not chosen that moment to stop. Why had he not gone as he said to watch the children playing cricket? But he did not speak; he looked; he nodded; he approved; he went on. He slipped seeing before him that hedge which had over and over again rounded some pause, signified some conclusion, seeing his wife and child, seeing again the urns with the trailing red geraniums which had so often decorated processes of thought, and bore, written up among their leaves, as if they were scraps of paper on which one scribbles notes in the rush of reading – he slipped, seeing all this, smoothly into speculation suggested by an article in *The Times* about the number of Americans who visit Shakespeare's house every year. If Shakespeare had never existed, he asked, would the world have differed much from what it is to-day? Does the progress of civilisation[44] depend upon great men? Is the lot of the average human being better now than in the time of the Pharaohs? Is the lot of the average human being, however, he asked himself, the criterion by which we judge the measure of civilisation? Possibly not. Possibly the greatest good requires the exist- ence of a slave class. The liftman in the Tube[45] is an eternal necessity. The thought was distasteful to him. He tossed his head. To avoid it, he would find some way of snubbing the predominance of the arts. He would argue that the world exists for the average human being; that the arts are merely a decoration imposed on the top of human life; they do not express it. Nor is Shakespeare necessary to it. Not knowing precisely why it was that he wanted to disparage Shakespeare and come to the rescue of the man who stands eternally in the door of the lift, he picked a leaf sharply from the hedge. All this would have to be dished up for the young men at Cardiff next month, he thought; here, on his terrace, he was merely foraging and picnicking (he threw away the leaf that he had picked so peevishly) like a man who reaches from his horse to pick a bunch of roses, or stuffs his pockets with nuts as he ambles at his ease through the lanes and fields of a country known to him from boyhood. It was all familiar; this turning, that stile, that cut across the fields. Hours he would spend thus, with his pipe, of an evening, thinking up and down and in and out of the old familiar lanes and commons, which were all stuck about with the history of that campaign there, the life of this statesman here, with poems and with anecdotes, with figures too, this thinker, that soldier; all very brisk and clear; but at length the lane, the field, the common, the fruitful nut-tree and the flowering hedge led him on to that further turn of the road where he dismounted always, tied his horse to a tree, and proceeded on foot alone. He reached the edge of the lawn and looked out on the bay beneath.

It was his fate, his peculiarity, whether he wished it or not, to come out thus on a spit of land which the sea is slowly eating away, and there to stand, like a desolate sea-bird, alone. It was his power, his gift, suddenly to shed all superfluities, to shrink and diminish so that he looked barer and felt sparer, even physically, yet lost none of his intensity of mind, and so to stand on his little ledge facing the dark of human ignorance, how we know nothing and the sea eats away the ground we stand on – that was his fate, his gift. But having thrown away, when he dismounted, all gestures and fripperies, all trophies of nuts and roses, and shrunk so that not only fame but even his own name was forgotten by him, he kept even in that desolation a vigilance which spared no phantom and luxuriated in no vision, and it was in this guise that he inspired in William Bankes (intermittently) and in Charles Tansley (obsequiously) and in his wife now, when she looked up and saw him standing at the edge of the lawn, profound reverence, and pity, and gratitude too, as a stake driven into the bed of a channel upon which the gulls perch and the waves beat inspires in merry boat-loads a feeling of gratitude for the duty it has taken upon itself of marking the channel out there in the floods alone.

'But the father of eight children has no choice. . . .' Muttering half aloud, so he broke off, turned, sighed, raised his eyes, sought the figure of his wife reading stories to the little boy; filled his pipe. He turned from the sight of human ignorance and human fate and the sea eating the ground we stand on, which, had he been able to contemplate it fixedly might have led to something; and found consolation in trifles so slight compared with the august theme just now before him that he was disposed to slur that comfort over, to deprecate it, as if to be caught happy in a world of misery was for an honest man the most despicable of crimes. It was true; he was for the most part happy; he had his wife; he had his children; he had promised in six weeks' time to talk 'some nonsense' to the young men of Cardiff about Locke, Hume, Berkeley,[46] and the causes of the French Revolution. But this and his pleasure in it, in the phrases he made, in the ardour of youth, in his wife's beauty, in the tributes that reached him from Swansea, Cardiff, Exeter, Southampton, Kidderminster, Oxford, Cambridge – all had to be deprecated and concealed under the phrase 'talking nonsense,' because, in effect, he had not done the thing he might have done. It was a disguise; it was the refuge of a man afraid to own his own feelings, who could not say, This is what I like – this is what I am; and rather pitiable and distasteful to William Bankes and Lily Briscoe, who wondered why such concealments should be necessary; why he needed always praise; why so brave a man in thought should be so timid in life; how strangely he was venerable and laughable at one and the same time.

Teaching and preaching is beyond human power, Lily suspected. (She was putting away her things.) If you are exalted you must somehow come a cropper. Mrs. Ramsay gave him what he asked too easily. Then the change must be so upsetting, Lily said. He comes in from his books and finds us all playing games and talking nonsense. Imagine what a change from the things he thinks about, she said.

He was bearing down upon them. Now he stopped dead and stood looking in silence at the sea. Now he had turned away again.

9

Yes, Mr. Bankes said, watching him go. It was a thousand pities. (Lily had said something about his frightening her –

he changed from one mood to another so suddenly.) Yes, said Mr. Bankes, it was a thousand pities that Ramsay could not behave a little more like other people. (For he liked Lily Briscoe; he could discuss Ramsay with her quite openly.) It was for that reason, he said, that the young don't read Carlyle.[47] A crusty old grumbler who lost his temper if the porridge was cold, why should he preach to us? was what Mr. Bankes understood that young people said nowadays. It was a thousand pities if you thought, as he did, that Carlyle was one of the great teachers of mankind. Lily was ashamed to say that she had not read Carlyle since she was at school. But in her opinion one liked Mr. Ramsay all the better for thinking that if his little finger ached the whole world must come to an end. It was not *that* she minded. For who could be deceived by him? He asked you quite openly to flatter him, to admire him, his little dodges deceived nobody. What she disliked was his narrowness, his blindness, she said, looking after him.

'A bit of a hypocrite?' Mr. Bankes suggested, looking, too, at Mr. Ramsay's back, for was he not thinking of his friendship, and of Cam refusing to give him a flower, and of all those boys and girls, and his own house, full of comfort, but, since his wife's death, quiet rather? Of course, he had his work ... All the same, he rather wished Lily to agree that Ramsay was, as he said, 'a bit of a hypocrite'.

Lily Briscoe went on putting away her brushes, looking up, looking down. Looking up, there he was – Mr. Ramsay – advancing towards them, swinging, careless, oblivious, remote. A bit of a hypocrite? she repeated. Oh no – the most sincere of men, the truest (here he was), the best; but, looking down, she thought, he is absorbed in himself, he is tyrannical, he is unjust; and kept looking down, purposely, for only so could she keep steady, staying with the Ramsays. Directly one looked up and saw them, what she called 'being in love' flooded them. They became part of that unreal but penetrating and exciting universe which is the world seen through the eyes of love. The sky stuck to them; the birds sang through them. And, what was even more exciting, she felt, too, as she saw Mr. Ramsay bearing down and retreating, and Mrs. Ramsay sitting with James in the window and the cloud moving and the tree bending, how life, from being made up of little separate incidents which one lived one by one, became curled and whole like a wave which bore one up with it and threw one down with it, there, with a dash on the beach.

Mr. Bankes expected her to answer. And she was about to say something criticising Mrs. Ramsay, how she was alarming, too, in her way, high-handed, or words to that effect, when Mr. Bankes made it entirely unnecessary for her to speak by his rapture. For such it was considering his age, turned sixty, and his cleanliness and his impersonality, and the white scientific coat which seemed to clothe him. For him to gaze as Lily saw him gazing at Mrs. Ramsay was a rapture, equivalent, Lily felt, to the loves of dozens of young men (and perhaps Mrs. Ramsay had never excited the loves of dozens of young men). It was love, she thought, pretending to move her canvas, distilled and filtered; love that never attempted to clutch its object; but, like the love which mathematicians bear their symbols, or poets their phrases, was meant to be spread over the world and become part of the human gain. So it was indeed. The world by all means should have shared it, could Mr. Bankes have said why that woman pleased him so; why the sight of her reading a fairy tale to her boy had upon him precisely the same effect as the solution of a scientific problem, so that he rested in contemplation of it, and felt, as he felt when he had proved something absolute about the digestive system of plants, that barbarity was tamed, the reign of chaos subdued.

Such a rapture – for by what other name could one call it? – made Lily Briscoe forget entirely what she had been about to say. It was nothing of importance; something about Mrs. Ramsay. It paled beside this 'rapture', this silent stare, for which she felt intense gratitude; for nothing so solaced her, eased her of the perplexity of life, and miraculously raised its burdens, as this sublime power, this heavenly gift, and one would no more disturb it, while it lasted, than break up the shaft of sunlight lying level across the floor.

That people should love like this, that Mr. Bankes should feel this for Mrs. Ramsay (she glanced at him musing) was helpful, was exalting. She wiped one brush after another upon a piece of old rag, menially, on purpose. She took shelter from the reverence which covered all women; she felt herself praised. Let him gaze; she would steal a look at her picture.

She could have wept. It was bad, it was bad, it was infinitely bad! She could have done it differently of course; the colour could have been thinned and faded; the shapes etherealised; that was how Paunceforte would have seen it. But then she did not see it like that. She saw the colour burning on a framework of steel; the light of a butterfly's wing lying upon the arches of a cathedral. Of all that only a few random marks scrawled upon the canvas remained. And it would never be seen; never be hung even, and there was Mr. Tansley whispering in her ear, 'Women can't paint, women can't write . . .'

She now remembered what she had been going to say about Mrs. Ramsay. She did not know how she would

have put it; but it would have been something critical. She
had been annoyed the other night by some highhandedness.
Looking along the level of Mr. Bankes' glance at her, she
thought that no woman could worship another woman in
the way he worshipped; they could only seek shelter under
the shade which Mr. Bankes extended over them both.
Looking along his beam she added to it her different ray,
thinking that she was unquestionably the loveliest of people
(bowed over her book); the best perhaps; but also, different
too from the perfect shape which one saw there. But why
different, and how different? she asked herself, scraping
her palette of all those mounds of blue and green which
seemed to her like clods with no life in them now, yet she
vowed, she would inspire them, force them to move, flow,
do her bidding tomorrow. How did she differ? What was
the spirit in her, the essential thing, by which, had you
found a glove in the corner of a sofa, you would have
known it, from its twisted finger, hers indisputably? She
was like a bird for speed, an arrow for directness. She was
wilful; she was commanding (of course, Lily reminded
herself, I am thinking of her relations with women, and I
am much younger, an insignificant person, living off the
Brompton Road). She opened bedroom windows. She shut
doors. (So she tried to start the tune of Mrs. Ramsay in her
head.) Arriving late at night, with a light tap on one's
bedroom door, wrapped in an old fur coat (for the setting
of her beauty was always that – hasty, but apt), she would
enact again whatever it might be – Charles Tansley losing
his umbrella; Mr. Carmichael snuffling and sniffing; Mr.
Bankes saying, 'the vegetable salts are lost'. All this she
would adroitly shape; even maliciously twist; and, moving
over to the window, in pretence that she must go, – it was
dawn, she could see the sun rising, – half turn back, more

intimately, but still always laughing, insist that she must, Minta must, they all must marry, since in the whole world, whatever laurels might be tossed to her (but Mrs. Ramsay cared not a fig for her painting), or triumphs won by her (probably Mrs. Ramsay had had her share of those), and here she saddened, darkened, and came back to her chair, there could be no disputing this: an unmarried woman (she lightly took her hand for a moment), an unmarried woman has missed the best of life. The house seemed full of children sleeping and Mrs. Ramsay listening; of shaded lights and regular breathing.

Oh but, Lily would say, there was her father; her home; even, had she dared to say it, her painting. But all this seemed so little, so virginal, against the other. Yet, as the night wore on, and white lights parted the curtains, and even now and then some bird chirped in the garden, gathering a desperate courage she would urge her own exemption from the universal law; plead for it; she liked to be alone; she liked to be herself; she was not made for that; and so have to meet a serious stare from eyes of unparalleled depth, and confront Mrs. Ramsay's simple certainty (and she was childlike now) that her dear Lily, her little Brisk, was a fool. Then, she remembered, she had laid her head on Mrs. Ramsay's lap and laughed and laughed and laughed, laughed almost hysterically at the thought of Mrs. Ramsay presiding with immutable calm over destinies which she completely failed to understand. There she sat, simple, serious. She had recovered her sense of her now – this was the glove's twisted finger. But into what sanctuary had one penetrated? Lily Briscoe had looked up at last, and there was Mrs. Ramsay, unwitting entirely what had caused her laughter, still presiding, but now with every trace of wilfulness abolished, and in its stead, something clear as the space which the clouds at last uncover – the little space of sky which sleeps beside the moon.

Was it wisdom? Was it knowledge? Was it, once more, the deceptiveness of beauty, so that all one's perceptions, half-way to truth, were tangled in a golden mesh? or did she lock up within her some secret which certainly Lily Briscoe believed people must have for the world to go on at all? Every one could not be as helter skelter, hand to mouth as she was. But if they knew, could they tell one what they knew? Sitting on the floor with her arms round Mrs. Ramsay's knees, close as she could get, smiling to think that Mrs. Ramsay would never know the reason of that pressure, she imagined how in the chambers of the mind and heart of the woman who was, physically, touching her, were stood, like the treasures in the tombs of kings, tablets bearing sacred inscriptions, which if one could spell them out would teach one everything, but they would never be offered openly, never made public. What art was there, known to love or cunning, by which one pressed through into those secret chambers? What device for becoming, like waters poured into one jar, inextricably the same, one with the object one adored? Could the body achieve it, or the mind, subtly mingling in the intricate passages of the brain? or the heart? Could loving, as people called it, make her and Mrs. Ramsay one? for it was not knowledge but unity that she desired, not inscriptions on tablets, nothing that could be written in any language known to men, but intimacy itself, which is knowledge, she had thought, leaning her head on Mrs. Ramsay's knee.

Nothing happened. Nothing! Nothing! as she leant her head against Mrs. Ramsay's knee. And yet, she knew knowledge and wisdom were stored in Mrs. Ramsay's heart. How then, she had asked herself, did one know one thing or another thing about people, sealed as they were? Only like a bee, drawn by some sweetness or sharpness in the air intangible to touch or taste, one haunted the dome-shaped hive, ranged the wastes of the air over the countries of the world alone, and then haunted the hives with their murmurs and their stirrings; the hives which were people. Mrs. Ramsay rose. Lily rose. Mrs. Ramsay went. For days there hung about her, as after a dream some subtle change is felt in the person one has dreamt of, more vividly than anything she said, the sound of murmuring and, as she sat in the wicker arm-chair in the drawing-room window she wore, to Lily's eyes, an august shape; the shape of a dome.

This ray passed level with Mr. Bankes's ray straight to Mrs. Ramsay sitting reading there with James at her knee. But now while she still looked, Mr. Bankes had done. He had put on his spectacles. He had stepped back. He had raised his hand. He had slightly narrowed his clear blue eyes, when Lily, rousing herself, saw what he was at, and winced like a dog who sees a hand raised to strike it. She would have snatched her picture off the easel, but she said to herself, One must. She braced herself to stand the awful trial of someone looking at her picture. One must, she said, one must. And if it must be seen, Mr. Bankes was less alarming than another. But that any other eyes should see the residue[48] of her thirty-three years, the deposit of each day's living, mixed with something more secret than she had ever spoken or shown in the course of all those days was an agony. At the same time it was immensely exciting.

Nothing could be cooler and quieter. Taking out a penknife, Mr. Bankes tapped the canvas with the bone handle. What did she wish to indicate by the triangular purple shape, 'just there?' he asked.

It was Mrs. Ramsay reading to James, she said. She

knew his objection – that no one could tell it for a human shape. But she had made no attempt at likeness, she said. For what reason had she introduced them then? he asked. Why indeed? – except that if there, in that corner, it was bright, here, in this, she felt the need of darkness. Simple, obvious, commonplace, as it was, Mr. Bankes was interested. Mother and child then – objects of universal veneration, and in this case the mother was famous for her beauty – might be reduced, he pondered, to a purple shadow without irreverence.

But the picture was not of them, she said. Or, not in his sense. There were other senses, too, in which one might reverence them. By a shadow here and a light there, for instance. Her tribute took that form, if, as she vaguely supposed, a picture must be a tribute. A mother and child might be reduced to a shadow without irreverence. A light here required a shadow there. He considered. He was interested. He took it scientifically in complete good faith. The truth was that all his prejudices were on the other side, he explained. The largest picture in his drawing-room, which painters had praised, and valued at a higher price than he had given for it, was of the cherry trees in blossom on the banks of the Kennet.[49] He had spent his honeymoon on the banks of the Kennet, he said. Lily must come and see that picture, he said. But now – he turned, with his glasses raised to the scientific examination of her canvas. The question being one of the relations of masses, of light and shadows, which, to be honest, he had never considered before, he would like to have it explained – what then did she wish to make of it? And he indicated the scene before them. She looked. She could not show him what she wished to make of it, could not see it even herself, without a brush in her hand. She took up once more her old painting position with the dim eyes and the absent-minded manner, subduing all her impressions as a woman to something much more general; becoming once more under the power of that vision which she had seen clearly once and must now grope for among hedges and houses and mothers and children – her picture. It was a question, she remembered, how to connect this mass on the right hand with that on the left. She might do it by bringing the line of the branch across so; or break the vacancy in the foreground by an object (James perhaps) so. But the danger was that by doing that the unity of the whole might be broken. She stopped; she did not want to bore him; she took the canvas lightly off the easel.

But it had been seen; it had been taken from her. This man had shared with her something profoundly intimate. And, thanking Mr. Ramsay for it and Mrs. Ramsay for it and the hour and the place, crediting the world with a power which she had not suspected, that one could walk away down that long gallery not alone any more but arm in arm with somebody – the strangest feeling in the world, and the most exhilarating – she nicked the catch of her paint-box to, more firmly than was necessary, and the nick seemed to surround in a circle for ever the paint-box, the lawn, Mr. Bankes, and that wild villain, Cam, dashing past.

10

For Cam grazed the easel by an inch; she would not stop for Mr. Bankes and Lily Briscoe; though Mr. Bankes, who would have liked a daughter of his own, held out his hand; she would not stop for her father, whom she grazed also by an inch; nor for her mother, who called 'Cam! I want you a moment!' as she dashed past. She was off like a bird, bullet, or arrow, impelled by what desire, shot by whom, at what directed, who could say? What, what? Mrs. Ramsay pondered, watching her. It might be a vision – of a shell, of a wheelbarrow, of a fairy kingdom on the far side of the hedge; or it might be the glory of speed; no one knew. But when Mrs. Ramsay called 'Cam!' a second time, the projectile dropped in mid career, and Cam came lagging back, pulling a leaf by the way, to her mother.

What was she dreaming about, Mrs. Ramsay wondered, seeing her engrossed, as she stood there, with some thought of her own, so that she had to repeat the message twice – ask Mildred if Andrew, Miss Doyle, and Mr. Rayley have come back? – The words seemed to be dropped into a well, where, if the waters were clear, they were also so extraordinarily distorting that, even as they descended, one saw them twisting about to make Heaven knows what pattern on the floor of the child's mind. What message would Cam give the cook? Mrs. Ramsay wondered. And indeed it was only by waiting patiently, and hearing that there was an old woman[50] in the kitchen with very red cheeks, drinking soup out of a basin, that Mrs. Ramsay at last prompted that parrot-like instinct which had picked up Mildred's words quite accurately and could now produce them, if one waited, in a colourless singsong. Shifting from foot to foot, Cam repeated the words, 'No, they haven't, and I've told Ellen to clear away tea.'

Minta Doyle and Paul Rayley had not come back then. That could only mean, Mrs. Ramsay thought, one thing. She must accept him, or she must refuse him. This going off after luncheon for a walk, even though Andrew was with them – what could it mean? except that she had decided, rightly, Mrs. Ramsay thought (and she was very, very fond of Minta), to accept that good fellow, who might not be brilliant, but then, thought Mrs. Ramsay, realising that James was tugging at her to make her go on reading aloud the Fisherman and his Wife, she did in her own heart infinitely prefer boobies to clever men who wrote dissertations; Charles Tansley for instance. Anyhow it must have happened, one way or the other, by now.

But she read, 'Next morning the wife awoke first, and it was just daybreak, and from her bed she saw the beautiful country lying before her. Her husband was still stretching himself . . .'

But how could Minta say now that she would not have him? Not if she agreed to spend whole afternoons trapesing about the country alone – for Andrew would be off after his crabs – but possibly Nancy was with them. She tried to recall the sight of them standing at the hall door after lunch. There they stood, looking at the sky, wondering about the weather, and she had said, thinking partly to cover their shyness, partly to encourage them to be off (for her sympathies were with Paul),

'There isn't a cloud anywhere within miles,' at which she could feel little Charles Tansley, who had followed them out, snigger. But she did it on purpose. Whether Nancy was there or not, she could not be certain, looking from one to the other in her mind's eye.

She read on: ' "Ah, wife," said the man, "why should we be King? I do not want to be King." "Well," said the wife, "if you won't be King, I will; go to the Flounder, for I will be King." '

'Come in or go out, Cam,' she said, knowing that Cam was attracted only by the word 'Flounder' and that in a moment she would fidget and fight with James as usual. Cam shot off. Mrs. Ramsay went on reading, relieved, for she and James shared the same tastes and were comfortable together.

'And when he came to the sea, it was quite dark grey, and the water heaved up from below, and smelt putrid. Then he went and stood by it and said,

> "Flounder, flounder, in the sea,
> Come, I pray thee, here to me;
> For my wife, good Ilsabil,
> Wills not as I'd have her will."

"Well, what does she want then?" said the Flounder.' And where were they now? Mrs. Ramsay wondered, reading and thinking, quite easily, both at the same time; for the story of the Fisherman and his Wife was like the bass gently accompanying a tune, which now and then ran up unexpectedly into the melody. And when should she be told? If nothing happened, she would have to speak seriously to Minta. For she could not go trapesing about all over the country, even if Nancy were with them (she tried again, unsuccessfully, to visualise their backs going down the path, and to count them). She was responsible to Minta's parents – the Owl and the Poker.[51] Her nicknames for them shot into her mind as she read. The Owl and the Poker – yes, they would be annoyed if they heard – and they were certain to hear – that Minta, staying with the Ramsays, had been seen etcetera, etcetera, etcetera. 'He wore a wig in the House of Commons and she ably assisted him at the head of the stairs,' she repeated, fishing them up out of her mind by a phrase which, coming back from some party, she had made to amuse her husband. Dear, dear, Mrs. Ramsay said to herself, how did they produce this incongruous daughter? this tomboy Minta, with a hole in her stocking? How did she exist in that portentous atmosphere where the maid was always removing in a dust-pan the sand that the parrot had scattered,

and conversation was almost entirely reduced to the ex-
ploits – interesting perhaps, but limited after all – of that
bird? Naturally, one had asked her to lunch, tea, dinner,
finally to stay with them up at Finlay, which had resulted
in some friction with the Owl, her mother, and more
calling, and more conversation, and more sand, and really
at the end of it, she had told enough lies about parrots to
last her a lifetime (so she had said to her husband that
night, coming back from the party). However, Minta came
. . . Yes, she came, Mrs. Ramsay thought, suspecting some
thorn in the tangle of this thought; and disengaging it
found it to be this: a woman had once accused her of
'robbing her of her daughter's affections'; something Mrs.
Doyle had said made her remember that charge again.
Wishing to dominate, wishing to interfere, making people
do what she wished – that was the charge against her, and
she thought it most unjust. How could she help being 'like
that' to look at? No one could accuse her of taking pains to
impress. She was often ashamed of her own shabbiness.
Nor was she domineering, nor was she tyrannical. It was
more true about hospitals and drains and the dairy. About
things like that she did feel passionately, and would, if she
had had the chance, have liked to take people by the scruff
of their necks and make them see. No hospital on the
whole island. It was a disgrace. Milk[52] delivered at your
door in London positively brown with dirt. It should be
made illegal. A model dairy and a hospital up here – those
two things she would have liked to do, herself. But how?
With all these children? When they were older, then perhaps
she would have time; when they were all at school.

Oh, but she never wanted James to grow a day older or
Cam either. These two she would have liked to keep for
ever just as they were, demons of wickedness, angels of

delight, never to see them grow up into long-legged mon-
sters. Nothing made up for the loss. When she read just
now to James, 'and there were numbers of soldiers with
kettle-drums and trumpets', and his eyes darkened, she
thought, why should they grow up, and lose all that? He
was the most gifted, the most sensitive of her children.[53] But
all, she thought, were full of promise. Prue, a perfect angel
with the others, and sometimes now, at night especially,
she took one's breath away with her beauty. Andrew –
even her husband admitted that his gift for mathematics
was extraordinary. And Nancy and Roger, they were both
wild creatures now, scampering about over the country all
day long. As for Rose, her mouth was too big, but she had
a wonderful gift with her hands. If they had charades, Rose
made the dresses; made everything; liked best arranging
tables, flowers, anything. She did not like it that Jasper
should shoot birds; but it was only a stage; they all went
through stages. Why, she asked, pressing her chin on
James's head, should they grow up so fast? Why should
they go to school? She would have liked always to have
had a baby. She was happiest carrying one in her arms.
Then people might say she was tyrannical, domineering,
masterful, if they chose; she did not mind. And, touching
his hair with her lips, she thought, he will never be so
happy again, but stopped herself, remembering how it
angered her husband that she should say that. Still, it was
true. They were happier now than they would ever be
again. A tenpenny tea set made Cam happy for days. She
heard them stamping and crowing on the floor above her
head the moment they woke. They came bustling along the
passage. Then the door sprang open and in they came,
fresh as roses, staring, wide awake, as if this coming into
the dining-room after breakfast, which they did every day

of their lives was a positive event to them; and so on, with one thing after another, all day long, until she went up to say good-night to them, and found them netted in their cots like birds among cherries and raspberries still making up stories about some little bit of rubbish – something they had heard, something they had picked up in the garden. They had all their little treasures ... And so she went down and said to her husband, Why must they grow up and lose it all? Never will they be so happy again. And he was angry. Why take such a gloomy view of life? he said. It is not sensible. For it was odd; and she believed it to be true; that with all his gloom and desperation he was happier, more hopeful on the whole, than she was. Less exposed to human worries – perhaps that was it. He had always his work to fall back on.[54] Not that she herself was 'pessimistic', as he accused her of being. Only she thought life – and a little strip of time presented itself to her eyes, her fifty years. There it was before her – life. Life: she thought but she did not finish her thought. She took a look at life, for she had a clear sense of it there, something real, something private, which she shared neither with her children nor with her husband. A sort of transaction went on between them, in which she was on one side, and life was on another, and she was always trying to get the better of it, as it was of her; and sometimes they parleyed (when she sat alone); there were, she remembered, great reconciliation scenes; but for the most part, oddly enough, she must admit that she felt this thing that she called life terrible, hostile, and quick to pounce on you if you gave it a chance. There were the eternal problems: suffering; death; the poor. There was always a woman dying of cancer even here. And yet she had said to all these children, You shall go through with it. To eight people she had said relentlessly that (and the bill for the greenhouse would be fifty pounds). For that reason, knowing what was before them – love and ambition and being wretched alone in dreary places – she had often the feeling, Why must they grow up and lose it all? And then she said to herself, brandishing her sword at life, nonsense. They will be perfectly happy. And here she was, she reflected, feeling life rather sinister again, making Minta marry Paul Rayley; because whatever she might feel about her own transaction and she had had experiences which need not happen to everyone (she did not name them to herself); she was driven on, too quickly she knew, almost as if it were an escape for her too, to say that people must marry; people must have children.

Was she wrong in this, she asked herself, reviewing her conduct for the past week or two, and wondering if she had indeed put any pressure upon Minta, who was only twenty-four, to make up her mind. She was uneasy. Had she not laughed about it? Was she not forgetting again how strongly she influenced people? Marriage needed – oh all sorts of qualities (the bill for the greenhouse would be fifty pounds); one – she need not name it – *that* was essential; the thing she had with her husband. Had they that?

'Then he put on his trousers and ran away like a madman,' she read. 'But outside a great storm was raging and blowing so hard that he could scarcely keep his feet; houses and trees toppled over, the mountains trembled, rocks rolled into the sea, the sky was pitch black, and it thundered and lightened, and the sea came in with black waves as high as church towers and mountains, and all with white foam at the top.'

She turned the page; there were only a few lines more, so that she would finish the story, though it was past bedtime. It was getting late. The light in the garden told her that; and the whitening of the flowers and something grey in the leaves conspired together to rouse in her a feeling of anxiety. What it was about she could not think at first. Then she remembered; Paul and Minta and Andrew had not come back. She summoned before her again the little group on the terrace in front of the hall door, standing looking up into the sky. Andrew had his net and basket. That meant he was going to catch crabs and things. That meant he would climb out on to a rock; he would be cut off. Or coming back single file on one of those little paths above the cliff one of them might slip. He would roll and then crash. It was growing quite dark.

But she did not let her voice change in the least as she finished the story, and added, shutting the book, and speaking the last words as if she had made them up herself, looking into James's eyes: 'And there they are living still at this very time.'

'And that's the end,'[55] she said, and she saw in his eyes, as the interest of the story died away in them, something else take its place; something wondering, pale, like the reflection of a light, which at once made him gaze and marvel. Turning, she looked across the bay, and there, sure enough, coming regularly across the waves first two quick strokes and then one long steady stroke, was the light of the Lighthouse. It had been lit.

In a moment he would ask her, 'Are we going to the Lighthouse?' And she would have to say, 'No: not to-morrow; your father says not.' Happily, Mildred came in to fetch them, and the bustle distracted them. But he kept looking back over his shoulder as Mildred carried him out, and she was certain that he was thinking, we are not going to the Lighthouse to-morrow; and she thought, he will remember that all his life.

11

No, she thought, putting together some of the pictures he had cut out – a refrigerator, a mowing machine, a gentleman in evening dress – children never forget. For this reason, it was so important what one said, and what one did, and it was a relief when they went to bed. For now she need not think about anybody. She could be herself, by herself. And that was what now she often felt the need of – to think; well not even to think. To be silent; to be alone. All the being and the doing, expansive, glittering, vocal, evaporated; and one shrunk, with a sense of solemnity, to being oneself, a wedge-shaped core of darkness, something invisible to others. Although she continued to knit, and sat upright, it was thus that she felt herself; and this self having shed its attachments was free for the strangest adventures. When life sank down for a moment, the range of experience seemed limitless. And to everybody there was always this sense of unlimited resources, she supposed; one after another, she, Lily, Augustus Carmichael, must feel, our apparitions, the things you know us by, are simply childish. Beneath it is all dark, it is all spreading, it is unfathomably deep; but now and again we rise to the surface and that is what you see us by. Her horizon seemed to her limitless. There were all the places she had not seen; the Indian plains; she felt herself pushing aside the thick leather curtain of a church in Rome.[56] This core of darkness could go anywhere, for no one saw it. They could not stop it, she thought, exulting. There was freedom, there was peace, there was, most welcome of all, a summoning together, a resting on a platform of stability. Not as oneself did one find rest ever, in her experience (she accomplished here something dexterous with her needles), but as a wedge of darkness. Losing personality, one lost the fret, the hurry, the stir; and there rose to her lips always some exclamation of triumph over life when things came together in this peace, this rest, this eternity; and pausing there she looked out to meet that stroke of the Lighthouse, the long steady stroke, the last of the three, which was her stroke, for watching them in this mood always at this hour one could not help attaching oneself to one thing especially of the things one saw; and this thing, the long steady stroke, was her stroke. Often she found herself sitting and looking, sitting and looking, with her work in her hands until she became the thing she looked at — that light for example. And it would lift up on it some little phrase or other which had been lying in her mind like that — 'Children don't forget, children don't forget' — which she would repeat and begin adding to it, It will end, It will end, she said. It will come, it will come, when suddenly she added, We are in the hands of the Lord.[57]

But instantly she was annoyed with herself for saying that. Who had said it? not she; she had been trapped into saying something she did not mean. She looked up over her knitting and met the third stroke and it seemed to her like her own eyes meeting her own eyes, searching as she alone could search into her mind and her heart, purifying out of existence that lie, any lie. She praised herself in praising the light, without vanity, for she was stern, she was searching, she was beautiful like that light. It was odd, she thought, how if one was alone, one leant to things, inanimate things; trees, streams, flowers; felt they expressed one; felt they became one; felt they knew one, in a sense were one; felt an irrational tenderness thus (she looked at that long steady light) as for oneself. There rose, and she looked and looked with her needles suspended, there curled up off the floor of the mind, rose from the lake of one's being, a mist, a bride to meet her lover.

What brought her to say that: 'We are in the hands of the Lord'? she wondered. The insincerity slipping in among the truths roused her, annoyed her. She returned to her knitting again. How could any Lord have made this world? she asked. With her mind she had always seized the fact that there is no reason, order, justice: but suffering, death, the poor. There was no treachery too base for the world to commit; she knew that. No happiness lasted; she knew that. She knitted with firm composure, slightly pursing her lips and, without being aware of it, so stiffened and composed the lines of her face in a habit of sternness that when her husband passed, though he was chuckling at the thought that Hume, the philosopher, grown enormously fat, had stuck in a bog, he could not help noting, as he passed, the sternness at the heart of her beauty. It saddened him, and her remoteness pained him, and he felt, as he passed, that he could not protect her, and, when he reached the hedge, he was sad. He could do nothing to help her. He must stand by and watch her. Indeed, the infernal truth was, he made things worse for her. He was irritable – he was touchy. He had lost his temper over the Lighthouse. He looked into the hedge, into its intricacy, its darkness.

Always, Mrs. Ramsay felt, one helped oneself out of solitude reluctantly by laying hold of some little odd or end, some sound, some sight. She listened, but it was all very still; cricket was over; the children were in their baths; there was only the sound of the sea. She stopped knitting; she held the long reddish-brown stocking dangling in her hands a moment. She saw the light again. With some irony in her interrogation, for when one woke at all, one's relations changed, she looked at the steady light, the pitiless, the remorseless, which was so much her, yet so little her, which had her at its beck and call (she woke in the night and saw it bent across their bed, stroking the floor), but for all that she thought, watching it with fascination, hypnotised, as if it were stroking with its silver fingers some sealed vessel in her brain whose bursting would flood her with delight, she had known happiness, exquisite happiness, intense happiness, and it silvered the rough waves a little more brightly, as daylight faded, and the blue went out of the sea and it rolled in waves of pure lemon which curved and swelled and broke upon the beach and the ecstasy burst in her eyes and waves of pure delight raced over the floor of her mind and she felt, It is enough! It is enough!

He turned and saw her. Ah! She was lovely, lovelier now than ever he thought. But he could not speak to her. He could not interrupt her. He wanted urgently to speak to her now that James was gone and she was alone at last. But he resolved, no; he would not interrupt her. She was aloof from him now in her beauty, in her sadness. He would let her be, and he passed her without a word, though it hurt him that she should look so distant, and he could not reach her, he could do nothing to help her. And again he would have passed her without a word had she not, at that very moment, given him of her own free will what she knew he would never ask, and called to him and taken the green shawl off the picture frame, and gone to him. For he wished, she knew, to protect her.

12

She folded the green shawl about her shoulders. She took his arm. His beauty was so great, she said, beginning to speak of Kennedy the gardener at once; he was so awfully handsome, that she couldn't dismiss him. There was a ladder against the greenhouse, and little lumps of putty stuck about, for they were beginning to mend the greenhouse roof. Yes, but as she strolled along with her husband, she felt that that particular source of worry had been placed. She had it on the tip of her tongue to say, as they strolled, 'It'll cost fifty pounds', but instead, for her heart failed her about money, she talked about Jasper shooting birds, and he said, at once, soothing her instantly, that it was natural in a boy, and he trusted he would find better ways of amusing himself before long. Her husband was so sensible, so just. And so she said, 'Yes; all children go through stages,' and began considering the dahlias in the big bed, and wondering what about next year's flowers, and had he heard the children's nickname for Charles Tansley, she asked. The atheist, they called him, the little atheist. 'He's not a polished specimen,' said Mr. Ramsay. 'Far from it,' said Mrs. Ramsay.

She supposed it was all right leaving him to his own devices, Mrs. Ramsay said, wondering whether it was any use sending down bulbs; did they plant them? 'Oh, he has his dissertation to write,' said Mr. Ramsay. She knew all about *that*, said Mrs. Ramsay. He talked of nothing else. It was about the influence of somebody upon something. 'Well, it's all he has to count on,' said Mr. Ramsay. 'Pray Heaven he won't fall in love with Prue,' said Mrs. Ramsay. He'd disinherit her if she married him, said Mr. Ramsay. He did not look at the flowers, which his wife was considering, but at a spot about a foot or so above them. There was no harm in him, he added, and was just about to say that anyhow he was the only young man in England who admired his – when he choked it back. He would not bother her again about his books. These flowers seemed creditable, Mr. Ramsay said, lowering his gaze and noticing something red, something brown. Yes, but then these she had put in with her own hands, said Mrs. Ramsay. The question was, what happened if she sent bulbs down; did Kennedy plant them? It was his incurable laziness; she added, moving on. If she stood over him all day long with a spade in her hand, he did sometimes do a stroke of work. So they strolled along, towards the red-hot pokers. 'You're teaching your daughters to exaggerate,' said Mr. Ramsay, reproving her. Her Aunt Camilla[58] was far worse than she was, Mrs. Ramsay remarked. 'Nobody ever held up your Aunt Camilla as a model of virtue that I'm aware of,' said Mr. Ramsay. 'She was the most beautiful woman I ever saw,' said Mrs. Ramsay. 'Somebody else was that,' said Mr. Ramsay. Prue was going to be far more beautiful than she was, said Mrs. Ramsay. He saw no trace of it, said Mr. Ramsay. 'Well, then, look to-night,' said Mrs. Ramsay. They paused. He wished Andrew could be induced to work harder. He would lose every chance of a scholarship[59] if he didn't. 'Oh scholarships!' she said. Mr. Ramsay thought her foolish for saying that, about a serious thing, like a scholarship. He should be very proud of Andrew if he got a scholarship, he said. She would be just as proud of him if he didn't, she answered. They disagreed always about this, but it did not matter. She liked him to believe in scholarships, and he liked her to be proud of Andrew whatever he did. Suddenly she remembered those little paths on the edge of the cliffs.

Wasn't it late? she asked. They hadn't come home yet. He flicked his watch carelessly open. But it was only just past seven. He held his watch open for a moment, deciding that he would tell her what he had felt on the terrace. To begin with, it was not reasonable to be so nervous. Andrew could look after himself. Then, he wanted to tell her that when he was walking on the terrace just now – here he became uncomfortable, as if he were breaking into that solitude, that aloofness, that remoteness of hers . . . But she pressed him. What had he wanted to tell her, she asked, thinking it was about going to the Lighthouse; and that he was sorry he had said 'Damn you'. But no. He did not like to see her look so sad, he said. Only wool-gathering, she protested, flushing a little. They both felt uncomfortable, as if they did not know whether to go on or go back. She had been reading fairy tales to James, she said. No, they could not share that; they could not say that.

They had reached the gap between the two clumps of red-hot pokers, and there was the Lighthouse again, but she would not let herself look at it. Had she known that he was looking at her, she thought, she would not have let herself sit there, thinking. She disliked anything that reminded her that she had been seen sitting thinking. So she looked over her shoulder, at the town. The lights were rippling and running as if they were drops of silver water held firm in a wind. And all the poverty, all the suffering had turned to that, Mrs. Ramsay thought. The lights of the town and of the harbour and of the boats seemed like a phantom net floating there to mark something which had sunk. Well, if he could not share her thoughts, Mr. Ramsay said to himself, he would be off, then, on his own. He wanted to go on thinking, telling himself the story how Hume was stuck in a bog; he wanted to laugh. But first it was nonsense to be anxious about Andrew. When he was Andrew's age he used to walk about the country[60] all day long, with nothing but a biscuit in his pocket and nobody bothered about him, or thought that he had fallen over a cliff. He said aloud he thought he would be off for a day's walk if the weather held. He had had about enough of Bankes and of Carmichael. He would like a little solitude. Yes, she said. It annoyed him that she did not protest. She knew that he would never do it. He was too old now to walk all day long with a biscuit in his pocket. She worried about the boys, but not about him. Years ago, before he had married, he thought, looking across the bay, as they stood between the clumps of red-hot pokers, he had walked all day. He had made a meal off bread and cheese in a public house. He had worked ten hours at a stretch; an old woman just popped her head in now and again and saw to the fire. That was the country he liked best, over there; those sandhills dwindling away into darkness. One could walk all day without meeting a soul. There was not a house scarcely, not a single village for miles on end. One could worry things out alone. There were little sandy beaches where no one had been since the beginning of time. The seals sat up and looked at you. It sometimes seemed to him that in a little house out there, alone – he broke off, sighing. He had no right. The father of eight children – he reminded himself. And he would have been a beast and a cur to wish a single thing altered. Andrew would be a better man than he had been. Prue would be a beauty, her mother said. They would stem the flood a bit. That was a good bit of work on the whole – his eight children. They showed he did not damn the poor little universe entirely, for on an evening like this, he thought, looking at the land dwindling away, the little island seemed pathetically small, half swallowed up in the sea.

'Poor little place,' he murmured with a sigh.

She heard him. He said the most melancholy things, but she noticed that directly he had said them he always seemed more cheerful than usual. All this phrase-making was a game, she thought, for if she had said half what he said, she would have blown her brains out by now.[61]

It annoyed her, this phrase-making, and she said to him, in a matter-of-fact way, that it was a perfectly lovely evening. And what was he groaning about, she asked, half laughing, half complaining, for she guessed what he was thinking – he would have written better books if he had not married.

He was not complaining, he said. She knew that he did not complain. She knew that he had nothing whatever to complain of. And he seized her hand and raised it to his lips and kissed it with an intensity that brought the tears to her eyes, and quickly he dropped it.

They turned away from the view and began to walk up the path where the silver-green spear-like plants grew, arm in arm. His arm was almost like a young man's arm, Mrs. Ramsay thought, thin and hard, and she thought with delight how strong he still was, though he was over sixty, and how untamed and optimistic, and how strange it was that being convinced, as he was, of all sorts of horrors, seemed not to depress him, but to cheer him. Was it not odd, she reflected? Indeed he seemed to her sometimes made differently from other people, born blind, deaf, and dumb, to the ordinary things, but to the extraordinary things, with an eye like an eagle's. His understanding often astonished her. But did he notice the flowers? No. Did he notice the view? No. Did he even notice his own daughter's beauty, or whether there was pudding on his plate or roast beef? He would sit at table with them like a person in a dream. And his habit of talking aloud, or saying poetry aloud, was growing on him, she was afraid; for sometimes it was awkward –

Best and brightest, come away![62]

poor Miss Giddings, when he shouted that at her, almost
jumped out of her skin. But then, Mrs. Ramsay, though
instantly taking his side against all the silly Giddingses in
the world, then, she thought, intimating by a little pressure
on his arm that he walked up hill too fast for her, and she
must stop for a moment to see whether those were fresh
mole-hills on the bank, then, she thought, stooping down
to look, a great mind like his must be different in every
way from ours. All the great men she had ever known, she
thought, deciding that a rabbit must have got in, were like
that, and it was good for young men (though the atmosphere of lecture-rooms was stuffy and depressing to her
beyond endurance almost) simply to hear him, simply to
look at him. But without shooting rabbits, how was one to
keep them down? she wondered. It might be a rabbit; it
might be a mole. Some creature anyhow was ruining her
evening primroses.[63] And looking up, she saw above the
thin trees the first pulse of the full-throbbing star, and
wanted to make her husband look at it; for the sight gave
her such keen pleasure. But she stopped herself. He never
looked at things. If he did, all he would say would be,
Poor little world, with one of his sighs.

At that moment, he said, 'Very fine', to please her, and
pretended to admire the flowers. But she knew quite well
that he did not admire them, or even realise that they were
there. It was only to please her ... Ah, but was that not
Lily Briscoe strolling along with William Bankes? She
focussed her short-sighted eyes upon the backs of a retreating couple. Yes, indeed it was. Did that not mean that they
would marry? Yes, it must! What an admirable idea! They
must marry!

13

He had been to Amsterdam,[64] Mr. Bankes was saying as he strolled across the lawn with Lily Briscoe. He had seen the Rembrandts. He had been to Madrid. Unfortunately, it was Good Friday and the Prado was shut. He had been to Rome. Had Miss Briscoe never been to Rome? Oh, she should— It would be a wonderful experience for her – the Sistine Chapel; Michael Angelo; and Padua, with its Giottos. His wife had been in bad health for many years, so that their sight-seeing had been on a modest scale.

She had been to Brussels; she had been to Paris, but only for a flying visit to see an aunt who was ill. She had been to Dresden; there were masses of pictures she had not seen; however, Lily Briscoe reflected, perhaps it was better not to see pictures: they only made one hopelessly discontented with one's own work. Mr. Bankes thought one could carry that point of view too far. We can't all be Titians and we can't all be Darwins,[65] he said; at the same time he doubted whether you could have your Darwin and your Titian if it weren't for humble people like ourselves. Lily would have liked to pay him a compliment; you're not humble, Mr. Bankes, she would have liked to have said. But he did not want compliments (most men do, she thought), and she was a little ashamed of her impulse and said nothing while he remarked that perhaps what he was saying did not apply to pictures. Anyhow, said Lily, tossing off her little insincerity, she would always go on painting, because it interested her. Yes, said Mr. Bankes, he was sure she would, and as they reached the end of the lawn he was asking her whether she had difficulty in finding subjects in London when they turned and saw the Ramsays. So that is marriage, Lily thought, a man and a woman looking at a girl throwing a ball. That is what Mrs. Ramsay tried to tell me the other night, she thought. For she was wearing a green shawl, and they were standing close together watching Prue and Jasper throwing catches. And suddenly the meaning which, for no reason at all, as perhaps they are stepping out of the Tube or ringing a doorbell, descends on people, making them symbolical,[66] making them representative, came upon them, and made them in the dusk standing, looking, the symbols of marriage, husband and wife. Then, after an instant, the symbolical outline which transcended the real figures sank down again, and they became, as they met them, Mr. and Mrs. Ramsay watching the children throwing catches. But still for a moment, though Mrs. Ramsay greeted them with her usual smile (oh, she's thinking we're going to get married, Lily thought) and said, 'I have triumphed to-night,' meaning that for once Mr. Bankes had agreed to dine with them and not run off to his own lodging where his man cooked vegetables properly; still, for one moment, there was a sense of things having been blown apart, of space, of irresponsibility as the ball soared high, and they followed it and lost it and saw the one star and the draped branches. In the failing light they all looked sharp-edged and ethereal and divided by great distances. Then, darting backwards over the vast space (for it seemed as if solidity had vanished altogether), Prue ran full tilt into them and caught the ball brilliantly high up in her left hand, and her mother said, 'Haven't they come back yet?' whereupon the spell was broken. Mr. Ramsay felt free now to laugh out loud at Hume, who had stuck in a bog and an old woman rescued him on condition he said the Lord's Prayer, and chuckling to himself he strolled off to his study. Mrs. Ramsay, bringing Prue back into the alliance of family life

again, from which she had escaped, throwing catches, asked,
'Did Nancy go with them?'

14

(Certainly, Nancy had gone with them, since Minta Doyle
had asked it with her dumb look, holding out her hand, as
Nancy made off, after lunch, to her attic, to escape the
horror of family life. She supposed she must go then. She
did not want to go. She did not want to be drawn into it
all. For as they walked along the road to the cliff Minta
kept on taking her hand. Then she would let it go. Then
she would take it again. What was it she wanted? Nancy
asked herself. There was something, of course, that people
wanted; for when Minta took her hand and held it, Nancy,
reluctantly, saw the whole world spread out beneath her, as
if it were Constantinople[67] seen through a mist, and then,
however heavy-eyed one might be, one must needs ask, 'Is
that Santa Sofia?' 'Is that the Golden Horn?' So Nancy
asked, when Minta took her hand, 'What is it that she
wants? Is it that?' And what was that? Here and there
emerged from the mist (as Nancy looked down upon life
spread beneath her) a pinnacle, a dome; prominent things,
without names. But when Minta dropped her hand, as she
did when they ran down the hillside, all that, the dome, the
pinnacle, whatever it was that had protruded through the
mist, sank down into it and disappeared.

Minta, Andrew observed, was rather a good walker. She
wore more sensible clothes than most women. She wore very
short skirts and black knickerbockers. She would jump
straight into a stream and flounder across. He liked her
rashness, but he saw that it would not do – she would kill
herself in some idiotic way one of these days. She seemed to be

afraid of nothing – except bulls. At the mere sight of a bull in a field she would throw up her arms and fly screaming, which was the very thing to enrage a bull of course. But she did not mind owning up to it in the least; one must admit that. She knew she was an awful coward about bulls, she said. She thought she must have been tossed in her perambulator when she was a baby. She didn't seem to mind what she said or did. Suddenly now she pitched down on the edge of the cliff and began to sing some song about

Damn your eyes, damn your eyes.

They all had to join in and sing the chorus, and shout out together:

Damn your eyes, damn your eyes,

but it would be fatal to let the tide come in and cover up all the good hunting-grounds before they got on to the beach.

'Fatal,' Paul agreed, springing up, and as they went slithering down, he kept quoting the guide-book about 'these islands being justly celebrated for their park-like prospects and the extent and variety of their marine curiosities'. But it would not do altogether, this shouting and damning your eyes, Andrew felt, picking his way down the cliff, this clapping him on the back, and calling him 'old fellow' and all that; it would not altogether do. It was the worst of taking women on walks. Once on the beach they separated, he going out on to the Pope's Nose,[68] taking his shoes off, and rolling his socks in them and letting that couple look after themselves; Nancy waded out to her own rocks and searched her own pools and let that couple look after themselves. She crouched low down and touched the smooth rubber-like sea anemones, who were stuck like

82

lumps of jelly to the side of the rock. Brooding, she changed the pool into the sea, and made the minnows into sharks and whales, and cast vast clouds over this tiny world by holding her hand against the sun, and so brought darkness and desolation, like God himself, to millions of ignorant and innocent creatures, and then took her hand away suddenly and let the sun stream down. Out on the pale criss-crossed sand, high-stepping, fringed, gauntletted, stalked some fantastic leviathan (she was still enlarging the pool), and slipped into the vast fissures of the mountain side. And then, letting her eyes slide imperceptibly above the pool and rest on that wavering line of sea and sky, on the tree trunks which the smoke of steamers made waver upon the horizon, she became with all that power sweeping savagely in and inevitably withdrawing, hypnotised, and the two senses of that vastness and this tininess (the pool had diminished again) flowering within it made her feel that she was bound hand and foot and unable to move by the intensity of feelings which reduced her own body, her own life, and the lives of all the people in the world, for ever, to nothingness. So listening to the waves, crouched over the pool, she brooded.

And Andrew shouted that the sea was coming in, so she leapt splashing through the shallow waves on to the shore and ran up the beach and was carried by her own impetuosity and her desire for rapid movement right behind a rock and there oh heavens! in each other's arms were Paul and Minta! kissing probably.[69] She was outraged, indignant. She and Andrew put on their shoes and stockings in dead silence without saying a thing about it. Indeed they were rather sharp with each other. She might have called him when she saw the crayfish or whatever it was, Andrew grumbled. However, they both felt, it's not our fault. They had not wanted this horrid nuisance to happen. All the same it irritated Andrew that Nancy should be a woman, and Nancy that Andrew should be a man and they tied their shoes very neatly and drew the bows rather tight.

It was not until they had climbed right up on to the top of the cliff again that Minta cried out that she had lost her grandmother's brooch[70] – her grandmother's brooch, the sole ornament she possessed – a weeping willow, it was (they must remember it) set in pearls. They must have seen it, she said, with the tears running down her cheeks, the brooch which her grandmother had fastened her cap with till the last day of her life. Now she had lost it. She would rather have lost anything than that! She would go back and look for it. They all went back. They poked and peered and looked. They kept their heads very low, and said things shortly and gruffly. Paul Rayley searched like a madman all about the rock where they had been sitting. All this pother about a brooch really didn't do at all, Andrew thought, as Paul told him to make a 'thorough search between this point and that'. The tide was coming in fast. The sea would cover the place where they had sat in a minute. There was not a ghost of a chance of their finding it now. 'We shall be cut off!' Minta shrieked, suddenly terrified. As if there were any danger of that! It was the same as the bulls all over again – she had no control over her emotions, Andrew thought. Women hadn't. The wretched Paul had to pacify her. The men (Andrew and Paul at once became manly, and different from usual) took counsel briefly and decided that they would plant Rayley's stick where they had sat and come back at low tide again. There was nothing more that could be done now. If the brooch was there, it would still be there in the morning, they assured her, but Minta still sobbed, all the way up to the top of the cliff. It was her grandmother's brooch; she would rather have lost anything but that, and yet Nancy felt, though it might be true that she minded losing her brooch, she wasn't crying only for that. She was crying for something else. We might all sit down and cry, she felt. But she did not know what for.

They drew ahead together, Paul and Minta, and he comforted her, and said how famous he was for finding things. Once when he was a little boy he had found a gold watch. He would get up at daybreak and he was positive he would find it. It seemed to him that it would be almost dark, and he would be alone on the beach, and somehow it would be rather dangerous. He began telling her, however, that he would certainly find it, and she said that she would not hear of his getting up at dawn: it was lost: she knew that: she had had a presentiment when she put it on that afternoon. And secretly he resolved that he would not tell her, but he would slip out of the house at dawn when they were all asleep and if he could not find it he would go to Edinburgh[71] and buy her another, just like it but more beautiful. He would prove what he could do. And as they came out on the hill and saw the lights of the town beneath them, the lights coming out suddenly one by one seemed like things that were going to happen to him – his marriage, his children, his house; and again he thought, as they came out on to the high road, which was shaded with high bushes, how they would retreat into solitude together, and walk on and on, he always leading her, and she pressing close to his side (as she did now). As they turned by the cross roads he thought what an appalling experience he had been through, and he must tell some one – Mrs. Ramsay of course, for it took his breath away to think what he had been and done. It had been far and away the worst moment of his life when he asked Minta to marry him. He would go straight to Mrs. Ramsay, because he felt somehow that she was the person who had made him do it. She had made him think he could do anything. Nobody else took him seriously. But she made him believe that he could do whatever he wanted. He had felt her eyes on him all day to-day, following him about (though she never said a word) as if she were saying, 'Yes, you can do it. I believe in you. I expect it of you.' She had made him feel all that, and directly they got back (he looked for the lights of the house above the bay) he would go to her and say, 'I've done it, Mrs. Ramsay; thanks to you.' And so turning into the lane that led to the house he could see lights moving about in the upper windows. They must be awfully late then. People were getting ready for dinner. The house was all lit up,[72] and the lights after the darkness made his eyes feel full, and he said to himself, childishly, as he walked up the drive, Lights, lights, lights, and repeated in a dazed way, Lights, lights, lights, as they came into the house, staring about him with his face quite stiff. But, good heavens, he said to himself, putting his hand to his tie, I must not make a fool of myself.)

15

'Yes,' said Prue, in her considering way, answering her mother's question, 'I think Nancy did go with them.'

16

Well then, Nancy had gone with them, Mrs. Ramsay supposed, wondering, as she put down a brush, took up a comb, and said 'Come in' to a tap at the door (Jasper and

Rose came in), whether the fact that Nancy was with them made it less likely or more likely that anything would happen; it made it less likely, somehow, Mrs. Ramsay felt, very irrationally, except that after all holocaust on such a scale was not probable. They could not all be drowned. And again she felt alone in the presence of her old antagonist, life.

Jasper and Rose said that Mildred wanted to know whether she should wait dinner.

'Not for the Queen of England,' said Mrs. Ramsay emphatically.

'Not for the Empress of Mexico,' she added, laughing at Jasper; for he shared his mother's vice: he, too, exaggerated.

And if Rose liked, she said, while Jasper took the message, she might choose which jewels she was to wear.[73] When there are fifteen people sitting down to dinner,[74] one cannot keep things waiting for ever. She was now beginning to feel annoyed with them for being so late; it was inconsiderate of them, and it annoyed her on top of her anxiety about them, that they should choose this very night to be out late, when, in fact, she wished the dinner to be particularly nice, since William Bankes had at last consented to dine with them; and they were having Mildred's masterpiece – Bœuf en Daube.[75] Everything depended upon things being served up the precise moment they were ready. The beef, the bayleaf, and the wine – all must be done to a turn. To keep it waiting was out of the question. Yet of course to-night, of all nights, out they went, and they came in late, and things had to be sent out, things had to be kept hot; the Bœuf en Daube would be entirely spoilt.

Jasper offered her an opal necklace; Rose a gold necklace. Which looked best against her black dress? Which did indeed? said Mrs. Ramsay absent-mindedly, looking at her neck and shoulders (but avoiding her face), in the glass. And then, while the children rummaged among her things, she looked out of the window at a sight which always amused her – the rooks trying to decide which tree to settle on. Every time, they seemed to change their minds and rose up into the air again, because, she thought, the old rook, the father rook, old Joseph was her name for him, was a bird of a very trying and difficult disposition. He was a disreputable old bird, with half his wing feathers missing. He was like some seedy old gentleman in a top hat she had seen playing the horn in front of a public house.

'Look!' she said, laughing. They were actually fighting. Joseph and Mary[76] were fighting. Anyhow they all went up again, and the air was shoved aside by their black wings and cut into exquisite scimitar shapes. The movement of the wings beating out, out, out – she could never describe it accurately enough to please herself – was one of the loveliest of all to her. Look at that, she said to Rose, hoping that Rose would see it more clearly than she could. For one's children so often gave one's own perceptions a little thrust forwards.

But which was it to be? They had all the trays of her jewel-case open. The gold necklace, which was Italian, or the opal necklace, which Uncle James had brought her from India; or should she wear her amethysts?

'Choose, dearests, choose,' she said, hoping that they would make haste.

But she let them take their time to choose: she let Rose, particularly, take up this and then that, and hold her jewels against the black dress, for this little ceremony of choosing jewels, which was gone through every night, was what

Rose liked best, she knew. She had some hidden reason of her own for attaching great importance to this choosing what her mother was to wear. What was the reason, Mrs. Ramsay wondered, standing still to let her clasp the necklace she had chosen, divining, through her own past, some deep, some buried, some quite speechless feeling that one had for one's mother at Rose's age. Like all feelings felt for oneself, Mrs. Ramsay thought, it made one sad. It was so inadequate, what one could give in return; and what Rose felt was quite out of proportion to anything she actually was. And Rose would grow up; and Rose would suffer, she supposed, with these deep feelings, and she said she was ready now, and they would go down, and Jasper, because he was the gentleman, should give her his arm, and Rose, as she was the lady, should carry her handkerchief (she gave her the handkerchief), and what else? oh, yes, it might be cold: a shawl. Choose me a shawl, she said, for that would please Rose, who was bound to suffer so. 'There,' she said, stopping by the window on the landing, 'there they are again.' Joseph had settled on another treetop. 'Don't you think they mind', she said to Jasper, 'having their wings broken?' Why did he want to shoot poor old Joseph and Mary? He shuffled a little on the stairs, and felt rebuked, but not seriously, for she did not understand the fun of shooting birds; that they did not feel; and being his mother she lived away in another division of the world, but he rather liked her stories about Mary and Joseph. She made him laugh. But how did she know that those were Mary and Joseph? Did she think the same birds came to the same trees every night? he asked. But here, suddenly, like all grown-up people, she ceased to pay him the least attention. She was listening to a clatter in the hall.

'They've come back!' she exclaimed, and at once she felt

much more annoyed with them than relieved. Then she wondered, had it happened? She would go down and they would tell her – but no. They could not tell her anything, with all these people about. So she must go down and begin dinner and wait. And, like some queen who, finding her people gathered in the hall, looks down upon them, and descends among them, and acknowledges their tributes silently, and accepts their devotion and their prostration before her (Paul did not move a muscle but looked straight before him as she passed), she went down, and crossed the hall and bowed her head very slightly, as if she accepted what they could not say: their tribute to her beauty.

But she stopped. There was a smell of burning. Could they have let the Bœuf en Daube overboil, she wondered? pray heaven not! when the great clangour of the gong announced solemnly, authoritatively, that all those scattered about, in attics, in bedrooms, on little perches of their own, reading, writing, putting the last smooth to their hair, or fastening dresses, must leave all that, and the little odds and ends on their washing-tables and dressing-tables, and the novels on the bed-tables, and the diaries which were so private, and assemble in the dining-room for dinner.

17

But what have I done with my life? thought Mrs. Ramsay, taking her place at the head of the table, and looking at all the plates making white circles on it. 'William, sit by me,' she said. 'Lily,' she said, wearily, 'over there.' They had that – Paul Rayley and Minta Doyle – she, only this – an infinitely long table and plates and knives. At the far end, was her husband, sitting down, all in a heap, frowning.

What at? She did not know. She did not mind. She could not understand how she had ever felt any emotion or any affection for him. She had a sense of being past everything, through everything, out of everything, as she helped the soup, as if there was an eddy – there – and one could be in it, or one could be out of it, and she was out of it. It's all come to an end, she thought, while they came in one after another, Charles Tansley – 'Sit there, please,' she said – Augustus Carmichael – and sat down. And meanwhile she waited, passively, for someone to answer her, for something to happen. But this is not a thing, she thought, ladling out soup, that one says.

Raising her eyebrows at the discrepancy – that was what she was thinking, this was what she was doing – ladling out soup – she felt, more and more strongly, outside that eddy; or as if a shade had fallen, and, robbed of colour, she saw things truly. The room (she looked round it) was very shabby. There was no beauty anywhere. She forebore to look at Mr. Tansley. Nothing seemed to have merged. They all sat separate. And the whole of the effort of merging and flowing and creating rested on her. Again she felt, as a fact without hostility, the sterility of men, for if she did not do it nobody would do it, and so, giving herself the little shake that one gives a watch that has stopped, the old familiar pulse began beating, as the watch begins ticking – one, two, three, one, two, three. And so on and so on, she repeated, listening to it, sheltering and fostering the still feeble pulse as one might guard a weak flame with a newspaper. And so then, she concluded, addressing herself by bending silently in his direction to William Bankes – poor man! who had no wife and no children, and dined alone in lodgings except for to-night; and in pity for him, life being now strong enough to bear her on again, she began all this business, as a sailor not without weariness sees the wind fill his sail and yet hardly wants to be off again and thinks how, had the ship sunk, he would have whirled round and round and found rest on the floor of the sea.

'Did you find your letters? I told them to put them in the hall for you,' she said to William Bankes.

Lily Briscoe watched her drifting into that strange no-man's land where to follow people is impossible and yet their going inflicts such a chill on those who watch them that they always try at least to follow them with their eyes as one follows a fading ship until the sails have sunk beneath the horizon.[77]

How old she looks, how worn she looks, Lily thought, and how remote. Then when she turned to William Bankes, smiling, it was as if the ship had turned and the sun had struck its sails again, and Lily thought with some amusement because she was relieved, Why does she pity him? For that was the impression she gave, when she told him that his letters were in the hall. Poor William Bankes, she seemed to be saying, as if her own weariness had been partly pitying people, and the life in her, her resolve to live again, had been stirred by pity. And it was not true, Lily thought; it was one of those misjudgments of hers that seemed to be instinctive and to arise from some need of her own rather than of other people's. He is not in the least pitiable. He has his work, Lily said to herself. She remembered, all of a sudden as if she had found a treasure, that she too had her work. In a flash she saw her picture, and thought, Yes, I shall put the tree further in the middle; then I shall avoid that awkward space. That's what I shall do. That's what has been puzzling me. She took up the salt cellar and put it down again on a flower in the pattern in the table-cloth, so as to remind herself to move the tree.

'It's odd that one scarcely gets anything worth having by post, yet one always wants one's letters,' said Mr. Bankes.

What damned rot they talk, thought Charles Tansley, laying down his spoon precisely in the middle of his plate, which he had swept clean, as if, Lily thought (he sat opposite to her with his back to the window precisely in the middle of the view), he were determined to make sure of his meals. Everything about him had that meagre fixity, that bare unloveliness. But nevertheless, the fact remained, it was almost impossible to dislike anyone if one looked at them. She liked his eyes; they were blue, deep set, frightening.

'Do you write many letters, Mr. Tansley?' asked Mrs. Ramsay, pitying him too, Lily supposed; for that was true of Mrs. Ramsay – she pitied men always as if they lacked something – women never, as if they had something. He wrote to his mother; otherwise he did not suppose he wrote one letter a month, said Mr. Tansley, shortly.

For he was not going to talk the sort of rot these people wanted him to talk. He was not going to be condescended to by these silly women. He had been reading in his room, and now he came down and it all seemed to him silly, superficial, flimsy. Why did they dress? He had come down in his ordinary clothes. He had not got any dress clothes. 'One never gets anything worth having by post' – that was the sort of thing they were always saying. They made men say that sort of thing. Yes, it was pretty well true, he thought. They never got anything worth having from one year's end to another. They did nothing but talk, talk, talk, eat, eat, eat. It was the women's fault. Women made civilisation impossible with all their 'charm', all their silliness.

'No going to the Lighthouse to-morrow, Mrs. Ramsay,' he said asserting himself. He liked her; he admired her; he still thought of the man in the drain-pipe looking up at her; but he felt it necessary to assert himself.

He was really, Lily Briscoe thought, in spite of his eyes, the most uncharming human being she had ever met. Then why did she mind what he said? Women can't write, women can't paint[78] – what did that matter coming from him, since clearly it was not true to him but for some reason helpful to him, and that was why he said it? Why did her whole being bow, like corn under a wind, and erect itself again from this abasement only with a great and rather painful effort? She must make it once more. There's the sprig on the table-cloth; there's my painting; I must move the tree to the middle; that matters – nothing else. Could she not hold fast to that, she asked herself, and not lose her temper, and not argue; and if she wanted a little revenge take it by laughing at him?

'Oh, Mr. Tansley,' she said, 'do take me to the Lighthouse with you. I should so love it.'

She was telling lies he could see. She was saying what she did not mean to annoy him, for some reason. She was laughing at him. He was in his old flannel trousers. He had no others. He felt very rough and isolated and lonely. He knew that she was trying to tease him for some reason; she didn't want to go to the Lighthouse with him; she despised him: so did Prue Ramsay; so did they all. But he was not going to be made a fool of by women, so he turned deliberately in his chair and looked out of the window and said, all in a jerk, very rudely, it would be too rough for her to-morrow. She would be sick.

It annoyed him that she should have made him speak like that, with Mrs. Ramsay listening. If only he could be alone in his room working, he thought, among his books. That was where he felt at his ease. And he had never run a penny into debt; he had never cost his father a penny since he was fifteen; he had helped them at home out of his savings; he was educating his sister. Still, he wished he had known how to answer Miss Briscoe properly; he wished it had not come out all in a jerk like that. 'You'd be sick.' He wished he could think of something to say to Mrs. Ramsay, something which would show her that he was not just a dry prig. That was what they all thought him. He turned to her. But Mrs. Ramsay was talking about people he had never heard of to William Bankes.

'Yes, take it away,' she said briefly, interrupting what she was saying to Mr. Bankes to speak to the maid. 'It must have been fifteen – no, twenty years ago – that I last saw her,' she was saying, turning back to him again as if she could not lose a moment of their talk, for she was absorbed by what they were saying. So he had actually heard from her this evening! And was Carrie still living at Marlow, and was everything still the same? Oh she could remember it as if it were yesterday – going on the river, feeling very cold. But if the Mannings made a plan they stuck to it. Never should she forget Herbert killing a wasp with a teaspoon on the bank! And it was still going on, Mrs. Ramsay mused, gliding like a ghost among the chairs and tables of that drawing-room on the banks of the Thames where she had been so very, very cold twenty years ago; but now she went among them like a ghost; and it fascinated her, as if, while she had changed, that particular day, now become very still and beautiful, had remained there, all these years. Had Carrie written to him herself? she asked.

'Yes. She says they're building a new billiard room,' he

said. No! No! That was out of the question! Building a billiard room! It seemed to her impossible.

Mr. Bankes could not see that there was anything very odd about it. They were very well off now. Should he give her love to Carrie?

'Oh,' said Mrs. Ramsay with a little start, 'No,' she added, reflecting that she did not know this Carrie who built a new billiard room. But how strange, she repeated, to Mr. Bankes's amusement, that they should be going on there still. For it was extraordinary to think that they had been capable of going on living all these years when she had not thought of them more than once all that time. How eventful her own life had been, during those same years. Yet perhaps Carrie Manning had not thought about her either. The thought was strange and distasteful.

'People soon drift apart,' said Mr. Bankes, feeling, how-ever, some satisfaction when he thought that after all he knew both the Mannings and the Ramsays. He had not drifted apart, he thought, laying down his spoon and wiping his clean-shaven lips punctiliously. But perhaps he was rather unusual, he thought, in this; he never let himself get into a groove. He had friends in all circles . . . Mrs. Ramsay had to break off here to tell the maid some-thing about keeping food hot. That was why he preferred dining alone. All these interruptions annoyed him. Well, thought William Bankes, preserving a demeanour of exqui-site courtesy and merely spreading the fingers of his left hand on the table-cloth as a mechanic examines a tool beautifully polished and ready for use in an interval of leisure, such are the sacrifices one's friends ask of one. It would have hurt her if he had refused to come. But it was not worth it for him. Looking at his hand he thought that if he had been alone dinner would have been almost over now; he would have been free to work. Yes, he thought, it is a terrible waste of time. The children were dropping in still. 'I wish one of you would run up to Roger's room,' Mrs. Ramsay was saying. How trifling it all is, how boring it all is, he thought, compared with the other thing – work. Here he sat drumming his fingers on the table-cloth when he might have been – he took a flashing bird's-eye view of his work. What a waste of time it all was to be sure! Yet, he thought, she is one of my oldest friends. I am by way of being devoted to her. Yet now, at this moment her presence meant absolutely nothing to him: her beauty meant nothing to him; her sitting with her little boy at the window – nothing, nothing. He wished only to be alone and to take up that book. He felt uncomfortable; he felt treacherous, that he could sit by her side and feel nothing for her. The truth was that he did not enjoy family life. It was in this sort of state that one asked oneself, What does one live for? Why, one asked oneself, does one take all these pains for the human race to go on? Is it so very desirable? Are we attractive as a species? Not so very, he thought, looking at those rather untidy boys. His favourite, Cam, was in bed, he supposed. Foolish questions, vain questions, questions one never asked if one was occupied. Is human life this? Is human life that? One never had time to think about it. But here he was asking himself that sort of question, because Mrs. Ramsay was giving orders to servants, and also because it had struck him, thinking how surprised Mrs. Ramsay was that Carrie Manning should still exist, that friendships, even the best of them, are frail things. One drifts apart. He reproached himself again. He was sitting beside Mrs. Ramsay and he had nothing in the world to say to her.

'I'm so sorry,' said Mrs. Ramsay, turning to him at last.

He felt rigid and barren, like a pair of boots that has been soaked and gone dry so that you can hardly force your feet into them. Yet he must force his feet into them. He must make himself talk. Unless he were very careful, she would find out this treachery of his; that he did not care a straw for her, and that would not be at all pleasant, he thought. So he bent his head courteously in her direction.

'How you must detest dining in this bear garden,' she said, making use, as she did when she was distracted, of her social manner. So, when there is a strife of tongues at some meeting, the chairman, to obtain unity, suggests that every one shall speak in French. Perhaps it is bad French; French may not contain the words that express the speaker's thoughts; nevertheless speaking French imposes some order, some uniformity. Replying to her in the same language, Mr. Bankes said, 'No, not at all,' and Mr. Tansley, who had no knowledge of this language, even spoken thus in words of one syllable, at once suspected its insincerity. They did talk nonsense, he thought, the Ramsays; and he pounced on this fresh instance with joy, making a note which, one of these days, he would read aloud, to one or two friends. There, in a society where one could say what one liked he would sarcastically describe 'staying with the Ramsays' and what nonsense they talked. It was worth while doing it once, he would say; but not again. The women bored one so, he would say. Of course Ramsay had dished himself by marrying a beautiful woman and having eight children. It would shape itself something like that, but now, at this moment, sitting stuck there with an empty seat beside him nothing had shaped itself at all. It was all in scraps and fragments. He felt extremely, even physically, uncomfortable. He wanted somebody to give him a chance of asserting himself. He wanted it so urgently that he fidgeted in his chair, looked at this person, then at that person, tried to break into their talk, opened his mouth and shut it again. They were talking about the fishing industry. Why did no one ask him his opinion? What did they know about the fishing industry?

Lily Briscoe knew all that. Sitting opposite him could she not see, as in an X-ray photograph, the ribs and thigh bones of the young man's desire to impress himself lying dark in the mist of his flesh – that thin mist which convention had laid over his burning desire to break into the conversation? But, she thought, screwing up her Chinese eyes, and remembering how he sneered at women, 'can't paint, can't write', why should I help him to relieve himself?

There is a code of behaviour she knew, whose seventh article (it may be) says that on occasions of this sort it behoves the woman, whatever her own occupation may be, to go to the help of the young man opposite so that he may expose and relieve the thigh bones, the ribs, of his vanity, of his urgent desire to assert himself; as indeed it is their duty, she reflected, in her old-maidenly fairness, to help us, suppose the Tube were to burst into flames. Then, she thought, I should certainly expect Mr. Tansley to get me out. But how would it be, she thought, if neither of us did either of these things? So she sat there smiling.

'You're not planning to go to the Lighthouse, are you, Lily?' said Mrs. Ramsay. 'Remember poor Mr. Langley; he had been round the world dozens of times, but he told me he never suffered as he did when my husband took him there. Are you a good sailor, Mr. Tansley?' she asked.

Mr. Tansley raised a hammer: swung it high in air; but realising, as it descended, that he could not smite that butterfly with such an instrument as this, said only that he had never been sick in his life. But in that one sentence lay compact, like gunpowder, that his grandfather was a fisherman; his father a chemist; that he had worked his way up entirely himself; that he was proud of it; that he was Charles Tansley – a fact that nobody there seemed to realise; but one of these days every single person would know it. He scowled ahead of him. He could almost pity these mild cultivated people, who would be blown sky high, like bales of wool and barrels of apples, one of these days by the gunpowder that was in him.

'Will you take me, Mr. Tansley?' said Lily, quickly, kindly, for, of course, if Mrs. Ramsay said to her, as in effect she did, 'I am drowning, my dear, in seas of fire. Unless you apply some balm to the anguish of this hour and say something nice to that young man there, life will run upon the rocks – indeed I hear the grating and the growling at this minute. My nerves are taut as fiddle strings. Another touch and they will snap' – when Mrs. Ramsay said all this, as the glance in her eyes said it, of course for the hundred and fiftieth time Lily Briscoe had to renounce the experiment – what happens if one is not nice to that young man there – and be nice.

Judging the turn in her mood correctly – that she was friendly to him now – he was relieved of his egotism, and told her how he had been thrown out of a boat when he was a baby; how his father used to fish him out with a boat-hook; that was how he had learnt to swim. One of his uncles kept the light on some rock or other off the Scottish coast, he said. He had been there with him in a storm. This was said loudly in a pause. They had to listen to him when he said that he had been with his uncle in a lighthouse in a storm. Ah, thought Lily Briscoe, as the conversation took this auspicious turn, and she felt Mrs. Ramsay's gratitude (for Mrs. Ramsay was free now to talk for a moment herself), ah, she thought, but what haven't I paid to get it for you? She had not been sincere.

She had done the usual trick – been nice. She would never know him. He would never know her. Human relations were all like that, she thought, and the worst (if it had not been for Mr. Bankes) were between men and women. Inevitably these were extremely insincere. Then her eye caught the salt cellar, which she had placed there to remind her, and she remembered that next morning she would move the tree further towards the middle, and her spirits rose so high at the thought of painting to-morrow that she laughed out loud at what Mr. Tansley was saying. Let him talk all night if he liked it.

'But how long do they leave men on a lighthouse?' she asked. He told her. He was amazingly well informed. And as he was grateful, and as he liked her, and as he was beginning to enjoy himself, so now, Mrs. Ramsay thought, she could return to that dream land, that unreal but fascinating place, the Mannings' drawing-room at Marlow twenty years ago; where one moved about without haste or anxiety, for there was no future to worry about. She knew what had happened to them, what to her. It was like reading a good book again, for she knew the end of that story, since it had happened twenty years ago, and life, which shot down even from this dining-room table in cascades, heaven knows where, was sealed up there, and lay, like a lake, placidly between its banks. He said they had built a billiard room – was it possible? Would William go on talking about the Mannings? She wanted him to. But no – for some reason he was no longer in the mood. She tried. He did not respond. She could not force him. She was disappointed.

'The children are disgraceful,' she said, sighing. He said something about punctuality being one of the minor virtues which we do not acquire until later in life.

'If at all,' said Mrs. Ramsay merely to fill up space, thinking what an old maid William was becoming. Conscious of his treachery, conscious of her wish to talk about something more intimate, yet out of mood for it at present, he felt come over him the disagreeableness of life, sitting there, waiting. Perhaps the others were saying something interesting? What were they saying?

That the fishing season was bad; that the men were emigrating. They were talking about wages and unemployment. The young man was abusing the government.[79] William Bankes, thinking what a relief it was to catch on to something of this sort when private life was disagreeable, heard him say something about 'one of the most scandalous acts of the present government.' Lily was listening; Mrs. Ramsay was listening; they were all listening. But already bored, Lily felt that something was lacking; Mr. Bankes felt that something was lacking. Pulling her shawl round her, Mrs. Ramsay felt that something was lacking. All of them bending themselves to listen thought, 'Pray heaven that the inside of my mind may not be exposed,' for each thought, 'The others are feeling this. They are outraged and indignant with the government about the fishermen. Whereas, I feel nothing at all.' But perhaps, thought Mr. Bankes, as he looked at Mr. Tansley, here is the man. One was always waiting for the man. There was always a chance. At any moment the leader might arise; the man of genius, in politics as in anything else. Probably he will be extremely disagreeable to us old fogies, thought Mr. Bankes, doing his best to make allowances, for he knew by some curious physical sensation, as of nerves erect in his spine, that he was jealous, for himself partly, partly more probably for his work, for his point of view, for his science; and therefore he was not entirely open-minded or altogether fair, for Mr. Tansley seemed to be saying, You have wasted your lives. You are all of you wrong. Poor old fogies, you're hopelessly behind the times. He seemed to be rather cocksure, this young man; and his manners were bad. But Mr. Bankes bade himself observe, he had courage; he had ability; he was extremely well up in the facts. Probably, Mr. Bankes thought, as Tansley abused the government, there is a good deal in what he says.

'Tell me now . . .' he said. So they argued about politics, and Lily looked at the leaf on the table-cloth; and Mrs. Ramsay, leaving the argument entirely in the hands of the two men, wondered why she was so bored by this talk, and wished, looking at her husband at the other end of the table, that he would say something. One word, she said to herself. For if he said a thing, it would make all the difference. He went to the heart of things. He cared about fishermen and their wages. He could not sleep for thinking of them. It was altogether different when he spoke; one did not feel then, pray heaven you don't see how little I care, because one did care. Then, realising that it was because she admired him so much that she was waiting for him to speak, she felt as if somebody had been praising her husband to her and their marriage, and she glowed all over without realising that it was she herself who had praised him. She looked at him thinking to find this shown in his face; he would be looking magnificent . . . But not in the least! He was screwing his face up, he was scowling and frowning, and flushing with anger. What on earth was it about? she wondered. What could be the matter? Only that poor old Augustus had asked for another plate of soup –

that was all. It was unthinkable, it was detestable (so he signalled to her across the table) that Augustus should be beginning his soup over again. He loathed people eating when he had finished. She saw his anger fly like a pack of hounds into his eyes, his brow, and she knew that in a moment something violent would explode, and then – but thank goodness! she saw him clutch himself and clap a brake on the wheel, and the whole of his body seemed to emit sparks but not words. He sat there scowling. He had said nothing, he would have her observe. Let her give him the credit for that! But why after all should poor Augustus not ask for another plate of soup? He had merely touched Ellen's arm and said:

'Ellen, please, another plate of soup,' and then Mr. Ramsay scowled like that.

And why not? Mrs. Ramsay demanded. Surely they could let Augustus have his soup if he wanted it. He hated people wallowing in food, Mr. Ramsay frowned at her. He hated everything dragging on for hours like this. But he had controlled himself, Mr. Ramsay would have her observe, disgusting though the sight was. But why show it so plainly, Mrs. Ramsay demanded (they looked at each other down the long table sending these questions and answers across, each knowing exactly what the other felt). Everybody could see, Mrs. Ramsay thought. There was Rose[80] gazing at her father, there was Roger gazing at his father; both would be off in spasms of laughter in another second, she knew, and so she said promptly (indeed it was time):

'Light the candles,' and they jumped up instantly and went and fumbled at the sideboard.

Why could he never conceal his feelings? Mrs. Ramsay wondered, and she wondered if Augustus Carmichael had noticed. Perhaps he had; perhaps he had not. She could not help respecting the composure with which he sat there, drinking his soup. If he wanted soup, he asked for soup. Whether people laughed at him or were angry with him he was the same. He did not like her, she knew that; but partly for that very reason she respected him, and looking at him, drinking soup, very large and calm in the failing light, and monumental, and contemplative, she wondered what he did feel then, and why he was always content and dignified; and she thought how devoted he was to Andrew, and would call him into his room, and, Andrew said, 'show him things'. And there he would lie all day long on the lawn brooding presumably over his poetry, till he reminded one of a cat watching birds, and then he clapped his paws together when he had found the word, and her husband said, 'Poor old Augustus – he's a true poet', which was high praise from her husband.[81]

Now eight candles were stood down the table, and after the first stoop the flames stood upright and drew with them into visibility the long table entire, and in the middle a yellow and purple dish of fruit. What had she done with it, Mrs. Ramsay wondered, for Rose's arrangement of the grapes and pears, of the horny pink-lined shell, of the bananas, made her think of a trophy fetched from the bottom of the sea, of Neptune's[82] banquet, of the bunch that hangs with vine leaves over the shoulder of Bacchus[83] (in some picture), among the leopard skins and the torches lolloping red and gold ... Thus brought up suddenly into the light it seemed possessed of great size and depth, was like a world in which one could take one's staff and climb up hills, she thought, and go down into valleys, and to her pleasure (for it brought them into sympathy momentarily) she saw that Augustus too feasted his eyes on the same plate of fruit, plunged in, broke off a bloom there, a tassel here, and returned, after feasting, to his hive. That was his way of looking, different from hers. But looking together united them.

Now all the candles were lit, and the faces on both sides of the table were brought nearer by the candle-light, and composed, as they had not been in the twilight, into a party round a table, for the night was now shut off by panes of glass, which, far from giving any accurate view of the outside world, rippled it so strangely that here, inside the room, seemed to be order and dry land; there, outside, a reflection in which things wavered and vanished, waterily.

Some change at once went through them all, as if this had really happened, and they were all conscious of making a party together in a hollow, on an island; had their common cause against that fluidity out there. Mrs. Ramsay, who had been uneasy, waiting for Paul and Minta to come in, and unable, she felt, to settle to things, now felt her uneasiness changed to expectation. For now they must come, and Lily Briscoe, trying to analyse the cause of the sudden exhilaration, compared it with that moment on the tennis lawn, when solidity suddenly vanished, and such vast spaces lay between them; and now the same effect was got by the many candles in the sparely furnished room, and the uncurtained windows, and the bright mask-like look of faces seen by candlelight. Some weight was taken off them; anything might happen, she felt. They must come now, Mrs. Ramsay thought, looking at the door, and at that instant, Minta Doyle, Paul Rayley, and a maid carrying a great dish in her hands came in together. They were awfully late; they were horribly late, Minta said, as they found their way to different ends of the table.

'I lost my brooch — my grandmother's brooch,' said

Minta with a sound of lamentation in her voice, and a suffusion in her large brown eyes, looking down, looking up, as she sat by Mr. Ramsay, which roused his chivalry so that he bantered her.

How could she be such a goose, he asked, as to scramble about the rocks in jewels?

She was by way of being terrified of him – he was so fearfully clever, and the first night when she had sat by him, and he talked about George Eliot, she had been really frightened, for she had left the third volume of *Middlemarch*[84] in the train and she never knew what happened in the end; but afterwards she got on perfectly, and made herself out even more ignorant than she was, because he liked telling her she was a fool. And so to-night, directly he laughed at her she was not frightened. Besides, she knew, directly she came into the room, that the miracle had happened; she wore her golden haze. Sometimes she had it; sometimes not. She never knew why it came or why it went, or if she had it until she came into the room and then she knew instantly by the way some man looked at her. Yes, to-night she had it, tremendously; she knew that by the way Mr. Ramsay told her not to be a fool. She sat beside him, smiling.

It must have happened then, thought Mrs. Ramsay; they are engaged. And for a moment she felt what she had never expected to feel again – jealousy. For he, her husband, felt it too – Minta's glow; he liked these girls, these golden-reddish girls, with something flying, something a little wild and harum-scarum about them, who didn't 'scrape their hair off', weren't, as he said about poor Lily Briscoe, 'skimpy'. There was some quality which she herself had not, some lustre, some richness, which attracted him, amused him, led him to make favourites of girls like

Minta. They might cut his hair for him, plait him watch-chains, or interrupt him at his work, hailing him (she heard them), 'Come along, Mr. Ramsay; it's our turn to beat them now,' and out he came to play tennis.

But indeed she was not jealous, only, now and then, when she made herself look in her glass a little resentful that she had grown old, perhaps, by her own fault. (The bill for the greenhouse and all the rest of it.) She was grateful to them for laughing at him ('How many pipes have you smoked to-day, Mr. Ramsay?' and so on), till he seemed a young man; a man very attractive to women, not burdened, not weighed down with the greatness of his labours and the sorrows of the world and his fame or his failure, but again as she had first known him, gaunt but gallant; helping her out of a boat, she remembered; with delightful ways, like that (she looked at him, and he looked astonishingly young, teasing Minta). For herself – 'Put it down there,' she said, helping the Swiss girl to place gently before her the huge brown pot in which was the Bœuf en Daube – for her own part she liked her boobies. Paul must sit by her. She had kept a place for him. Really, she sometimes thought she liked the boobies best. They did not bother one with their dissertations. How much they missed, after all, these very clever men! How dried up they did become, to be sure. There was something, she thought as he sat down, very charming about Paul. His manners were delightful to her, and his sharp-cut nose and his bright blue eyes. He was so considerate. Would he tell her – now that they were all talking again – what had happened?

'We went back to look for Minta's brooch,' he said, sitting down by her. 'We' – that was enough. She knew from the effort, the rise in his voice to surmount a difficult word that it was the first time he had said 'we'. 'We' did this, 'we' did that. They'll say that all their lives, she thought, and an exquisite scent of olives and oil and juice rose from the great brown dish as Marthe, with a little flourish, took the cover off. The cook had spent three days over that dish. And she must take great care, Mrs. Ramsay thought, diving into the soft mass, to choose a specially tender piece for William Bankes. And she peered into the dish, with its shiny walls and its confusion of savoury brown and yellow meats, and its bay leaves and its wine, and thought, This will celebrate the occasion – a curious sense rising in her, at once freakish and tender, of celebrating a festival, as if two emotions were called up in her, one profound – for what could be more serious than the love of man for woman, what more commanding, more impressive, bearing in its bosom the seeds of death; at the same time these lovers, these people entering into illusion glittering-eyed, must be danced round with mockery, decorated with garlands.

'It is a triumph,' said Mr. Bankes, laying his knife down for a moment. He had eaten attentively. It was rich; it was tender. It was perfectly cooked. How did she manage these things in the depths of the country? he asked her. She was a wonderful woman. All his love, all his reverence had returned; and she knew it.

'It is a French recipe[85] of my grandmother's,' said Mrs. Ramsay, speaking with a ring of great pleasure in her voice. Of course it was French. What passes for cookery in England is an abomination (they agreed). It is putting cabbages in water. It is roasting meat till it is like leather. It is cutting off the delicious skins of vegetables. 'In which', said Mr. Bankes, 'all the virtue of the vegetable is contained.' And the waste, said Mrs. Ramsay. A whole French family could live on what an English cook throws away. Spurred on by her sense that William's affection had come back to her, and that everything was all right again, and that her suspense was over, and that now she was free both to triumph and to mock, she laughed, she gesticulated, till Lily thought, How childlike, how absurd she was, sitting up there with all her beauty opened again in her, talking about the skins of vegetables. There was something frightening about her. She was irresistible. Always she got her own way in the end, Lily thought. Now she had brought this off – Paul and Minta, one might suppose, were engaged. Mr. Bankes was dining here. She put a spell on them all, by wishing, so simply, so directly, and Lily contrasted that abundance with her own poverty of spirit, and supposed that it was partly that belief (for her face was all lit up – without looking young, she looked radiant) in this strange, this terrifying thing, which made Paul Rayley, the centre of it, all of a tremor, yet abstract, absorbed, silent. Mrs. Ramsay, Lily felt, as she talked about the skins of vegetables, exalted that, worshipped that; held her hands over it to warm them, to protect it, and yet, having brought it all about, somehow laughed, led her victims, Lily felt, to the altar. It came over her too now – the emotion, the vibration of love. How inconspicuous she felt herself by Paul's side! He, glowing, burning; she, aloof, satirical; he, bound for adventure; she, moored to the shore; he, launched, incautious; she solitary, left out – and, ready to implore a share, if it were disaster, in his disaster, she said shyly:

'When did Minta lose her brooch?'

He smiled the most exquisite smile, veiled by memory, tinged by dreams. He shook his head. 'On the beach,' he said.

'I'm going to find it,' he said, 'I'm getting up early.'

This being kept secret from Minta, he lowered his voice, and turned his eyes to where she sat, laughing, beside Mr. Ramsay.

Lily wanted to protest violently and outrageously her desire to help him, envisaging how in the dawn on the beach she would be the one to pounce on the brooch half-hidden by some stone, and thus herself be included among the sailors and adventurers. But what did he reply to her offer? She actually said with an emotion that she seldom let appear, 'Let me come with you'; and he laughed. He meant yes or no – either perhaps. But it was not his meaning – it was the odd chuckle he gave, as if he had said, Throw yourself over the cliff if you like, I don't care. He turned on her cheek the heat of love, its horror, its cruelty, its unscrupulosity. It scorched her, and Lily, looking at Minta being charming to Mr. Ramsay at the other end of the table, flinched for her exposed to those fangs, and was thankful. For at any rate, she said to herself, catching sight of the salt cellar on the pattern, she need not marry, thank Heaven: she need not undergo that degradation. She was saved from that dilution. She would move the tree rather more to the middle.

Such was the complexity of things. For what happened to her, especially staying with the Ramsays, was to be made to feel violently two opposite things at the same time; that's what you feel, was one; that's what I feel was the other, and then they fought together in her mind, as now. It is so beautiful, so exciting, this love, that I tremble on the verge of it, and offer, quite out of my own habit, to look for a brooch on a beach; also it is the stupidest, the most barbaric of human passions, and turns a nice young man with a profile like a gem (Paul's was exquisite) into a bully with a crowbar (he was swaggering, he was insolent) in the Mile End Road.[86] Yet she said to herself, from the dawn of time odes have been sung to love; wreaths heaped and roses; and if you asked nine people out of ten they would say they wanted nothing but this; while the women, judging from her own experience, would all the time be feeling, This is not what we want; there is nothing more tedious, puerile, and inhumane than love; yet it is also beautiful and necessary. Well then, well then? she asked, somehow expecting the others to go on with the argument, as if in an argument like this one threw one's own little bolt which fell short obviously and left the others to carry it on. So she listened again to what they were saying in case they should throw any light upon the question of love.

'Then,' said Mr. Bankes, 'there is that liquid the English call coffee.'

'Oh coffee!' said Mrs. Ramsay. But it was much rather a question (she was thoroughly roused, Lily could see, and talked very emphatically) of real butter and clean milk. Speaking with warmth and eloquence she described the iniquity of the English dairy system, and in what state milk was delivered at the door, and was about to prove her charges, for she had gone into the matter, when all round the table, beginning with Andrew in the middle, like a fire leaping from tuft to tuft of furze, her children laughed; her husband laughed; she was laughed at, fire-encircled, and forced to vail her crest, dismount her batteries, and only retaliate by displaying the raillery and ridicule of the table to Mr. Bankes as an example of what one suffered if one attacked the prejudices of the British Public.

Purposely, however, for she had it on her mind that Lily, who had helped her with Mr. Tansley, was out of things, she exempted her from the rest; said 'Lily anyhow agrees with me,' and so drew her in, a little fluttered, a little startled. (For she was thinking about love.) They were both out of things, Mrs. Ramsay had been thinking, both Lily and Charles Tansley. Both suffered from the glow of the other two. He, it was clear, felt himself utterly in the cold; no woman would look at him with Paul Rayley in the room. Poor fellow! Still, he had his dissertation, the influence of somebody upon something: he could take care of himself. With Lily it was different. She faded, under Minta's glow; became more inconspicuous than ever, in her little grey dress with her little puckered face and her little Chinese eyes. Everything about her was so small. Yet, thought Mrs. Ramsay, comparing her with Minta, as she claimed her help (for Lily should bear her out she talked no more about her dairies than her husband did about his boots – he would talk by the hour about his boots), of the two Lily at forty will be the better. There was in Lily a thread of something; a flare of something; something of her own which Mrs. Ramsay liked very much indeed, but no man would, she feared. Obviously, not, unless it were a much older man, like William Bankes. But then he cared, well, Mrs. Ramsay sometimes thought that he cared, since his wife's death, perhaps for her. He was not 'in love' of course; it was one of those unclassified affections of which there are so many. Oh but nonsense, she thought; William must marry Lily. They have so many things in common. Lily is so fond of flowers. They are both cold and aloof and rather self-sufficing. She must arrange for them to take a long walk together.

Foolishly, she had set them opposite each other. That could be remedied to-morrow. If it were fine, they should go for a picnic. Everything seemed possible. Everything seemed right. Just now (but this cannot last, she thought, dissociating herself from the moment while they were all talking about boots) just now she had reached security; she hovered like a hawk suspended; like a flag floated in an element of joy which filled every nerve of her body fully and sweetly, not noisily, solemnly rather, for it arose, she thought, looking at them all eating there, from husband and children and friends; all of which rising in this profound stillness (she was helping William Bankes to one very small piece more and peered into the depths of the earthenware pot) seemed now for no special reason to stay there like a smoke, like a fume rising upwards, holding them safe together. Nothing need be said; nothing could be said. There it was, all round them. It partook, she felt, carefully helping Mr. Bankes to a specially tender piece, of eternity; as she had already felt about something different once before that afternoon; there is a coherence in things, a stability; something, she meant, is immune from change, and shines out (she glanced at the window with its ripple of reflected lights) in the face of the flowing, the fleeting, the spectral, like a ruby; so that again to-night she had the feeling she had had once to-day already, of peace, of rest. Of such moments, she thought, the thing is made that remains for ever after. This would remain.

'Yes,' she assured William Bankes, 'there is plenty for everybody.'

'Andrew,' she said, 'hold your plate lower, or I shall spill it.' (The Bœuf en Daube was a perfect triumph.) Here, she felt, putting the spoon down, was the still space that lies about the heart of things, where one could move or rest; could wait now (they were all helped) listening; could then, like a hawk which lapses suddenly from its high station, flaunt and sink on laughter easily, resting her whole weight upon what at the other end of the table her husband was saying about the square root of one thousand two hundred and fifty-three, which happened to be the number on his railway ticket.

What did it all mean? To this day she had no notion. A square root? What was that? Her sons knew. She leant on them; on cubes and square roots; that was what they were talking about now; on Voltaire[87] and Madame de Staël;[88] on the character of Napoleon;[89] on the French system of land tenure;[90] on Lord Rosebery;[91] on Creevey's Memoirs:[92] she let it uphold her and sustain her, this admirable fabric of the masculine intelligence, which ran up and down, crossed this way and that, like iron girders spanning the swaying fabric, upholding the world, so that she could trust herself to it utterly, even shut her eyes, or flicker them for a moment, as a child staring up from its pillow winks at the myriad layers of the leaves of a tree. Then she woke up. It was still being fabricated. William Bankes was praising the Waverley novels.[93]

He read one of them every six months, he said. And why should that make Charles Tansley angry? He rushed in (all, thought Mrs. Ramsay, because Prue will not be nice to him) and denounced the Waverley novels when he knew nothing about it, nothing about it whatsoever, Mrs. Ramsay thought, observing him rather than listening to what he said. She could see how it was from his manner – he wanted to assert himself, and so it would always be with him till he got his Professorship or married his wife, and so need not be always saying, 'I—I—I.'[94] For that was what his criticism of poor Sir Walter, or perhaps it was Jane Austen, amounted to. 'I—I—I.' He was thinking of himself and the impression he was making, as she could tell by the sound of his voice, and his emphasis and his uneasiness. Success would be good for him. At any rate they were off again. Now she need not listen. It could not last she knew, but at the moment her eyes were so clear that they seemed to go round the table unveiling each of these people, and their thoughts and their feelings, without effort like a light stealing under water so that its ripples and the reeds in it and the minnows balancing themselves, and the sudden silent trout are all lit up hanging, trembling. So she saw them; she heard them; but whatever they said had also this quality, as if what they said was like the movement of a trout when, at the same time, one can see the ripple and the gravel, something to the right, something to the left; and the whole is held together; for whereas in active life she would be netting and separating one thing from another; she would be saying she liked the Waverley novels or had not read them; she would be urging herself forward; now she said nothing. For the moment she hung suspended.

'Ah, but how long do you think it'll last?' said somebody. It was as if she had antennae trembling out from her, which, intercepting certain sentences, forced them upon her attention. This was one of them. She scented danger for her husband. A question like that would lead, almost certainly, to something being said which reminded him of his own failure. How long would he be read – he would think at once. William Bankes (who was entirely free from all such vanity) laughed, and said he attached no importance to changes in fashion. Who could tell what was going to last – in literature or indeed in anything else?

'Let us enjoy what we do enjoy,' he said. His integrity seemed to Mrs. Ramsay quite admirable. He never seemed for a moment to think, But how does this affect me? But then if you had the other temperament, which must have praise, which must have encouragement, naturally you began (and she knew that Mr. Ramsay was beginning) to be uneasy; to want somebody to say, Oh, but your work will last, Mr. Ramsay, or something like that. He showed his uneasiness quite clearly now by saying, with some irritation, that, anyhow, Scott (or was it Shakespeare?) would last him his lifetime. He said it irritably. Everybody, she thought, felt a little uncomfortable, without knowing why. Then Minta Doyle, whose instinct was fine, said bluffly, absurdly, that she did not believe that any one really enjoyed reading Shakespeare. Mr. Ramsay said grimly (but his mind was turned away again) that very few people liked it as much as they said they did. But, he added, there is considerable merit in some of the plays nevertheless, and Mrs. Ramsay saw that it would be all right for the moment anyhow; he would laugh at Minta, and she, Mrs. Ramsay saw, realising his extreme anxiety about himself, would, in her own way, see that he was taken care of, and praise him, somehow or other. But she wished it was not necessary: perhaps it was her fault that it was necessary. Anyhow, she was free now to listen to what Paul Rayley was trying to say about books one had read as a boy. They lasted, he said. He had read some of Tolstoi[95] at school. There was one he always remembered, but he had forgotten the name. Russian names were impossible, said Mrs. Ramsay. 'Vronsky,' said Paul. He remembered that because he always thought it such a good name for a villain. 'Vronsky,' said Mrs. Ramsay; 'O, *Anna Karenina*,' but that did not take them very far; books were not in their line. No, Charles Tansley would put them both right in a second about books, but it was all so mixed up with, Am I saying the right thing? Am I making a good impression? that, after all, one knew more about him than about Tolstoi, whereas what Paul said was about the thing simply, not himself.

Like all stupid people, he had a kind of modesty too, a consideration for what you were feeling, which, once in a way at least, she found attractive. Now he was thinking, not about himself or about Tolstoi, but whether she was cold, whether she felt a draught, whether she would like a pear.

No, she said, she did not want a pear. Indeed she had been keeping guard over the dish of fruit (without realising it) jealously, hoping that nobody would touch it. Her eyes had been going in and out among the curves and shadows of the fruit, among the rich purples of the lowland grapes, then over the horny ridge of the shell, putting a yellow against a purple, a curved shape against a round shape, without knowing why she did it, or why, every time she did it, she felt more and more serene; until, oh, what a pity that they should do it − a hand reached out, took a pear, and spoilt the whole thing. In sympathy she looked at Rose. She looked at Rose sitting between Jasper and Prue. How odd that one's child should do that!

How odd to see them sitting there, in a row, her children, Jasper, Rose, Prue, Andrew, almost silent, but with some joke of their own going on, she guessed, from the twitching at their lips. It was something quite apart from everything else, something they were hoarding up to laugh over in their own room. It was not about their father, she hoped. No, she thought not. What was it, she wondered, sadly rather, for it seemed to her that they would laugh when she was not there. There was all that hoarded behind those rather set, still, mask-like faces, for they did not join in easily; they were like watchers, surveyors, a little raised or set apart from the grown-up people. But when she looked at Prue to-night, she saw that this was not now quite true of her. She was just beginning, just moving, just descending. The faintest light was on her face, as if the glow of Minta opposite, some excitement, some anticipation of happiness was reflected in her, as if the sun of the love of men and women rose over the rim of the table-cloth, and without knowing what it was she bent towards it and greeted it. She kept looking at Minta, shyly, yet curiously, so that Mrs. Ramsay looked from one to the other and said, speaking to Prue in her own mind, You will be as happy as she is one of these days. You will be much happier, she added, because you are my daughter, she meant; her own daughter must be happier than other people's daughters. But dinner was over. It was time to go. They were only playing with things on their plates. She would wait until they had done laughing at some story her husband was telling. He was having a joke with Minta about a bet. Then she would get up.

She liked Charles Tansley, she thought, suddenly; she liked his laugh. She liked him for being so angry with Paul and Minta. She liked his awkwardness. There was a lot in that young man after all. And Lily, she thought, putting her napkin beside her plate, she always has some joke of her own. One need never bother about Lily. She waited. She tucked her napkin under the edge of her plate. Well, were they done now? No. That story had led to another story. Her husband was in great spirits to-night, and wishing, she supposed, to make it all right with old Augustus after that scene about the soup, had drawn him in — they were telling stories about some one they had both known at college. She looked at the window in which the candle flames burnt brighter now that the panes were black, and looking at that outside the voices came to her very strangely, as if they were voices at a service in a cathedral, for she did not listen to the words. The sudden bursts of laughter and then one voice (Minta's) speaking alone, reminded her of men and boys crying out the Latin words of a service in some Roman Catholic cathedral. She waited. Her husband spoke. He was repeating something, and she knew it was poetry from the rhythm and the ring of exaltation and melancholy in his voice:

> Come out and climb the garden path,
>> Luriana Lurilee.
> The China rose is all abloom and buzzing with the yellow bee.[96]

The words (she was looking at the window) sounded as if they were floating like flowers on water out there, cut off from them all, as if no one had said them, but they had come into existence of themselves.

> And all the lives we ever lived and all the lives to be
> Are full of trees and changing leaves.

She did not know what they meant, but, like music, the words seemed to be spoken by her own voice, outside her self, saying quite easily and naturally what had been in her mind the whole evening while she said different things. She knew, without looking round, that every one at the table was listening to the voice saying:

> I wonder if it seems to you
>> Luriana, Lurilee

with the same sort of relief and pleasure that she had, as if this were, at last, the natural thing to say, this were their own voice speaking.

But the voice stopped. She looked round. She made herself get up. Augustus Carmichael had risen and, holding his table napkin so that it looked like a long white robe he stood chanting:

To see the Kings go riding by
Over lawn and daisy lea
With their palm leaves and cedar sheaves,
    Luriana, Lurilee,

and as she passed him he turned slightly towards her
repeating the last words:

    Luriana, Lurilee,

and bowed to her as if he did her homage. Without
knowing why, she felt that he liked her better than he had
ever done before; and with a feeling of relief and gratitude
she returned his bow and passed through the door which
he held open for her.

It was necessary now to carry everything a step further.
With her foot on the threshold she waited a moment
longer in a scene which was vanishing even as she looked,
and then, as she moved and took Minta's arm and left the
room, it changed, it shaped itself differently; it had become,
she knew, giving one last look at it over her shoulder,
already the past.

18

As usual, Lily thought. There was always something that
had to be done at that precise moment, something that
Mrs. Ramsay had decided for reasons of her own to do
instantly, it might be with every one standing about making
jokes, as now, not being able to decide whether they were
going into the smoking-room, into the drawing-room, up
to the attics. Then one saw Mrs. Ramsay in the midst of
this hubbub standing there with Minta's arm in hers,
bethink her 'Yes, it is time for that now,' and so make off at

once with an air of secrecy to do something alone. And directly she went a sort of disintegration set in; they wavered about, went different ways, Mr. Bankes took Charles Tansley by the arm and went off to finish on the terrace the discussion they had begun at dinner about politics, thus giving a turn to the whole poise of the evening, making the weight fall in a different direction, as if, Lily thought, seeing them go, and hearing a word or two about the policy of the Labour Party,[97] they had gone up on to the bridge of the ship and were taking their bearings; the change from poetry to politics struck her like that; so Mr. Bankes and Charles Tansley went off, while the others stood looking at Mrs. Ramsay going upstairs in the lamplight alone. Where, Lily wondered, was she going so quickly?

Not that she did in fact run or hurry; she went indeed rather slowly. She felt rather inclined just for a moment to stand still after all that chatter, and pick out one particular thing; the thing that mattered; to detach it; separate it off; clean it of all the emotions and odds and ends of things, and so hold it before her, and bring it to the tribunal where, ranged about in conclave, sat the judges she had set up to decide these things. Is it good, is it bad, is it right or wrong? Where are we going to? and so on. So she righted herself after the shock of the event, and quite unconsciously and incongruously, used the branches of the elm trees outside to help her to stabilise her position. Her world was changing: they were still. The event had given her a sense of movement. All must be in order. She must get that right and that right, she thought, insensibly approving of the dignity of the trees' stillness, and now again of the superb upward rise (like the beak of a ship up a wave) of the elm branches as the wind raised them. For it was windy (she stood a moment to look out). It was windy, so that the leaves now and then brushed open a star, and the stars themselves seemed to be shaking and darting light and trying to flash out between the edges of the leaves. Yes, that was done then, accomplished; and as with all things done, become solemn. Now one thought of it, cleared of chatter and emotion, it seemed always to have been, only was shown now, and so being shown struck everything into stability. They would, she thought, going on again, however long they lived, come back to this night; this moon; this wind; this house: and to her too. It flattered her, where she was most susceptible of flattery, to think how, wound about in their hearts, however long they lived she would be woven; and this, and this, and this, she thought, going upstairs, laughing, but affectionately, at the sofa on the landing (her mother's[98]) at the rocking-chair (her father's); at the map of the Hebrides. All that would be revived again in the lives of Paul and Minta; 'the Rayleys' — she tried the new name over; and she felt, with her hand on the nursery door, that community of feeling with other people which emotion gives as if the walls of partition had become so thin that practically (the feeling was one of relief and happiness) it was all one stream, and chairs, tables, maps, were hers, were theirs, it did not matter whose, and Paul and Minta would carry it on when she was dead.

She turned the handle, firmly, lest it should squeak, and went in, pursing her lips slightly, as if to remind herself that she must not speak aloud. But directly she came in she saw, with annoyance, that the precaution was not needed. The children were not asleep. It was most annoying. Mildred should be more careful. There was James wide awake and Cam sitting bolt upright, and Mildred out of bed in her bare feet, and it was almost eleven and they were all talking. What was the matter? It was that horrid skull[99] again. She had told Mildred to move it, but Mildred, of course, had forgotten, and now there was Cam wide awake and James wide awake quarrelling when they ought to have been asleep hours ago. What had possessed Edward to send them this horrid skull? She had been so foolish as to let them nail it up there. It was nailed fast, Mildred said, and Cam couldn't go to sleep with it in the room, and James screamed if she touched it.

Then Cam must go to sleep (it had great horns said Cam –) must go to sleep and dream of lovely palaces, said Mrs. Ramsay, sitting down on the bed by her side. She could see the horns, Cam said, all over the room. It was true. Wherever they put the light (and James could not sleep without a light) there was always a shadow somewhere.

'But think, Cam, it's only an old pig,' said Mrs. Ramsay, 'a nice black pig like the pigs at the farm.' But Cam thought it was a horrid thing, branching at her all over the room.

'Well then,' said Mrs. Ramsay, 'we will cover it up,' and they all watched her go to the chest of drawers, and open the little drawers quickly one after another, and not seeing anything that would do, she quickly took her own shawl off and wound it round the skull, round and round and round, and then she came back to Cam and laid her head almost flat on the pillow beside Cam's and said how lovely it looked now; how the fairies would love it; it was like a bird's nest; it was like a beautiful mountain such as she had seen abroad, with valleys and flowers and bells ringing and birds singing and little goats and antelopes . . . She could see the words[100] echoing as she spoke them rhythmically in Cam's mind, and Cam was repeating after her how it was like a mountain, a bird's nest, a garden, and there were little antelopes, and her eyes were opening and shutting, and Mrs. Ramsay went on saying still more monotonously, and more rhythmically and more nonsensically, how she must shut her eyes and go to sleep and dream of mountains and valleys and stars falling and parrots and antelopes and gardens, and everything lovely, she said, raising her head very slowly and speaking more and more mechanically, until she sat upright and saw that Cam was asleep.

Now, she whispered, crossing over to his bed, James must go to sleep too, for see, she said, the boar's skull was still there; they had not touched it; they had done just what he wanted; it was there quite unhurt. He made sure that the skull was still there under the shawl. But he wanted to ask her something more. Would they go to the Lighthouse to-morrow?

No, not to-morrow, she said, but soon, she promised him; the next fine day. He was very good. He lay down. She covered him up. But he would never forget, she knew, and she felt angry with Charles Tansley, with her husband, and with herself, for she had raised his hopes. Then feeling for her shawl and remembering that she had wrapped it round the boar's skull, she got up, and pulled the window down another inch or two, and heard the wind, and got a breath of the perfectly indifferent chill night air and mur-mured good-night to Mildred and left the room and let the tongue of the door slowly lengthen in the lock and went out.

She hoped he would not bang his books on the floor above their heads, she thought, still thinking how annoying Charles Tansley was. For neither of them slept well; they were excitable children, and since he said things like that about the Lighthouse, it seemed to her likely that he would knock a pile of books over, just as they were going to sleep, clumsily sweeping them off the table with his elbow. For she supposed that he had gone upstairs to work. Yet he looked so desolate; yet she would feel relieved when he went; yet she would see that he was better treated to-morrow; yet he was admirable with her husband; yet his manners certainly wanted improving; yet she liked his laugh – thinking this, as she came downstairs, she noticed that she could now see the moon itself through the staircase window – the yellow harvest moon – and turned, and they saw her, standing above them on the stairs.

'That's my mother,' thought Prue. Yes; Minta should look at her; Paul Rayley should look at her. That is the thing itself, she felt, as if there were only one person like that in the world; her mother. And, from having been quite grown up, a moment before, talking with the others, she became a child again, and what they had been doing was a game, and would her mother sanction their game, or condemn it, she wondered. And thinking what a chance it was for Minta and Paul and Lily to see her, and feeling what an extraordinary stroke of fortune it was for her to have her, and how she would never grow up and never leave home, she said, like a child, 'We thought of going down to the beach to watch the waves.'

Instantly, for no reason at all, Mrs. Ramsay became like a girl of twenty, full of gaiety. A mood of revelry suddenly took possession of her. Of course they must go; of course they must go, she cried, laughing; and running down the last three or four steps quickly, she began turning from one to the other and laughing and drawing Minta's wrap round her and saying she only wished she could come too, and would they be very late, and had any of them got a watch?

'Yes, Paul has,' said Minta. Paul slipped a beautiful gold watch out of a little wash-leather case to show her. And as he held it in the palm of his hand before her, he felt 'She knows all about it. I need not say anything.' He was saying to her as he showed her the watch, 'I've done it, Mrs. Ramsay. I owe it all to you.' And seeing the gold watch lying in his hand, Mrs. Ramsay felt, How extraordinarily lucky Minta is! She is marrying a man who has a gold watch in a wash-leather bag!

'How I wish I could come with you!' she cried. But she was withheld by something so strong that she never even thought of asking herself what it was. Of course it was impossible for her to go with them. But she would have liked to go, had it not been for the other thing, and tickled by the absurdity of her thought (how lucky to marry a man with a wash-leather bag for his watch) she went with a smile on her lips into the other room, where her husband sat reading.

19

Of course, she said to herself, coming into the room, she had to come here to get something she wanted. First she wanted to sit down in a particular chair under a particular lamp. But she wanted something more, though she did not know, could not think what it was that she wanted. She looked at her husband (taking up her stocking and beginning to knit), and saw that he did not want to be interrupted – that was clear. He was reading something that moved him very much. He was half smiling and then she knew he was controlling his emotion. He was tossing the pages over. He was acting it – perhaps he was thinking himself the person in the book. She wondered what book it was.

Oh, it was one of old Sir Walter's,[101] she saw, adjusting the shade of her lamp so that the light fell on her knitting. For Charles Tansley had been saying (she looked up as if she expected to hear the crash of books on the floor above) had been saying that people don't read Scott any more. Then her husband thought, 'That's what they'll say of me'; so he went and got one of those books. And if he came to the conclusion 'That's true' what Charles Tansley said, he would accept it about Scott. (She could see that he was weighing, considering, putting this with that as he read.) But not about himself. He was always uneasy about himself. That troubled her. He would always be worrying about his own books – will they be read, are they good, why aren't they better, what do people think of me? Not liking to think of him so, and wondering if they had guessed at dinner why he suddenly became irritable when they talked about fame and books lasting, wondering if the children were laughing at that, she twitched the stocking out, and all the fine gravings came drawn with steel instruments about her lips and forehead, and she grew still like a tree which has been tossing and quivering and now, when the breeze falls, settles, leaf by leaf, into quiet.

It didn't matter, any of it, she thought. A great man, a great book, fame – who could tell? She knew nothing about it. But it was his way with him, his truthfulness – for instance at dinner she had been thinking quite instinctively, If only he would speak! She had complete trust in him. And dismissing all this, as one passes in diving now a weed, now a straw, now a bubble, she felt again, sinking deeper, as she had felt in the hall when the others were talking, There is something I want – something I have come to get, and she fell deeper and deeper without knowing quite what it was, with her eyes closed. And she waited a little, knitting, wondering, and slowly those words they had said at dinner, 'the China rose is all abloom and buzzing with the honey bee,' began washing from side to side of her mind rhythmically, and as they washed, words, like little shaded lights, one red, one blue, one yellow, lit up in the dark of her mind, and seemed leaving their perches up there to fly across and across, or to cry out and to be echoed; so she turned and felt on the table beside her for a book.[102]

> And all the lives we ever lived
> And all the lives to be,
> Are full of trees and changing leaves,

she murmured, sticking her needles into the stocking. And she opened the book and began reading here and there at random, and as she did so she felt that she was climbing backwards, upwards, shoving her way up under petals that curved over her, so that she only knew this is white, or this is red. She did not know at first what the words meant at all.

> Steer, hither steer your winged pines, all beaten Mariners[103]

she read and turned the page, swinging herself, zigzagging this way and that, from one line to another as from one branch to another, from one red and white flower to another, until a little sound roused her – her husband slapping his thighs. Their eyes met for a second; but they did not want to speak to each other. They had nothing to say, but something seemed, nevertheless, to go from him to her. It was the life, it was the power of it, it was the tremendous humour, she knew, that made him slap his thighs. Don't interrupt me, he seemed to be saying, don't say anything; just sit there. And he went on reading. His lips twitched. It filled him. It fortified him. He clean forgot all the little rubs and digs of the evening, and how it bored him unutterably to sit still while people ate and drank interminably, and his being so irritable with his wife and so touchy and minding when they passed his books over as if they didn't exist at all. But now, he felt, it didn't matter a damn who reached Z (if thought ran like an alphabet from A to Z). Somebody would reach it – if not he, then another. This man's strength and sanity, his feeling for straightforward simple things, these fishermen, the poor old crazed creature in Mucklebackit's cottage made him feel so vigorous, so relieved of something that he felt roused and triumphant and could not choke back his tears. Raising the book a little to hide his face he let them fall and shook his head from side to side and forgot himself completely (but not one or two reflections about morality and French novels and English novels and Scott's hands being tied but his view perhaps being as true as the other view) forgot his own bothers and failures completely in poor Steenie's drowning and Mucklebackit's sorrow (that was Scott at his best) and the astonishing delight and feeling of vigour that it gave him.

Well, let them improve upon that, he thought as he finished the chapter. He felt that he had been arguing with somebody, and had got the better of him. They could not improve upon that, whatever they might say; and his own position became more secure. The lovers were fiddlesticks, he thought, collecting it all in his mind again. That's fiddlesticks, that's first-rate, he thought, putting one thing beside another. But he must read it again. He could not remember the whole shape of the thing. He had to keep his judgement in suspense. So he returned to the other thought – if young men did not care for this, naturally they did not care for him either. One ought not to complain, thought Mr. Ramsay, trying to stifle his desire to complain to his wife that young men did not admire him. But he was determined; he would not bother her again. Here he looked at her reading. She looked very peaceful, reading. He liked to think that every one had taken themselves off and that he and she were alone. The whole of life did not consist in going to bed with a woman, he thought, returning to Scott and Balzac, to the English novel and the French novel.

Mrs. Ramsay raised her head and like a person in a light sleep seemed to say that if he wanted her to wake she would, she really would, but otherwise, might she go on sleeping, just a little longer, just a little longer? She was climbing up those branches, this way and that, laying hands on one flower and then another.

Nor praise the deep vermilion in the rose,

she read, and so reading she was ascending, she felt, on to the top, on to the summit. How satisfying! How restful! All the odds and ends of the day stuck to this magnet; her mind felt swept, felt clean. And then there it was, suddenly entire shaped in her hands, beautiful and reasonable, clear and complete, the essence sucked out of life and held rounded here – the sonnet.[104]

But she was becoming conscious of her husband looking at her. He was smiling at her, quizzically, as if he were ridiculing her gently for being asleep in broad daylight, but at the same time he was thinking, Go on reading. You don't look sad now, he thought. And he wondered what she was reading, and exaggerated her ignorance, her simplicity, for he liked to think that she was not clever, not book-learned at all. He wondered if she understood what she was reading. Probably not, he thought. She was astonishingly beautiful. Her beauty seemed to him, if that were possible, to increase.

> Yet seem'd it winter still, and, you away,
> As with your shadow I with these did play,

she finished.

'Well?' she said, echoing his smile dreamily, looking up from her book.

> As with your shadow I with these did play,

she murmured putting the book on the table.

What had happened she wondered, as she took up her knitting, since she had last seen him alone? She remembered dressing, and seeing the moon; Andrew holding his plate too high at dinner; being depressed by something William had said; the birds in the trees; the sofa on the landing; the children being awake; Charles Tansley waking them with his books falling – oh no, that she had invented; and Paul having a wash-leather case for his watch. Which should she tell him about?

'They're engaged,' she said, beginning to knit, 'Paul and Minta.'

'So I guessed,' he said. There was nothing very much to be said about it. Her mind was still going up and down, up and down with the poetry; he was still feeling very vigorous, very forthright, after reading about Steenie's funeral. So they sat silent. Then she became aware that she wanted him to say something.

Anything, anything, she thought, going on with her knitting. Anything will do.

'How nice it would be to marry a man with a wash-leather bag for his watch,' she said, for that was the sort of joke they had together.

He snorted. He felt about this engagement as he always felt about any engagement; the girl is much too good for that young man. Slowly it came into her head, why is it then that one wants people to marry? What was the value, the meaning of things? (Every word they said now would be true.) Do say something, she thought, wishing only to hear his voice. For the shadow, the thing folding them in was beginning, she felt, to close round her again. Say anything, she begged, looking at him, as if for help.

He was silent, swinging the compass[105] on his watch-chain to and fro, and thinking of Scott's novels and Balzac's novels. But through the crepuscular walls of their intimacy, for they were drawing together, involuntarily, coming side by side, quite close, she could feel his mind like a raised hand shadowing her mind; and he was beginning now that her thoughts took a turn he disliked — towards this 'pessimism' as he called it — to fidget, though he said nothing, raising his hand to his forehead, twisting a lock of hair, letting it fall again.

'You won't finish that stocking to-night,' he said, pointing to her stocking. That was what she wanted — the asperity in his voice reproving her. If he says it's wrong to be pessimistic probably it is wrong, she thought; the marriage will turn out all right.

'No,' she said, flattening the stocking out upon her knee, 'I shan't finish it.'

And what then? For she felt that he was still looking at her, but that his look had changed. He wanted something — wanted the thing she always found it so difficult to give him; wanted her to tell him that she loved him. And that, no, she could not do. He found talking so much easier than she did. He could say things — she never could. So naturally it was always he that said the things, and then for some reason he would mind this suddenly, and would reproach her. A heartless woman he called her; she never told him that she loved him. But it was not so – it was not so. It was only that she never could say what she felt. Was there no crumb on his coat? Nothing she could do for him? Getting up she stood at the window with the reddish-brown stocking in her hands, partly to turn away from him, partly because she did not mind looking now, with him watching, at the Lighthouse. For she knew that he had turned his head as she turned; he was watching her. She knew that he was thinking, You are more beautiful than ever. And she felt herself very beautiful. Will you not tell me just for once that you love me? He was thinking that, for he was roused, what with Minta and his book, and its being the end of the day and their having quarrelled about going to the Lighthouse. But she could not do it; she could not say it. Then, knowing that he was watching her, instead of saying anything she turned, holding her stocking, and looked at him. And as she looked at him she began to smile, for though she had not said a word, he knew, of course he knew, that she loved him. He could not deny it. And smiling she looked out of the window and said (thinking to herself, Nothing on earth can equal this happiness) –

'Yes, you were right. It's going to be wet to-morrow.' She had not said it, but he knew it. And she looked at him smiling. For she had triumphed again.

II

TIME PASSES[1]

'Well, we must wait for the future to show,' said Mr. Bankes, coming in from the terrace.

'It's almost too dark to see,' said Andrew, coming up from the beach.

'One can hardly tell which is the sea and which is the land,' said Prue.

'Do we leave that light burning?' said Lily as they took their coats off indoors.

'No,' said Prue, 'not if everyone's in.'

'Andrew,' she called back, 'just put out the light in the hall.'

One by one the lamps were all extinguished, except that Mr. Carmichael, who liked to lie awake a little reading Virgil,³ kept his candle burning rather longer than the rest.

2

So with the lamps all put out, the moon sunk, and a thin rain drumming on the roof a downpouring of immense darkness began. Nothing, it seemed, could survive the flood, the profusion of darkness which, creeping in at keyholes and crevices, stole round window blinds, came into bedrooms, swallowed up here a jug and basin, there a bowl of red and yellow dahlias, there the sharp edges and firm bulk of a chest of drawers. Not only was furniture confounded; there was scarcely anything left of body or mind by which one could say 'This is he' or 'This is she.' Sometimes a hand was raised as if to clutch something or ward off something, or somebody groaned, or somebody laughed aloud as if sharing a joke with nothingness.

Nothing stirred in the drawing-room or in the dining-room or on the staircase. Only through the rusty hinges and swollen sea-moistened woodwork certain airs, detached from the body of the wind (the house was ramshackle after all) crept round corners and ventured indoors. Almost one might imagine them, as they entered the drawing-room, questioning and wondering, toying with the flap of hanging wall-paper, asking, would it hang much longer, when would it fall? Then smoothly brushing the walls, they passed on musingly as if asking the red and yellow roses on the wall-paper whether they would fade, and questioning (gently, for there was time at their disposal) the torn letters in the wastepaper basket, the flowers, the books, all of which were now open to them and asking, Were they allies?[4] Were they enemies? How long would they endure?

So some random light directing them from some uncovered star, or wandering ship, or the Lighthouse even, with its pale footfall upon stair and mat, the little airs mounted the staircase and nosed round bedroom doors. But here surely, they must cease. Whatever else may perish and disappear what lies here is steadfast. Here one might say to those sliding lights, those fumbling airs, that breathe and bend over the bed itself, here you can neither touch nor destroy. Upon which, wearily, ghostlily as if they had feather-light fingers and the light persistency of feathers, they would look, once, on the shut eyes and the loosely clasping fingers, and fold their garments wearily and disappear. And so, nosing, rubbing, they went to the window on the staircase, to the servants' bedrooms, to the boxes in the attics; descending, blanched the apples on the dining-room table, fumbled the petals of roses, tried the picture

on the easel, brushed the mat and blew a little sand along
the floor. At length, desisting, all ceased together, gathered together, all sighed together; all together gave off
an aimless gust of lamentation to which some door in
the kitchen replied; swung wide; admitted nothing; and
slammed to.

[Here Mr. Carmichael, who was reading Virgil, blew out
his candle. It was past midnight.]

3

But what after all is one night? A short space, especially
when the darkness dims so soon, and so soon a bird sings,
a cock crows, or a faint green quickens, like a turning leaf,
in the hollow of the wave. Night, however, succeeds to
night. The winter holds a pack of them in store and deals
them equally, evenly, with indefatigable fingers. They
lengthen; they darken. Some of them hold aloft clear
planets, plates of brightness. The autumn trees, ravaged as
they are, take on the flash of tattered flags kindling in the
gloom of cool cathedral caves where gold letters on marble
pages describe death in battle and how bones bleach and
burn far away in Indian sands. The autumn trees gleam in
the yellow moonlight, in the light of harvest moons, the
light which mellows the energy of labour, and smooths the
stubble, and brings the wave lapping blue to the shore.

It seemed now as if, touched by human penitence and all
its toil, divine goodness had parted the curtain and displayed behind it, single, distinct, the hare erect; the wave
falling; the boat rocking, which, did we deserve them,
should be ours always. But alas, divine goodness, twitching
the cord, draws the curtain; it does not please him; he
covers his treasures in a drench of hail, and so breaks

them, so confuses them that it seems impossible that their calm should ever return or that we should ever compose from their fragments a perfect whole or read in the littered pieces the clear words of truth. For our penitence deserves a glimpse only; our toil respite only.

The nights now are full of wind and destruction; the trees plunge and bend and their leaves fly helter skelter until the lawn is plastered with them and they lie packed in gutters and choke rain pipes and scatter damp paths. Also the sea tosses itself and breaks itself, and should any sleeper fancying that he might find on the beach an answer to his doubts, a sharer of his solitude, throw off his bedclothes and go down by himself to walk on the sand, no image with semblance of serving and divine promptitude comes readily to hand bringing the night to order and making the world reflect the compass[5] of the soul. The hand dwindles in his hand; the voice bellows in his ear. Almost it would appear that it is useless in such confusion to ask the night those questions as to what, and why, and wherefore, which tempt the sleeper from his bed to seek an answer.

[Mr. Ramsay stumbling along a passage stretched his arms out one dark morning, but, Mrs. Ramsay having died rather suddenly the night before, he stretched his arms out. They remained empty.[6]]

4

So with the house empty and the doors locked and the mattresses rolled round, those stray airs, advance guards of great armies, blustered in, brushed bare boards, nibbled and fanned, met nothing in bedroom or drawing-room that wholly resisted them but only hangings that flapped, wood that creaked, the bare legs of tables, saucepans and china already furred, tarnished, cracked. What people had shed and left – a pair of shoes, a shooting cap, some faded skirts and coats in wardrobes – those alone kept the human shape and in the emptiness indicated how once they were filled and animated; how once hands were busy with hooks and buttons; how once the looking-glass had held a face; had held a world hollowed out in which a figure turned, a hand flashed, the door opened, in came children rushing and tumbling; and went out again. Now, day after day, light turned, like a flower reflected in water, its clear image on the wall opposite. Only the shadows of the trees, flourishing in the wind, made obeisance on the wall, and for a moment darkened the pool in which light reflected itself; or birds, flying, made a soft spot flutter slowly across the bedroom floor.

So loveliness reigned and stillness, and together made the shape of loveliness itself, a form from which life had parted; solitary like a pool at evening, far distant, seen from a train window, vanishing so quickly that the pool, pale in the evening, is scarcely robbed of its solitude, though once seen. Loveliness and stillness clasped hands in the bedroom, and among the shrouded jugs and sheeted chairs even the prying of the wind, and the soft nose of the clammy sea airs, rubbing, snuffling, iterating, and reiterating their questions – 'Will you fade? Will you perish?' – scarcely disturbed the peace, the indifference, the air of pure integrity, as if the question they asked scarcely needed that they should answer: we remain.

Nothing it seemed could break that image, corrupt that innocence, or disturb the swaying mantle of silence which, week after week, in the empty room, wove into itself the falling cries of birds, ships hooting, the drone and hum of the fields, a dog's bark, a man's shout, and folded them round the house in silence. Once only a board sprang on the landing; once in the middle of the night with a roar, with a rupture, as after centuries of quiescence, a rock rends itself from the mountain and hurtles crashing into the valley, one fold of the shawl loosened and swung to and fro. Then again peace descended; and the shadow wavered; light bent to its own image in adoration on the bedroom wall; when Mrs. McNab,[7] tearing the veil of silence with hands that had stood in the wash-tub, grinding it with boots that had crunched the shingle, came as directed to open all windows, and dust the bedrooms.

5

As she lurched (for she rolled like a ship at sea) and leered (for her eyes fell on nothing directly, but with a sidelong glance that deprecated the scorn and anger of the world – she was witless, she knew it), as she clutched the banisters and hauled herself upstairs and rolled from room to room, she sang. Rubbing the glass of the long looking-glass and leering sideways at her swinging figure a sound issued from her lips – something that had been gay twenty years before on the stage perhaps, had been hummed and danced to, but now, coming from the toothless, bonneted, care-taking woman, was robbed of meaning, was like the voice of witlessness, humour, persistency itself, trodden down but springing up again, so that as she lurched, dusting, wiping, she seemed to say how it was one long sorrow and trouble, how it was getting up and going to bed again, and bringing things out and putting them away again. It was not easy or snug this world she had known for close on seventy years. Bowed down she was with weariness. How long, she asked, creaking and groaning on her knees under the bed, dusting the boards, how long shall it endure? but hobbled to her feet again, pulled herself up, and again with her sidelong leer which slipped and turned aside even from her own face, and her own sorrows, stood and gaped in the glass, aimlessly smiling, and began again the old amble and hobble, taking up mats, putting down china, looking sideways in the glass, as if, after all, she had her consolations, as if indeed there twined about her dirge some incorrigible hope. Visions of joy there must have been at the wash-tub, say with her children (yet two had been base-born and one had deserted her), at the public-house, drinking; turning over scraps in her drawers. Some cleavage of the dark there must have been, some channel in the depths of obscurity through which light enough issued to twist her face grinning in the glass and make her, turning to her job again, mumble out the old music hall song. Meanwhile the mystic, the visionary, walked the beach, stirred a puddle, looked at a stone, and asked themselves 'What am I?' 'What is this?' and suddenly an answer was vouchsafed them (what it was they could not say): so that they were warm in the frost and had comfort in the desert. But Mrs. McNab continued to drink and gossip as before.

6

The spring without a leaf to toss, bare and bright like a virgin fierce in her chastity, scornful in her purity, was laid out on fields wide-eyed and watchful and entirely careless of what was done or thought by the beholders.

[Prue Ramsay, leaning on her father's arm, was given in marriage that May. What, people said, could have been more fitting? And, they added, how beautiful she looked!]

As summer neared, as the evenings lengthened, there came to the wakeful, the hopeful, walking the beach, stirring the pool, imaginations of the strangest kind – of flesh turned to atoms which drove before the wind, of stars flashing in their hearts, of cliff, sea, cloud, and sky brought purposely together to assemble outwardly the scattered parts of the vision within. In those mirrors, the minds of men, in those pools of uneasy water, in which clouds for ever turn and shadows form, dreams persisted, and it was impossible to resist the strange intimation which every gull, flower, tree, man and woman, and the white earth itself seemed to declare (but if questioned at once to withdraw) that good triumphs, happiness prevails, order rules; or to resist the extraordinary stimulus to range hither and thither in search of some absolute good, some crystal of intensity, remote from the known pleasures and familiar virtues, something alien to the processes of domestic life, single, hard, bright, like a diamond in the sand, which would render the possessor secure. Moreover, softened and acquiescent, the spring with her bees humming and gnats dancing threw her cloak about her, veiled her eyes, averted her head, and among passing shadows and flights of small rain seemed to have taken upon her a knowledge of the sorrows of mankind.

[Prue Ramsay died that summer in some illness connected with childbirth, which was indeed a tragedy, people said. They said nobody deserved happiness more.]

And now in the heat of summer the wind sent its spies about the house again. Flies wove a web in the sunny rooms; weeds that had grown close to the glass in the night tapped methodically at the window pane. When darkness fell, the stroke of the Lighthouse, which had laid itself with such authority upon the carpet in the darkness, tracing its pattern, came now in the softer light of spring mixed with moonlight gliding gently as if it laid its caress and lingered stealthily and looked and came lovingly again. But in the very lull of this loving caress, as the long stroke leant upon the bed, the rock was rent asunder; another fold of the shawl loosened; there it hung, and swayed. Through the short summer nights and the long summer days, when the empty rooms seemed to murmur with the echoes of the fields and the hum of flies, the long streamer waved gently, swayed aimlessly; while the sun so striped and barred the rooms and filled them with yellow haze that Mrs. McNab, when she broke in and lurched about, dusting, sweeping, looked like a tropical fish oaring its way through sun-lanced waters.

But slumber and sleep though it might there came later in the summer ominous sounds like the measured blows of hammers dulled on felt, which, with their repeated shocks still further loosened the shawl and cracked the tea-cups. Now and again some glass tinkled in the cupboard as if a giant voice had shrieked so loud in its agony that tumblers stood inside a cupboard vibrated too. Then again silence fell; and then, night after night, and sometimes in plain mid-day when the roses were bright and light turned on the wall its shape clearly there seemed to drop into this silence this indifference, this integrity, the thud of something falling.

[A shell exploded. Twenty or thirty young men were blown up in France, among them Andrew Ramsay, whose death, mercifully, was instantaneous.]

At that season those who had gone down to pace the beach and ask of the sea and sky what message they reported or what vision they affirmed had to consider among the usual tokens of divine bounty – the sunset on the sea, the pallor of dawn, the moon rising, fishing-boats against the moon, and children pelting each other with handfuls of grass, something out of harmony with this jocundity, this serenity. There was the silent apparition of an ashen-coloured ship[8] for instance, come, gone; there was a purplish stain upon the bland surface of the sea as if something had boiled and bled, invisibly, beneath. This intrusion into a scene calculated to stir the most sublime reflections and lead to the most comfortable conclusions stayed their pacing. It was difficult blandly to overlook them, to abolish their significance in the landscape; to continue, as one walked by the sea, to marvel how beauty outside mirrored beauty within.

Did Nature supplement what man advanced? Did she complete what he began? With equal complacence she saw his misery, condoned his meanness, and acquiesced in his torture. That dream, then, of sharing, completing, finding in solitude on the beach an answer, was but a reflection in a mirror, and the mirror itself was but the surface glassiness which forms in quiescence when the nobler powers sleep beneath? Impatient, despairing yet loth to go (for beauty offers her lures, has her consolations), to pace the beach was impossible; contemplation was unendurable; the mirror was broken.

[Mr. Carmichael brought out a volume of poems that spring, which had an unexpected success. The war, people said, had revived their interest in poetry.]

7

Night after night, summer and winter, the torment of storms, the arrow-like stillness of fine weather, held their court without interference. Listening (had there been any one to listen) from the upper rooms of the empty house only gigantic chaos streaked with lightning could have been heard tumbling and tossing, as the winds and waves disported themselves like the amorphous bulks of leviathans whose brows are pierced by no light of reason, and mounted one on top of another, and lunged and plunged in the darkness or the daylight (for night and day, month and year ran shapelessly together) in idiot games, until it seemed as if the universe were battling and tumbling, in brute confusion and wanton lust aimlessly by itself.

In spring the garden urns, casually filled with wind-blown plants, were gay as ever. Violets came and daffodils. But the stillness and the brightness of the day were as strange as the chaos and tumult of night, with the trees standing there, and the flowers standing there, looking before them, looking up, yet beholding nothing, eyeless, and so terrible.

8

Thinking no harm, for the family would not come, never again, some said, and the house would be sold at Michaelmas perhaps, Mrs. McNab stooped and picked a bunch of flowers to take home with her. She laid them on the table while she dusted. She was fond of flowers. It was a pity to let them waste. Suppose the house were sold (she stood arms akimbo in front of the looking-glass) it would want seeing to – it would. There it had stood all these years without a soul in it. The books and things were mouldy, for, what with the war and help being hard to get, the house had not been cleaned as she could have wished. It was beyond one person's strength to get it straight now. She was too old. Her legs pained her. All those books needed to be laid out on the grass in the sun; there was plaster fallen in the hall; the rain-pipe had blocked over the study window and let the water in; the carpet was ruined quite. But people should come themselves; they should have sent somebody down to see. For there were clothes in the cupboards; they had left clothes in all the bedrooms. What was she to do with them? They had the moth in them – Mrs. Ramsay's things. Poor lady! She would never want *them* again. She was dead, they said; years ago, in London. There was the old grey cloak she wore gardening. (Mrs. McNab fingered it.) She could see her, as she came up the drive with the washing, stooping over her flowers (the garden was a pitiful sight now, all run to riot, and rabbits scuttling at you out of the beds) – she could see her with one of the children by her in that grey cloak. There were boots and shoes; and a brush and comb left on the dressing-table, for all the world as if she expected to come back to-morrow. (She had died very sudden at the end, they said.) And once they had been coming, but had put off coming, what with the war, and travel being so difficult these days; they had never come all these years; just sent her money; but never wrote, never came, and expected to find things as they had left them, ah dear! Why the dressing-table drawers were full of things (she pulled them open), handkerchiefs, bits of ribbon. Yes, she could see Mrs. Ramsay as she came up the drive with the washing.

'Good-evening, Mrs. McNab,' she would say.

She had a pleasant way with her. The girls all liked her. But dear, many things had changed since then (she shut the drawer); many families had lost their dearest. So she was dead; and Mr. Andrew killed; and Miss Prue dead too, they said, with her first baby; but every one had lost some one these years. Prices had gone up[9] shamefully, and didn't come down again neither. She could well remember her in her grey cloak.

'Good-evening, Mrs. McNab,' she said, and told cook to keep a plate of milk soup for her – quite thought she wanted it, carrying that heavy basket all the way up from town. She could see her now, stooping over her flowers; (and faint and flickering, like a yellow beam or the circle at the end of a telescope, a lady in a grey cloak, stooping over her flowers, went wandering over the bedroom wall, up the dressing-table, across the wash-stand, as Mrs. McNab hobbled and ambled, dusting, straightening).

And cook's name now? Mildred? Marian? – some name like that. Ah, she had forgotten – she did forget things. Fiery, like all red-haired women. Many a laugh they had had. She was always welcome in the kitchen. She made them laugh, she did. Things were better then than now.

She sighed; there was too much work for one woman. She wagged her head this side and that. This had been the nursery. Why, it was all damp in here; the plaster was falling. Whatever did they want to hang a beast's skull there for? gone mouldy too. And rats in all the attics. The rain came in. But they never sent; never came. Some of the locks had gone, so the doors banged. She didn't like to be up here at dusk alone neither. It was too much for one woman, too much, too much. She creaked, she moaned. She banged the door. She turned the key in the lock, and left the house shut up, locked, alone.

9

The house was left; the house was deserted. It was left like a shell on a sandhill to fill with dry salt grains now that life had left it. The long night seemed to have set in; the trifling airs, nibbling, the clammy breaths, fumbling, seemed to have triumphed. The saucepan had rusted and the mat decayed. Toads had nosed their way in. Idly, aimlessly, the swaying shawl swung to and fro. A thistle thrust itself between the tiles in the larder. The swallows nested in the drawing-room; the floor was strewn with straw; the plaster fell in shovelfuls; rafters were laid bare; rats carried off this and that to gnaw behind the wainscots. Tortoise-shell butterflies burst from the chrysalis and pattered their life out on the window-pane. Poppies sowed themselves among the dahlias; the lawn waved with long grass; giant artichokes towered among roses; a fringed carnation flowered among the cabbages; while the gentle tapping of a weed at the window had become, on winters' nights, a drumming from sturdy trees and thorned briars which made the whole room green in summer.

What power could now prevent the fertility, the insensibility of nature? Mrs. McNab's dream of a lady, of a child, of a plate of milk soup? It had wavered over the walls like a spot of sunlight and vanished. She had locked the door; she had gone. It was beyond the strength of one woman, she said. They never sent. They never wrote. There were things up there rotting in the drawers – it was a shame to leave them so, she said. The place was gone to rack and ruin. Only the Lighthouse beam entered the rooms for a moment, sent its sudden stare over bed and wall in the darkness of winter, looked with equanimity at the thistle and the swallow, the rat and the straw. Nothing[10] now withstood them; nothing said no to them. Let the wind blow; let the poppy seed itself and the carnation mate with the cabbage. Let the swallow build in the drawing-room, and the thistle thrust aside the tiles, and the butterfly sun itself on the faded chintz of the arm-chairs. Let the broken glass and the china lie out on the lawn and be tangled over with grass and wild berries.

For now had come that moment, that hesitation when dawn trembles and night pauses, when if a feather alight in the scale it will be weighed down. One feather, and the house, sinking, falling, would have turned and pitched downwards to the depths of darkness. In the ruined room, picnickers would have lit their kettles; lovers sought shelter there, lying on the bare boards; and the shepherd stored his dinner on the bricks, and the tramp slept with his coat round him to ward off the cold. Then the roof would have fallen; briars and hemlocks would have blotted out path, step, and window; would have grown, unequally but lustily over the mound, until some trespasser, losing his way, could have told only by a red-hot poker among the nettles, or a scrap of china in the hemlock, that here once some one had lived; there had been a house.

If the feather had fallen, if it had tipped the scale downwards, the whole house would have plunged to the depths to lie upon the sands of oblivion. But there was a force working; something not highly conscious; something that leered, something that lurched; something not inspired to go about its work with dignified ritual or solemn chanting. Mrs. McNab groaned; Mrs. Bast[11] creaked. They were old; they were stiff; their legs ached. They came with their brooms and pails at last; they got to work. All of a sudden, would Mrs. McNab see that the house was ready, one of the young ladies wrote: would she get this done; would she get that done; all in a hurry. They might be coming for the summer; had left everything to the last; expected to find things as they had left them. Slowly and painfully, with broom and pail, mopping, scouring, Mrs. McNab, Mrs. Bast stayed the corruption and the rot;

rescued from the pool of Time that was fast closing over them now a basin, now a cupboard; fetched up from oblivion all the Waverley novels and a tea-set one morning; in the afternoon restored to sun and air a brass fender and a set of steel fire-irons. George, Mrs. Bast's son, caught the rats, and cut the grass. They had the builders. Attended with the creaking of hinges and the screeching of bolts, the slamming and banging of damp-swollen woodwork, some rusty laborious birth seemed to be taking place, as the women, stooping, rising, groaning, singing, slapped and slammed, upstairs now, now down in the cellars. Oh, they said, the work!

They drank their tea in the bedroom sometimes, or in the study; breaking off work at mid-day with the smudge on their faces, and their old hands clasped and cramped with the broom handles. Flopped on chairs they contemplated now the magnificent conquest over taps and bath; now the more arduous, more partial triumph over long rows of books, black as ravens once, now white-stained, breeding pale mushrooms and secreting furtive spiders. Once more, as she felt the tea warm in her, the telescope fitted itself to Mrs. McNab's eyes, and in a ring of light she saw the old gentleman, lean as a rake, wagging his head, as she came up with the washing, talking to himself, she supposed, on the lawn. He never noticed her. Some said he was dead; some said she was dead. Which was it? Mrs. Bast didn't know for certain either. The young gentleman was dead. That she was sure. She had read his name in the papers.

There was the cook now, Mildred, Marian, some such name as that — a red-headed woman, quick-tempered like all her sort, but kind, too, if you knew the way with her. Many a laugh they had had together. She saved a plate of soup for Maggie; a bite of ham, sometimes; whatever was over. They lived well in those days. They had everything they wanted (glibly, jovially, with the tea hot in her, she unwound her ball of memories, sitting in the wicker arm-chair by the nursery fender). There was always plenty doing, people in the house, twenty staying sometimes, and washing up till long past midnight.

Mrs. Bast (she had never known them; had lived in Glasgow at that time) wondered, putting her cup down, whatever they hung that beast's skull there for? Shot in foreign parts no doubt.

It might well be, said Mrs. McNab, wantoning on with her memories; they had friends in eastern countries; gentle-men staying there, ladies in evening dress; she had seen them once through the dining-room door all sitting at dinner. Twenty she dared say in all their jewellery, and she asked to stay help wash up, might be till after midnight.

Ah, said Mrs. Bast, they'd find it changed. She leant out of the window. She watched her son George scything the grass. They might well ask, what had been done to it? seeing how old Kennedy was supposed to have charge of it, and then his leg got so bad after he fell from the cart; and perhaps then no one for a year, or the better part of one; and then Davie Macdonald, and seeds might be sent, but who should say if they were ever planted? They'd find it changed.

She watched her son scything. He was a great one for work – one of those quiet ones. Well they must be getting along with the cupboards, she supposed. They hauled themselves up.

At last, after days of labour within, of cutting and digging without, dusters were flicked from the windows, the windows were shut to, keys were turned all over the house; the front door was banged; it was finished.

And now as if the cleaning and the scrubbing and the scything and the mowing had drowned it there rose that half-heard melody, that intermittent music which the ear half catches but lets fall; a bark, a bleat; irregular, intermittent, yet somehow related; the hum of an insect, the tremor of cut grass, dissevered yet somehow belonging; the jar of a dor beetle, the squeak of a wheel, loud, low, but mysteriously related; which the ear strains to bring together and is always on the verge of harmonising but they are never quite heard, never fully harmonised, and at last, in the evening, one after another the sounds die out, and the harmony falters, and silence falls. With the sunset sharpness was lost, and like mist rising, quiet rose, quiet spread, the wind settled; loosely the world shook itself down to sleep, darkly here without a light to it, save what came green suffused through leaves, or pale on the white flowers by the window.

[Lily Briscoe[12] had her bag carried up to the house late one evening in September. Mr. Carmichael came by the same train.]

10

Then indeed peace had come. Messages of peace breathed from the sea to the shore. Never to break its sleep any more, to lull it rather more deeply to rest and whatever the dreamers dreamt holily, dreamt wisely, to confirm – what else was it murmuring – as Lily Briscoe laid her head on the pillow in the clean still room and heard the sea. Through the open window the voice of the beauty of the world came murmuring, too softly to hear exactly what it said – but what mattered if the meaning were plain? – entreating the sleepers (the house was full again; Mrs.

Beckwith was staying there, also Mr. Carmichael), if they would not actually come down to the beach itself at least to lift the blind and look out. They would see then night flowing down in purple; his head crowned; his sceptre jewelled; and how in his eyes a child might look. And if they still faltered (Lily was tired out with travelling and slept almost at once; but Mr. Carmichael read a book by candlelight), if they still said no, that it was vapour this splendour of his, and the dew had more power than he, and they preferred sleeping; gently then without complaint, or argument, the voice would sing its song. Gently the waves[13] would break (Lily heard them in her sleep); tenderly the light fell (it seemed to come through her eyelids). And it all looked, Mr. Carmichael thought, shutting his book, falling asleep, much as it used to look years ago.

Indeed the voice might resume, as the curtains of dark wrapped themselves over the house, over Mrs. Beckwith, Mr. Carmichael, and Lily Briscoe so that they lay with several folds of blackness on their eyes, why not accept this, be content with this, acquiesce and resign? The sigh of all the seas breaking in measure round the isles soothed them; the night wrapped them; nothing broke their sleep, until, the birds beginning and the dawn weaving their thin voices in to its whiteness, a cart grinding, a dog somewhere barking, the sun lifted the curtains, broke the veil on their eyes, and Lily Briscoe stirring in her sleep clutched at her blankets as a faller clutches at the turf on the edge of a cliff. Her eyes opened wide. Here she was again, she thought, sitting bolt upright in bed. Awake.

III

THE LIGHTHOUSE

What does it mean then, what can it all mean? Lily Briscoe asked herself, wondering whether, since she had been left alone, it behoved her to go to the kitchen to fetch another cup of coffee or wait here. What does it mean? – a catchword that was, caught up from some book, fitting her thought loosely, for she could not, this first morning with the Ramsays, contract her feelings, could only make a phrase resound to cover the blankness of her mind until these vapours had shrunk. For really, what did she feel, come back after all these years and Mrs. Ramsay dead? Nothing, nothing – nothing that she could express at all.

She had come late last night when it was all mysterious, dark. Now she was awake, at her old place at the breakfast table, but alone. It was very early too, not yet eight. There was this expedition – they were going to the Lighthouse, Mr. Ramsay, Cam, and James. They should have gone already – they had to catch the tide or something. And Cam was not ready and James was not ready and Nancy had forgotten to order the sandwiches and Mr. Ramsay had lost his temper and banged out of the room.

'What's the use of going now?' he had stormed.

Nancy had vanished. There he was, marching up and down the terrace in a rage. One seemed to hear doors slamming and voices calling all over the house. Now Nancy burst in, and asked, looking round the room, in a queer half dazed, half desperate way, 'What does one send to the Lighthouse?' as if she were forcing herself to do what she despaired of ever being able to do.

What does one send to the Lighthouse indeed! At any other time Lily could have suggested reasonably tea, tobacco, newspapers. But this morning everything seemed so extraordinarily queer that a question like Nancy's – What does one send to the Lighthouse? – opened doors in one's mind that went banging and swinging to and fro and made one keep asking, in a stupefied gape, What does one send? What does one do? Why is one sitting here after all?

Sitting alone (for Nancy went out again) among the clean cups at the long table she felt cut off from other people, and able only to go on watching, asking, wondering. The house, the place, the morning, all seemed strangers to her. She had no attachment here, she felt, no relations with it, anything might happen, and whatever did happen, a step outside, a voice calling ('It's not in the cupboard; it's on the landing,' some one cried), was a question, as if the link that usually bound things together had been cut, and they floated up here, down there, off, anyhow. How aimless it was, how chaotic, how unreal it was, she thought, looking at her empty coffee cup. Mrs. Ramsay dead; Andrew killed;[1] Prue dead too – repeat it as she might, it roused no feeling in her. And we all get together in a house like this on a morning like this, she said, looking out of the window – it was a beautiful still day.

Suddenly Mr. Ramsay raised his head as he passed and looked straight at her, with his distraught wild gaze which was yet so penetrating, as if he saw you, for one second, for the first time, for ever; and she pretended to drink out of her empty coffee cup so as to escape him – to escape his demand on her, to put aside a moment longer that imperious need. And he shook his head at her, and strode on ('Alone' she heard him say, 'Perished'[2] she heard him say) and like everything else this strange morning the words became symbols, wrote themselves all over the grey-green walls. If only she could put them together, she felt, write them out in some sentence, then she would have got at the truth of things. Old Mr. Carmichael came padding softly in, fetched his coffee, took his cup and made off to sit in the sun. The extraordinary unreality was frightening; but it was also exciting. Going to the Lighthouse. But what does one send to the Lighthouse? Perished. Alone. The grey-green light on the wall opposite. The empty places. Such were some of the parts, but how bring them together? she asked. As if any interruption would break the frail shape she was building on the table she turned her back to the window lest Mr. Ramsay should see her. She must escape somehow, be alone somewhere. Suddenly she remembered. When she had sat there last ten years ago there had been a little sprig or leaf pattern on the table-cloth, which she had looked at in a moment of revelation. There had been a problem about a foreground of a picture.[3] Move the tree to the middle, she had said. She had never finished that picture. It had been knocking about in her mind all these years. She would paint that picture now. Where were her paints, she wondered? Her paints, yes. She had left them in the hall last night. She would start at once. She got up quickly, before Mr. Ramsay turned.

She fetched herself a chair. She pitched her easel with her precise old-maidish movements on the edge of the lawn, not too close to Mr. Carmichael, but close enough for his protection. Yes, it must have been precisely here that she had stood ten years ago. There was the wall; the hedge; the tree. The question was of some relation between those masses. She had borne it in her mind all these years. It seemed as if the solution had come to her: she knew now what she wanted to do.

But with Mr. Ramsay bearing down on her, she could do nothing. Every time he approached – he was walking up and down the terrace – ruin approached, chaos approached. She could not paint. She stooped, she turned; she took up this rag; she squeezed that tube. But all she did was to ward him off a moment. He made it impossible for her to do anything. For if she gave him the least chance, if he saw her disengaged a moment, looking his way a moment, he would be on her, saying, as he had said last night, 'You find us much changed.' Last night he had got up and stopped before her, and said that. Dumb and staring though they had all sat, the six children whom they used to call after the Kings and Queens of England – the Red, the Fair, the Wicked, the Ruthless, – she felt how they raged under it. Kind old Mrs. Beckwith said something sensible. But it was a house full of unrelated passions – she had felt that all the evening. And on top of this chaos Mr. Ramsay got up, pressed her hand, and said: 'You will find us much changed' and none of them had moved or had spoken; but had sat there as if they were forced to let him say it. Only James (certainly the Sullen) scowled at the lamp; and Cam screwed her handkerchief round her finger. Then he reminded them that they were going to the Lighthouse to-morrow. They must be ready, in the hall, on the stroke of half-past seven. Then, with his hand on the door, he stopped; he turned upon them. Did they not want to go? he demanded. Had they dared say No (he had some reason for wanting it) he would have flung himself tragically backwards into the bitter waters of despair. Such a gift he had for gesture. He looked like a king in exile. Doggedly James said yes. Cam stumbled more wretchedly. Yes, oh yes, they'd both be ready, they said. And it struck her, this was tragedy – not palls, dust, and the shroud; but children coerced, their spirits subdued. James was sixteen, Cam seventeen, perhaps. She had looked round for someone who was not there, for Mrs. Ramsay, presumably. But there was only kind Mrs. Beckwith turning over her sketches under the lamp. Then, being tired, her mind still rising and falling with the sea, the taste and smell that places have after long absence possessing her, the candles wavering in her eyes, she had lost herself and gone under. It was a wonderful night, starlit; the waves sounded as they went upstairs; the moon surprised them, enormous, pale, as they passed the staircase window. She had slept at once.

She set her clean canvas firmly upon the easel, as a barrier, frail, but she hoped sufficiently substantial to ward off Mr. Ramsay and his exactingness. She did her best to look, when his back was turned, at her picture; that line there, that mass there. But it was out of the question. Let him be fifty feet away, let him not even speak to you, let him not even see you, he permeated, he prevailed, he imposed himself. He changed everything. She could not see the colour; she could not see the lines; even with his back turned to her, she could only think, But he'll be down on me in a moment, demanding – something she felt she could not give him. She rejected one brush; she chose another. When would those children come? When would they all be off? she fidgeted. That man, she thought, her anger rising in her, never gave; that man took. She, on the other hand, would be forced to give. Mrs. Ramsay had given. Giving, giving, giving, she had died – and had left all this. Really, she was angry with Mrs. Ramsay. With the brush slightly trembling in her fingers she looked at the hedge, the step, the wall. It was all Mrs. Ramsay's doing. She was dead. Here was Lily, at forty-four, wasting her time, unable to do a thing, standing there, playing at painting, playing at the one thing one did not play at, and it was all Mrs. Ramsay's fault. She was dead. The step where she used to sit was empty. She was dead.

But why repeat this over and over again? Why be always trying to bring up some feeling she had not got? There was a kind of blasphemy in it. It was all dry: all withered: all spent. They ought not to have asked her; she ought not to have come. One can't waste one's time at forty-four, she thought. She hated playing at painting. A brush, the one dependable thing in a world of strife, ruin, chaos – that one should not play with, knowingly even: she detested it. But he made her. You shan't touch your canvas, he seemed to say, bearing down on her, till you've given me what I want of you. Here he was, close upon her again, greedy, distraught. Well, thought Lily in despair, letting her right hand fall at her side, it would be simpler then to have it over. Surely she could imitate from recollection the glow, the rhapsody, the self-surrender she had seen on so many women's faces (on Mrs. Ramsay's, for instance) when on some occasion like this they blazed up – she could remember the look on Mrs. Ramsay's face – into a rapture of sympathy, of delight in the reward they had, which, though the reason of it escaped her, evidently conferred on them the most supreme bliss of which human nature was capable. Here he was, stopped by her side. She would give him what she could.

2

She seemed to have shrivelled slightly, he thought. She looked a little skimpy, wispy; but not unattractive. He liked her. There had been some talk of her marrying

William Bankes once, but nothing had come of it. His wife had been fond of her. He had been a little out of temper too at breakfast. And then, and then – this was one of those moments when an enormous need urged him, without being conscious what it was, to approach any woman, to force them, he did not care how, his need was so great, to give him what he wanted: sympathy.

Was anybody looking after her? he said. Had she everything she wanted?

'Oh, thanks, everything,' said Lily Briscoe nervously. No; she could not do it. She ought to have floated off instantly upon some wave of sympathetic expansion: the pressure on her was tremendous. But she remained stuck. There was an awful pause. They both looked at the sea. Why, thought Mr. Ramsay, should she look at the sea when I am here? She hoped it would be calm enough for them to land at the Lighthouse, she said. The Lighthouse! The Lighthouse! What's that got to do with it? he thought impatiently. Instantly, with the force of some primeval gust (for really he could not restrain himself any longer), there issued from him such a groan that any other woman in the whole world would have done something, said something – all except myself, thought Lily, girding at herself bitterly, who am not a woman, but a peevish, ill-tempered, dried-up old maid presumably.

Mr. Ramsay sighed to the full. He waited. Was she not going to say anything? Did she not see what he wanted from her? Then he said he had a particular reason for wanting to go to the Lighthouse. His wife used to send the men things. There was a poor boy with a tuberculous hip, the lightkeeper's son. He sighed profoundly. He sighed significantly. All Lily wished was that this enormous flood of grief, this insatiable hunger for sympathy, this demand that she should surrender herself up to him entirely, and even so he had sorrows enough to keep her supplied for ever, should leave her, should be diverted (she kept looking at the house, hoping for an interruption) before it swept her down in its flow.

'Such expeditions,' said Mr. Ramsay, scraping the ground with his toe, 'are very painful.' Still Lily said nothing. (She is a stock, she is a stone, he said to himself.) 'They are very exhausting,' he said, looking, with a sickly look that nauseated her (he was acting, she felt, this great man was dramatising himself), at his beautiful hands. It was horrible, it was indecent. Would they never come, she asked, for she could not sustain this enormous weight of sorrow, support these heavy draperies of grief (he had assumed a pose of extreme decrepitude; he even tottered a little as he stood there) a moment longer.

Still she could say nothing; the whole horizon seemed swept bare of objects to talk about; could only feel, amazedly, as Mr. Ramsay stood there, how his gaze seemed to fall dolefully over the sunny grass and discolour it, and cast over the rubicund, drowsy, entirely contented figure of Mr. Carmichael, reading a French novel on a deck-chair, a veil of crape, as if such an existence, flaunting its prosperity in a world of woe, were enough to provoke the most dismal thoughts of all. Look at him, he seemed to be saying, look at me; and indeed, all the time he was feeling, Think of me, think of me. Ah, could that bulk only be wafted alongside of them, Lily wished; had she only pitched her easel a yard or two closer to him; a man, any man, would staunch this effusion, would stop these lamentations. A woman, she had provoked this horror; a woman, she should have known how to deal with it. It was immensely to her discredit, sexually, to stand there dumb. One said –

what did one say? – Oh, Mr. Ramsay! Dear Mr. Ramsay! That was what that kind old lady who sketched, Mrs. Beckwith, would have said instantly, and rightly. But no. They stood there, isolated from the rest of the world. His immense self-pity, his demand for sympathy poured and spread itself in pools at her feet, and all she did, miserable sinner that she was, was to draw her skirts a little closer round her ankles, lest she should get wet. In complete silence she stood there, grasping her paint brush.

Heaven could never be sufficiently praised! She heard sounds in the house. James and Cam must be coming. But Mr. Ramsay, as if he knew that his time ran short, exerted upon her solitary figure the immense pressure of his concentrated woe; his age; his frailty; his desolation; when suddenly, tossing his head impatiently, in his annoyance – for, after all, what woman could resist him? – he noticed that his boot-laces were untied. Remarkable boots they were too, Lily thought, looking down at them: sculptured; colossal; like everything that Mr. Ramsay wore, from his frayed tie to his half-buttoned waistcoat, his own indisputably. She could see them walking to his room of their own accord, expressive in his absence of pathos, surliness, ill-temper, charm.

'What beautiful boots!' she exclaimed. She was ashamed of herself. To praise his boots when he asked her to solace his soul; when he had shown her his bleeding hands, his lacerated heart, and asked her to pity them, then to say, cheerfully, 'Ah, but what beautiful boots you wear!' deserved, she knew, and she looked up expecting to get it, in one of his sudden roars of ill-temper, complete annihilation.

Instead, Mr. Ramsay smiled. His pall, his draperies, his infirmities fell from him. Ah yes, he said, holding his foot

up for her to look at, they were first-rate boots. There was
only one man in England who could make boots like that.
Boots are among the chief curses of mankind, he said.
'Bootmakers make it their business,' he exclaimed, 'to
cripple and torture the human foot.' They are also the
most obstinate and perverse of mankind. It had taken him
the best part of his youth to get boots made as they should
be made. He would have her observe (he lifted his right
foot and then his left) that she had never seen boots made
quite that shape before. They were made of the finest
leather in the world, also. Most leather was mere brown
paper and cardboard. He looked complacently at his foot,
still held in the air. They had reached, she felt, a sunny
island where peace dwelt, sanity reigned and the sun for
ever shone, the blessed island of good boots. Her heart
warmed to him. 'Now let me see if you can tie a knot,' he
said. He poohpoohed her feeble system. He showed her his
own invention. Once you tied it, it never came undone.
Three times he knotted her shoe; three times he unknotted
it.

Why, at this completely inappropriate moment, when he
was stooping over her shoe, should she be so tormented
with sympathy for him that, as she stooped too, the blood
rushed to her face, and, thinking of her callousness (she
had called him a play-actor) she felt her eyes swell and
tingle with tears? Thus occupied he seemed to her a figure
of infinite pathos. He tied knots. He bought boots. There
was no helping Mr. Ramsay on the journey he was going.
But now just as she wished to say something, could have
said something, perhaps, here they were – Cam and James.[4]
They appeared on the terrace. They came, lagging, side by
side, a serious, melancholy couple.

But why was it like *that* they came? She could not help

feeling annoyed with them; they might have come more cheerfully; they might have given him what, now that they were off, she would not have the chance of giving him. For she felt a sudden emptiness; a frustration. Her feeling had come too late; there it was ready; but he no longer needed it. He had become a very distinguished, elderly man, who had no need of her whatsoever. She felt snubbed. He slung a knapsack round his shoulders. He shared out the parcels – there were a number of them, ill tied, in brown paper. He sent Cam for a cloak. He had all the appearance of a leader making ready for an expedition. Then, wheeling about, he led the way with his firm military tread, in those wonderful boots, carrying brown paper parcels, down the path, his children following him. They looked, she thought, as if fate had devoted them to some stern enterprise, and they went to it, still young enough to be drawn acquiescent in their father's wake, obediently, but with a pallor in their eyes which made her feel that they suffered something beyond their years in silence. So they passed the edge of the lawn, and it seemed to Lily that she watched a procession go, drawn on by some stress of common feeling which made it, faltering and flagging as it was, a little company bound together and strangely impressive to her. Politely, but very distantly, Mr. Ramsay raised his hand and saluted her as they passed.

But what a face, she thought, immediately finding the sympathy which she had not been asked to give troubling her for expression. What had made it like that? Thinking, night after night, she supposed – about the reality of kitchen tables, she added, remembering the symbol which in her vagueness as to what Mr. Ramsay did think about Andrew had given her. (He had been killed by the splinter of a shell instantly, she bethought her.) The kitchen table was something visionary, austere; something bare, hard, not ornamental. There was no colour to it; it was all edges and angles; it was uncompromisingly plain. But Mr. Ramsay kept always his eyes fixed upon it, never allowed himself to be distracted or deluded, until his face became worn too and ascetic and partook of this unornamented beauty which so deeply impressed her. Then, she recalled (standing where he had left her, holding her brush), worries had fretted it – not so nobly. He must have had his doubts about that table, she supposed; whether the table was a real table; whether it was worth the time he gave to it; whether he was able after all to find it. He had had doubts, she felt, or he would have asked less of people. That was what they talked about late at night sometimes, she suspected; and then next day Mrs. Ramsay looked tired, and Lily flew into a rage with him over some absurd little thing. But now he had nobody to talk to about that table, or his boots, or his knots; and he was like a lion seeking whom he could devour, and his face had that touch of desperation, of exaggeration in it which alarmed her, and made her pull her skirts about her. And then, she recalled, there was that sudden revivication, that sudden flare (when she praised his boots), that sudden recovery of vitality and interest in ordinary human things, which too passed and changed (for he was always changing, and hid nothing) into that other final phase which was new to her and had, she owned, made herself ashamed of her own irritability, when it seemed as if he had shed worries and ambitions, and the hope of sympathy and the desire for praise, had entered some other region, was drawn on, as if by curiosity, in dumb colloquy, whether with himself or another, at the head of that little procession out of one's range. An extraordinary face! The gate banged.

3

So they're gone, she thought, sighing with relief and disappointment. Her sympathy seemed to fly back in her face, like a bramble sprung. She felt curiously divided, as if one part of her were drawn out there – it was a still day, hazy; the Lighthouse looked this morning at an immense distance; the other had fixed itself doggedly, solidly, here on the lawn. She saw her canvas as if it had floated up and placed itself white and uncompromising directly before her. It seemed to rebuke her with its cold stare for all this hurry and agitation; this folly and waste of emotion; it drastically recalled her and spread through her mind first a peace, as her disorderly sensations (he had gone and she had been so sorry for him and she had said nothing) trooped off the field; and then, emptiness. She looked blankly at the canvas, with its uncompromising white stare; from the canvas to the garden. There was something (she stood screwing up her little Chinese eyes in her small puckered face) something she remembered in the relations of those lines cutting across, slicing down, and in the mass of the hedge with its green cave of blues and browns, which had stayed in her mind; which had tied a knot in her mind so that at odds and ends of time, involuntarily, as she walked along the Brompton Road, as she brushed her hair, she found herself painting that picture, passing her eye over it, and untying the knot in imagination. But there was all the difference in the world between this planning airily away from the canvas, and actually taking her brush and making the first mark.

She had taken the wrong brush in her agitation at Mr. Ramsay's presence, and her easel, rammed into the earth so nervously, was at the wrong angle. And now that she had put that right, and in so doing had subdued the impertinences and irrelevances that plucked her attention and made her remember how she was such and such a person, had such and such relations to people, she took her hand and raised her brush. For a moment it stayed trembling in a painful but exciting ecstasy in the air. Where to begin? – that was the question; at what point to make the first mark? One line placed on the canvas committed her to innumerable risks, to frequent and irrevocable decisions. All that in idea seemed simple became in practice immediately complex; as the waves shape themselves symmetrically from the cliff top, but to the swimmer among them are divided by steep gulfs, and foaming crests. Still the risk must be run; the mark made.

With a curious physical sensation, as if she were urged forward and at the same time must hold herself back, she made her first quick decisive stroke. The brush descended. It flickered brown over the white canvas; it left a running mark. A second time she did it – a third time. And so pausing and so flickering, she attained a dancing rhythmical movement, as if the pauses were one part of the rhythm and the strokes another, and all were related; and so, lightly and swiftly pausing, striking, she scored her canvas with brown running nervous lines which had no sooner settled there than they enclosed (she felt it looming out at her) a space. Down in the hollow of one wave she saw the next wave towering higher and higher above her. For what could be more formidable than that space? Here she was again, she thought, stepping back to look at it, drawn out of gossip, out of living, out of community with people into the presence of this formidable ancient enemy of hers – this other thing, this truth, this reality, which suddenly laid hands on her, emerged stark at the back of appearances and commanded her attention. She was half unwilling, half reluctant. Why always be drawn out and haled away? Why not left in peace, to talk to Mr. Carmichael on the lawn? It was an exacting form of intercourse anyhow. Other worshipful objects were content with worship; men, women, God, all let one kneel prostrate; but this form, were it only the shape of a white lamp-shade looming on a wicker table, roused one to perpetual combat, challenged one to a fight in which one was bound to be worsted. Always (it was in her nature, or in her sex, she did not know which) before she exchanged the fluidity of life for the concentration of painting she had a few moments of nakedness when she seemed like an unborn soul, a soul reft of body, hesitating on some windy pinnacle and exposed without protection to all the blasts of doubt. Why then did she do it? She looked at the canvas, lightly scored with running lines. It would be hung in the servants' bedrooms. It would be rolled up and stuffed under a sofa. What was the good of doing it then, and she heard some voice saying she couldn't paint, saying she couldn't create, as if she were caught up in one of those habitual currents which after a certain time experience forms in the mind, so that one repeats words without being aware any longer who originally spoke them.

Can't paint, can't write, she murmured monotonously, anxiously considering what her plan of attack should be. For the mass loomed before her; it protruded; she felt it pressing on her eyeballs. Then, as if some juice necessary for the lubrication of her faculties were spontaneously squirted, she began precariously dipping among the blues and ambers, moving her brush hither and thither, but it was now heavier and went slower, as if it had fallen in with some rhythm which was dictated to her (she kept looking at the hedge, at the canvas) by what she saw, so that while her hand quivered with life, this rhythm was strong enough to bear her along with it on its current. Certainly she was losing consciousness of outer things. And as she lost consciousness of outer things, and her name and her personality and her appearance, and whether Mr. Carmichael was there or not, her mind kept throwing up from its depths, scenes, and names, and sayings, and memories and ideas, like a fountain spurting over that glaring, hideously difficult white space, while she modelled it with greens and blues.

Charles Tansley[5] used to say that, she remembered, women can't paint, can't write. Coming up behind her he had stood close beside her, a thing she hated, as she painted here on this very spot. 'Shag tobacco', he said, 'fivepence an ounce', parading his poverty, his principles. (But the war had drawn the sting of her femininity. Poor devils, one thought, poor devils of both sexes, getting into such messes.) He was always carrying a book about under his arm – a purple book. He 'worked'. He sat, she remembered, working in a blaze of sun. At dinner he would sit right in the middle of the view. And then, she reflected, there was that scene on the beach. One must remember that. It was a windy morning. They had all gone to the beach. Mrs. Ramsay sat and wrote letters by a rock. She wrote and wrote. 'Oh,' she said, looking up at last at something floating in the sea, 'is it a lobster pot? Is it an upturned boat?' She was so short-sighted that she could not see, and then Charles Tansley became as nice as he could possibly be. He began playing ducks and drakes. They chose little flat black stones and sent them skipping over the waves. Every now and then Mrs. Ramsay looked up over her spectacles and laughed at them. What they said she could not remember, but only she and Charles throwing stones and getting on very well all of a sudden and Mrs.

Ramsay watching them. She was highly conscious of that. Mrs. Ramsay, she thought, stepping back and screwing up her eyes. (It must have altered the design a good deal when she was sitting on the step with James. There must have been a shadow.) Mrs. Ramsay. When she thought of herself and Charles throwing ducks and drakes and of the whole scene on the beach, it seemed to depend somehow upon Mrs. Ramsay sitting under the rock, with a pad on her knee, writing letters. (She wrote innumerable letters, and sometimes the wind took them and she and Charles just saved a page from the sea.) But what a power was in the human soul! she thought. That woman sitting there, writing under the rock resolved everything into simplicity; made these angers, irritations fall off like old rags; she brought together this and that and then this, and so made out of that miserable silliness and spite (she and Charles squabbling, sparring, had been silly and spiteful) something — this scene on the beach for example, this moment of friendship and liking — which survived, after all these years, complete, so that she dipped into it to re-fashion her memory of him, and it stayed in the mind almost like a work of art.

'Like a work of art,' she repeated, looking from her canvas to the drawing-room steps and back again. She must rest for a moment. And, resting, looking from one to the other vaguely, the old question which traversed the sky of the soul perpetually, the vast, the general question which was apt to particularise itself at such moments as these, when she released faculties that had been on the strain, stood over her, paused over her, darkened over her. What is the meaning of life? That was all — a simple question; one that tended to close in on one with years. The great revelation had never come. The great revelation perhaps never did come. Instead there were little daily miracles, illuminations, matches struck unexpectedly in the dark; here was one. This, that, and the other; herself and Charles Tansley and the breaking wave; Mrs. Ramsay bringing them together; Mrs. Ramsay saying 'Life stand still here'; Mrs. Ramsay making of the moment[6] something permanent (as in another sphere Lily herself tried to make of the moment something permanent) – this was of the nature of a revelation. In the midst of chaos there was shape; this eternal passing and flowing (she looked at the clouds going and the leaves shaking) was struck into stability. Life stand still here, Mrs. Ramsay said. 'Mrs. Ramsay! Mrs. Ramsay!' she repeated. She owed this revelation to her.

All was silence. Nobody seemed yet to be stirring in the house. She looked at it there sleeping in the early sunlight with its windows green and blue with the reflected leaves. The faint thought she was thinking of Mrs. Ramsay[7] seemed in consonance with this quiet house; this smoke; this fine early morning air. Faint and unreal, it was amazingly pure and exciting. She hoped nobody would open the window or come out of the house, but that she might be left alone to go on thinking, to go on painting. She turned to her canvas. But impelled by some curiosity, driven by the discomfort of the sympathy which she held undischarged, she walked a pace or so to the end of the lawn to see whether, down there on the beach, she could see that little company setting sail. Down there among the little boats which floated, some with their sails furled, some slowly, for it was very calm, moving away, there was one rather apart from the others. The sail was even now being hoisted. She decided that there in that very distant and entirely silent little boat Mr. Ramsay was sitting with Cam and James. Now they had got the sail up; now after a little flagging and hesitation the sails filled and, shrouded in profound silence, she watched the boat take its way with deliberation past the other boats out to sea.

4

The sails flapped over their heads. The water chuckled and slapped the sides of the boat, which drowsed motionless in the sun. Now and then the sails rippled with a little breeze in them, but the ripple ran over them and ceased. The boat made no motion at all. Mr. Ramsay sat in the middle of the boat. He would be impatient in a moment, James thought, and Cam thought, looking at their father, who sat in the middle of the boat between them (James steered; Cam sat alone in the bow) with his legs tightly curled. He hated hanging about. Sure enough, after fidgeting a second or two, he said something sharp to Macalister's boy, who got out his oars and began to row. But their father, they knew, would never be content until they were flying along. He would keep looking for a breeze, fidgeting, saying things under his breath, which Macalister and Macalister's boy would overhear, and they would both be made horribly uncomfortable. He had made them come. He had forced them to come. In their anger they hoped that the breeze would never rise, that he might be thwarted in every possible way, since he had forced them to come against their wills.

All the way down to the beach they had lagged behind together, though he bade them 'Walk up, walk up', without speaking. Their heads were bent down, their heads were pressed down by some remorseless gale. Speak to him they could not. They must come; they must follow. They must walk behind him carrying brown paper parcels.[8] But they vowed, in silence, as they walked, to stand by each other and carry out the great compact – to resist tyranny to the death. So there they would sit, one at one end of the boat, one at the other, in silence. They would say nothing, only look at him now and then where he sat with his legs twisted, frowning and fidgeting, and pishing and pshawing and muttering things to himself, and waiting impatiently for a breeze. And they hoped it would be calm. They hoped he would be thwarted. They hoped the whole expedition would fail, and they would have to put back, with their parcels, to the beach.

But now, when Macalister's boy had rowed a little way out, the sails slowly swung round, the boat quickened itself, flattened itself, and shot off. Instantly, as if some great strain had been relieved, Mr. Ramsay uncurled his legs, took out his tobacco pouch, handed it with a little grunt to Macalister, and felt, they knew, for all they suffered, perfectly content. Now they would sail on for hours like this, and Mr. Ramsay would ask old Macalister a question – about the great storm last winter probably – and old Macalister would answer it, and they would puff their pipes together, and Macalister would take a tarry rope in his fingers, tying or untying some knot, and the boy would fish, and never say a word to any one. James would be forced to keep his eye all the time on the sail. For if he forgot, then the sail puckered, and shivered, and the boat slackened, and Mr. Ramsay would say sharply, 'Look out! Look out!' and old Macalister would turn slowly on his seat. So they heard Mr. Ramsay asking some question about the great storm at Christmas. 'She comes driving round the point,' old Macalister said, describing the great storm last Christmas, when ten ships had been driven into the bay for shelter, and he had seen 'one there, one there, one there' (he pointed slowly round the bay. Mr. Ramsay followed him, turning his head). He had seen three men clinging to the mast. Then she was gone. 'And at last we shoved her off,' he went on (but in their anger and their silence they only caught a word here and there, sitting at opposite ends of the boat, united by their compact to fight tyranny to the death). At last they had shoved her off, they had launched the lifeboat, and they had got her out past the point – Macalister told the story; and though they only caught a word here and there, they were conscious all the time of their father – how he leant forward, how he brought his voice into tune with Macalister's voice; how, puffing at his pipe, and looking there and there where Macalister pointed, he relished the thought of the storm and the dark night and the fishermen striving there.[9] He liked that men should labour and sweat on the windy beach at night, pitting muscle and brain against the waves and the wind; he liked men to work like that, and women to keep house, and sit beside sleeping children indoors, while men were drowned, out there in a storm. So James could tell, so Cam could tell (they looked at him, they looked at each other), from his toss and his vigilance and the ring in his voice, and the little tinge of Scottish accent which came into his voice, making him seem like a peasant himself, as he questioned Macalister about the eleven ships that had been driven into the bay in a storm. Three had sunk.

He looked proudly where Macalister pointed;[10] and Cam thought, feeling proud of him without knowing quite why, had he been there he would have launched the lifeboat, he would have reached the wreck, Cam thought. He was so brave, he was so adventurous, Cam thought. But she remembered. There was the compact; to resist tyranny to the death. Their grievance weighed them down. They had been forced; they had been bidden. He had borne them down once more with his gloom and his authority, making them do his bidding, on this fine morning, come, because he wished it, carrying these parcels, to the Lighthouse; take part in those rites he went through for his own pleasure in memory of dead people, which they hated, so that they lagged after him, and all the pleasure of the day was spoilt.

Yes, the breeze was freshening. The boat was leaning, the water was sliced sharply and fell away in green cascades, in bubbles, in cataracts. Cam looked down into the foam, into the sea with all its treasure in it, and its speed hypnotised her, and the tie between her and James sagged a little. It slackened a little. She began to think, How fast it goes. Where are we going? and the movement hypnotised her, while James, with his eye fixed on the sail and on the horizon, steered[11] grimly. But he began to think as he steered that he might escape; he might be quit of it all. They might land somewhere; and be free then. Both of them, looking at each other for a moment, had a sense of escape and exaltation, what with the speed and the change. But the breeze bred in Mr. Ramsay too the same excitement, and, as old Macalister turned to fling his line overboard, he cried aloud, 'We perished,' and then again, 'each alone.' And then with his usual spasm of repentance or shyness, pulled himself up, and waved his hand towards the shore.

'See the little house,' he said pointing, wishing Cam to look. She raised herself reluctantly and looked. But which was it? She could no longer make out, there on the hillside, which was their house. All looked distant and peaceful and strange. The shore seemed refined, far away, unreal. Already the little distance they had sailed had put them far from it and given it the changed look, the composed look, of something receding in which one has no longer any part. Which was their house? She could not see it.

'But I beneath a rougher sea,' Mr. Ramsay murmured. He had found the house and so seeing it, he had also seen himself there; he had seen himself walking on the terrace, alone. He was walking up and down between the urns; and he seemed to himself very old, and bowed. Sitting in the boat he bowed, he crouched himself, acting instantly his part – the part of a desolate man, widowed, bereft; and so called up before him in hosts people sympathising with him; staged for himself as he sat in the boat, a little drama; which required of him decrepitude and exhaustion and sorrow (he raised his hands and looked at the thinness of them, to confirm his dream) and then there was given him in abundance women's sympathy, and he imagined how they would soothe him and sympathise with him, and so getting in his dream some reflection of the exquisite pleasure women's sympathy was to him, he sighed and said gently and mournfully,

> But I beneath a rougher sea
> Was whelmed in deeper gulfs than he,

so that the mournful words were heard quite clearly by them all. Cam half started on her seat. It shocked her – it outraged her. The movement roused her father; and he shuddered, and broke off, exclaiming: 'Look! Look!' so urgently that James also turned his head to look over his shoulder at the island. They all looked. They looked at the island.

But Cam could see nothing. She was thinking how all those paths and the lawn, thick and knotted with the lives they had lived there, were gone: were rubbed out; were past; were unreal, and now this was real; the boat and the sail with its patch; Macalister with his earrings; the noise of the waves – all this was real. Thinking this, she was murmuring to herself 'We perished, each alone', for her father's words broke and broke again in her mind, when her father, seeing her gazing so vaguely, began to tease her. Didn't she know the points of the compass? he asked. Didn't she know the North from the South? Did she really think they lived right out there? And he pointed again, and showed her where their house was, there, by those trees. He wished she would try to be more accurate, he said: 'Tell me – which is East, which is West?' he said, half laughing at her, half scolding her, for he could not understand the state of mind of any one, not absolutely imbecile, who did not know the points of the compass. Yet she did not know. And seeing her gazing, with her vague, now rather frightened, eyes fixed where no house was Mr. Ramsay forgot his dream; how he walked up and down between the urns on the terrace; how the arms were stretched out to him. He thought, women are always like that; the vagueness of their minds is hopeless; it was a thing he had never been able to understand; but so it was. It had been so with her – his wife. They could not keep anything clearly fixed in their minds. But he had been wrong to be angry with her; moreover, did he not rather like this vagueness in women? It was part of their extraordinary charm. I will make her smile at me, he thought. She looks frightened. She was so silent. He clutched his fingers, and determined that his voice and his face and all the quick expressive gestures which had been at his command making people pity him and praise him all these years should subdue themselves. He would make her smile at him. He would find some simple easy thing to say to her. But what? For, wrapped up in his work as he was, he forgot the sort of thing one said. There was a puppy. They had a puppy. Who was looking after the puppy to-day? he asked. Yes, thought James pitilessly, seeing his sister's head against the sail, now she will give way. I shall be left to fight the tyrant alone. The compact would be left to him to carry out. Cam would never resist tyranny to the death, he thought grimly, watching her face, sad, sulky, yielding. And as sometimes happens when a cloud falls on a green hillside and gravity descends and there among all the surrounding hills is gloom and sorrow, and it seems as if the hills themselves must ponder the fate of the clouded, the darkened, either in pity, or maliciously rejoicing in her dismay: so Cam now felt herself overcast, as she sat there among calm, resolute people and wondered how to answer her father about the puppy; how to resist his entreaty – forgive me, care for me; while James the lawgiver, with the tablets of eternal wisdom laid open on his knee (his hand on the tiller had become symbolical to her), said, Resist him. Fight him. He said so rightly; justly. For they must fight tyranny to the death, she thought. Of all human qualities she reverenced justice most. Her brother was most god-like, her father most suppliant. And to which did she yield, she thought, sitting between them, gazing at the shore whose points were all unknown to her, and thinking how the lawn and the terrace and the house were smoothed away now and peace dwelt there.

'Jasper,' she said sullenly. He'd look after the puppy.

And what was she going to call him? her father persisted. He had had a dog when he was a little boy, called Frisk. She'll give way, James thought, as he watched a look come upon her face, a look he remembered. They look down, he thought, at their knitting or something. Then suddenly they look up. There was a flash of blue, he remembered, and then somebody sitting with him laughed, surrendered, and he was very angry. It must have been his mother, he thought, sitting on a low chair, with his father standing over her. He began to search among the infinite series of impressions which time had laid down, leaf upon leaf, fold upon fold softly, incessantly upon his brain; among scents, sounds; voices, harsh, hollow, sweet; and lights passing, and brooms tapping; and the wash and hush of the sea, how a man had marched up and down and stopped dead, upright, over them. Meanwhile, he noticed, Cam dabbled her fingers in the water, and stared at the shore and said nothing. No, she won't give way, he thought; she's different, he thought. Well, if Cam would not answer him, he would not bother her, Mr. Ramsay decided, feeling in his pocket for a book.[12] But she would answer him; she wished, passionately, to move some obstacle that lay upon her tongue and to say, Oh yes, Frisk. I'll call him Frisk. She wanted even to say, Was that the dog that found its way over the moor alone? But try as she might, she could think of nothing to say like that, fierce and loyal to the compact, yet passing on to her father, unsuspected by James, a private token of the love she felt for him. For she thought, dabbling her hand (and now Macalister's boy had caught a mackerel, and it lay kicking on the floor, with blood on its gills) for she thought, looking at James who kept his eyes dispassionately on the sail, or glanced now and then for a second at the horizon, you're not exposed to it, to this pressure and division of feeling, this extraordinary temptation. Her father was feeling in his pockets; in another second, he would have found his book. For no one attracted her more; his hands were beautiful to her and his feet,[13] and his voice, and his words, and his haste, and his temper, and his oddity, and his passion, and his saying straight out before every one, we perish, each alone, and his remoteness. (He had opened his book.) But what remained intolerable, she thought, sitting upright, and watching Macalister's boy tug the hook out of the gills of another fish, was that crass blindness and tyranny[14] of his which had poisoned her childhood and raised bitter storms, so that even now she woke in the night trembling with rage and remembered some command of his; some insolence: 'Do this', 'Do that'; his dominance: his 'Submit to me'.

So she said nothing, but looked doggedly and sadly at the shore, wrapped in its mantle of peace; as if the people there had fallen asleep, she thought; were free like smoke, were free to come and go like ghosts. They have no suffering there, she thought.

5

Yes, that is their boat, Lily Briscoe decided, standing on the edge of the lawn. It was the boat with greyish-brown sails, which she saw now flatten itself upon the water and shoot off across the bay. There he sits, she thought, and the children are quite silent still. And she could not reach him either. The sympathy she had not given him weighed her down. It made it difficult for her to paint.

She had always found him difficult. She had never been able to praise him to his face, she remembered. And that reduced their relationship to something neutral, without that element of sex in it which made his manner to Minta so gallant, almost gay. He would pick a flower for her, lend her his books. But could he believe that Minta read them? She dragged them about the garden, sticking in leaves to mark the place.

'D'you remember, Mr. Carmichael?' she was inclined to ask, looking at the old man. But he had pulled his hat half over his forehead; he was asleep, or he was dreaming, or he was lying there catching words, she supposed.

'D'you remember?' she felt inclined to ask him as she passed him, thinking again of Mrs. Ramsay on the beach; the cask bobbing up and down; and the pages flying. Why, after all these years had that survived, ringed round, lit up, visible to the last detail, with all before it blank and all after it blank, for miles and miles?

'Is it a boat? Is it a cork?' she would say, Lily repeated, turning back, reluctantly again, to her canvas. Heaven be praised for it, the problem of space remained, she thought, taking up her brush again. It glared at her. The whole mass of the picture was poised upon that weight. Beautiful and bright it should be on the surface, feathery and evanescent, one colour melting into another like the colours on a butterfly's wing; but beneath the fabric must be clamped together with bolts of iron. It was to be a thing you could ruffle with your breath; and a thing you could not dislodge with a team of horses. And she began to lay on a red, a grey, and she began to model her way into the hollow there. At the same time, she seemed to be sitting beside Mrs. Ramsay on the beach.

'Is it a boat? Is it a cask?' Mrs. Ramsay said. And she began hunting round for her spectacles. And she sat, having found them, silent, looking out to sea. And Lily, painting steadily, felt as if a door had opened, and one went in and stood gazing silently about in a high cathedral-like place, very dark, very solemn. Shouts came from a world far away. Steamers vanished in stalks of smoke on the horizon. Charles threw stones and sent them skipping.

Mrs. Ramsay sat silent. She was glad, Lily thought, to

rest in silence, uncommunicative; to rest in the extreme obscurity of human relationships. Who knows what we are, what we feel? Who knows even at the moment of intimacy, This is knowledge? Aren't things spoilt then, Mrs. Ramsay may have asked (it seemed to have happened so often, this silence by her side) by saying them? Aren't we more expressive thus? The moment at least seemed extraordinarily fertile. She rammed a little hole in the sand and covered it up, by way of burying in it the perfection of the moment. It was like a drop of silver in which one dipped and illumined the darkness of the past.

Lily stepped back to get her canvas – so – into perspective. It was an odd road to be walking, this of painting. Out and out one went, further and further, until at last one seemed to be on a narrow plank, perfectly alone, over the sea. And as she dipped into the blue paint, she dipped too into the past there. Now Mrs. Ramsay got up, she remembered. It was time to go back to the house – time for luncheon. And they all walked up from the beach together, she walking behind with William Bankes, and there was Minta in front of them with a hole in her stocking. How that little round hole of pink heel seemed to flaunt itself before them! How William Bankes deplored it, without, so far as she could remember, saying anything about it! It meant to him the annihilation of womanhood, and dirt and disorder, and servants leaving and beds not made at midday – all the things he most abhorred. He had a way of shuddering and spreading his fingers out as if to cover an unsightly object, which he did now – holding his hand in front of him. And Minta walked on ahead, and presumably Paul met her and she went off with Paul in the garden.

The Rayleys, thought Lily Briscoe, squeezing her tube of green paint. She collected her impressions of the Rayleys.

Their lives appeared to her in a series of scenes; one, on the staircase at dawn. Paul had come in and gone to bed early; Minta was late. There was Minta, wreathed, tinted, garish on the stairs about three o'clock in the morning. Paul came out in his pyjamas carrying a poker in case of burglars. Minta was eating a sandwich, standing half-way up by a window, in the cadaverous early morning light, and the carpet had a hole in it. But what did they say? Lily asked herself, as if by looking she could hear them. Something violent. Minta went on eating her sandwich, annoyingly, while he spoke. He spoke indignant, jealous words, abusing her, in a mutter so as not to wake the children, the two little boys. He was withered, drawn; she flamboyant, careless. For things had worked loose after the first year or so; the marriage had turned out rather badly.

And this, Lily thought, taking the green paint on her brush, this making up scenes about them, is what we call 'knowing' people, 'thinking' of them, 'being fond' of them! Not a word of it was true; she had made it up; but it was what she knew them by all the same. She went on tunnelling her way into her picture, into the past.

Another time, Paul said he 'played chess in coffeehouses'. She had built up a whole structure of imagination on that saying too. She remembered how, as he said it, she thought how he rang up the servant, and she said 'Mrs. Rayley's out, sir', and he decided that he would not come home either. She saw him sitting in the corner of some lugubrious place where the smoke attached itself to the red plush seats, and the waitresses got to know you, playing chess with a little man who was in the tea trade and lived at Surbiton, but that was all Paul knew about him. And then Minta was out when he came home and then there was that scene on the stairs, when he got the poker in case of burglars (no doubt to frighten her too) and spoke so bitterly, saying she had ruined his life. At any rate when she went down to see them at a cottage near Rickmansworth, things were horribly strained. Paul took her down the garden to look at the Belgian hares which he bred, and Minta followed them, singing, and put her bare arm on his shoulder, lest he should tell her anything.

Minta was bored by hares, Lily thought. But Minta never gave herself away. She never said things like that about playing chess in coffee-houses. She was far too conscious, far too wary. But to go on with their story – they had got through the dangerous stage by now. She had been staying with them last summer some time and the car broke down and Minta had to hand him his tools. He sat on the road mending the car, and it was the way she gave him the tools – business-like, straightforward, friendly – that proved it was all right now. They were 'in love' no longer; no, he had taken up with another woman, a serious woman, with her hair in a plait and a case in her hand (Minta had described her gratefully, almost admiringly), who went to meetings and shared Paul's views (they had got more and more pronounced) about the taxation of land values[15] and a capital levy. Far from breaking up the marriage, that alliance had righted it. They were excellent friends, obviously, as he sat on the road and she handed him his tools.

So that was the story of the Rayleys, Lily smiled. She imagined herself telling it to Mrs. Ramsay, who would be full of curiosity to know what had become of the Rayleys. She would feel a little triumphant, telling Mrs. Ramsay that the marriage had not been a success.

But the dead, thought Lily, encountering some obstacle in her design which made her pause and ponder, stepping back a foot or so, Oh the dead! she murmured, one pitied them, one brushed them aside, one had even a little contempt for them. They are at our mercy. Mrs. Ramsay has faded and gone, she thought. We can over-ride her wishes, improve away her limited, old-fashioned ideas. She recedes further and further from us. Mockingly she seemed to see her there at the end of the corridor of years saying, of all incongruous things, 'Marry, marry!' (sitting very upright early in the morning with the birds beginning to cheep in the garden outside). And one would have to say to her, It has all gone against your wishes. They're happy like that; I'm happy like this. Life has changed completely. At that all her being, even her beauty, became for a moment, dusty and out of date. For a moment Lily, standing there, with the sun hot on her back, summing up the Rayleys, triumphed over Mrs. Ramsay, who would never know how Paul went to coffee-houses and had a mistress; how he sat on the ground and Minta handed him his tools; how she stood here painting, had never married, not even William Bankes.

Mrs. Ramsay had planned it. Perhaps, had she lived, she would have compelled it. Already that summer he was 'the kindest of men'. He was 'the first scientist of his age, my husband says'. He was also 'poor William – it makes me so unhappy, when I go to see him, to find nothing nice in his house – no one to arrange the flowers'. So they were sent for walks together, and she was told, with that faint touch of irony that made Mrs. Ramsay slip through one's fingers, that she had a scientific mind; she liked flowers; she was so exact. What was this mania of hers for marriage?[16] Lily wondered, stepping to and fro from her easel.

(Suddenly, as suddenly as a star slides in the sky, a reddish light seemed to burn in her mind, covering Paul

Rayley, issuing from him. It rose like a fire sent up in token of some celebration by savages on a distant beach. She heard the roar and the crackle. The whole sea for miles round ran red and gold. Some winy smell mixed with it and intoxicated her, for she felt again her own headlong desire to throw herself off the cliff and be drowned looking for a pearl brooch on a beach. And the roar and the crackle repelled her with fear and disgust, as if while she saw its splendour and power she saw too how it fed on the treasure of the house, greedily, disgustingly, and she loathed it. But for a sight, for a glory it surpassed everything in her experience, and burnt year after year like a signal fire on a desert island at the edge of the sea, and one had only to say 'in love' and instantly, as happened now, up rose Paul's fire again. And it sank and she said to herself, laughing, 'The Rayleys'; how Paul went to coffee-houses and played chess.)

She had only escaped by the skin of her teeth though, she thought. She had been looking at the table-cloth, and it had flashed upon her that she would move the tree to the middle, and need never marry anybody, and she had felt an enormous exultation. She had felt, now she could stand up to Mrs. Ramsay – a tribute to the astonishing power that Mrs. Ramsay had over one. Do this, she said, and one did it. Even her shadow at the window with James was full of authority. She remembered how William Bankes had been shocked by her neglect of the significance of mother and son. Did she not admire their beauty? he said. But William, she remembered, had listened to her with his wise child's eyes when she explained how it was not irreverence: how a light there needed a shadow there and so on. She did not intend to disparage a subject which, they agreed, Raphael[17] had treated divinely. She was not cynical. Quite the contrary.

Thanks to his scientific mind he understood – a proof of disinterested intelligence which had pleased her and comforted her enormously. One could talk of painting then seriously to a man. Indeed, his friendship had been one of the pleasures of her life. She loved William Bankes.

They went to Hampton Court[18] and he always left her, like the perfect gentleman he was, plenty of time to wash her hands, while he strolled by the river. That was typical of their relationship. Many things were left unsaid. Then they strolled through the courtyards, and admired, summer after summer, the proportions and the flowers, and he would tell her things, about perspective, about architecture, as they walked, and he would stop to look at a tree, or the view over the lake, and admire a child (it was his great grief – he had no daughter) in the vague aloof way that was natural to a man who spent so much time in laboratories that the world when he came out seemed to dazzle him, so that he walked slowly, lifted his hand to screen his eyes and paused, with his head thrown back, merely to breathe the air. Then he would tell her how his housekeeper was on her holiday; he must buy a new carpet for the staircase. Perhaps she would go with him to buy a new carpet for the staircase. And once something led him to talk about the Ramsays and he had said how when he first saw her she had been wearing a grey hat; she was not more than nineteen or twenty. She was astonishingly beautiful. There he stood looking down the avenue at Hampton Court, as if he could see her there among the fountains.

She looked now at the drawing-room step. She saw, through William's eyes,[19] the shape of a woman, peaceful and silent, with downcast eyes. She sat musing, pondering (she was in grey that day, Lily thought). Her eyes were bent. She would never lift them. Yes, thought Lily, looking intently, I must have seen her look like that, but not in grey; nor so still, nor so young, nor so peaceful. The figure came readily enough. She was astonishingly beautiful, William said. But beauty was not everything. Beauty had this penalty – it came too readily, came too completely. It stilled life – froze it. One forgot the little agitations; the flush, the pallor, some queer distortion, some light or shadow, which made the face unrecognisable for a moment and yet added a quality one saw for ever after. It was simpler to smooth that all out under the cover of beauty. But what was the look she had, Lily wondered, when she clapped her deer-stalker's hat on her head, or ran across the grass, or scolded Kennedy, the gardener? Who could tell her? Who could help her?

Against her will she had come to the surface, and found herself half out of the picture, looking, a little dazedly, as if at unreal things, at Mr. Carmichael. He lay on his chair with his hands clasped above his paunch not reading, or sleeping, but basking like a creature gorged with existence. His book had fallen on to the grass.

She wanted to go straight up to him and say, 'Mr. Carmichael!' Then he would look up benevolently as always, from his smoky vague green eyes. But one only woke people if one knew what one wanted to say to them. And she wanted to say not one thing, but everything. Little words that broke up the thought and dismembered it said nothing. 'About life, about death; about Mrs. Ramsay' – no, she thought, one could say nothing to nobody. The urgency of the moment always missed its mark. Words fluttered sideways and struck the object inches too low. Then one gave it up; then the idea sunk back again; then one became like most middle-aged people, cautious, furtive, with wrinkles between the eyes and a look of perpetual apprehension. For how could one express in words these emotions of the body? express that emptiness there? (She was looking at the drawing-room steps; they looked extraordinarily empty.) It was one's body feeling, not one's mind. The physical sensations that went with the bare look of the steps had become suddenly extremely unpleasant. To want and not to have, sent all up her body a hardness, a hollowness, a strain. And then to want and not to have – to want and want – how that wrung the heart, and wrung it again and again! Oh Mrs. Ramsay! she called out silently, to that essence which sat by the boat, that abstract one made of her, that woman in grey, as if to abuse her for having gone, and then having gone, come back again. It had seemed so safe, thinking of her. Ghost, air, nothingness, a thing you could play with easily and safely at any time of day or night, she had been that, and then suddenly she put her hand out and wrung the heart thus. Suddenly, the empty drawing-room steps, the frill of the chair inside, the puppy tumbling on the terrace, the whole wave and whisper of the garden became like curves and arabesques flourishing round a centre of complete emptiness.

'What does it mean? How do you explain it all?' she wanted to say, turning to Mr. Carmichael again. For the whole world seemed to have dissolved in this early morning hour into a pool of thought, a deep basin of reality, and one could almost fancy that had Mr. Carmichael spoken, a little tear would have rent the surface of the pool. And then? Something would emerge. A hand[20] would be shoved up, a blade would be flashed. It was nonsense of course.

A curious notion came to her that he did after all hear the things she could not say. He was an inscrutable old man, with the yellow stain on his beard, and his poetry, and his puzzles, sailing serenely through a world which satisfied all his wants, so that she thought he had only to put down his hand where he lay on the lawn to fish up anything he wanted. She looked at her picture. That would have been his answer, presumably – how 'you' and 'I' and 'she' pass and vanish; nothing stays; all changes; but not words, not paint. Yet it would be hung in the attics, she thought; it would be rolled up and flung under a sofa; yet even so, even of a picture[21] like that, it was true. One might say, even of this scrawl, not of that actual picture, perhaps, but of what it attempted, that it 'remained for ever', she was going to say, or, for the words spoken sounded even to herself, too boastful, to hint, wordlessly; when, looking at the picture, she was surprised to find that she could not see it. Her eyes were full of a hot liquid (she did not think of tears at first) which, without disturbing the firmness of her lips, made the air thick, rolled down her cheeks. She had perfect control of herself – Oh yes! – in every other way. Was she crying then for Mrs. Ramsay, without being aware of any unhappiness? She addressed old Mr. Carmichael again. What was it then? What did it mean? Could things thrust their hands up and grip one; could the blade cut; the fist grasp? Was there no safety? No learning by heart of the ways of the world? No guide, no shelter, but all was miracle, and leaping from the pinnacle of a tower into the air? Could it be, even for elderly people, that this was life? – startling, unexpected, unknown? For one moment she felt that if they both got up, here, now on the lawn, and demanded an explanation, why was it so short, why was it so inexplicable, said it with violence, as two fully equipped human beings from whom nothing should be hid might speak, then, beauty would roll itself up; the space would fill; those empty flourishes would form into shape; if they shouted loud enough Mrs. Ramsay would return. 'Mrs. Ramsay!' she said aloud, 'Mrs. Ramsay!' The tears ran down her face.

6

[Macalister's boy took one of the fish and cut a square out of its side to bait his hook with. The mutilated body (it was alive still) was thrown back into the sea.]

7

'Mrs. Ramsay!' Lily cried, 'Mrs. Ramsay!' But nothing happened. The pain increased. That anguish could reduce one to such a pitch of imbecility, she thought! Anyhow the old man had not heard her. He remained benignant, calm — if one chose to think it, sublime. Heaven be praised, no one had heard her cry that ignominious cry, stop pain, stop! She had not obviously taken leave of her senses. No one had seen her step off her strip of board into the waters of annihilation. She remained a skimpy old maid, holding a paint-brush on the lawn.

And now slowly the pain of the want, and the bitter anger (to be called back, just as she thought she would never feel sorrow for Mrs. Ramsay again. Had she missed her among the coffee cups at breakfast? not in the least) lessened; and of their anguish left, as antidote, a relief that was balm in itself, and also, but more mysteriously, a sense of some one there, of Mrs. Ramsay, relieved for a moment of the weight that the world had put on her, staying lightly by her side and then (for this was Mrs. Ramsay in all her beauty) raising to her forehead a wreath of white flowers with which she went. Lily squeezed her tubes again. She attacked that problem of the hedge. It was strange how clearly she saw her, stepping with her usual quickness across fields among whose folds, purplish and soft, among whose flowers, hyacinths or lilies, she vanished. It was some trick of the painter's eye. For days after she had heard of her death[22] she had seen her thus, putting her wreath to her forehead and going unquestioningly with her companion, a shadow, across the fields. The sight, the phrase, had its power to console. Wherever she happened to be, painting, here, in the country or in London, the vision would come to her, and her eyes, half closing, sought something to base her vision on. She looked down the railway carriage, the omnibus; took a line from shoulder or cheek; looked at the windows opposite; at Piccadilly, lamp-strung in the evening. All had been part of the fields of death. But always something – it might be a face, a voice, a paper boy crying *Standard, News*[23] – thrust through, snubbed her, waked her, required and got in the end an effort of attention, so that the vision must be perpetually remade. Now again, moved as she was by some instinctive need of distance and blue, she looked at the bay beneath her, making hillocks of the blue bars of the waves, and stony fields of the purpler spaces. Again she was roused as usual by something incongruous. There was a brown spot in the middle of the bay. It was a boat. Yes, she realised that after a second. But whose boat? Mr. Ramsay's boat, she replied. Mr. Ramsay; the man who had marched past her, with his hand raised, aloof, at the head of a procession, in his beautiful boots, asking her for sympathy, which she had refused. The boat was now half way across the bay.

So fine was the morning except for a streak of wind here and there that the sea and sky looked all one fabric, as if sails were stuck high up in the sky, or the clouds had dropped down into the sea. A steamer far out at sea had drawn in the air a great scroll of smoke which stayed there curving and circling decoratively, as if the air were a fine gauze which held things and kept them softly in its mesh, only gently swaying them this way and that. And as happens sometimes when the weather is very fine, the cliffs looked as if they were conscious of the ships, and the ships looked as if they were conscious of the cliffs, as if they signalled to each other some secret message of their own. For sometimes quite close to the shore, the Lighthouse looked this morning in the haze an enormous distance away.

'Where are they now?' Lily thought, looking out to sea. Where was he, that very old man who had gone past her silently, holding a brown paper parcel under his arm? The boat was in the middle of the bay.

8

They don't feel a thing there, Cam thought, looking at the shore, which, rising and falling, became steadily more distant and more peaceful. Her hand cut a trail in the sea, as her mind made the green swirls and streaks into patterns and, numbed and shrouded, wandered in imagination in that underworld of waters where the pearls stuck in clusters to white sprays, where in the green light a change came over one's entire mind and one's body shone half transparent enveloped in a green cloak.

Then the eddy slackened round her hand. The rush of the water ceased; the world became full of little creaking and squeaking sounds. One heard the waves breaking and flapping against the side of the boat as if they were anchored in harbour. Everything became very close to one. For the sail, upon which James had his eyes fixed until it had become to him like a person whom he knew, sagged entirely; there they came to a stop, flapping about waiting for a breeze, in the hot sun, miles from shore, miles from the Lighthouse. Everything in the whole world seemed to stand still. The Lighthouse became immovable, and the line of the distant shore became fixed. The sun grew hotter and everybody seemed to come very close together and to feel each other's presence, which they had almost forgotten. Macalister's fishing line went plumb down into the sea. But Mr. Ramsay went on reading with his legs curled under him.

He was reading a little shiny book with covers mottled like a plover's egg. Now and again, as they hung about in that horrid calm, he turned a page. And James felt that each page was turned with a peculiar gesture aimed at him: now assertively, now commandingly; now with the intention of making people pity him; and all the time, as his father read and turned one after another of those little pages, James kept dreading the moment when he would look up and speak sharply to him about something or other. Why were they lagging about here? he would demand, or something quite unreasonable like that. And if he does, James thought, then I shall take a knife and strike him to the heart.

He had always kept this old symbol of taking a knife and striking his father to the heart. Only now, as he grew older, and sat staring at his father in an impotent rage, it was not him, that old man reading, whom he wanted to kill, but it was the thing that descended on him – without his knowing it perhaps: that fierce sudden black-winged harpy, with its talons and its beak all cold and hard, that struck and struck at you (he could feel the beak on his bare legs, where it had struck when he was a child) and then made off, and there he was again, an old man, very sad, reading his book. That he would kill, that he would strike to the heart. Whatever he did – (and he might do anything, he felt, looking at the Lighthouse and the distant shore) whether he was in a business, in a bank, a barrister, a man at the head of some enterprise, that he would fight, that he would track down and stamp out – tyranny, despotism, he called it – making people do what they did not want to do, cutting off their right to speak. How could any of them say, But I won't, when he said, Come to the Lighthouse. Do this. Fetch me that. The black wings spread, and the hard beak tore. And then next moment, there he sat reading his book; and he might look up – one never knew quite reasonably. He might talk to the Macalisters. He might be pressing a sovereign into some frozen old woman's hand in the street, James thought; he might be shouting out at some fisherman's sports; he might be waving his arms in the air with excitement. Or he might sit at the head of the table dead silent from one end of dinner to the other. Yes, thought James, while the boat slapped and dawdled there in the hot sun; there was a waste of snow and rock very lonely and austere; and there he had come to feel, quite often lately, when his father said something which surprised the others, were two pairs of footprints only; his own and his father's. They alone knew each other. What then was this terror, this hatred? Turning back among the many leaves which the past had folded in him, peering into the heart of that forest where light and shade so chequer each other that all shape is distorted, and one blunders, now with the sun in one's eyes, now with a dark shadow, he sought an image to cool and detach and round off his feeling in a concrete shape. Suppose then that as a child sitting helpless in a perambulator, or on someone's

knee, he had seen a waggon crush ignorantly and inno-
cently, someone's foot? Suppose he had seen the foot first,
in the grass, smooth, and whole; then the wheel; and the
same foot, purple, crushed. But the wheel was innocent. So
now, when his father came striding down the passage
knocking them up early in the morning to go to the
Lighthouse down it came over his foot, over Cam's foot,
over anybody's foot. One sat and watched it.

But whose foot[24] was he thinking of, and in what
garden[25] did all this happen? For one had settings for these
scenes; trees that grew there; flowers; a certain light; a few
figures. Everything tended to set itself in a garden where
there was none of this gloom and none of this throwing of
hands about; people spoke in an ordinary tone of voice.
They went in and out all day long. There was an old
woman gossiping in the kitchen; and the blinds were
sucked in and out by the breeze; all was blowing, all was
growing; and over all those plates and bowls and tall
brandishing red and yellow flowers a very thin yellow veil
would be drawn, like a vine leaf, at night. Things became
stiller and darker at night. But the leaf-like veil was so fine
that lights lifted it, voices crinkled it; he could see through
it a figure stooping, hear, coming close, going away, some
dress rustling, some chain tinkling.

It was in this world that the wheel went over the
person's foot. Something, he remembered, stayed and darkened over him; would not move; something flourished up
in the air, something arid and sharp descended even there,
like a blade, a scimitar, smiting through the leaves and
flowers even of that happy world and making them shrivel
and fall.

'It will rain,' he remembered his father saying. 'You
won't be able to go to the Lighthouse.'

The Lighthouse was then a silvery, misty-looking tower with a yellow eye that opened suddenly and softly in the evening. Now——

James looked at the Lighthouse.[26] He could see the white-washed rocks; the tower, stark and straight; he could see that it was barred with black and white; he could see windows in it; he could even see washing spread on the rocks to dry. So that was the Lighthouse, was it?

No, the other was also the Lighthouse. For nothing was simply one thing. The other was the Lighthouse too. It was sometimes hardly to be seen across the bay. In the evening one looked up and saw the eye opening and shutting and the light seemed to reach them in that airy sunny garden where they sat.

But he pulled himself up. Whenever he said 'they' or 'a person', and then began hearing the rustle of some one coming, the tinkle of some one going, he became extremely sensitive to the presence of whoever might be in the room. It was his father now. The strain became acute. For in one moment if there was no breeze, his father would slap the covers of his book together, and say: 'What's happening now? What are we dawdling about here for, eh?' as, once before he had brought his blade down among them on the terrace and she had gone stiff all over, and if there had been an axe handy, a knife, or anything with a sharp point he would have seized it and struck his father through the heart. His mother had gone stiff all over, and then, her arm slackening, so that he felt she listened to him no longer, she had risen somehow and gone away and left him there, impotent, ridiculous, sitting on the floor grasping a pair of scissors.

Not a breath of wind blew. The water chuckled and gurgled in the bottom of the boat where three or four mackerel beat their tails up and down in a pool of water not deep enough to cover them. At any moment Mr. Ramsay (James scarcely dared look at him) might rouse himself, shut his book, and say something sharp; but for the moment he was reading, so that James stealthily, as if he were stealing downstairs on bare feet, afraid of waking a watch-dog by a creaking board, went on thinking what was she like, where did she go that day? He began following her from room to room and at last they came to a room where in a blue light, as if the reflection came from many china dishes, she talked to somebody; he listened to her talking. She talked to a servant, saying simply whatever came into her head. 'We shall need a big dish to-night. Where is it – the blue dish?' She alone spoke the truth;[27] to her alone could he speak it. That was the source of her everlasting attraction for him, perhaps; she was a person to whom one could say what came into one's head. But all the time he thought of her, he was conscious of his father following his thought, shadowing it, making it shiver and falter.

At last he ceased to think; there he sat with his hand on the tiller in the sun, staring at the Lighthouse, powerless to move, powerless to flick off these grains of misery which settled on his mind one after another. A rope seemed to bind him there, and his father had knotted it and he could only escape by taking a knife and plunging it . . . But at that moment the sail swung slowly round, filled slowly out, the boat seemed to shake herself, and then to move off half conscious in her sleep, and then she woke and shot through the waves. The relief was extraordinary. They all seemed to fall away from each other again and to be at their ease and the fishing-lines slanted taut across the side of the boat. But his father did not rouse himself. He only raised his right hand mysteriously high in the air, and let it fall upon his knee again as if he were conducting some secret symphony.

9

[The sea without a stain on it, thought Lily Briscoe, still standing and looking out over the bay. The sea is stretched like silk across the bay. Distance had an extraordinary power; they had been swallowed up in it, she felt, they were gone for ever, they had become part of the nature of things. It was so calm; it was so quiet. The steamer itself had vanished, but the great scroll of smoke still hung in the air and drooped like a flag mournfully in valediction.]

10

It was like that then, the island, thought Cam, once more drawing her fingers through the waves. She had never seen it from out at sea before. It lay like that on the sea, did it, with a dent in the middle and two sharp crags, and the sea swept in there, and spread away for miles and miles on either side of the island. It was very small; shaped something like a leaf stood on end. So we took a little boat, she thought, beginning to tell herself a story of adventure about escaping from a sinking ship. But with the sea streaming through her fingers, a spray of seaweed vanishing behind them, she did not want to tell herself seriously a story; it was the sense of adventure and escape that she wanted, for she was thinking, as the boat sailed on, how her father's anger about the points of the compass, James's obstinacy about the compact, and her own anguish, all had slipped, all had passed, all had streamed away. What then came next? Where were they going? From her hand, ice cold, held deep in the sea, there spurted up a fountain of joy at the change, at the escape, at the adventure (that she should be alive, that she should be there). And the drops falling from this sudden and unthinking fountain of joy fell here and there on the dark, the slumbrous shapes in her mind; shapes of a world not realised[28] but turning in their darkness, catching here and there, a spark of light; Greece, Rome, Constantinople. Small as it was, and shaped something like a leaf stood on end with the gold sprinkled waters flowing in and about it, it had, she supposed, a place in the universe – even that little island? The old gentlemen[29] in the study she thought could have told her. Sometimes she strayed in from the garden purposely to catch them at it. There they were (it might be Mr. Carmichael or Mr. Bankes, very old, very stiff) sitting opposite each other in their low arm-chairs. They were crackling in front of them the pages of *The Times*, when she came in from the garden, all in a muddle, about something some one had said about Christ; a mammoth had been dug up in a London street; what was the great Napoleon[30] like? Then they took all this with their clean hands (they wore grey coloured clothes; they smelt of heather) and they brushed the scraps together, turning the paper, crossing their knees, and said something now and then very brief. In a kind of trance she would take a book from the shelf and stand there, watching her father write, so equally, so neatly from one side of the page to another, with a little cough now and then, or something said briefly to the other old gentleman opposite. And she thought, standing there with her book open, here one could let whatever one thought expand like a leaf in water; and if it did well here, among the old gentlemen smoking and *The Times* crackling, then it was right. And watching her father as he wrote in his study, she thought (now sitting in the boat) he was most lovable, he was most wise; he was not vain nor a tyrant. Indeed, if he saw she was there, reading a book, he would ask her, as gently as any one could, Was there nothing he could give her?

Lest this should be wrong, she looked at him reading the little book with the shiny cover mottled like a plover's egg. No; it was right. Look at him now, she wanted to say aloud to James. (But James had his eye on the sail.) He is a sarcastic brute, James would say. He brings the talk round to himself and his books, James would say. He is intolerably egotistical. Worst of all, he is a tyrant. But look! she said, looking at him. Look at him now. She looked at him reading the little book with his legs curled; the little book whose yellowish pages she knew, without knowing what was written on them. It was small; it was closely printed; on the fly-leaf, she knew, he had written that he had spent fifteen francs on dinner; the wine had been so much; he had given so much to the waiter; all was added up neatly at the bottom of the page. But what might be written in the book which had rounded its edges off in his pocket, she did not know. What he thought they none of them knew. But he was absorbed in it, so that when he looked up, as he did now for an instant, it was not to see anything; it was to pin down some thought more exactly. That done, his mind flew back again and he plunged into his reading. He read, she thought, as if he were guiding something, or wheedling a large flock of sheep, or pushing his way up and up a single narrow path; and sometimes he went fast and straight, and broke his way through the thicket, and sometimes it seemed a branch struck at him, a bramble blinded him, but he was not going to let himself be beaten by that; on he went, tossing over page after page. And she went on telling herself a story about escaping from a sinking ship, for she was safe, while he sat there; safe, as she felt herself when she crept in from the garden, and took a book down, and the old gentleman, lowering the paper suddenly, said something very brief over the top of it about the character of Napoleon.

She gazed back over the sea, at the island. But the leaf was losing its sharpness. It was very small; it was very distant. The sea was more important now than the shore. Waves were all round them, tossing and sinking, with a log wallowing down one wave; a gull riding on another. About here, she thought, dabbling her fingers in the water, a ship had sunk, and she murmured, dreamily, half asleep, how we perished, each alone.

I I

So much depends then, thought Lily Briscoe, looking at the sea which had scarcely a stain on it, which was so soft that the sails and the clouds seemed set in its blue, so much depends, she thought, upon distance: whether people are near us or far from us; for her feeling for Mr. Ramsay changed as he sailed further and further across the bay. It seemed to be elongated, stretched out; he seemed to become more and more remote. He and his children seemed to be swallowed up in that blue, that distance; but here, on the lawn, close at hand, Mr. Carmichael suddenly grunted. She laughed. He clawed his book up from the grass. He settled into his chair again puffing and blowing like some sea monster. That was different altogether, because he was so near. And now again all was quiet. They must be out of bed by this time, she supposed, looking at the house, but nothing appeared there. But then, she remembered, they had always made off directly a meal was over, on business of their own. It was all in keeping with this silence, this emptiness, and the unreality of the early morning hour. It was a way things had sometimes, she thought, lingering for a moment and looking at the long glittering windows and the plume of blue smoke: they became unreal. So coming back from a journey, or after an illness, before habits had spun themselves across the surface, one felt that same unreality, which was so startling; felt something emerge. Life was most vivid then. One could be at one's ease. Mercifully one need not say, very briskly, crossing the lawn to greet old Mrs. Beckwith, who would be coming out to find a corner to sit in, 'Oh good-morning, Mrs. Beckwith! What a lovely day! Are you going to be so bold as to sit in the sun? Jasper's hidden the chairs. Do let me find you one!' and all the rest of the usual chatter. One need not speak at all. One glided, one shook one's sails (there was a good deal of movement in the bay, boats were starting off) between things, beyond things. Empty it was not, but full to the brim. She seemed to be standing up to the lips in some substance, to move and float and sink in it, yes, for these waters were unfathomably deep. Into them had spilled so many lives. The Ramsays'; the children's; and all sorts of waifs and strays of things besides. A washerwoman with her basket; a rook; a red-hot poker; the purples and grey-greens of flowers: some common feeling which held the whole together.

It was some such feeling of completeness perhaps which, ten years ago, standing almost where she stood now, had made her say that she must be in love with the place. Love had a thousand shapes. There might be lovers whose gift it was to choose out the elements of things and place them together and so, giving them a wholeness not theirs in life, make of some scene, or meeting of people (all now gone and separate), one of those globed compacted things over which thought lingers, and love plays.

Her eyes rested on the brown speck of Mr. Ramsay's sailing boat. They would be at the Lighthouse by lunch time she supposed. But the wind had freshened, and, as the sky changed slightly and the sea changed slightly and the boats altered their positions, the view, which a moment before had seemed miraculously fixed, was now unsatisfactory. The wind had blown the trail of smoke about; there was something displeasing about the placing of the ships.

The disproportion there seemed to upset some harmony in her own mind. She felt an obscure distress. It was confirmed when she turned to her picture. She had been wasting her morning. For whatever reason she could not achieve that razor edge of balance between two opposite forces; Mr. Ramsay and the picture; which was necessary. There was something perhaps wrong with the design? Was it, she wondered, that the line of the wall wanted breaking, was it that the mass of the trees was too heavy? She smiled ironically; for had she not thought, when she began, that she had solved her problem?

What was the problem then? She must try to get hold of something that evaded her. It evaded her when she thought of Mrs. Ramsay; it evaded her now when she thought of her picture. Phrases came. Visions came. Beautiful pictures. Beautiful phrases. But what she wished to get hold of was that very jar on the nerves, the thing itself[31] before it has been made anything. Get that and start afresh; get that and start afresh; she said desperately, pitching herself firmly again before her easel. It was a miserable machine, an inefficient machine, she thought, the human apparatus for painting or for feeling; it always broke down at the critical moment; heroically, one must force it on. She stared, frowning. There was the hedge, sure enough. But one got nothing by soliciting urgently. One got only a glare in the eye from looking at the line of the wall, or from thinking – she wore a grey hat. She was astonishingly beautiful. Let it come, she thought, if it will come. For there are moments when one can neither think nor feel. And if one can neither think nor feel, she thought, where is one?

Here on the grass, on the ground, she thought, sitting down, and examining with her brush a little colony of plantains. For the lawn was very rough. Here sitting on the world, she thought, for she could not shake herself free from the sense that everything this morning was happening for the first time, perhaps for the last time, as a traveller, even though he is half asleep, knows, looking out of the train window, that he must look now, for he will never see that town, or that mule-cart, or that woman at work in the fields, again. The lawn was the world; they were up here together, on this exalted station, she thought, looking at old Mr. Carmichael, who seemed (though they had not said a word all this time) to share her thoughts. And she would never see him again perhaps. He was growing old. Also, she remembered, smiling at the slipper that dangled from his foot, he was growing famous.[32] People said that his poetry was 'so beautiful.' They went and published things he had written forty years ago. There was a famous man now called Carmichael, she smiled, thinking how many shapes one person might wear, how he was that in the newspapers, but here the same as he had always been. He looked the same – greyer, rather. Yes, he looked the same, but somebody had said, she recalled, that when he had heard of Andrew Ramsay's death (he was killed in a second by a shell; he should have been a great mathematician) Mr.

Carmichael had 'lost all interest in life'. What did it mean –
that? she wondered. Had he marched through Trafalgar
Square grasping a big stick? Had he turned pages over and
over, without reading them, sitting in his room in St.
John's Wood alone? She did not know what he had done,
when he heard that Andrew was killed, but she felt it in
him all the same. They only mumbled at each other on
staircases; they looked up at the sky and said it will be fine
or it won't be fine. But this was one way of knowing
people, she thought: to know the outline, not the detail, to
sit in one's garden and look at the slopes of a hill running
purple down into the distant heather. She knew him in that
way. She knew that he had changed somehow. She had
never read a line of his poetry. She thought that she knew
how it went though, slowly and sonorously. It was sea-
soned and mellow. It was about the desert and the camel.
It was about the palm tree and the sunset. It was extremely
impersonal; it said something about death; it said very little
about love. There was an aloofness about him. He wanted
very little of other people. Had he not always lurched
rather awkwardly past the drawing-room window with
some newspaper under his arm, trying to avoid Mrs.
Ramsay whom for some reason he did not much like? On
that account, of course, she would always try to make him
stop. He would bow to her. He would halt unwillingly and
bow profoundly. Annoyed that he did not want anything
of her, Mrs. Ramsay would ask him (Lily could hear her)
wouldn't he like a coat, a rug, a newspaper? No, he wanted
nothing. (Here he bowed.) There was some quality in her
which he did not much like. It was perhaps her masterful-
ness, her positiveness, something matter-of-fact in her. She
was so direct.

(A noise drew her attention to the drawing-room

window – the squeak of a hinge. The light breeze was toying with the window.)

There must have been people who disliked her[33] very much, Lily thought (Yes; she realised that the drawing-room step was empty, but it had no effect on her whatever. She did not want Mrs. Ramsay now). – People who thought her too sure, too drastic. Also her beauty offended people probably. How monotonous, they would say, and the same always! They preferred another type – the dark, the vivacious. Then she was weak with her husband. She let him make those scenes. Then she was reserved. Nobody knew exactly what had happened to her. And (to go back to Mr. Carmichael and his dislike) one could not imagine Mrs. Ramsay standing painting, lying reading, a whole morning on the lawn. It was unthinkable. Without saying a word, the only token of her errand a basket on her arm, she went off to the town, to the poor, to sit in some stuffy little bedroom. Often and often Lily had seen her go silently in the midst of some game, some discussion, with her basket on her arm, very upright. She had noted her return. She had thought, half laughing (she was so methodical with the tea cups) half moved (her beauty took one's breath away), eyes that are closing in pain have looked on you. You have been with them there.

And then Mrs. Ramsay would be annoyed because somebody was late, or the butter not fresh, or the teapot chipped. And all the time she was saying that the butter was not fresh one would be thinking of Greek temples, and how beauty had been with them there. She never talked of it – she went, punctually, directly. It was her instinct to go, an instinct like the swallows for the south, the artichokes for the sun, turning her infallibly to the human race, making her nest in its heart. And this, like all instincts, was a little distressing to people who did not share it; to Mr. Carmichael perhaps, to herself certainly. Some notion was in both of them about the ineffectiveness of action, the supremacy of thought. Her going was a reproach to them, gave a different twist to the world, so that they were led to protest, seeing their own prepossessions disappear, and clutch at them vanishing. Charles Tansley did that too: it was part of the reason why one disliked him. He upset the proportions of one's world. And what had happened to him, she wondered, idly stirring the plantains with her brush. He had got his fellowship. He had married; he lived at Golders Green.

She had gone one day into a Hall and heard him speaking during the war. He was denouncing something: he was condemning somebody. He was preaching brotherly love. And all she felt was how could he love his kind who did not know one picture from another, who had stood behind her smoking shag ('fivepence an ounce, Miss Briscoe') and making it his business to tell her women can't write, women can't paint, not so much that he believed it, as that for some odd reason he wished it? There he was, lean and red and raucous, preaching love from a platform (there were ants crawling about among the plantains which she disturbed with her brush – red, energetic ants, rather like Charles Tansley). She had looked at him ironically from her seat in the half-empty hall, pumping love into that chilly space, and suddenly, there was the old cask or whatever it was bobbing up and down among the waves and Mrs. Ramsay looking for her spectacle case among the pebbles. 'Oh dear! What a nuisance! Lost again. Don't bother, Mr. Tansley. I lose thousands every summer,' at which he pressed his chin back against his collar, as if afraid to sanction such exaggeration, but could stand it in her whom he liked, and smiled very charmingly. He must have confided in her on one of those long expeditions when people got separated and walked back alone. He was educating his little sister, Mrs. Ramsay had told her. It was immensely to his credit. Her own idea of him was grotesque, Lily knew well, stirring the plantains with her brush. Half one's notions of other people were, after all, grotesque. They served private purposes of one's own. He did for her instead of a whipping-boy.[34] She found herself flagellating his lean flanks when she was out of temper. If she wanted to be serious about him she had to help herself to Mrs. Ramsay's sayings, to look at him through her eyes.

She raised a little mountain for the ants to climb over. She reduced them to a frenzy of indecision by this interference in their cosmogony. Some ran this way, others that.

One wanted fifty pairs of eyes to see with, she reflected. Fifty pairs of eyes were not enough to get round that one woman with, she thought. Among them, must be one that was stone blind to her beauty. One wanted most some secret sense, fine as air, with which to steal through keyholes and surround her where she sat knitting, talking, sitting silent in the window alone; which took to itself and treasured up like the air which held the smoke of the steamer, her thoughts, her imaginations, her desires. What did the hedge mean to her, what did the garden mean to her, what did it mean to her when a wave broke? (Lily looked up, as she had seen Mrs. Ramsay look up; she too heard a wave falling on the beach.) And then what stirred and trembled in her mind when the children cried, 'How's that? How's that?' cricketing? She would stop knitting for a second. She would look intent. Then she would lapse again, and suddenly Mr. Ramsay stopped dead in his pacing in front of her, and some curious shock passed through her and seemed to rock her in profound agitation on its breast when stopping there he stood over her, and looked down at her. Lily could see him.

He stretched out his hand and raised her from her chair. It seemed somehow as if he had done it before; as if he had once bent in the same way and raised her from a boat which, lying a few inches off some island, had required that the ladies should thus be helped on shore by the gentlemen. An old-fashioned scene that was, which required, very nearly, crinolines and peg-top trousers.[35] Letting herself be helped by him, Mrs. Ramsay had thought (Lily supposed) the time has come now; Yes, she would say it now. Yes, she would marry him. And she stepped slowly, quietly on shore. Probably she said one word only, letting her hand rest still in his. I will marry you, she might have said, with her hand in his; but no more. Time after time the same thrill had passed between them – obviously it had, Lily thought, smoothing a way for her ants. She was not inventing; she was only trying to smooth out something she had been given years ago folded up; something she had seen. For in the rough and tumble of daily life, with all those children about, all those visitors, one had constantly a sense of repetition – of one thing falling where another had fallen, and so setting up an echo which chimed in the air and made it full of vibrations.

But it would be a mistake, she thought, thinking how they walked off together, she in her green shawl, he with his tie flying, arm in arm, past the greenhouse, to simplify their relationship. It was no monotony of bliss – she with her impulses and quicknesses; he with his shudders and glooms. Oh no. The bedroom door would slam violently early in the morning. He would whizz his plate through the window. Then all through the house there would be a sense of doors slamming and blinds fluttering as if a gusty wind were blowing and people scudded about trying in a hasty way to fasten hatches and make things shipshape. She had met Paul Rayley like that one day on the stairs. They had laughed and laughed, like a couple of children, all because Mr. Ramsay, finding an earwig in his milk at breakfast had sent the whole thing flying through the air on to the terrace outside. 'An earwig,' Prue murmured, awestruck, 'in his milk.' Other people might find centipedes. But he had built round him such a fence of sanctity,[36] and occupied the space with such a demeanour of majesty that an earwig in his milk was a monster.

But it tired Mrs. Ramsay, it cowed her a little – the plates whizzing and the doors slamming. And there would fall between them sometimes long rigid silences, when, in a state of mind which annoyed Lily in her, half plaintive, half resentful, she seemed unable to surmount the tempest calmly, or to laugh as they laughed, but in her weariness perhaps concealed something. She brooded and sat silent. After a time he would hang stealthily about the places where she was – roaming under the window where she sat writing letters or talking, for she would take care to be busy when he passed, and evade him, and pretend not to see him. Then he would turn smooth as silk, affable, urbane, and try to win her so. Still she would hold off, and now she would assert for a brief season some of those prides and airs the due of her beauty which she was generally utterly without; would turn her head; would look so, over her shoulder, always with some Minta, Paul, or William Bankes at her side. At length, standing outside the group the very figure of a famished wolfhound (Lily got up off the grass and stood looking at the steps, at the window, where she had seen him), he would say her name,[37] once only, for all the world like a wolf barking in the snow, but still she held back; and he would say it once more, and this time something in the tone would rouse her, and she would go to him, leaving them all of a sudden, and they would walk off together among the pear trees, the cabbages, and the raspberry beds. They would have it out together. But with what attitudes and with what words? Such a dignity[38] was theirs in this relationship that, turning away, she and Paul and Minta would hide their curiosity and their discomfort, and begin picking flowers, throwing balls, chattering, until it was time for dinner, and there they were, he at one end of the table, she at the other, as usual.

'Why don't some of you take up botany? ... With all those legs and arms why doesn't one of you ...?' So they would talk as usual, laughing, among the children. All would be as usual, save only for some quiver, as of a blade in the air, which came and went between them as if the usual sight of the children sitting round their soup plates had freshened itself in their eyes after that hour among the pears and the cabbages. Especially, Lily thought, Mrs. Ramsay would glance at Prue. She sat in the middle between brothers and sisters, always so occupied, it seemed, seeing that nothing went wrong that she scarcely spoke herself. How Prue must have blamed herself for that earwig in the milk! How white she had gone when Mr. Ramsay threw his plate through the window! How she drooped under those long silences between them! Anyhow, her mother now would seem to be making it up to her; assuring her that everything was well; promising her that one of these days that same happiness would be hers. She had enjoyed it for less than a year, however.

She had let the flowers fall from her basket, Lily thought,

screwing up her eyes and standing back as if to look at her picture, which she was not touching, however, with all her faculties in a trance, frozen over superficially but moving underneath with extreme speed.

She let her flowers fall from her basket, scattered and tumbled them on to the grass and, reluctantly[39] and hesitatingly, but without question or complaint – had she not the faculty of obedience to perfection? – went too. Down fields, across valleys, white, flower-strewn – that was how she would have painted it. The hills were austere. It was rocky; it was steep. The waves sounded hoarse on the stones beneath. They went, the three of them together, Mrs. Ramsay walking rather fast in front, as if she expected to meet some one round the corner.

Suddenly the window at which she was looking was whitened by some light stuff behind it. At last then somebody had come into the drawing-room; somebody was sitting in the chair.[40] For Heaven's sake, she prayed, let them sit still there and not come floundering out to talk to her. Mercifully, whoever it was stayed still inside; had settled by some stroke of luck so as to throw an odd-shaped triangular shadow over the step. It altered the composition of the picture a little. It was interesting. It might be useful. Her mood was coming back to her. One must keep on looking without for a second relaxing the intensity of emotion, the determination not to be put off, not to be bamboozled. One must hold the scene – so – in a vice and let nothing come in and spoil it. One wanted, she thought, dipping her brush deliberately, to be on a level with ordinary experience, to feel simply that's a chair, that's a table, and yet at the same time, It's a miracle, it's an ecstasy. The problem might be solved after all. Ah, but what had happened? Some wave of white went over the window pane. The air must have stirred some flounce in the room. Her heart leapt at her and seized her and tortured her.

'Mrs. Ramsay! Mrs. Ramsay!' she cried, feeling the old horror come back – to want and want and not to have. Could she inflict that still? And then, quietly, as if she refrained, that too became part of ordinary experience, was on a level with the chair, with the table. Mrs. Ramsay – it was part of her perfect goodness to Lily – sat there quite simply, in the chair, flicked her needles to and fro, knitted her reddish-brown stocking, cast her shadow on the step. There she sat.

And as if she had something she must share, yet could hardly leave her easel, so full her mind was of what she was thinking, of what she was seeing, Lily went past Mr. Carmichael holding her brush to the edge of the lawn. Where was that boat now? Mr. Ramsay? She wanted him.

12

Mr. Ramsay had almost done reading. One hand hovered over the page as if to be in readiness to turn it the very instant he had finished it. He sat there bareheaded with the wind blowing his hair about, extraordinarily exposed to everything. He looked very old. He looked, James thought, getting his head now against the Lighthouse, now against the waste of waters running away into the open, like some old stone lying on the sand; he looked as if he had become physically what was always at the back of both of their minds – that loneliness which was for both of them the truth about things.

He was reading very quickly, as if he were eager to get to the end. Indeed they were very close to the Lighthouse now. There it loomed up, stark and straight, glaring white and black, and one could see the waves breaking in white splinters like smashed glass upon the rocks. One could see lines and creases in the rocks. One could see the windows clearly; a dab of white on one of them, and a little tuft of green on the rock. A man had come out and looked at them through a glass and gone in again. So it was like that, James thought, the Lighthouse one had seen across the bay all these years; it was a stark tower on a bare rock. It satisfied him.[41] It confirmed some obscure feeling of his about his own character. The old ladies, he thought, thinking of the garden at home, went dragging their chairs about on the lawn. Old Mrs. Beckwith, for example, was always saying how nice it was and how sweet it was and how they ought to be so proud and they ought to be so happy, but as a matter of fact James thought, looking at the Lighthouse stood there on its rock, it's like that. He looked at his father reading fiercely with his legs curled tight. They shared that knowledge. 'We are driving before a gale — we must sink,' he began saying to himself, half aloud exactly as his father said it.

Nobody seemed to have spoken for an age. Cam was tired of looking at the sea. Little bits of black cork had floated past; the fish were dead in the bottom of the boat. Still her father read, and James looked at him and she looked at him, and they vowed that they would fight tyranny to the death, and he went on reading quite unconscious of what they thought. It was thus that he escaped, she thought. Yes, with his great forehead and his great nose, holding his little mottled book firmly in front of him, he escaped. You might try to lay hands on him, but then like a bird, he spread his wings, he floated off to settle out of your reach somewhere far away on some desolate stump. She gazed at the immense expanse of the sea. The island had grown so small that it scarcely looked like a leaf any longer. It looked like the top of a rock which some big wave would cover. Yet in its frailty were all those paths, those terraces, those bedrooms — all those innumerable things. But as, just before sleep, things simplify themselves so that only one of all the myriad details has power to assert itself, so, she felt, looking drowsily at the island, all those paths and terraces and bedrooms were fading and disappearing, and nothing was left but a pale blue censer swinging rhythmically this way and that across her mind. It was a hanging garden; it was a valley, full of birds, and flowers, and antelopes . . . She was falling asleep.

'Come now,' said Mr. Ramsay, suddenly shutting his book.

Come where? To what extraordinary adventure? She woke with a start. To land somewhere, to climb somewhere? Where was he leading them? For after his immense silence the words startled them. But it was absurd. He was hungry, he said. It was time for lunch. Besides, look, he said. There's the Lighthouse. 'We're almost there.'

'He's doing very well,' said Macalister, praising James. 'He's keeping her very steady.'

But his father never praised him, James thought grimly.

Mr. Ramsay opened the parcel and shared out the sandwiches[42] among them. Now he was happy, eating bread and cheese with these fishermen. He would have liked to live in a cottage and lounge about in the harbour spitting with the other old men, James thought, watching him slice his cheese into thin yellow sheets with his penknife.

This is right, this is it, Cam kept feeling, as she peeled her hard-boiled egg. Now she felt as she did in the study when the old men were reading *The Times*. Now I can go on thinking whatever I like, and I shan't fall over a precipice or be drowned, for there he is, keeping his eye on me, she thought.

At the same time they were sailing so fast along by the rocks that it was very exciting – it seemed as if they were doing two things at once; they were eating their lunch here in the sun and they were also making for safety in a great storm after a shipwreck. Would the water last? Would the provisions last? she asked herself, telling herself a story but knowing at the same time what was the truth.

They would soon be out of it, Mr. Ramsay was saying to old Macalister; but their children would see some strange things. Macalister said he was seventy-five last March; Mr. Ramsay was seventy-one. Macalister said he had never seen a doctor; he had never lost a tooth. And that's the way I'd like my children to live – Cam was sure that her father was thinking that, for he stopped her throwing a sandwich into the sea and told her, as if he were thinking of the fishermen and how they live, that if she did not want it she should put it back in the parcel. She should not waste it. He said it so wisely, as if he knew so well all the things that happened in the world, that she put it back at once, and then he gave her, from his own parcel, a gingerbread nut, as if he were a great Spanish gentleman, she thought, handing a flower to a lady at a window (so courteous his manner was). But he was shabby, and simple, eating bread and cheese; and yet he was leading them on a great expedition where, for all she knew, they would be drowned.

'That was where she sunk,' said Macalister's boy suddenly.

'Three men were drowned where we are now,' said the old man. He had seen them clinging to the mast himself. And Mr. Ramsay taking a look at the spot was about, James and Cam were afraid, to burst out:

But I beneath a rougher sea,

and if he did, they could not bear it; they would shriek aloud; they could not endure another explosion of the passion that boiled in him; but to their surprise all he said was 'Ah' as if he thought to himself, But why make a fuss about that? Naturally men are drowned in a storm, but it is a perfectly straightforward affair, and the depths of the sea (he sprinkled the crumbs from his sandwich paper over them) are only water after all. Then having lighted his pipe he took out his watch. He looked at it attentively; he made, perhaps, some mathematical calculation. At last he said, triumphantly:

'Well done!' James had steered them like a born sailor.

There! Cam thought, addressing herself silently to James. You've got it at last. For she knew that this was what James had been wanting, and she knew that now he had got it he was so pleased that he would not look at her or at his father or at any one. There he sat with his hand on the tiller sitting bolt upright, looking rather sulky and frowning slightly. He was so pleased that he was not going to let anybody take away a grain of his pleasure. His father had praised him. They must think that he was perfectly indifferent. But you've got it now, Cam thought.

They had tacked, and they were sailing swiftly, buoyantly on long rocking waves which handed them on from one to another with an extraordinary lilt and exhilaration beside the reef. On the left a row of rocks showed brown through the water which thinned and became greener and on one, a higher rock, a wave incessantly broke and spurted a little column of drops which fell down in a shower. One could hear the slap of the water and the patter of falling drops and a kind of hushing and hissing sound from the waves rolling and gambolling and slapping the rocks as if they were wild creatures who were perfectly free and tossed and tumbled and sported like this for ever.

Now they could see two men on the Lighthouse, watching them and making ready to meet them.

Mr. Ramsay buttoned his coat, and turned up his trousers. He took the large, badly packed, brown paper parcel which Nancy had got ready and sat with it on his knee. Thus in complete readiness to land he sat looking back at the island. With his long-sighted eyes perhaps he could see the dwindled leaf-like shape standing on end on a plate of gold quite clearly. What could he see? Cam wondered. It was all a blur to her. What was he thinking now? she wondered. What was it he sought, so fixedly, so intently, so silently? They watched him, both of them, sitting bareheaded with his parcel on his knee staring and staring at the frail blue shape which seemed like the vapour of something that had burnt itself away. What do you want? they both wanted to ask. They both wanted to say, Ask us anything and we will give it you. But he did not ask them anything. He sat and looked at the island and he might be thinking, We perished, each alone, or he might be thinking, I have reached it. I have found it, but he said nothing.

Then he put on his hat.

'Bring those parcels,' he said, nodding his head at the things Nancy had done up for them to take to the Lighthouse. 'The parcels for the Lighthouse men,' he said. He rose and stood in the bow of the boat, very straight and tall, for all the world, James thought, as if he were saying, 'There is no God,' and Cam thought, as if he were leaping into space, and they both rose to follow him as he sprang, lightly like a young man, holding his parcel, on to the rock.

13

'He must have reached it,' said Lily Briscoe aloud, feeling suddenly completely tired out. For the Lighthouse had become almost invisible, had melted away into a blue haze, and the effort of looking at it and the effort of thinking of him landing there, which both seemed to be one and the same effort, had stretched her body and mind to the utmost. Ah, but she was relieved. What-ever she had wanted to give him, when he left her that morning, she had given him at last.

'He has landed,' she said aloud. 'It is finished.' Then, surging up, puffing slightly, old Mr. Carmichael stood beside her, looking like an old pagan god, shaggy, with weeds in his hair and the trident (it was only a French novel) in his hand. He stood by her on the edge of the lawn, swaying a little in his bulk, and said, shading his eyes with his hand: 'They will have landed,' and she felt that she had been right. They had not needed to speak. They had been thinking the same things and he had answered her without her asking him anything. He stood there spreading his hands over all the weakness and suffering of mankind; she thought he was surveying, tolerantly, compassionately, their final destiny. Now he has crowned the occasion, she thought, when his hand slowly fell, as if she had seen him let fall from his great height a wreath of violets and asphodels which, fluttering slowly, lay at length upon the earth.

Quickly, as if she were recalled by something over there, she turned to her canvas. There it was – her picture. Yes, with all its greens and blues, its lines running up and across, its attempt at something. It would be hung in the attics, she thought; it would be destroyed. But what did that matter? she asked herself, taking up her brush again. She looked at the steps; they were empty; she looked at her canvas; it was blurred. With a sudden intensity, as if she saw it clear for a second, she drew a line there, in the centre. It was done; it was finished.[43] Yes, she thought, laying down her brush in extreme fatigue, I have had my vision.

THE END

Notes

1. There are no section titles in *MS*.

2. *the expedition*: see Quentin Bell, *Virginia Woolf*, I, p. 32 (Hogarth Press, 1972). *Hyde Park Gate News*, 12 September 1892: 'On Saturday morning Master Hilary Hunt and Master Basil Smith came up to Talland House and asked Master Thoby and Miss Virginia Stephen to accompany them to the light-house as Freeman the boatman said that there was a perfect tide and wind for going there. Master Adrian Stephen was much disappointed at not being allowed to go.'

3. *Army and Navy Stores*: large all-purpose department store in Victoria Street, much patronized by the middle classes.

4. *Our frail barks*: a faint echo of Shakespeare's Sonnet 116, in which love is 'the star to every wand'ring bark'.

5. *tuberculous hip*: TB was a very common illness especially among the poor, and could affect the joints. It was often caught from drinking unpasteurized milk, so Mrs Ramsay's concern for the lighthouse-keeper's son is related to her concern about the milk, p. 112. In *Mausoleum*, p. 63, Leslie Stephen describes Julia's dedication to the poor and sick of St Ives.

6. *the atheist Tansley*: in *MS*, Tansley's atheism is more emphasized and contrasted with Lily's belief (*MS*, p. 34, 'She worshipped God').

7. *the Hebrides*: islands off the west coast of Scotland, which include the Isle of Skye. Woolf transfers the house from Talland House, St Ives, where the Stephen family spent their summers from 1882–95, the year of Julia Stephen's death. The Stephen children revisited the house in 1905. Talland House is described in *Moments of Being*, pp. 110–12 (including

its 'view of the bay to Godrevy Lighthouse'), and in *Mausoleum*, p. 62: 'a small but roomy house, with a garden of an acre or two all up and down hill, with quaint little terraces divided by hedges of escallonia, a grape-house and kitchen-garden and a so-called "orchard" beyond ... Every corner of the house and garden is full of memories for me – I could hardly bear to look at it again, I think.'

8. *ruled India*: there are a number of references in *TL* to the Indian empire. Julia Stephen was born in India and was the daughter of one of the Pattle sisters. Her mother married a doctor with a practice in Calcutta; her aunt, Sarah Pattle, married a distinguished administrator of British colonial rule in India, Thoby Pattle.

9. *she looked in the glass*: perhaps a faint echo of Hardy's poem:

> I look into my glass
> And view my wasted skin
> And say, would god it came to pass
> My heart had grown as thin.

('I look into my glass', *Complete Poems of Thomas Hardy*, Macmillan, 1976, p. 81.)

10. *Prolegomena*: an abstract of a thesis. Latin verses were entered for prizes at Oxford and Cambridge, but in this gossip about Balliol College, Oxford, it is not made clear which university Mr Ramsay attended. Leslie Stephen was at Cambridge.

11. *the passing of the Reform Bill*: in 'Social Life in England' (*Essays*, II, 1916 pp. 64–6), Woolf reviews a series of lectures by Dr Foakes Jackson on the period 1750–1850. The lectures drew on Thomas Creevey's (1768–1838) *Memoirs*, lively accounts of the Georgian era and of Brussels at the time of the Battle of Waterloo (cf. the reference to Creevey's *Memoirs* on p. 115). The review uses the phrase 'the passing of the Reform Bill'; Jackson had commented that 'The ruling aristocracy came to an end when the Reform Bill was passed in 1832, but their prestige remained.' This echo suggests that the Ramsay children may have been discussing the history of

their parents' vanishing mid-Victorian age; or they may have been having more topical conversations about the moves towards the Liberal Government's Parliament Act of 1911.

12. *the Grisons*: a canton of Switzerland.

13. *Italian house*: Julia Stephen's ancestors were French; her mother was descended from the Chevalier d'Etang. In *MS*, p. 15, she is descended from the French house of Clareville. While writing *TL*, Woolf wrote an introduction to a book of photographs by her great-aunt, Julia Margaret Cameron (*Victorian Photographs of Famous Men and Fair Women*, Hogarth Press, 1926), and wrote to Vita Sackville-West trying to prove Cameron's aristocratic French ancestry (*Letters*, III, 19 July 1926, pp. 278–80). Cameron's photographs of Julia Stephen, which had been hung on the walls of Gordon Square in 1905, were, thus, in Woolf's mind while writing the novel.

14. *an affair at Oxford . . . Hindustanee*: in *MS*, pp. 39–40, there is more detail about Augustus Carmichael's awful marriage and on his translating proverbs from the Persian. In *Moments of Being*, p. 87, Woolf refers to her mother's fondness for her uncle Thoby Prinsep, who used to 'read his translations from the Persian poets'. She also describes a family friend, Professor Wolstenholme (*Moments of Being*, pp. 73, 142; Bell, op. cit., I, p. 32) who has a strong resemblance to Carmichael: 'We called him "The Woolly One"'. In *Mausoleum*, p. 79, Leslie Stephen describes Julia's kindness to 'poor old Wolstenholme, called "the woolly" by you irreverent children, a man whom I had first known as a brilliant mathematician at Cambridge, whose Bohemian tastes and heterodox opinions had made a Cambridge career unadvisable, who had tried to become a hermit in Wastdale. He had emerged, married an uncongenial and rather vulgar Swiss girl . . . was despondent and dissatisfied and consoled himself with mathematics and opium.' There may also be something of T. S. Eliot's marriage (*Diary*, II, 21 June 1924, p. 304) in the character.

15. *a working man*: in *MS*, there is more detail on Tansley's class hostility to the Ramsays, here and at the dinner party: his

'commitment to social injustice' (p. 16); his wanting to teach 'working men like himself' (p. 20); he reads Meredith and Tolstoi but thinks that literature is not 'a pasttime for idle hours' (pp. 135, 173).

16. *Ibsen*: Henrik Ibsen (1828–1906), dealt with serious political subjects of the sort that would interest Tansley (as well as using symbolical images like the wild duck, or the tower in *The Master Builder*, which are not unlike the lighthouse).

17. *hoary*: white.

18. *Mr. Paunceforte*: in the 1890s St Ives became a centre for artists, including Whistler and Sickert. See Frances Spalding, *Vanessa Bell* (Weidenfeld & Nicolson, 1983, p. 11).

19. *her grandmother's friends ... moist*: Julia's aunt, Sara Prinsep, entertained the Pre-Raphaelite painters at Little Holland House. Julia spent much of her youth there and was proposed to by two of the painters. In *MS*, p. 21, there is more detail about their painting techniques, and their signed photographs are hanging in the house (*MS*, p. 54). When Vanessa Bell reads *TL* she is 'a little doubtful about covering paints with damp cloths' (*Letters*, III, appendix, p. 573). Woolf replies: 'I think Watts used to buy lapiz lazuli, break it up with a small hammer, and keep it under damp cloths. I think, too, the pre-raphaelites thought it more like nature to use garden clay, whenever possible; to serve for colours' (Letter to Vanessa Bell, 22 May 1927, *Letters*, III, p. 379).

20. *a picture ... Garter*: Mrs Ramsay is often identified with Victorian monarchy and empire, and seen as a Queen or an Empress. (In *Moments of Being*, p. 35, Julia Stephen is compared to 'some commanding Empress'.) The Garter is the highest order of British knighthood, worn by the sovereign. In *MS*, p. 22, the picture is of the Queen as a widow.

21. *tap of balls*: cricket was the summer game at St Ives and an important part of the Stephen family childhood. In her first notes for *TL*, Woolf lists under 'Topics that may come in': 'The waves breaking. Tapping of cricket balls. The bark "How's that?"' (*MS*, appendix A, p. 49.)

22. *an impulse of terror*: in *MS*, p. 24, Mrs Ramsay has a wish at this point 'that she might die first'.

23. *Stormed at with shot and shell*: Mr Ramsay quotes from verses two and three of Tennyson's 'The Charge of the Light Brigade' (1854), which commemorates (and glorifies) a futile and disastrous charge at the Battle of Balaclava in the Crimean War:

> Forward, the Light Brigade!
> Was there a man dismayed?
> Not though the soldiers knew
> Some one had blundered:
> Their's not to make reply,
> Their's not to reason why,
> Their's but to do and die:
> Into the valley of Death
> Rode the six hundred.
>
> Cannon to right of them,
> Cannon to left of them,
> Cannon in front of them
> Volleyed and thundered;
> Stormed at with shot and shell,
> Boldly they rode and well,
> Into the jaws of Death,
> Into the mouth of Hell
> Rode the six hundred.

24. *jacmanna*: or *jacmanii*, purple clematis which flowers all summer long. The engagement of Kitty Lushington and Leo Maxse 'under the jackmanii in the Love Corner at St Ives was my first introduction to the passion of love' (*Moments of Being*, p. 143).

25. *Subject and object and the nature of reality*: Leslie Stephen was a rationalist metaphysician who, in a work such as *The Science of Ethics* (1882), which failed to establish him as a successful speculative philosopher (Gordon, op. cit., p. 25), was

determined to separate ethics from religion. Mr Ramsay's 'work' is even more baffling in *MS*, p. 31: 'truth, good, things subject & object. Meaning. The Nature of Reality (here Lily repeated words she had seen in one of Mr Ramsay's books, purloined to read, but utterly unintelligible).' In *An Agnostic's Apology* (1893), p. 137, Stephen writes: ' "This is a table" is a phrase which in the first place asserts that I have a certain set of organized sense-impressions.'

Woolf's account of Mr Ramsay's epistemology may have been influenced by the discussions of Thoby's Cambridge friends on the ethics of G. E. Moore and Goldsworthy Lowes Dickinson; cf. the argument over the cow in E. M. Forster's *The Longest Journey* (1907): ' "The cow is there," said Ansell ... "You have not proved it" ... It was philosophy. They were discussing the existence of objects. Do they exist only when there is someone to look at them? or have they a real existence of their own? It is all very interesting, but at the same time it is difficult. Hence the cow. She seemed to make things easier' (*The Longest Journey*, The Abinger Edition, Edward Arnold, 1984, p. 3).

26. *a valet*: a valet who can also cook vegetables properly, see p. 80.

27. *one old woman*: Mrs McNab.

28. *Helen*: in *MS*, p. 55, Woolf writes in the margin, after the reference to Helen: 'Old Jones had written about the face that launched a thousand ships', an allusion to Marlowe's *Doctor Faustus* and the speech in praise of Helen's beauty. Greek allusions, direct and indirect, are frequent in the novel.

29. *Croom on the Mind and Bates on the Savage Customs of Polynesia*: in *MS*, p. 55, it is 'Crooms translation of the sagas, or Jones on Mind'. George Croom Robinson (1842–92) was a close friend of Leslie Stephen, Professor of Philosophy at University College, London and editor of the philosophical journal *Mind*. The relation between the mind and savage customs had a bearing on Leslie Stephen's work, who argued that 'Evolution replaces God' (Noel Annan, *Leslie Stephen: The Godless*

Victorian, Weidenfeld & Nicolson, 1984, pp. 282, 289) and, in *The Science of Ethics*, that societies which permitted intellectual freedom were more likely to survive.

30. *Marie*: becomes Marthe, p. 109.

31. *Never did anybody look so sad*: in *MS*, p. 57, more explanation is given for her sadness: 'was it true that somebody whom she was to marry had blown his brains out or had died, [less dramatically] in India? There had been [something; but] Nobody knew/could say. Mrs Ramsay [never] made [a] sign.' In *Moments of Being*, p. 82, Woolf says that her mother 'looked very sad'.

32. *The Graces ... asphodel*: in classical mythology the three Graces were the goddesses who bestowed beauty. Asphodel is the lily plant, planted on graves, associated in Greek myth with death and the underworld. The image of the goddess and the flowers of death is used later in the novel, suggesting the story of Demeter and Persephone; cf. *Diary*, II, 16 Jan. 1923, p. 226, on Katherine Mansfield's death: 'Visual impressions kept coming & coming before me – always of Katherine putting on a white wreath, & leaving us, called away; made dignified, chosen.' For the myths of Demeter and Persephone and their association with ancient matriarchal mythology, in which there is 'a strange equation of marriage and death, the bridal chamber and the grave', see Joseph Blotner, 'Mythic Patterns in *To the Lighthouse*' (PMLA, No. 71, 1956, pp. 547ff.). Woolf's friend, the classical anthropologist Jane Harrison, described in *Prolegomena to the Study of Greek Religion*, (CUP, 1903, 1908, 1922), which Woolf read (see *Diary*, II, 12 Sept. 1921, p. 136), the 'matriarchal' mythology of Demeter, Kore and Persephone, and the Greek ritual festivals in which 'before they were bidden to depart the ghosts were feasted', and 'at the end of the meal the priest rose from the table and hunted out the souls of the dead'.

33. *Knitting*: this is one of the attitudes Woolf remembers her mother in, 'knitting on the hall step while we play cricket' (*Moments of Being*, p. 84).

34. *Michael Angelo*: in *MS*, p. 54, the picture is on an easel. In *Moments of Being*, p. 84, Woolf remembers her mother sitting under an engraving of Beatrice; cf. other references to great Renaissance paintings and to Michael Angelo in the Sistine Chapel, p. 79.

35. *he quivered*: at this point in *MS*, p. 60, he is named as 'Rhoderick Ramsay'.

36. *in June he gets out of tune*: a version of the old rhyme about the cuckoo:

> In April he shows his bill
> In May he sings all day [or 'he's here to stay']
> In June he'll change his tune
> In July away he'll fly.

(Iona and Peter Opie, *Oxford Nursery Rhyme Book*, Oxford, 1955, p. 54.)

37. *Polar region*: R. F. Scott's *The Voyage of the Discovery* was published in 1905 to enormous publicity, after his first antarctic expedition of 1902–4. His second, in 1910, ended in tragedy.

Mr Ramsay's struggle to reach 'R', and his anxiety about his own failure, may have been drawn in part from Leslie Stephen's account of his feelings about his work in *Mausoleum*. On the *Dictionary of National Biography* he wrote 'It became a burthen and yet, as I must confess, I took a pride in it and had a kind of dogged resolution to see it through as far as I could' (p. 87). On his achievements he wrote 'The sense in which I do take myself to be a failure is this: I have scattered myself too much. I think that I had it in me to make something like a real contribution to philosophical or ethical thought. Unluckily, what with journalism and dictionary making, I have been a jack of all trades ... if the history of English thought in the nineteenth century should ever be written, my name will only be mentioned in small type and footnotes whereas, had my energies been wisely directed, I might have had the honour of a paragraph in full sized type or even a section in a chapter all to myself' (p. 93). He goes on to describe Julia's support and his 'extortion' of compliments from her.

38. *He stood . . . by the urn*: there was a point on the terrace of Talland House known as 'The Lookout Place' (*Moments of Being*, p. 111). Woolf's language for Mr Ramsay here is a faint echo of Hardy's portrayal of his friend Leslie Stephen in his poem 'The Schreckhorn', about the Alpine mountain (which Stephen climbed):

> Aloof, as if a thing of mood and whim;
> Now that its spare and desolate figure gleams
> Upon my nearing vision, less it seems
> A looming Alp-height than a guise of him
> Who scaled its horn with ventured life and limb
> (*Poems of Thomas Hardy*, Macmillan, 1974, p. 107.)

39. *Shakespeare*: a frequent figure in Mr Ramsay's thoughts (cf. pp. 48, 117) who also was read by Mrs Ramsay.

40. *His own little light*: at this point in *MS*, p. 68, Mr Ramsay misquotes from Matthew Arnold's 'Thyrsis', his elegy for the lost scholar, Arthur Clough, and the lost Arcadia. Mr Ramsay says:

> Roam on. The light we sought is
> shining still. I wandered till I died.

The lines are:

> Why faintest thou? I wandered till I died.
> Roam on! The light we sought is shining still.

41. *his wife and son*: in *MS*, p. 69, this is a long passage comparing the vision of wife and child to 'the profound spirit brooding over the waters of life'. The language closely resembles De Quincey's on the 'burthen of solitude': 'thou broodest, like the spirit of God moving upon the surface of the deeps, over every heart that sleeps in the nurseries of Christendom' (*Suspiria de Profundis* (1845), in *Confessions of an English Opium Eater and Other Writings*, OUP, 1985, p. 114). See notes 57, 102.

42. *Grimm's fairy story*: in the Brothers Grimm story of 'The Fisherman and his Wife' (*Grimm's Household Tales*, translated and edited by Margaret Hunt with an introduction by Andrew Lang, Bohn's Standard Library, George Bell & Son, London, 1884), the poor fisherman who lives in a pigsty catches and releases a golden Flounder, who is a Prince in disguise. He is urged by his bullying wife to ask the fish, first for a little hut, and then, successively, for more and more exorbitant requests: he must be king, emperor, Pope, and, at last, like God. Each request is granted in stormier weather, and, at the final blasphemy, the Flounder sends them back to their original pigsty. The throwing of the mutilated fish into the sea by Macalister's boy, p. 196, seems to echo the story of the Flounder.

43. *a book*: in *MS*, p. 77, it is a copy of the *Spectator*.

44. *civilisation*: in *MS*, p. 80, the idea is developed into 'what relation the arts bear to human life'.

45. *the Tube*: referred to again in the novel on pp. 80, 99.

46. *Locke, Hume, Berkeley*: in Annan, op. cit., p. 223: 'Leslie Stephen set out to rescue the English empiricists, Locke, Berkeley and Hume, from Taine's contention that they were insignificant.' In Stephen's *The History of English Thought in the Eighteenth Century* (2 vols., 1876, 1902), Hume was one of his 'rationalist heroes' (Annan, p. 225). In *English Literature and Society in the Eighteenth Century* (1903, 1904) Stephen lectured on the English philosophers and their intellectual relationship to the Revolution. Annan comments that Stephen would 'never have come out on the side of the Jacobins' but appreciated that Paine, for instance, 'really feels for the people' (p. 226). In *MS*, p. 135, Charles Tansley has been reading 'the second volume of Sorel's history of the French Revolution'; later in the novel, Cam thinks of the old gentlemen talking about Napoleon, p. 205.

47. *Carlyle*: closely identified by Woolf with Leslie Stephen. Stephen greatly admired Carlyle (though the admiration was not reciprocated), calling him 'a really noble old cove and by

far the best specimen of the literary gent we can at present produce' (Annan, op. cit., p. 172). He wrote his biography for the *Dictionary of National Biography*. In his *Mausoleum*, an autobiographical account of his marriage written for his children, he hopes that he has not behaved as badly as Carlyle (p. 89) in his domestic life ('I was not as bad as Carlyle, was I?' she remembers (1908) his saying to Stella Duckworth, *Moments of Being*, p. 41). Woolf read 'masses' of Carlyle in her youth (*Diary*, II, 15 Aug. 1924, p. 310) and associated him with her father, remembering, for instance, visiting Anny Thackeray who told 'a story of Carlyle and father; Carlyle saying he'd as soon wash his face in a dirty puddle as write journalism' (*Diary*, I, 5 March 1919, p. 248). She was interested in the Carlyles' difficult and extraordinary marriage. See 'More Carlyle Letters', (*Essays*, I, pp. 259–61) and 'Geraldine and Jane' (*CE*, IV, pp. 27–39). Rereading him in 1921, she thinks of him as 'an old toothless grave digger' (*Diary*, II, 29 April 1921, p. 115).

In *A Room of One's Own* (1928), ch.2, she says 'we do know what Carlyle went through when he wrote the *French Revolution*.'

48. *residue*: in *MS*, p. 92, it is 'what had been in her mind as a baby, [&] what was the residue of [all] her thirty three years', and so very like the way Woolf describes the contents of her own memories in *Moments of Being*.

49. *Kennet*: in Wiltshire.

50. *an old woman*: Mrs McNab remembers, on pp. 152–3, the cook ('Mildred, Marian, some such name as that') saving her 'a plate of soup'.

51. *The Owl and the Poker*: the faint nonsense-poem or nursery-rhyme effect of this (as if from Edward Lear) is accentuated in *MS*, p. 96: 'Mrs Ramsay always thought of them as a poker & a stuffed owl.'

52. *Milk*: Julia Stephen's short book on advice for nurses, drawn from her own experience, is very precise with instructions about milk: 'The nurse must see the milkman herself and impress on him the importance of sweet fresh milk from one

cow being always brought' (*Notes from Sick Rooms*, Smith Elder & Co., London, 1883, p. 39).

53. *her children*: in *MS*, p. 99, the children are more distinctly characterized here: 'Nancy was fond of reading, & Roger, she believed, had a real feeling for architecture.' Timothy (who becomes Jasper) had 'her love of music'.

54. *He had always his work to fall back on*: in *MS*, p. 101, Mrs Ramsay's line of thought is rather different here, and incorporates the image from Mr Ramsay's mind: in spite of their lack of money, she is determined that he 'should never [desert his have] to give up his own [special] work, his philosophy – [that] pursuit of the letter Z [which still escaped him].'

55. *the end*: in *MS*, p. 103, Cam does not go out, and Mrs Ramsay reads the whole story to both children.

56. *a church in Rome*: cf. 'some Roman Catholic Cathedral', p. 120; 'a cathedral-like place', p. 186. Woolf visited Rome in April 1927 and wrote 'I like the Roman Catholic religion . . . I am sure Rome is the city where I shall come to die' (*Letters*, III, 9 April 1927, pp. 360–61). In *MS*, p. 110, Lily imagines converting to Roman Catholicism.

57. *We are in the hands of the Lord*: in *MS*, p. 105, Mrs Ramsay remembers her own mother saying this. The 'quotation' may have several sources: 'We will fall into the hands of the Lord, and not into the hands of men; for as His majesty is, so is His mercy' (Eccles., 2:18); 'It is a fearful thing to fall into the hands of the living God' (Heb., 10:13); 'Father, into thy hands I commend my spirit' (Luke, 23:46); 'Into thy hands I commend my spirit' (*PB*, 31:6). In De Quincey's *Suspiria de Profundis*, which Woolf was writing about at the same time as *TL* (see Note 102), a very similar passage occurs:

Said but once, said but softly, not marked at all, words revive before me in darkness and solitude; and they arrange themselves gradually into sentences, but through an effort sometimes of a distressing kind, to which I am in a manner forced to become a party.

After the death of his sister, passages from the funeral service about the dead being 'taken unto' the Lord come into his mind in this way. Like Mrs Ramsay, 'annoyed with herself for saying that', De Quincey is 'incensed' and 'offended' by finding these words in his mind, though he acknowledges their 'consolatory' power (De Quincey, op. cit., pp. 117–19).

58. *Aunt Camilla*: the Pattle sisters, Julia Stephen's mother and aunts, were legendary beauties.

59. *scholarship*: to Oxford or Cambridge. In *MS*, p. 113, to 'Balloil [*sic*] or Trinity'.

60. *to walk about the country*: see Annan, op. cit., pp. 30, 97, on Leslie Stephen as a great walker (as well as cross-country runner and mountaineer) and organizer of the 'Sunday Tramps', a group of Sunday walking friends which lasted for fifteen years and achieved 252 walks. Woolf's 'Cornwall Diary' for 1905 records her own taste for 'solitary tramping', rambling over uncharted territory and reciting poems to herself like her father, like 'A blinding mist came down and hid the land' (from Kingsley's 'The Sands of Dee': 'The rolling mist came down and hid the land/And never home came she'). (Virginia Woolf, *A Passionate Apprentice*, Chatto and Windus, 1990, p. 286.)

61. *she would have blown her brains out by now*: in *MS*, p. 116, the feeling is attributed to Mr, not Mrs Ramsay: 'If he had believed what he said, he should have shot himself long ago.'

62. *Best and brightest, come away!*: Shelley, 'To Jane: The Invitation' (1822): 'Best and brightest, come away!/ Fairer far than this fair Day ...' The poet compares the 'radiant sister of the Day' to 'the brightest hour of unborn Spring', who 'like a prophetess of May/ Strewed flowers upon the barren way, / Making the wintry world appear/ Like one on whom thou smilest, dear.' Leaving a notice on his door for his 'accustomed' visitors (Reflection, Care, Death) he invites her 'away' to 'the wild woods and the plains', a pastoral paradise 'where

the earth and ocean meet/ And all things seem only one/ In the universal sun.'

63. *evening primroses*: in 'Reading' (*Essays*, III, 1919, p. 150) the 'yellow of the Evening Primroses' is imagined on 'a hot summer morning'. But in letters to Vita Sackville-West, 13 May and 22 May 1927, she writes: 'An old creature writes to say that all my fauna and flora of the Hebrides is totally inaccurate'; 'my horticulture is in every instance wrong: there are no rooks, elms, or dahlias in the Hebrides; my sparrows are wrong; so are my carnations . . .' (*Letters*, III, pp. 374, 379.)

64. *He had been to Amsterdam ... Giottos*: Mr Bankes has been to the Rijksmuseum in Amsterdam and the Prado in Madrid. In *MS*, p. 119, Woolf has 'Siena', not Padua, with its Giottos. Their conversation about great paintings is one of several references to Renaissance art, especially to madonnas; cf. pp. 35, 105.

65. *Darwin*: Leslie Stephen was acquainted with, and profoundly influenced by, Darwin, so (like Carlyle) they were associated in Woolf's mind.

66. *symbolical*: in *MS*, p. 120, 'Crucified, & transcendent'.

67. *Constantinople ... Santa Sofia*: images of the East and of a Byzantine 'golden dome' recur (cf. p. 205). Constantinople and the dome of Santa Sophia are two of the settings in *Orlando* (ch. 3). Woolf visited it on the journey of 1906 in which Vanessa and Thoby Stephen both caught typhoid and after which Thoby died. In her travel diary for 1906 (*A Passionate Apprentice*, p. 347) she saw Santa Sophia like 'a treble globe of bubbles frozen solid, floating out to meet us. For it is fashioned in the shape of some fine substance, thin as glass, blown in plump curves; save that it is also substantial as a pyramid.' Lyndall Gordon (op. cit., p. 111) compares this to her ideas of form in *TL*. In *MS*, p. 320, when the image of Byzantium recurs, Cam thinks more explicitly about 'how [the] world had come into existence; about the ancient civilizations of Egyptians; Greeks & Romans; the Byzantine Empire.'

68. *Pope's Nose*: in *MS*, p. 124, 'the pope's nose rocks'.

69. *Paul and Minta! kissing probably*: in *MS*, pp. 125–6, Nancy is more disgusted by this sight ('the lust and the warmth, the ravening and the cruelty'), like Rachel coming across the lovers in *The Voyage Out* ('I don't like that', ch. 11). In *Moments of Being*, p. 105, Woolf remembers the courtship of Stella Duckworth and Jack Hills at Hyde Park Gate in 1895, as her 'first vision of love between man and woman'. See also Note 24.

70. *brooch*: in *Moments of Being*, p. 114, Woolf remembers the town crier at St Ives advertising for one of their guests' lost brooch. While writing *TL*, Woolf lost her 'little mother of pearl brooch' after a visit to Cookham, near Marlow (*Diary*, III, 3 March 1926, p. 64).

71. *Edinburgh*: not an easy day's journey from the Isle of Skye. In *MS*, p. 172, he plans to go by boat.

72. *The house was all lit up*: cf. 'How Should One Read a Book?', written in 1926 (a fragment of it is drafted in *MS*): 'Shall we read [biographies and autobiographies] to satisfy that curiosity which possesses us sometimes when in the evening we linger in front of a house where the lights are lit and the blinds not yet drawn, and each floor of the house shows us a different section of human life in being?' (*CE*, II, p. 3.)

73. *choose which jewels she was to wear*: in *Moments of Being*, p. 95, Woolf remembers that it was 'one of those snatched moments' with her mother 'that was so amusing and for some reason so soothing and yet exciting', when one 'chose the jewels she was to wear'.

74. *fifteen people sitting down to dinner*: in fact fourteen: Mr and Mrs Ramsay, William Bankes, Charles Tansley, Augustus Carmichael, Lily Briscoe, Paul Rayley, Minta Doyle, Andrew, Prue, Nancy, Rose, Roger and Jasper.

75. *Bœuf en Daube*: a very slow-cooking beef casserole. Instructions for cooking are given in *MS*, p. 129: 'You stand it in water for 24 hours: you stir continuously; you add a little bay leaf, and then a dash of sherry: the whole never being allowed, of course, to come to the boil.' Vanessa Bell in a letter to Woolf

on 11 May 1927, comments: 'But how do you make Bœuf en Daube? Does it have to be eaten on the moment after cooking 3 days?' (*Letters*, III, appendix, p. 573.)

76. *Joseph and Mary*: in *MS*, pp. 130–31, the old 'father rook' is mentioned, but the rooks are not given these holy names.

77. *follows a fading ship . . . horizon*: a faint echo of Tennyson's 'Tears, Idle Tears' (1847):

> Fresh as the first beam glittering on a sail,
> That brings our friends up from the underworld,
> Sad as the last which reddens over one
> That sinks with all we love below the verge;
> So sad, so fresh, the days that are no more.

In *Essays* (II, 1916, p. 49), she remarks of this poem, 'the beauty of it is so much greater than we remembered.'

78. *Women can't write, women can't paint*: in *MS*, p. 138, Lily finds it difficult to argue with this because 'she had no militancy in her and could not bear to be be [*sic*] called, as she might have been called had she come out with her views a feminist.' This is like Woolf's later argument with herself over *A Room of One's Own* (is there 'a shrill feminine tone', *Diary*, III, 23 Oct. 1929, p. 262).

79. *the government*: in *MS*, p. 152, there is more detail about the fishermen emigrating to America. Of the political discussion, Bankes feels that 'in sciences, there is creation; in art, creation, but in this art [politics] there is nothing but abuse.' The sufferings of the fishermen sets up the connection with Scott's *The Antiquary*, see Note 101.

80. *Rose*: in *MS*, p. 161, there is more detail about the children's ages here: Nancy is sixteen, Prue is eighteen.

81. *She could not help . . . from her husband*: in *MS*, pp. 154–6, there is a much longer account of Carmichael's character here, his failure at governing India, his twiddling thumbs, his refusal to hurry, either when meeting a bear in the Himalayas or doing acrostics. The 'things' he shows Andrew are described as 'the sacred relics in a little box such as one keeps studs in.'

82. *Neptune*: Mr Carmichael is later compared to an old pagan god with a trident, p. 225.

83. *Bacchus*: Woolf seems to be conflating two paintings, Caravaggio's self-portrait as *Adolescent Bacchus*, a half-naked torso draped in a white robe, vine leaves in his dark hair, with wine and a fruit bowl, in the Uffizi (which she visited in 1904 and 1909), and Titian's 'Bacchus and Ariadne', with Bacchus's chariot, in his procession of gods, nymphs, satyrs and animals, drawn by leopards (or cheetahs) as he encounters Ariadne by the seashore. Titian derives his subject from Catullus and Ovid's *Ars Amatoria*. The painting is in the National Gallery, which Woolf told Vanessa Bell in 1918 (*Letters*, II, p. 260) she did not enjoy visiting.

84. *Middlemarch*: see 'George Eliot' (*CE*, I, 1919, p. 201), where Woolf calls it 'one of the few English novels written for grown-up people'. In *MS*, p. 164, Minta has left it 'in the Tube'. In *Moments of Being*, p. 146, Woolf remembers (in 1920/21) that her half-brother George Duckworth mastered the first volume of *Middlemarch* in order to impress Flora Russell, daughter of the grand hostess Lady Arthur Russell, and was immensely relieved 'when he left the second volume in a train and got my father, whose set was ruined, to declare that in his opinion one volume of *Middlemarch* was enough.'

85. *a French recipe*: Woolf forgets here that she has given Mrs Ramsay Italian ancestors. See Note 13.

86. *Mile End Road*: a rough district of East London. In *MS*, p. 170, it is the Old Kent Road, and Paul is imagined as a type who might 'break down the doors of timid maiden ladies'.

87. *Voltaire*: freethinking Deist French philosopher and satirist (1694–1778). Leslie Stephen derived his arguments against Christianity from Voltaire, though he dissociated himself from Voltaire's 'obscenity' (Annan, op. cit., p. 254). Voltaire was admired by Woolf as 'scathing, wild and witty' (*Essays*, I, 'Fantasy', 1921, p. 317).

88. *Madame de Staël*: French critic, novelist and intellectual hostess (1766–1817). Author of *Corinne* (1807) and of *L'Allemagne*, a

book on German nationalism, banned by Napoleon. Woolf is funny about her eloquence in an essay on Maria Edgeworth (*Essays*, I, 1909, p. 317). But in a letter to Richard Aldington, she says she has never read Madame de Staël (*Letters*, III, 26 Jan. 1926, p. 233).

89. *Napoleon*: see p. 205 and 'The Lighthouse', Note 30. The recurring references to Napoleon and the French Revolution suggest that a subliminal comparison is being drawn between Mr Ramsay and Napoleon. At the dinner table, the children are presented as conspirators, and in 'The Lighthouse' they are in a contract to 'resist tyranny to the death' (p. 178). In *MS*, p. 153, more emphasis is given to the idea of Tansley as a new kind of 'leader', later linked in Lily's mind with the thought that everyone is striving after something, whether 'a republic without [war or] crime' or 'attempts at union'. The 'masculine' conversation at the dinner in *MS*, p. 173, is also about 'Talleyrand' and 'the French Revolution'.

90. *the French system of land tenure*: the French Revolution brought about a great upheaval in the ownership of land; when Napoleon came to power he found large stocks of land not sold or granted away, and from this he endowed a (largely middle-class) group of new landowners.

91. *Lord Rosebery*: Archibald Primrose, 5th Earl of Rosebery (1847–1929). Foreign Secretary, 1886; Liberal PM, 1894–5; resigned as leader of the Liberal Party, 1896. Author of books on Pitt, Chatham and Napoleon (1922), he praised Stephen's *Dictionary of National Biography* as 'the monumental literary work of Her Majesty's Reign' (Annan, op. cit., p. 2).

92. *Creevey's Memoirs*: see Note 11.

93. *Waverley Novels*: there is a set of Scott's novels in the house, from which Mr Ramsay selects *The Antiquary* (see Note 101) after dinner, and which is 'fetched up from oblivion' in 'Time Passes', p. 152.

94. *I—I—I*: in *A Room of One's Own* (1928), the dominance of the letter 'I' casts a dark shadow over the page of 'Mr A's' novel. In *The Years* (1937), a woman listening to a man talking at a

party thinks 'She had heard it all before, I, I, I, – he went on' ('Present Day').

95. *Tolstoi*: in *MS*, p. 179, Charles Tansley praises Tolstoi ('what he meant was Tolstoi would have approved of me, but not of you') and Paul Rayley prefers 'Trollope to Dickens' ('A very stupid remark, Mrs Ramsay knew that'). In a letter to Vita Sackville-West, Woolf describes hearing Tatiana Tolstoi lecturing, and then feeling that 'I hated us all, for being prosperous & comfortable, & wished to be a working woman, & wished to be able to excuse my life to Tolstoi' (*Letters*, 31 Jan. 1926, III, p. 236).

96. *Come out . . . yellow bee*: 'Luriana Lurilee' by Charles Elton, published posthumously in *Another World Than This* (eds. Vita Sackville-West and Harold Nicolson, Michael Joseph, 1945). In *MS*, p. 181, Augustus Carmichael quotes it before Mr Ramsay, and a phrase from it is taken up in the passage about Mrs McNab in 'Time Passes' (*MS*, p. 165). The poem in full reads:

> Come out and climb the garden path
> Luriana Lurilee,
> The China rose is all abloom
> And buzzing with the yellow bee.
> We'll swing you on a cedar bough,
> Luriana Lurilee.
>
> I wonder if it seems to you
> Luriana Lurilee,
> That all the lives we ever lived
> And all the lives to be
> Are full of trees and changing leaves,
> Luriana Lurilee.
>
> How long it seems since you and I,
> Luriana Lurilee,
> Roamed in the forest where our kind
> Had just begun to be,
> And laughed and chattered in the flowers,
> Luriana Lurilee.

How long since you and I went out,
Luriana Lurilee,
To see the kings go riding by
Over lawn and daisy lea,
With their palm leaves and their cedar sheaves,
Luriana Lurilee.

Swing, swing, swing on a bough,
Luriana Lurilee,
Till you sleep in a humble heap
Or under a gloomy churchyard tree,
And then fly back to swing on a bough,
Luriana Lurilee.

In a letter to Vita Sackville-West, Woolf refers to Clive Bell's heart as 'turning to honey, in which the yellow bee *blooms*' (*Letters*, 23 Dec. 1925, III, p. 225).

97. *Labour Party*: George Dangerfield's *The Strange Death of Liberal England* (1934) and G. D. H. Cole's *A History of the Labour Party from 1914* (1948) described the rise of the Labour Party in the early years of the century as a gradual and inevitable turning away of the working class from the Liberal Party, dating from the 1890s. More recent historians of the party (e.g. K. Laybourn, *The Rise of Labour*, Edward Arnold, 1988) have placed more emphasis on the alliance between Labour and the Trade Union movement and have explained the demise of the Liberal Party as a product of the cultural and social changes of the First World War. The Independent Labour Party was founded in 1893 and Labour was created as a party in the General Election of 1906, which resulted in an overwhelming Liberal majority. Labour was a minority party which largely supported the Liberals, and did not stand for 'socialism' up to the First World War, but the working-class voter, especially in industrial areas, looked increasingly to the Labour Party for representation. Leonard Woolf was active in the Fabian Society and the Labour Party from 1912 onwards, stood unsuccessfully for election in 1922, and was

closely involved with Labour's response to the General Strike in May 1926.

The recollections on which *TL* is based come from the 1890s, but the first part of *TL* must, strictly speaking, be set around 1908, since ten years pass in 'Time Passes' and 'The Lighthouse' is set just after the end of the war. (However, in *MS*, p. 2, in a note to herself of 6 August 1925, Woolf said: 'There need be no specification of date'). During this time Asquith's Liberal Government was in power and Ramsay Macdonald was heading Labour's pacifist opposition to entry into the war, until the last moment.

98. *her mother's*: in *MS*, p. 167, there is a 'bust' of her mother on the landing.

99. *that horrid skull*: see *Moments of Being*, p. 78: 'The night nursery was vast too. In winter I would slip in before bed to take a look at the fire. I was very anxious to see that the fire was low, because it frightened me if it burnt after we went to bed. I dreaded that little flickering flame on the walls; but Adrian liked it; and to make a compromise, Nurse folded a towel over the fender.' The skull, like Uncle James's opals, is evidently a gift from another of Mrs Ramsay's brothers in the colonies. In *Jacob's Room*, Jacob insists on taking a sheep's skull home from the beach.

100. *the words*: Cam remembers these words, p. 221. In *Moments of Being*, p. 82, Woolf remembers (1939/40) that her mother would send her to sleep as a child by telling her 'to think of all the lovely things I could imagine. Rainbows and bells . . .'

101. *Sir Walter*: in 'Impressions of Sir Leslie Stephen' (*Essays*, I, 1906, p. 128) she wrote: 'My father always loved reading aloud, and of all books, I think, he loved Scott's the best.' She goes on to describe his rereading the Waverley Novels 'with quiet satisfaction' in the last years of his life. Stephen wrote on Scott in *Hours in a Library* (3 vols., 1874, 1876, 1909) and for the *DNB*. He praises him for his 'healthy animalism' and for his associations with 'the pleasure of that healthy open-air life' of Scotland.

Mr Ramsay goes to chapters 26, 29, 31, 32 and 34 of *The Antiquary* (1816) which recount the sudden death by drowning of the fisherman Mucklebackit's young son Steenie, the grief of the family and the emotions of the antiquary, Jonathan Oldbuck, who, like Mr Ramsay, in spite of his 'Stoic' maxims can't restrain his tears.

In *MS*, pp. 194–5, *The Antiquary* is named as the novel Mr Ramsay is reading, and there is more detail on there being no sexual interest in Scott and on Mr Ramsay 'mouthing' the Scottish dialect to himself as he reads.

Mr Ramsay's pleasure in, and reservations about, Scott are very like Woolf's, who wrote several essays on him: 'Across the Border' (*Essays*, II, 1918, pp. 217ff.); 'Scott's Character' (*Essays*, III, 1921, pp. 301ff.); '*The Antiquary*' (*Essays*, III, 1924, pp. 454ff.); 'Gas at Abbotsford' (*CE*, I, 1940, pp. 134ff.). (This last essay followed a journey to Scotland and the Borders when Woolf 'glutted her passion for Scott on his tomb'. See *Letters*, VI, 1938, p. 247; *Diary*, V, 1938, pp. 151–2.) In her essay on *The Antiquary*, she praises the 'immense vivacity' with which he treats 'the common people whom he loved', and his use of 'that Scottish dialect which is at once so homely and so pungent, so colloquial and so passionate, so shrewd and so melancholy.' 'The Waverley novels are as unmoral as Shakespeare's plays ... you may read them over and over again ... and never know for certain what Scott himself thought.' Like Mr Ramsay, she admires 'the scene in the cottage where Steenie Mucklebackit lies dead; the father's grief, the mother's irritability, the minister's consolations, all come together, tragic, irrelevant, comic, drawn, one knows not how, to make a whole, a complete presentation of life, which, as always, Scott creates carelessly, without a word of comment, as if the parts grew together without his willing it, and broke into ruin again without his caring' (*Essays*, III, p. 457).

In *Moments of Being*, p. 86, Woolf remembers (1939/40) that it was her mother who had 'a passion' for Scott.

102. *a book*: in *MS*, p. 194, it is 'an anthology of poems', and Mrs Ramsay is described as 'never reading at all, except in this way'. Every night she reads 'some poetry . . . and the Opium Eater'. In *Moments of Being*, p. 86, De Quincey is described as Julia Stephen's favourite writer (so by cutting this reference from *MS*, she is making Mrs Ramsay less like her mother). Woolf was writing on De Quincey while writing *TL*, and published an essay on De Quincey's 'Impassioned Prose' in 1926 (*Diary*, III, 11 May 1926, p. 83; *CE*, I, pp. 165ff.; *CE*, IV, pp. 1ff.). Her account of De Quincey's treatment of 'that side of the mind which is exposed in solitude' (*CE*, I, p. 166) is very like Mrs Ramsay's thought process. See also Note 57.

103. *Steer . . . all beaten Mariners*: 'The Sirens' Song', William Browne of Tavistock (1591–1643), from *Inner Temple Masque*, in *Works* (1772).

> Steer, hither steer your winged pines,
> All beaten mariners!
> Here lie Love's undiscovered mines,
> A prey to passengers;
> Perfumes far sweeter than the best
> Which make the Phoenix' urn and nest.
> Fear not your ships,
> Nor any to oppose you save our lips;
> But come on shore,
> Where no joy dies till Love hath gotten more.
>
> For swelling waves our panting breasts,
> Where never storms arise,
> Exchange, and be awhile our guests:
> For stars gaze on our eyes.
> The compass Love shall hourly sing,
> And as he goes about the ring,
> We will not miss
> To tell each point he nameth with a kiss.
> Then come on shore,
> Where no joy dies till Love hath gotten more.

Woolf was also reading Herrick while writing *TL* (she copied out several of the 'Hesperides' in *MS*, appendix A, p. 43). In an essay on 'Sir Walter Raleigh' and the Elizabethans, she describes their characteristic poetry as haunted by 'the sound of the sea', 'the meditative mood fostered by long days at sea, sleep and dreams under strange stars, and lonely effort in the face of death.'

104. *the sonnet*: Shakespeare, Sonnet 98:

> From you have I been absent in the Spring,
> When proud-pied April, dress'd in all his trim,
> Hath put a spirit of youth in every thing,
> That heavy Saturn laugh'd and leap'd with him.
> Yet nor the lays of birds, nor the sweet smell
> Of different flowers in odour and in hue,
> Could make me any summer's story tell,
> Or from their proud lap pluck them where they grew;
> Nor did I wonder at the lily's white,
> Nor praise the deep vermilion in the rose:
> They were but sweet, but figures of delight,
> Drawn after you, you pattern of all those.
> Yet seem'd it winter still, and, you away,
> As with your shadow I with these did play.

In *MS*, the sonnet is not specified; cf. p. 194, where Mrs Ramsay seems to Lily 'ghost, air, nothingness, a thing you could play with'.

105. *the compass*: cf. the steering of the mariners by Love's compass (Note 103), and the compass points on p. 182. In *MS*, p. 30, in the passage where Lily and Mr Bankes are watching Mr Ramsay while he recites 'The Charge of the Light Brigade', there is a drawing of compass points.

TIME PASSES

1. in *MS*, an 'Outline' for 'Time Passes' is included (appendix B, p. 51), which reads:

[Tie?] *Ten Chapters*

Now the question of the ten years.

[Tie?]

The Seasons.

The Skull

The gradual dissolution of everything

This is to be contrasted with the permanence of – what?

Sun, moon & stars.

Hopeless gulfs of misery.

Cruelty.

The War.

Change. Oblivion. Human vitality. Old woman

Cleaning up. The bobbed up, valorous, as of a principle

of human life projected

We are handed on by our children?

Shawls & shooting caps. A green handled brush.

The devouringness of nature.

But all the time, this passes, accumulates.

Darkness.

The welter of winds & waves

What then is the medium through wh. we regard human

beings?

Tears. [di?]

[Sleep th] Slept through life.

2. this section 'I' is not in *MS*.

3. *Virgil*: Woolf went to Latin classes and read Virgil in the 1890s (*Letters*, I, pp. 2, 20) and was reading Virgil again in 1906 (*Letters*, I, p. 215). She found the 'purest Romance' in him (*Essays*, II, 1917, p. 74). Possibly Mr Carmichael is reading the *Eclogues*, Virgil's pastoral love poems and laments.

4. *Were they allies?*: the suggested allusion to the war here is not in *MS*, where the 'certain airs' are personified as 'ghostly confidantes', 'nameless comforters' and then as the 'counterpart' or 'sharer' to the dreaming sleeper (p. 200).

5. *the compass*: see 'The Window', Note 105, and p. 182.

6. [*Mr. Ramsay . . . remained empty.*]: the bracketed deaths are not in *MS*. See De Quincey, *Suspiria de Profundis*, for the temptation of suicide when we 'stretch out our arms in darkness' (De Quincey, op. cit., p. 120); cf. 'The Window', Note 102. The Ramsay deaths reflect the shocks of bereavement in Woolf's childhood and early adulthood: her mother died in 1895, her half-sister, Stella, in 1897, and her brother, Thoby, in 1906.

7. *Mrs. McNab*: in *MS*, p. 214, there is more detail on Mrs McNab as an ordinary victim of the war, with a reference back to 'Luriana Lurilee': she 'was nothing but a mat for kings & kaisers to tread on, who would indeed stand patiently in the streets to see the kings go riding by, & whose sugar & tea were [now cut down by their passions &] reduced at their command.' She is more emphatically contrasted in *MS* to the walker on the beach, the 'crazed, the mystic, the visionary', the kind of person who 'makes abstract' and 'mounts the pulpit' and makes everything 'simple'.

8. *ashen-coloured ship*: in *MS*, p. 221, a 'murderous looking ship' with a 'black snout', making the reference to the war more explicit.

9. *Prices had gone up*: cf. Note 7 on Mrs McNab. On wartime prices and hoarding, see Letter to Vanessa Bell, 3 July 1917 (*Letters*, II, p. 160): 'We were able to get you 2 lbs of icing sugar . . . I don't think we can get more than 1 lb a week for you regularly . . . I will get it & hoard it, unless you think its too expensive – 9d a 1lb.'

10. *Nothing*: in *MS*, pp. 277–8, a reference back here to 'the watchers, the preachers', who have been silenced by the 'cannonading' and the 'black snout' of the ship and have 'gone in despair'; again more emphasis on the war.

11. *Mrs. Bast*: in *MS*, p. 229, Mrs Bast (her name possibly an echo of Leonard Bast in E. M. Forster's *Howards End*) and Mrs McNab are even more moronic, with references to their 'craziness' and 'vacancy of mind'.

12. *Lily Briscoe*: in *MS*, Lily does not arrive in 'Time Passes'.

13. *Gently the waves*: in *MS*, p. 235, this passage of 'acquiescence' (like the whole of 'Time Passes') is more extended and anticipates more clearly *The Waves*, with the line (which becomes the last sentence of *The Waves*) 'The wave breaks on the shore.'

THE LIGHTHOUSE

1. *Andrew killed*: in *MS*, p. 241, 'killed in battle', in quotation marks. (This is the first of several points in *MS* where the war is more explicitly invoked, eg, p. 296, 'What would she have thought, [say] about [the War] it?') Lily, at this point in *MS*, has extended thoughts on the aimlessness of life: 'We don't "see people" for months. Then they're dead.'

2. *'Alone' . . . 'Perished'*: William Cowper (1731–1800), 'The Castaway' (1799). The eleven-stanza poem describing the plight of the man 'washed headlong from on board' ('such a destined wretch as I') who 'waged with death a lasting strife' ends:

> But misery still delights to trace
> Its semblance in another's case.
>
> No voice divine the storm allayed,
> No light propitious shone,
> When, snatched from all effectual aid,
> We perished, each alone;
> But I beneath a rougher sea,
> And whelmed in deeper gulfs than he.

In 'Cowper and Lady Austen' (*CE*, III, 1929, pp. 181–7), Woolf describes Cowper's sad life, his religious mania and his suicide attempt: 'He sank from gloom to gloom, and died in misery.'

3. *a picture*: in *MS*, p. 245, Lily does not remember, at this point, the ten-year-old picture, she starts a new one. Only later when she starts to paint, is it described as 'a picture she had attempted before'.

4. *Cam and James*: in their relation to Mr Ramsay in 'The Lighthouse', they resemble the Stephen children after Julia Stephen's death. See *Moments of Being*, pp. 40–41.

5. *Charles Tansley*: in *MS*, p. 259, there is more detail on Tansley's wartime – presumably pacifist and socialist – activities and on how he has got married and had children. The phrase about the war drawing the 'sting of her femininity' is not in *MS*, instead, Lily feels that everything has become 'simpler'.

6. *the moment*: this concept, very important for Woolf (see *Moments of Being*), is much extended in *MS*, where the moment 'threw out like radium its meaning'.

7. *faint thought she was thinking of Mrs. Ramsay*: in *MS*, p. 262, there is more emphasis on Mrs Ramsay as a ghost, 'an essence', 'stealing back', 'faintly almost imperceptivly [*sic*] she made herself felt. She had put off the robe of flesh and taken on another'.

8. *brown paper parcels*: in *MS*, p. 264, they are 'intolerable', 'sacred [relics] tokens, wrapped up in that odious mixture of gloom and sorrow.' There is more emphasis here on the 'rituals' of Mr Ramsay's 'grim altar' (p. 266).

9. *the fishermen striving there*: see *Moments of Being*, p. 113, for Leslie Stephen's 'great respect' for fishermen.

10. *He looked proudly where Macalister pointed*: in *MS*, p. 265, Mr Ramsay flings out his hand, 'white, chiselled and shaped', with a ring on the little finger, compared to Macalister's 'brown thick mass' of hand.

11. *while James . . . steered*: in *Moments of Being*, p. 115, on holidays at St Ives: 'Perhaps every ten days we would go sailing. Thoby would be allowed to steer. He had to keep the sail filled with wind, and father said, "Show them you can bring her in, my boy", and setting his face, flushing with the effort, he sat there, bringing us round the point.'

Macalister's boat would have been one of the last of the Scottish (or Cornish) fishermen's sailboats. By 1910 more boats were being fitted with paraffin motors and by 1914 the traditional line-fishing in the Hebrides (especially Skye) had almost died out (See Malcolm Gray, *The Fishing Industries of Scotland, 1790–1914*, OUP, 1978).

12. *a book*: cf. pp. 199, 206. In *MS*, there is more detail about which book Mr Ramsay is reading ('not with English words', p. 323; 'Aristotle, Plato, Greek, was it?', p. 352), but the book is not named. In 'Impressions of Sir Leslie Stephen' (*Essays*, I, 1906, p. 129) she remembers 'his little *Plato*, which, being of a convenient size for his pocket, went with him on his journeys, and travelled to America and back.' Susan Dick informs me that Leslie Stephen's copy of vol. III of Plato's *Opera Omnia*, in Washington State University Library, is annotated by him at the front, like Mr Ramsay's book.

13. *his feet*: 'How beautiful are thy feet with shoes' (S. of S., 7:1).

14. *tyranny*: In *MS*, p. 313, Cam's thoughts about his tyranny recur at the very end of the journey, before her vision of the frailty of the island. At this point, she has a memory (cancelled in *TL*) of her father giving her mother a yellow flower, who received it with a little cry ('Three drops of pleasure – Ah – ahah'), a memory which she sets against his 'Do this: do that'. This is an example of the very considerable rearrangement and condensing of 'The Lighthouse' (more than in 'The Window') from *MS* to *TL*.

15. *land values*: under the influence of the American land-reformer Henry George in the 1880s, Liberal opinion began to favour 'a tax on land values as a remedy for social inequality. Lloyd George's proposals for land taxes were the most outrageous feature of his 1909 'People's Budget', and forced an election in 1910. Proposals for land-value taxation were never enacted because of the war. The argument surfaced again in the 1920s and in 1924 Lloyd George's government produced a report on 'The Land and the Nation', proposing land nationalization.

16. *marriage*: *MS*, p. 272, Lily expands the thought: 'Why did [they] in [those days] believe in their sepulchral union – [believed] in locking people up in the catacombs and turning the key on them for ever?' The whole of this section about the Rayleys is very much reordered from *MS* to *TL*.

In *Mausoleum*, pp. 75, 77, Leslie Stephen describes Julia as 'a bit of a matchmaker', with 'exalted views of love and marriage'.

17. *Raphael*: great painter (1483–1520), of the High Renaissance, perhaps best known for the *Sistine Madonna*. Woolf remembered her mother being described as a mixture of 'the Madonna and a woman of the world' (*Moments of Being*, p. 90; *Diary*, III, 4 May 1928, p. 183); cf. 'The Window', Note 34.

18. *Hampton Court*: Virginia and Leonard Woolf visited Hampton Court in wartime (*Diary*, I, Jan. 1918, p. 106). She would set a scene there in *The Waves*.

19. *through William's eyes*: in *MS*, p. 223, it is Lily herself who can only conjure up a 'ghost' of 'astonishing beauty', but feels that 'Mrs Ramsay was not like that': 'Why had death given her the part to play that was none of hers in life?'

20. *a hand*: a faint echo of Excalibur being snatched by a magic hand from the lake at the end of Tennyson's *Morte d'Arthur*:

> So flashed and fell the brand Excalibur:
> But ere he dipt the surface, rose an arm
> Clothed in white samite, mystic, wonderful,
> And caught him by the hilt.

The story slightly resembles the magic Flounder coming out of the sea.

21. *a picture*: in *MS*, p. 280, there is a much longer passage on whether 'Pictures are more important than people', and how the relationship in art is more 'immortal' than between lovers: 'It was an awful marriage; forever.'

22. *her death*: in *MS*, pp. 303–4, 'She had never heard how she had died: only "suddenly"'. She imagines her going across fields with her 'wreath' of flowers as 'the Bride of Death'.

23. *Standard, News*: the two London evening-papers.

24. *But whose foot*: in *MS*, p. 269, 'Presumably, if he were quite honest, he meant his mother'.

25. *in what garden*: in *MS*, p. 309, more explicitly the Garden of Eden: 'that miraculous garden, where [everything to begin

with] where before the [f] fall of the world (& he did really
divide time into the space before catastrophe, & the space
after) [all the] if it was not actual fine weather, at any rate
nobody was gloomy like this.'

26. *Lighthouse*: in *MS*, p. 312, a more explicit connection is made
between the 'grey & stark Lighthouse' and the world after
the fall, which James has to accept: 'And this being the
[noble] nature of truth, it was not to be gainsaid.'

27. *the truth*: in *MS*, p. 315, there is a long passage from James's
thoughts on how the loss of her 'truth' after her death leads
to a wartime family life of darkness and distortion, the
children having to accompany their father to 'tabernacles in
the city' where 'his father, standing up very stiff and straight,
proved conclusively (but James could never keep his attention
fixed) that there is no God.'

28. *shapes of a world not realised*: cf. 'Blank misgivings of a
creature/Moving about in worlds not realised' (Wordsworth,
'Ode, Intimations of Immortality from Recollections of Early
Childhood', 1807). In *MS*, p. 320, Cam is thinking more
explicitly in this passage about the evolution of civilization.

29. *The old gentlemen*: in *Moments of Being*, pp. 142–3, Woolf
remembers (1920/21) the 'old gentlemen' (including Professor
Wolstenholme, on whom Carmichael is based) calling on her
father, 'eating very slowly, staying very late' and discussing
'all things under the sun'. In *MS*, pp. 322–3, Cam's family
memories are more extensive, including 'a scene of the most
terrible kind – when James stood there with his sums &
argued, & her father argued & they once dashed about the
room & she could only [laugh], drawing aside into the
window, & look at the peaceful lawn, the grass, the flowers
& [contrast that peace] think of that happiness & this entire
complete misery'. This passage is cut in *TL*.

30. *Napoleon*: see 'The Window', Note 89.

31. *The thing itself*: in *MS*, p. 329, she adds: 'the germ, in painting,
in knowing, of all art and affection'.

32. *he was growing famous*: in *MS*, p. 330, more details are given

about Mr Carmichael's work: 'It was said that a book he wrote in the 70s about travelling in Burma was a masterpiece ... People were beginning to say that Mr. Carmichael who had always been known to a few enthusiasts, as one of the finest translators of our time: & so on.'

33. *people who disliked her*: in *MS*, p. 332, partly because 'she had no religious beliefs'.

34. *a whipping-boy*: in *MS*, p. 338, more explicitly an argument between the sexes: 'The antagonism was eternal.' In Lily's mind Tansley becomes 'a symbol', a 'mere fork-shaped root'.

35. *crinolines and peg-top trousers*: mid-Victorian fashions, wide petticoats and tapering trousers. In *Moments of Being*, p. 86, Woolf describes the world of her aunt and uncle, the Prinseps, at Little Holland House, as 'a summer afternoon world' with a 'stream of ladies in crinolines and little straw hats; they are attended by gentlemen in peg-top trousers and whiskers. The date is round about 1860.'

36. *a fence of sanctity*: in *MS*, p. 342, after this, Mr Ramsay is described as letting them into his study to show 'his book of birds; or his immense map of the Hebrides; or [his] some curious instrument which he kept in his study & never allowed anyone to touch for [measuring].'

37. *he would say her name*: in *MS*, p. 6, Mrs Ramsay's name is 'Sara'. In *MS*, p. 343, his calling of her name is more ominous: 'at length, standing outside the group, [like] the very figure of a lean watch dog, a [hungry & passionate wolf which sees] a [*sic*] famished [but] wolf, he would say her name, once, only for all the world like a wolf barking in the snow; & he would [ba] say it once more, [but] & this time with something of menace in the tone, which would arous [*sic*] [the] some deep instinct in her.'

38. *Such a dignity*: in *MS*, p. 262, it adds: 'for there was a greatness in the relationship between the Ramsays which made all these glimpses of it, naked, alarming.'

39. *reluctantly*: in *MS*, p. 345, it adds 'how could one wish to die

at twenty-five?' (See 'The Window', Note 32, on Demeter and Persephone.)

40. *somebody was sitting in the chair*: in *MS*, p. 346: 'It might be Rose; it might be Nancy; it might be that old woman, whats her name, finishing her novel.' A long section in *MS*, pp. 346–8, follows, trying to get right the 'apparition' of Mrs Ramsay in the window.

41. *It satisfied him*: in *MS*, p. 349, '& seemed to him to [be] on his side in the war against tyranny'. A longer passage follows on James imagining his future.

42. *the sandwiches*: in *MS*, pp. 359–60, eating the sandwiches (ham in *MS*, not cheese) prompts Mr Ramsay to reminisce about being offered milk when he went walking, and how when he 'was young one could sleep in the open'; how 'he would like to come back again after a hundred years ... to see what they'd made of it.' Cam feels that 'the old wizard' had 'put off his magic', 'he knew perfectly well what he was doing', had thrown off 'his being a great man' and was now 'telling them stories round a camp fire'.

43. *it was finished*: in *MS*, p. 386: '[It was done] It was over. But she had had her vision.' In margin: 'The white shape stayed perfectly still.'

Appendix I

Substantive emendations adopted or conjectured in this edition.

The first reading is the one printed in this edition. The italic
entry immediately following the square bracket indicates whether
this reading is that of the first British edition (*1927*), the first
American edition (*A1927*), the 1930 'New Edition' (*1930*), or the
present edition (*this edn*). When an emendation has been adopted
in this edition, the original reading of *1927* is also given for
purposes of comparison. When the present editor has allowed
the reading of *1927* to stand but conjectures an emendation, the
formula *conj. this edn* is used. Page and line numbers are for this
edition.

11.7	washing it, when] *1930*; washing, when *1927*
11.9	chased them to – or] *1930*; chased them – or *1927*
11.10	with them in – the] *1930*; with them – in the *1927*
15.10	their husband's labours] *1927*; their husbands' labours *conj. this edn*
16.8	she asked] *1927*; she had asked *conj. this edn*
16.18	men smoked on] *1930*; men did in *1927*
24.12	with this all] *1927*; with all this *conj. this edn*
32.21	got shabbier and got shabbier] *1927*; got shabbier and shabbier *conj. this edn*
	cf. *MS*, p. 55 (deletions not recorded): 'But the whole effect, she concluded was becoming summer by summer shabbier & shabbier & paler'.
36.11	in which to regain *this edn*; into which to regain *1927*
	cf. *MS*, p. 60 (deletions not recorded): 'as if he wrapped himself about & that he needed privacy in which to regain his equilibrium'.
92.32	flower in the pattern] *1930*; flower in pattern *1927*

93.8   middle of the view   *this edn*;   middle of view   *1927*
cf. 174.19: 'At dinner he would sit right in the middle of the view.'

122.3   ways, Mr. Bankes]   *1927*;   ways. Mr. Bankes   *conj. this edn*

140.23   but, Mrs. Ramsay having died rather suddenly the night before, he stretched his arms out. They]   *1930*;   but Mrs. Ramsay having died rather suddenly the night before he stretched his arms out. They   *1927*;   but, Mrs. Ramsay having died rather suddenly the night before he stretched his arms out, they   *conj. this edn*

149.20   skull there for?]   *this edn*;   skull there?   *1927*
cf. 153.10: 'whatever they hung that beast's skull there for?'

151.7   ruined rooms]   *this edn*;   ruined room   *1927*
cf. *MS*, p. 229 (deletions not recorded): 'picnickers, would have boiled their kettles in its ruined rooms'.

162.10   You find us]   *1927*;   'You will find us   *conj. this edn*
cf. *MS*, p. 243: '"You find things much altered." Dumb & staring though they had all sat she had felt (knowing them scarcely at all, all these children, six children, James, Nancy Cam, Roger,) how they raged under it.' But cf. 162.18 (identical in *MS*, p. 243): '"You will find us much changed."' Perhaps Virginia Woolf originally followed her holograph draft, then decided that Mr Ramsay should twice make the same statement (the second one that he makes in the holograph draft), and then imperfectly emended either her typescript or her proof.

164.28   2]   *A1927* (II);   3   *1927*

171.1   3]   *A1927* (III);   4   *1927*

173.21   experience forms]   *A1927*;   forms experience   *1927*

177.5   4]   *A1927* (IV);   5   *1927*

185.16   5]   *A1927* (V);   6   *1927*

186.11   cork]   *1927*;   cask   *conj. this edn*
cf. *MS*, p. 295: 'There was the old cork dipping & bobbing in the sea; Charles Tansley throwing stones; a

wave breaking; racing almost up to the rock where Mrs. Ramsay sat, writing, writing, in that little round rapid hand that was so illegible. [new paragraph] "Is it a boat, is it a cork?" Mrs. Ramsay would say looking up,'; and *MS*, p. 337: 'Then, suddenly the old cork or whatever it was began bobbing up & down among the waves;'. Susan Dick's transcript of the holograph here supports *1927*; but *1927*'s recurrent 'cask' (186.7, 186.25, 213.27) strongly suggests that 'cask' was the word that Virginia Woolf intended at 186.11. Common sense also suggests the conjectured emendation: a floating cork could hardly be confused with a floating cask, and even if it could it would not be visible to Mrs. Ramsay's short-sighted eyes.

190.19	painting, had] *1927*; painting, and had *conj. this edn*	
196.3	6] *A 1927* (VI); 7 *1927*	
196.7	7] *A 1927* (VII); 8 *1927*	
198.16	8] *A 1927* (VIII); 9 *1927*	
200.17	fisherman's] *1927*; fishermen's *conj. this edn*	
204.4	9] *A 1927* (IX); 10 *1927*	
204.13	10] *A 1927* (X); 11 *1927*	
207.15	11] *A 1927* (XI); 12 *1927*	
219.17	12] *A 1927* (XII); 13 *1927*	
225.1	13] *A 1927* (XIII); 14 *1927*	
225.29	greens] *A 1927*; green *1927*	

cf. 174.9: 'while she modelled it with greens and blues'.

Appendix II

A selection from the substantive variant readings in the first British (*1927*) and first American (*A 1927*) editions. Page and line numbers are for this edition.

11.6   raising from the mud a beggar's dirty foot and washing, when she thus] *1927*; raising from the mud to wash a beggar's dirty foot, when she thus   *A 1927*

12.10   disparage them, put them all on edge somehow with his acid way of peeling the flesh and blood off everything, he was not satisfied.] *1927*; disparage them – he was not satisfied.   *A 1927*

14.25   otherwise milk-white. He wanted nothing, he murmured.] *1927*; otherwise milk white. No, nothing, he murmured.   *A 1927*

16.30   to say how he had been to Ibsen with the Ramsays.] *1927*; to say how he had gone not to the circus but to Ibsen with the Ramsays.   *A 1927*

19.3   looked at her; Charles Tansley felt] *1927*; looked at her; for the first time in his life Charles Tansley felt   *A 1927*

20.8   (as she sat in the window), that] *1927*; (as she sat in the window which opened on the terrace), that   *A 1927*

24.14   impossible. One could not say what one meant. So now] *1927*; impossible. So now   *A 1927*

27.25   over his shoulder, as over her father's, to look at] *1927*; over his shoulder, to look at   *A 1927*

30.2   You have none.] *1927*; Mr. Bankes has none.   *A 1927*

32.26   things must spoil. What was the use of flinging a green Cashmere shawl over the edge of a picture frame? In two weeks it would be the colour of pea soup. But it

was the doors that annoyed her; every door was left
open.] *1927*; things must spoil. Every door was left
open. *A 1927*

34.21   end of the line, Greek, blue-eyed, straight-nosed.]
1927; end of the line very clearly Greek, straight, blue-
eyed. *A 1927*

39.22   three resonant taps on the ram's horn which made the
handle of the urn,] *1927*; three resonant taps on the
handle of the urn, *A 1927*

41.13   (He looked into the darkness, into the intricacy of the
twigs.)] *1927*; (He looked into the hedge, into the
intricacy of the twigs.) *A 1927*

51.5   his pleasure in it, in the phrases] *1927*; his pleasure in
it, his glory in the phrases *A 1927*

55.17   found a glove] *1927*; found a crumpled glove *A 1927*

66.32   You shall go through with it.] *1927*; You shall go
through it all. *A 1927*

67.21   one – she need not name it – *that* was essential;]
1927; one – she need not name it – that was essential;
A 1927

70.28   one leant to things, inanimate things;] *1927*; one leant
to inanimate things; *A 1927*

80.33   bringing Prue back into the alliance of family life again,
from which she had escaped, throwing catches, asked-
,] *1927*; bringing Prue back into throwing catches
again, from which she had escaped, asked, *A 1927*

94.17   if she wanted a little revenge] *1927*; if she wanted revenge *A 1927*

104.6   and then – but thank goodness! she saw him clutch
himself] *1927*; and then – thank goodness! she saw
him clutch himself *A 1927*

108.1   They might cut his hair for him,] *1927*; They might
cut his hair from him, *A 1927*

110.16   Paul Rayley, the centre of it, all of a tremor,] *1927*; Paul
Rayley, sitting at her side, all of a tremor, *A 1927*

112.4   nothing but this; while the women,]   *1927*;   nothing
        but this – love; while the women   *A 1927*

114.22 the thing is made that remains for ever after. This would
        remain.]   *1927*;   the thing is made that endures.   *A 1927*

115.1   one thousand two hundred and fifty-three, which hap-
        pened to be the number on his railway ticket.]   *1927*;   one
        thousand two hundred and fifty-three. That was the
        number, it seemed, on his watch.   *A 1927*

117.33 the thing simply, not himself.]   *1927*;   the thing, simply,
        not himself, nothing else.   *A 1927*

131.20 suddenly entire shaped in her hands,]   *1927*;   suddenly
        entire; she held it in her hands,   *A 1927*

134.8   partly because she did not mind looking now, with him
        watching, at the Lighthouse. For she knew]   *1927*; partly
        because she remembered how beautiful it often is – the
        sea at night. But she knew   *A 1927*

134.25 It's going to be wet to-morrow.' She had not said it, but
        he knew it. And she looked at him smiling. For she had
        triumphed again.]   *1927*;   It's going to be wet tomor-
        row. You won't be able to go.' And she looked at him
        smiling. For she had triumphed again. She had not said
        it: yet he knew.   *A 1927*

138.18 So some random light directing them from some uncov-
        ered star, or wandering ship, or the Lighthouse even,
        with its pale footfall upon stair and mat, the little airs
        mounted the staircase]   *1927*;   So some random light
        directing them with its pale footfall upon stair and mat,
        from some uncovered star, or wandering ship, or the
        Lighthouse even, the little airs mounted the stairca-
        se   *A 1927*

140.22 Mr. Ramsay stumbling along a passage stretched his
        arms out one dark morning, but Mrs. Ramsay having
        died rather suddenly the night before he stretched his
        arms out. They remained empty.]   *1927*;   Mr. Ramsay,
        stumbling along a passage one dark morning, stretched
        his arms out, but Mrs. Ramsay having died rather suddenly

the night before, his arms, though stretched out, remained empty. *A1927*

143.17   Meanwhile the mystic, the visionary, walked the beach, stirred a puddle, looked at a stone, and asked themselves 'What am I?' 'What is this?' and suddenly an answer was vouchsafed them (what it was they could not say): so that] *1927*; The mystic, the visionary, walking the beach on a fine night, stirring a puddle, looking at a stone, asking themselves 'What am I,' 'What is this?' had suddenly an answer vouchsafed them: (they could not say what it was) so that *A1927*

144.26   a tragedy, people said. They said nobody deserved happiness more.] *1927*; a tragedy, people said, everything, they said, had promised so well. *A1927*

146.2   children pelting each other with handfuls of grass, something out of harmony with this jocundity, this serenity.] *1927*; children making mud pies or pelting each other with handfuls of grass, something out of harmony with this jocundity and this serenity. *A1927*

146.15   With equal complacence she saw his misery, condoned his meanness, and acquiesced in his torture. That dream, then, of sharing, completing, finding in solitude on the beach an answer, was but a reflection in a mirror,] *1927*; With equal complacence she saw his misery, his meanness, and his torture. That dream, of sharing, completing, of finding in solitude on the beach an answer, was then but a reflection in a mirror, *A1927*

149.26   left the house shut up, locked, alone.] *1927*; left the house alone, shut up, locked. *A1927*

154.16   the white flowers by the window.] *1927*; the white flowers in the bed by the window. *A1927*

154.18   late one evening in September. Mr. Carmichael came by the same train.] *1927*; late one evening in September. *A1927*

155.15   much as it used to look years ago.] *1927*; much as it used to look. *A1927*

155.26   Lily Briscoe stirring in her sleep clutched at her blankets]
1927;   Lily Briscoe stirring in her sleep. She clutched at
her blankets   *A1927*

161.13   She must escape somehow, be alone somewhere.]
1927;   She must escape somewhere, be alone somewhere.
A1927

161.19   that picture. It had been knocking about in her mind all
these years. She would paint that picture now. Where
were]   *1927*;   that picture. She would paint that picture
now. It had been knocking about in her mind all these
years. Where were   *A1927*

171.4   seemed to fly back in her face, like a bramble sprung.]
1927;   seemed to be cast back on her, like a bramble
sprung across her face.   *A1927*

173.20   one of those habitual currents which after a certain time
forms experience in the mind,]   *1927*;   one of those
habitual currents in which after a certain time experience
forms in the mind,   *A1927*

188.9   as if by looking she could hear them. Something violent.
Minta went on eating her sandwich, annoyingly, while
he spoke. He spoke indignant, jealous words, abusing
her,]   *1927*;   as if by looking she could hear them.
Minta went on eating her sandwich, annoyingly, while
he spoke something violent, abusing her,   *A1927*

188.29   got to know you, playing chess with a little man]
1927;   got to know you, and he played chess with a
little man   *A1927*

189.27   Lily smiled.]   *1927*;   Lily thought.   *A1927*

201.30   making them shrivel and fall.]   *1927*;   making it shrivel
and fall.   *A1927*

216.3   She had met Paul Rayley like that one day on the stairs.
They had laughed and laughed, like a couple of children,
all because Mr. Ramsay, finding an earwig in his milk at
breakfast had sent the whole thing flying through the air
on to the terrace outside. 'An earwig,' Prue murmured,
awestruck, 'in his milk.' Other people might find

centipedes. But he had built round him such a fence of sanctity, and occupied the space with such a demeanour of majesty that an earwig in his milk was a monster.] *1927*;   She had met Paul Rayley like that one day on the stairs. It had been an earwig, apparently. Other people might find centipedes. They had laughed and laughed. *A1927*